Butterfly Assassins

Steve Walsh

In memory of my Dad.
He was the light I saw that night.
But every night I guess, thinking back.

Chapter 1

Looking back

Do you remember Sally Bennett? The schoolgirl injured in the car accident outside Davenport train station? The twelve-year-old whose life was saved when Wilson clamped a punctured artery with the pliers on a multi-tool?

Well, I have a confession to make. That incident was no accident! It was all stage-managed under the auspices of The Powers That Be and orchestrated by a Brimstone butterfly.

In other words, a textbook case of divine intervention.

You see, *without* her traumatic injuries, Sally would never have been able to reveal that Wilson was in the white room, in limbo-land, which in turn would have meant Wilson *not* being resurrected by Daisy. So on that fateful October afternoon, the shepherding of the flock engendered a curious circle of life in which the convex of Wilson's yang locked perfectly on the concave of Sally's yin.

And more to the point, they both ended up in Stockport Infirmary, which was *my* objective all along.

Sally Bennett was an orphan and an only child. Tragically and incomprehensibly, at the age of ten, both of her parents died in quick succession; her mother from breast cancer and two months later her father from a heart attack, or more likely, from heartbreak.

Proof, some would say, that fate plays our cards blind. One can be dealt three buses in a row, a run of traffic lights on red

1

or a pair of deaths; it all depends on the shuffle.

In Sally's case however, her cards were marked the day she was born, the deck was rigged and all the odds stacked in favour of an intervention by Auntie Kay; the elder sister from her mother's side and a Queen of Hearts from the Lewis Carroll side.

Kay was a successful and famously feisty TV executive who worked for the BBC at Media City in Salford and lived in a tumbledown vicarage in the village of Cheadle, ten miles south of Manchester. A petite woman with features of child-like proportion and a porcelain complexion, Kay was a Mancunian, rather than a Manchurian, china doll.

Looks can be deceptive however, because bantamweight Kay was in a class of her own when it came to producing hard-hitting news features. A trade magazine once described her as, 'taut like piano wire and as highly strung'. A compliment that not only caused Kay to buff her fingernails on the lapel of her jacket; she framed the article and hung it in the downstairs loo.

Kay was still grieving the death of her sister when eight weeks later, the catastrophic aftershock of her brother-in-law passing away left in its wake an apocalyptic landscape beyond all recognition. Not for a second did Kay hesitate in moving in with Sally to give all the comfort and support needed while a plan to rebuild two shattered lives was formulated. Several emotionally charged weeks slipped by as Kay waded through the interviews, paperwork and background checks relating to fast track guardianship.

Towards the end of this process, some bureaucratic nonsense regarding a police caution for clipping a neighbour's overgrown hedge and an argument with the Director of Social

Services, whom Kay lambasted as 'that dilatory jobsworth', caused Sally to temporarily fall through a gap in the system.

Banishment to a children's home in Buxton turned up like a cruel-faced joker and though Kay visited twice daily, Sally endured four nights in a shared dormitory, alone and confused in a world that seemed unable to hold its axis.

Early on the day she was scheduled to leave the children's home, at around four-thirty in the morning, Sally woke from fitful sleep to the sounds of muffled laughter and craned her neck to identify the source. Moonlight pouring through a skylight confirmed that all four roommates were fast asleep, yet flurries of giggles continued to waft through the air like a giddy breeze. Two voices could be identified, excited children's voices: one whispering, the other chuckling, and at that ungodly hour the subject matter could only have been mischief-making. Propping herself on one elbow, and with the senses of sight and sound now aligned, Sally followed the laughter like notes on sheet music and soon reached the conclusion the merriment was unfolding in the corridor outside. This sound of funny business beckoned like the Pied Piper's flute as Sally scrambled out of bed and slipped into a dressing gown. Slowly, she opened the dormitory door, took a tentative step forward and peered in one direction, then the other. Curiously, there was not a soul to be seen.

Running the length of the corridor to the left, a bookcase held a variety of titles, toys and board games stacked neatly on shelves. A display of spidery artworks, hand-drawn in wax crayon, were pinned like specimens to cork boards on the opposite wall. A pencil beam of light ran beneath the office door at the far end. Looking to the right, the empty corridor tumbled over the lip of a staircase and down to the day room and the reception area below. At the top of the stairs, the night lady's armchair sat empty with a magazine splayed over the armrest. Sally assumed she was ushering the mischief-makers back to bed. The fun and games appeared to be over.

Somewhat miffed at missing out on the revelry, but out of bed and awake nevertheless, Sally realised she needed to pee. A threadbare teddy slumped on a shelf, monitored proceedings like a drowsy night-watchman as Sally tiptoed past in bare feet. Pushing open the bathroom door, a movement sensor instantly acknowledged the visitor and a fluorescent light spluttered into life to reveal the whitewashed walls and linoleum flooring of a room designed in the institutional style. Sally entered the first cubicle and turned to close the flimsy door. The lock was broken and the door swung back lazily. She kicked it shut repeatedly and angrily. Sitting on a cold toilet seat, in the middle of the night, in a random home for unfortunate displaced children, Sally wondered if the persecution would ever end? The light clicked off and moments later, her tears began to fall.

Sally must have fallen asleep, because some time later her eyes once again blinked open to the sound of muted laughter and cupped hand to ear mutterings. This time the culprits seemed almost within touching distance, just a metre or so away, somewhere in the void of pitch-black space beyond the open cubicle door. The voices were definitely those of children and registered as an older boy and a younger girl. The whispering and giggling continued for a few seconds more and then abruptly stopped, suggesting a dare had been issued and the challenge accepted. Sally was acutely aware of her embarrassing situation. She suspected the unruly kids from earlier had entered the toilet block after she'd nodded off on the loo. They'd seen her sitting there, the light had gone out and now they were somewhere out in the darkness revelling in her predicament. Sally raised a foot to kick the cubicle door shut. In doing so, the movement detector once again reacted with a stuttering start and spat out a single strobe of light.

The older child was indeed a boy, aged about ten. He was scrawny and scruffy in ill-fitting school clothes. Short trousers, two sizes too big flared below his knees and the folds of a coarse cotton shirt were roughly tucked into the waistband. A belt of knotted cord pulled everything tight to his narrow waist like the drawstring on a rucksack. The scuffed shoes were clearly oversized hand-me-downs as were the baggy socks sagging around sparrow legs. The younger child was aged about five or six. She was wearing the pleated skirt and short-sleeved blouse of a summer term, school uniform. The tangle of corkscrew ringlets, the rag doll clamped firmly under her arm and the thumb stuck in her mouth all suggested she was missing the loving touch of her mother.

Though the image was captured in the time frame of a lightning burst, Sally would never forget the detail. How the boy's face carried a look of shock with his mouth and eyes open wide. The girl's face, frozen in the moment, was set with the defiant stare the young employ to mask vulnerability. It was as though a 'special effect' flash had been selected on a camera and in the instant of exposure, their presence had been embossed with incandescence. As if a sparkler in dexterous hands had sketched an outline of their essential features against a Bonfire Night sky. The fleeting impression was consumed by light when a second pulse of photons chased the first away.

Reflections on life, viewed through the prism of a sleepless night, often refract at distorted angles. And so it was, an hour later, as Sally lay awake in a room harbouring unfamiliar shapes and shadows, she was presented with the here and now from an entirely different perspective altogether. The green shoots of the notion stemmed from the movie she'd watched with her mum a few days before she passed away. *The Truman Show,* in which a man's life, all of his life in fact, is played out live on TV like an all-day soap opera. Friends and family are in on the act and all know the script, apart from the man. Sally lay in bed and tried to scope the dimensions of the idea as it might apply to her situation, rather like a mime artist trying to define an invisible object. The egocentric concept of a day, a month, one's lifetime being choreographed in advance was intriguing and led Sally to a startling possibility. What if the plate shifts, the extraordinary events that had turned her own world upside down, the sudden deaths of both parents, were not simply the cruel result of random chance? What if every outcome and eventuality was being manipulated by a malignant force, by an influence outside of her control; by some crazy, behind the scenes *Christof* character or a supreme puppeteer manipulating the strings of her life? The cockeyed thought pitched itself lucidly and in seriousness and Sally rolled over on to her front to bury her face and the ludicrous idea in the pillow; but there was no escaping the family of supporting arguments that quickly followed; each hectoring with their own particular viewpoint and reiterating the whispers she'd overheard at the funerals.

"It all seems very suspicious if you want my opinion. I mean, *both* parents dying within a few weeks of each other!

Has that ever . . . I mean what are the chances of that?"

"And! Somebody told me there was no clear cause of death on her father's death certificate."

"She didn't show any emotion whatsoever, never cried even. That's not normal for a ten-year-old! She just took everything in her stride, so matter of fact, like she was there, but not *all there,* if you know what I mean."

"Poor girl, with no brothers or sisters and having to live with Kay. Can you imagine, such a self-centred woman becoming a guardian? At least Sally won't have to change schools!"

And what about the mix-up that meant I had to stay here for four nights? Auntie Kay said it was beyond comprehension in this day and age.

Sally once again rolled over in frustration and let her head thump down on the pillow as though it were an egg timer and unwanted thoughts would trickle back out.

Peering into the granular darkness, solid lumps of charcoal acquired new identities. Three dressing gowns hanging on a wall became monks hunched in prayer. A narrow wardrobe stood to attention like a sentry box. The spindles on a bedstead were now the bars of a prison cell. Sally's gaze shifted to a red glow which she assumed was coming from a bulb in a thermostat or the 'on' light on a plug socket. Or a firefly! Or a fairy fly! Because the red light suddenly rose upwards to assume a new position where it momentarily hovered, drone like yet silent, before slowly advancing forwards and increasing in size quite markedly. Sally blinked to recalibrate her vision, to refocus the light back to its original size and location but the aerobatics continued. A metre or so from Sally's face and just out of reach, the light came to a halt for a second time. The fuzzy glow now resembled a bicycle reflector on a foggy night and continued to increase in scale and definition until it morphed into what looked like a foil balloon floating on an invisible string. Inching herself higher up the bed, Sally cast sideways glances across the dorm as if to ask, "can anyone else see this?" A shimmering, ripple effect unsettled the mirrored surface of the balloon as though a raindrop had fallen on a puddle and a picture began to form like a photograph developing in a darkroom tray. To Sally's astonishment, the picture then stuttered into life with the jerky camera work of a home movie and as the view panned out, the cameraman adjusted the focus to present a broader panorama in sharp detail.

Sally instantly recognised the person standing in sunlight; the female figure alone on a deserted beach with sand as white as sugar under a cloudless sky of azure blue. It was her lovely, beautiful mum and she was alive again. Fronds of palm trees were swaying in the background as though waving hello. Her mother's hair, woven into braids, resembled golden dreadlocks and wispy strands reflected sunbeams in flashing pixels of rainbow colour. She was smiling, on holiday somewhere and beckoning to Sally with laughing eyes and outstretched arms to join her. She looked happy and full of life, so different to the weak, emaciated figure gasping for shallow breath in a hospice bed. Sally smiled, captivated with the serenity of the vision and instinctively reached out to take her mother's hand, to accept the invitation, to once again canter through crashing waves on seahorses together; but as Sally's fingertips pierced the illusory surface, the balloon popped like a soap bubble and the apparition dissolved.

Two hours later, as the first yawn of morning light stretched over the skylight, Sally refused sleep in order to retain the cherished memory of the animated postcard. She knew the vision had been both real and prophetic, something otherworldly and beyond her control; an encounter that even the strongest emotions in league with the deepest yearnings of her imagination could never have conceived. Sally had sensed the spiritual presence of her mother reaching out from another dimension; from an incomprehensibly different aspect of existence. Her mother had called from beyond the grave, from heaven itself, with an invitation to join her in the afterlife. This promise, that a wonderful reunion was waiting at the end of her life's journey, was destined to prejudice Sally's thoughts and behaviour from that moment on.

Fate was playing its hand and having led with a heart, the face card of her mother, Sally had no other option but to follow suit.

Chapter 2

The old vicarage

Later that morning, as Sally zipped up the contents of her trolley bag, Kay strode into the foyer of the children's home brandishing the required paperwork and with little ceremony re-claimed guardianship of her niece. Sally waved goodbye to the girls from the dorm as the car pulled out of the gates and headed back to south Manchester.

Kay's home was built in Victorian times as a residence for the rector of Christ Church, Cheadle. The three-storey red brick property featured a steep slate roof, a crenellated turret, a pair of spires topped with weathervanes and arched, mullioned windows with leaded glass portraying colourful scenes from the bible. The architect must have had a dark sense of humour though, because the abundance of Neo-Gothic detailing suggested *The Adams Family* might also have lived there. On closer inspection, the peeling paintwork, blocked gutters, the crumbling brick fascia, missing roof tiles and the unkempt gardens suggested that nobody lived there. The postman referred to the house as 'Faulty Towers'.

The vicarage was hidden from view by a perimeter of rhododendron bushes of Amazonian proportions. A tarmac driveway, pock marked with frost damage and resembling the cratered surface of the moon led directly from the main road through two crooked gate posts, with no gate, before sweeping round to the back of the house and the main entrance. From there, a long narrow lawn, moss choked in the summer and boggy in the winter, ran into a dense thicket of brambles and an orchard. The fruit trees were always a place of worship for young heathens come Harvest Festival time.

As the car pulled to a halt outside the vicarage, Kay took a deep breath, switched off the engine and exhaled a sigh of relief.

"Well Sally, this is officially your new home now. Not where you want to be, I know. But I'll do everything to give you the safe and loving environment your mum and dad would have wanted."

Kay's wan smile held firm and resolute until the corners of her mouth began to tremble and droop, the tears began to flow and her self-composure collapsed in waves of shoulder shaking sobs. Sally unclipped her seatbelt, stretched awkwardly over the centre console and gave Kay a hug.

"It's alright Auntie Kay. Don't be upset. I have sad moments all the time, but it helps if you think about all the other people much worse off than us. Starving children in Africa, families trapped in the middle of wars, the other children in the home. What's happened has happened and we can't change things, so we just have to accept it and be strong and think positively about the future. And in comparison I'm lucky, because I have you."

Sally's words cosseted Kay's heart like a comfort blanket and she was struck by the emotional juxtaposition, by the role reversal of an orphaned child giving solace to a no-nonsense career woman known for a lack of empathy. In fact, Kay was so taken with the incongruity, she failed to register the detached, otherworldly tone in Sally's voice and had she looked up, the

11

dissonance would have been further compounded by clear, dry eyes staring through the car windscreen at something in the middle distance of a ten-year-old mind.

"Can I tell you something Auntie Kay? And you can give me your advice?"

Kay spluttered out a hybrid sound, both sob and laugh and nodded her head.

"I think everything is going to be okay! I had a really strange experience, well two actually, if you count the other one. And I know my mum and dad have gone, but they sent me a message last night to say they're together again and want me to join them on a holiday. I can tell you more if you want?"

Kay began dabbing her eyes with a tissue and confirmed she was still listening. Sally sat back and continued.

"Okay. The first part started when I went for a pee and the toilet door wouldn't lock properly. That made me upset and weepy cos I was frustrated with everything. Anyway, I must have fallen asleep because when I woke up I heard the children who'd been playing in the corridor and now they were laughing at me while I was sitting on the loo! So I kicked the door again and just as the light came on I saw them, but not as real people, they were more like a glowing drawing. I could see the outlines of their bodies and clothes and faces."

Sally giggled at how ridiculous she was sounding. Kay pulled a comical face and placed a hand on Sally's forehead to feign checking her temperature.

"Auntie Kay, it was so weird, but not frightening. Do you think they could have been ghosts?"

Kay moved a lock of stray hair from Sally's eyes and felt the tiny jolt of static.

"Sounds like a nightmare to be honest love, falling asleep

on the loo, but having said that, something similar happened to me once at university. I'll tell you about that when you're older. Anyway, sorry, you were saying. What was the second experience?"

"Okay, right, now this is the other bit."

Sally adjusted her seating position.

"So when I went back to bed, I couldn't sleep because I kept thinking about *The Truman Show*; it was Mum's favourite film. Anyway, I was kind of looking around the room in the dark, just thinking about things and everything that's happened, when I saw this red light. Like a small light on a switch. But then after a few seconds the light moved towards me and became bigger and it was kind of floating like a shiny balloon. Seriously Auntie Kay, I wasn't dreaming this, it was hovering, and then became a sort of picture ball. That's the only way I can describe it. And do you know what happened?"

Sally hesitated, fearful of revealing the details in case Kay was able to ascribe an ordinary explanation to her wonderful, extraordinary experience.

"Go on. I'm listening" said Kay.

"I saw Mum, and she looked so happy. She was on a beach and it was beautiful and sunny like a paradise and her hair was really long and tied in golden braids that sparkled in the sunlight. Dad wasn't there, I mean I couldn't see him, perhaps he was taking the video. Anyway, Mum reached out to me like she wanted me to join her and as I went to touch her hand, the balloon popped and the red light went out and I couldn't see her anymore. And that's what happened."

Sally turned to face Kay.

"It felt like it was real because I was in bed and wide awake, I wasn't sleepwalking or dreaming. What do you think it meant? Was it a message from Mum in heaven?"

Kay held a tissue firmly over her nose and mouth to stop the explosion of grief and all she could do by way of reply was raise an eyebrow in order to say,

"I've absolutely no idea Sally."

They sat in silence for a few minutes, preparing mentally for the next step; a small yet significant stride that would see them cross the threshold of a new life together.

Still visibly upset, Kay retrieved the trolley bag from the boot of the car. Sally was peering up at the vicarage and smiling.

"I remember being here a few times when I was little, but now it looks different, your house is amazing Auntie Kay."

Sally's bedroom was on the first floor at the back of the vicarage and overlooked the garden. The room was spacious and airy and dominated by an original sash window with a wide sill that made the perfect bench seat. The window was impressive, but flattered to deceive, because it couldn't actually be opened. Both pulley cords had snapped and layers of paint, the decorative strata of a hundred years, had fused sash to frame. *'Window repairs (in general)'* was at the top of Kay's *'to do'* list. Outside, below the window, there was a patio of crazy paving caked in green algae that was as treacherous as ice after rain. The white plastic furniture, indelibly stained with skeletal leaf imprints, was unlikely to ever scrub up well. Beyond the lawn to the left, Sally could see fruit trees protected by coils of barbed briar and just visible to the right, through a gap between the rhododendron bushes, a rusty iron gate offered access from the vicarage into a church field overgrown with meadow grass a metre tall. A foot worn path skirted the remnants of an old tennis court and continued rising up the field until the trail ran alongside a stone wall weathered black with acid rain and disappeared from view. Beyond, Sally could see a graveyard and a church with a steep spire and a white faced clock that stood out against sooty stonework.

Distant chimes registered the hour as Sally opened an old biscuit tin containing the cherished last photograph of them all together as a family. Mum, Dad and daughter; three happy, sunburnt faces, eating ice cream on Bournemouth pier on a perfect summer's day.

After placing the frame on the bedside table and then adjusting the angle to face her pillow, Sally was startled to see flaking skin and a fiery red rash erupting over the inside of her forearm. The journey to Davenport station was about to begin.

Chapter 3

Felix the cat

Sally had been living with Kay for six months and was in the final year of junior school as the first Christmas without her parents approached. Friends and teachers knew it would be a challenging time so meaning well, they voted unanimously for Sally to play the lead role of Snow White in the school pantomime, and turned a deaf ear to the fact her voice fell flat on higher notes.

The subject of the pantomime was broached one afternoon as Sally sat at the kitchen table writing Christmas cards to classmates. Despite encouragement from Kay, the prospect of being Snow White and having to sing, in fact just standing on stage in front of an audience, filled her with dread.

"But you like singing Sally, you sing along with songs on the radio all the time; I've no idea what the songs are mind you, but your voice is beautiful."

"Auntie Kay, I was singing in the car last week and you got into a paddy and told me to stop because I was tone deaf. So which one is it, I can't be both?"

"Look, it's only a school pantomime. It's not the final of 'Britain's Got Talent'. If you're going to get all stressed, ask for a different part. Ask to be one of the seven dwarfs, a part that doesn't involve singing. What about Grumpy? That would be perfect casting for you!"

"Ha! Very funny! And you'd be perfect as the wicked witch. You probably wouldn't have to wear any special make-up either."

Kay started laughing and then began to cackle as she reached for her make-up compact.

"Mirror, mirror in my hand, who's the best TV producer in the land?"

Kay dabbed a black spot on the tip of her nose with an eyebrow pencil.

"That's a wart Sally, all the best wicked witches have one."

Sally was not amused.

"But I really want to be Snow White. To show everyone I'm a strong person and that I'm okay, after . . . you know, Mum and Dad. I just don't want anyone to be embarrassed if I forget my words or if I can't sing the high notes properly."

"Look love, what if I try and organise a singing lesson? We've plenty of time before the pantomime, a bit of tuition might give you a lift, help you reach the top notes and you'll surprise everyone."

"Thanks, but I think I need more than a couple of singing lessons. They all voted for me to do this, and I know why, they thought it would . . . well anyway, they asked for it, so they're going to get it."

"Yeh, that's the attitude Sal, you show 'em. Make the best of what you've got. Just like we all have to do in life – I'm a bloody expert in that respect. Plus, you can have a wart on your nose like mine and show them that *our* Snow White is no Little Miss Perfect. Then if your voice goes off course, pretend it's all part of the act. A modern day, kick ass Snow White – warts and all! Actually, come to think of it, it's not a wart. Let's call it a beauty spot!"

That night, Sally fell asleep rehearsing the words to the

17

song 'Someday My Prince Will Come'. For an hour or so she tossed and turned, tormented by thoughts of freezing on stage or forgetting her lines; but as her eyelids began to flutter and the phase of sleep shifted an octave, Snow White journeyed over the seven jewelled hills, beyond the seventh wall and discovered the magical kingdom known to some as The Market Square.

Initially, Sally thought she'd travelled back in time, to the eye test at the opticians three days earlier. Everything was blurred and ill-defined, with no specific detail to suggest where she might be. Sally was lost in a world of soft focus movement and colour, as though viewing her dream through frosted glass.

"Worse!" she said, instinctively.

The unseen hand of the optician made an adjustment and the image sharpened.

"A little bit better."

The prescription was revised and clarity increased by another notch.

"Much better, but still not perfect."

Progressive lenses were fitted and the scene settled into 20/20 focus.

"Perfect."

Sally was perched on a stool in a vast open-plan space with a low ceiling. A music teacher, or possibly a voice coach, with an Italian accent, a pink shirt, and a paisley patterned cravat sat facing her with his arms crossed. He'd been *'la, laa, laaa'ing'* for what felt like a year and was growing increasingly frustrated with Sally's inability to follow his vocal footsteps. As a by-product, he was constantly mopping beads of sweat from his flustered red face with a hand towel.

"No, no, no!"

The voice coach threw his hands in the air.

"Devi cantare con le orecchie! You have to learn to sing with your ears child!"

Sally considered the instruction and gave the obvious reply.

"But then how will people be able to hear me?"

"Mama mia, per l'amor di Dio. I don't actually mean *sing* with your ears. Your ears will take you to the correct pitch. Unless you listen to what your ears are saying, vocal training is useless. You just sang a note I've never even heard before!"

Twenty minutes later, the tutor declared Sally's voice to be "in a class of its own" and threw in the damp towel. It seems that even The Market Square can do nothing to correct the wonky stringing of vocal cords.

Looking across the room, Sally assessed her surroundings. She was in some sort of recording studio crossed with a music rehearsal space. To the right stood a glass panelled booth, rather like a telephone box, in which a chunky microphone was suspended on an adjustable arm. A mixing desk with rows of knobs and buttons and slider controls could be seen in a room beyond the booth. The ceiling was soundproofed with what appeared to be the acoustic equivalent of egg boxes and the walls, covered with a fluffy, flock material, were adorned with framed photos of Sally's favourite pop stars. The floor was carpeted with tiles in a chessboard pattern and crisscrossed with cables snaking from power sockets to stacks of amplifiers and black box speakers. A girl with pink streaks in a buzz cut, bashed through scales on a drum kit. A boy with heavy metal tattoos was tuning his electric guitar. Clusters of students were texting and tweeting and taking selfies as they perfected dance steps copied from YouTube. All were dressed in the street style of the latest music videos. To Sally's left, on a crude wooden stage that resembled the one in Cheadle village hall, a string quartet were rehearsing a piece of classical music under the guidance of a conductor in black tie and tails. Directly across the room, a group of four girls looking remarkably like Perry, Jessy, Jade and Leigh-Anne from *Little Mix* were gathered around a piano singing 'Move', which is their best song, in Sally's opinion. The pianist was struggling to play more than a few opening bars though, because the girls kept breaking into fits of giggles and slapping each other for singing out of time.

Sally was in awe, as any schoolgirl in the company of super-cool older kids and pop stars would be. She contemplated walking over to ask Jade for a selfie but was nervous and fearful of ridicule. Sally wasn't certain if she had a part to play in her dream. The question was resolved however, when the optician introduced a soft blur filter to the vision and the room once again lost all definition. For a few seconds, only vague outlines and diffused colours registered, as though the dream was continuing behind a steamy window but then came the tinkle of piano keys and as Sally turned to track the source of the sound, the dream morphed and 20/20 vision returned.

Sally was still perched on the stool but the music room was now silent and empty. For no apparent reason, the light then began to fade in steady increments, as though responding to the turn of a dimmer switch, and with silent motion, the ceiling panels retracted in a series of sliding steps to expose the infinite blackness of an open air night sky. As darkness continued to encroach on all four sides, the sudden clunk of a lever summoned a spotlight and the resultant cone of soft illumination encircled a magnificent Steinway grand piano positioned in the centre of the floor. The Italian music teacher with the pink shirt and the cravat cracked his knuckles and beckoned Sally to join him. When he gestured for a second time, insistent, but with a friendly smile, Sally pushed herself off the stool and walked over to join him.

Sally's fingers were far better at following instruction than her vocal cords and after ten minutes, or it may well have been hours in dreamtime, she could race through the major and minor scales with her eyes closed. The translation of sheet music into finger movement was also accomplished with alacrity and Sally was just about to tackle a Grade 5 piece based on an Ariana Grande song when the haunting, plaintive notes of a violin sliced through the air and called her attention.

The string quartet had returned to the stage and a boy wearing a school blazer with a large orange sun embroidered on the breast pocket sat bathed in a pool of light playing a solo piece like a virtuoso. He reminded Sally of someone from school.

He looks just like that new boy who sits at the front of the class, the one with the broken glasses, what's his name? Felix!

Felix was from Somalia and a refugee. Mrs Hill, the Headmistress, had introduced him to the school during assembly and explained that Felix, his parents and his elder brother were the victims of a war in Africa and had fled to England leaving their home and all their possessions behind. Using a map pinned to a cork board, Mrs Hill illustrated their journey and pointed out the route Felix and his family had taken.

"But now Felix and his family are safe here in England, we're going to make him more than welcome at Cheadle Juniors aren't we children?"

"Yes Mrs Hill."

Felix and his family lived hand to mouth in a cramped, sparsely furnished flat above a Chinese takeaway in Gatley – but Mrs Hill didn't tell the school children that.

A quiet, sensitive looking boy, Felix was small for his age, thin, frail even, with perfect teeth that gleamed like polished opals and undoubtedly clever. He was able to speak English fluently within a few weeks of arriving at the school. Sally was intrigued by Felix the moment she saw him standing timidly at Mrs Hill's side. Something about him called her attention and never more so than the moment she recognised him playing the violin in her dream!

Sally walked towards the stage and drawing closer, her familiarity with the damaged spectacles, clumsily repaired with sticky tape, dispelled any doubts.

That really is Felix and he's brilliant on the violin.

His eyes were closed and graceful sweeps of the bow caressed soulful, melancholic notes from the instrument. Sally was mesmerised by the flawless performance. She raised her hand to catch Felix's attention but he was lost in the mournful chords of the Bach concerto. A few seconds later, as he nodded for a page of sheet music to be turned over, her wave hit its target. Felix abruptly ceased playing, placed the instrument carefully on the floor, jumped off the stage and marched over to Sally. The flabbergasted conductor stood open mouthed, his baton frozen in mid-air, as though a wizard had cast a spell on himself.

Sally tucked stray locks of hair behind her ears to help Felix recognise her face but it wasn't necessary.

"Hi, you're Sally aren't you? The girl who sits at the back of my class. I haven't seen you here before."

Sally hesitated for a moment, mindful of the fact that she was about to hold a conversation with her sleeping self.

"No, this is my first time. I think. Actually, I don't really know where I am. I was worried about something when I went to bed. I have to sing in the school pantomime as Snow White and Auntie Kay said that singing lessons might help, so I think that's why I'm having this dream."

"Yeh, I know, I'm in the same class remember. I voted for you, everyone did, cos your singing isn't always that bad. I'm sorry about what happened to your mum and dad."

Sally was taken aback by the brazen introduction of her parents into a conversation with someone she barely knew and her spontaneous response also came as a surprise.

"That's okay. Shit happens."

Sally had heard Kay use the phrase loads of time, usually when she was on the phone to the office and thought it would make her sound grown up.

"I wish my dad was dead as well."

"What?" exclaimed Sally.

"I hate him, he's always hitting my mum and when I try to stop him, he hits me. He broke my glasses again and now I can't get new ones because the optician said I don't look after

23

them properly. Mum hasn't got any money so I had to fix them myself. Look."

Felix removed his glasses and pointed out the all too obvious repair.

"I told you that straight away because I didn't want you to think I was a total loser, wearing broken glasses."

Sally searched for appropriate words with which to placate Felix; about his dad, the sticky tape repair, the difficulties and hardship but the sentence wouldn't come.

"Come on," he said, grabbing her by the hand, "I'm bored with music class, let's see what's happening in The Market Square."

Felix led the way out of the music room, up two flights of stairs and then down a long corridor with classrooms either side. The walls were a lovely rose pink colour so the scent of fresh flowers could well have been Sally's nose playing tricks. The voice of a teacher in a classroom on the left led to children's laughter. In the next classroom, on the right, students were reciting a poem in French. In another, pupils could be heard learning Latin verbs. At the end of the corridor, three steps down brought them into a foyer, where a sliding window allowed communication with the elderly lady poking at a typewriter in the small office beyond. In the centre of the foyer, a huge bouquet of flaming red poppies stood in a crystal vase on a polished mahogany table with ball and claw feet. Beyond that, a pair of wooden swing doors with shiny brass push plates were identified by an illuminated sign as the 'Exit'. Sally grabbed Felix by the elbow just as he was about to barge through.

"Felix, wait, where are we going?"

Sally didn't sense her dream was about to evolve into a

nightmare but felt the need for a degree of preparedness nevertheless.

"It's okay. This is L'Ecole. That's French for school. In here you learn about all kinds of subjects, but out there, in The Market Square, the dreams are much better. It's where you go to have an *adventure*."

As Sally listened to Felix, a notion from earlier came calling once again.

From where exactly, are the words I'm putting into Felix's mouth coming? How does my sleeping brain know to say these things without pausing to think? How do I know what to tell Felix to say in order for him to repeat it back to me? And how do I know that those doors will lead to a different part of the dream when we're outside?

"So it will still be my dream, won't it Felix, I mean, what's happening outside, when we go through the doors?"

"Yeh! Sort of."

Felix placed both palms on a brass plate, took a step back, pushed the door with all the force he could muster and stepped into The Market Square where the *adventure,* was in full swing.

Sally followed Felix into bright sunlight, down a flight of stone steps and through a wrought iron gate – laughing out loud as she recognised where this new segment of dream was coming from. Felix removed his glasses, adjusted the running repair and put them back in place.

"What's going on?" he asked, squinting up at Sally.

A huge banner hanging between flagpoles and stretching from one side of The Market Square to the other spelled out the reply.

'Cruft's Mouse Show.'

"It's like that dog show on television Felix, but this one's for mice. I should have brought Mr Jinx."

That would have been inappropriate though, because Sally's pet mouse was tiny and the mice in The Market Square were bigger than Labrador dogs. Giant white mice, with jewel encrusted collars and leads of coloured ribbon, were on parade with their proud owners in an arena covered with sawdust and wood shavings. One mouse was racing through an obstacle course of hurdles and tunnels. Another was galloping inside a giant exercise wheel, going nowhere fast. A lady wearing a knitted twin-set, clipboard in hand, was appraising the giant mouse standing on the table in front of her. Its whiskers were over a foot long and the tips were curled like watch springs. Fur had been artfully shaved in places, poodle style, and the mouse's tail stood erect like a pink javelin.

"Come on," said Sally clutching Felix's hand, "let's get closer."

As they passed the Clock Tower, under the solemn gaze of the statue of Mr Abingdon or possibly Mr Ludlow, Felix stopped and brought Sally's attention to a stone monument about two metres in height. He was mumbling about something he'd read on the internet as Sally left his side to take a closer look.

The square slab of black granite appeared to be a war memorial and the rows of names and dates embossed in gold leaf confirmed as such. A carved inscription running across the top read:

'In memory of the 11s who died to save The Secret'

Underneath, four long columns listed the names of the

fallen but gave no detail of rank or title. There was no reference to captain this, or major that, or private somebody, it seemed the names were those of civilians rather than soldiers.

Philip Edwards 1932 - 1952
Sasha Malik 1940 - 1953
Karla Dupre 1927 - 1958
Brian Kendrick 1938 - 1962

Sally made a rough calculation and arrived at just over three hundred people. Beneath the columns, running along the base of the monument, a final epitaph read:

With little to lose, they had so much to gain. The Powers That Be salute you.

At the foot of the fourth column, three sets of parallel lines had been traced in fine blue chalk in readiness for the addition of new names. A stonemason's chisel and a lump hammer lay on the floor. Sally understood how a pet mouse could have influenced her dream but where was this backdrop coming from? And something about the dates struck Sally as odd. The names, the people, they'd all died at a relatively young age; when some were still in their teens. Also, none appeared to have fallen at the same time as they would have done if fighting in a battle or a war together. Every life seemed to have been lost at a singular, individual moment and those moments spanned hundreds of years.

The first name on the list, 'Carlo Marrenti', was born in 1537 and lived until 1558.

"So, he was twenty-one when he died, ten years older than me." Sally pointed out the fact to Felix. "That was nearly five hundred years ago, but the most recent . . . "

Felix stepped forward and placed his finger on the carved lettering for James Chang. 1993 - 2015

" . . . he died this year."

Sally could see that although the dates were different, the years in which the people had died were in chronological order, as though they'd emerged from the trenches in single file stretching over centuries.

"I searched for James Chang and those dates on the internet in the library" Felix said. "I found out what happened to him. He was electrocuted on a railway line in a tube station in London six weeks ago."

Felix confirmed the fact with a nod.

"It's true, check it for yourself."

He tugged the cuff of Sally's sweater and turned on his heels.

"Come on, let's see if the Number 11 Club's open."

They skirted around the mouse show, past the butchers, the bakers, the candlestick makers and beyond Sampson's Motorcycle Workshop, to the upper left corner of The Market Square. Here Felix pulled up at an alleyway barely wide enough for two people. Sally looked down the seemingly never ending rat run and her vision went haywire. Tilting her head from side to side, she tried to focus, but it made no difference. The narrow thoroughfare was an optical illusion. The brick walls converged at such a steep angle that the meeting point in infinity may well have been just a few metres away. The perspective was all horribly wrong; like one of those rooms that assumes the proportions of a doll's house the moment you step inside. Daylight quickly began to ebb as though another dimmer switch had been turned down and Sally felt a pang of anxiety.

Earlier The Market Square had been alive with activity, but now all was eerily quiet. The mouse show was over and the sawdust floor had been swept away. Sombre light and flickering shadow from an ornate gaslight gave meagre reassurance all was well. A mackerel sky with luminescent flanks of violet and gold fled towards the horizon with nightfall in pursuit. Had they inadvertently crossed a border and stepped into a darker side of The Market Square? Felix sensed Sally's trepidation.

"It's okay," he said, pointing down the alley, "look, that's where we're going. It's not far."

Sally couldn't see any sort of rallying point. The alley appeared to go on forever or go nowhere at all and following Felix's directive made her go cross-eyed.

"I'm not going down there Felix. Are you mad?"

Somewhere deep inside the tunnel, maybe fifty metres or possibly five hundred metres away, a slit tore through the darkness and released the sound of laughter muffled by distance. The sliver of light then thinned to nothing like a candle going out, or, to be more accurate, the door closing on a party.

As though a starting pistol had been fired, Felix set off down the passageway and after a moment's hesitation Sally followed; cautiously keeping three or four steps behind and fully prepared for flight, not fight.

Perspective continued to play tricks. The walls grew higher as the way ahead stretched forwards with a push me, pull you sort of rhythm. Sally caught up with Felix and reached for his hand, for his own safety of course, and it was at that moment she heard the tinkle of a piano followed by the hum of conversation and shrieks of laughter. Forging on with new optimism, the hubbub increased in volume as the sound of people beckoned like a homing beacon. Yet Sally couldn't pinpoint where the noise was coming from. After a further thirty or forty steps, she began to question the merits of a seemingly fruitless endeavour and that's when Felix stopped, turned to his left and pointed upwards.

"Look. I told you it'd be okay. We're here" he said.

The neon sign jutted out at a right angle from above a featureless black door and depicted two yellow dice bouncing on a baize green background. The face of one die was flashing on six, the other die was flashing on five. The 'Number 11 Club' lettering glowed in electric blue.

Sally's jaw dropped. She looked back up the alleyway to try and gauge how far they'd walked but found it impossible to judge distance in a passageway that was both visually incoherent and impenetrable to gaslight. Utterly confused, she questioned the existence of the sign.

So how come I didn't see the glow? It's brighter than a Christmas tree? This place just popped-up out of nowhere.

Felix took a step forward and rapped smartly on the door.

After five seconds, the shutter to a small viewing window slid back and a pair of bulbous eyes peered out and then down. Sally half considered making a run for it and leaving Felix to fend for himself.

Following the clunk of a sliding lock, the door opened inwards.

"Ah, Mr Felix, good evening sir, it's so good to see you again."

The greeting came from a barrel-chested man with a shiny

bald head and a face as round as a bowling ball. His walrus moustache was waxed at the tips and he wore the formal evening attire of dress shirt, dinner jacket and bow tie. His beaming smile revealed a gold tooth.

"Your seat at the bar is waiting as always sir."

The doorman encouraged Felix to enter, first with a bow and then with the sweep of his hand.

"Thank you Charles. It's good to be back."

Felix nonchalantly pressed something into the doorman's hand, trod lightly down a short flight of stairs, pulled a black velvet curtain to one side and slipped inside the Number 11 Club like James Bond junior in school uniform and with bust glasses.

Sally's jaw almost unhinged itself.

A second bow and another exaggerated sweep of the hand encouraged *her* to enter.

"Good evening madam, welcome to the Number 11" said Charles.

Sally stepped forward with no trepidation whatsoever. *Who the heck does Felix think he is and more to the point, what's he up to?*

The steps led down to a small foyer and the carpet was soft and deep beneath Sally's feet, like walking on marshmallow.

"Good evening madam," said the girl in the white silk blouse standing behind the cloakroom hatch, "may I take your coat?"

"But I'm not wearing a coat."

"Oh, but you are madam."

And she was.

Sally was wearing an ankle length, white fur coat with three large pink buttons in the shape of mouse noses. The fur coat was luxuriously soft and silky to the touch, just like stroking Mr Jinx. Sally slipped out of the coat and the cloakroom attendant gave her a ticket stamped with a number eleven.

Charles parted the velvet curtains with a smile as Sally followed in the footsteps of Felix.

The Number 11 Club reminded Sally of a cocktail bar in a five-star hotel. The Lowry in Manchester to be specific, because she'd been there once with Kay on a fundraising 'Fun Day' in support of homeless teenagers.

The Number 11 Club had a similar, minimalist interior, with subdued lighting and black leather sofas and fancy, chrome frame chairs with matching coffee tables. The cocktail hour jazz from a grand piano made the perfect backing track for the easy conversation and laughter. The elegant women and well groomed men had been lifted straight from the pages of Kay's Vogue magazine. A table of four were being served fish fingers sandwiches and ice cream floats.

Sally's eyes quickly honed in on their target – they could hardly miss him.

Felix was sitting at a bar, on a stool almost as tall as himself, sipping a drink from a Champagne flute with a fat cigar wedged between his fingers. His school tie had been replaced by a huge, black, bow tie.

A bat attacking his throat would be better.

Sally was becoming increasingly annoyed with the antics of her own dream. Felix beckoned her with an insouciant flick of the head which was the equivalent of a red rag to a bull. She shot over like a ballistic missile.

"Felix, what the hell do you think you're doing? You're

smoking a cigar and you're drinking Champagne. You're going to get into so much trouble."

"No I won't. Smoking's not banned in the Number 11 Club" he replied dismissively, totally missing Sally's point.

"What can I get you madam?"

A waiter with slicked back hair and wearing a bib apron branded with the bouncing dice logo stood in front of Sally polishing a glass.

"She'll have the same as me Arthur, a Sprite on the rocks."

"Very good Mr Felix, any nibbles?"

"Yes, we'll have six packets of Cheesy Wotsits."

"Very good sir."

Felix turned to Sally. She was speechless.

"Mum says we can't afford Cheesy Wotsits so I always ask for lots of packets when I'm here."

Sally still couldn't think of anything to say and simply stared at Felix in disbelief as he sucked away at his cigar, in his daft glasses, sipping Sprite like some stupid little ... whatever!

"You're just incredible Felix."

"I know," said Felix, before releasing a fat smoke ring that hung in the air like a halo.

Sally had thought she liked Felix. He was kind, never tried to show off, was always friendly with everyone in the class, but now she was irked by the discovery of an irritating side to his character.

"You know smoking stunts your growth? And you're not even that tall to begin with!" Sally punctuated her sarcasm with a nasally snort.

"Very funny," said Felix, blowing a second smoke ring and without a care in the world.

The conductor of the quartet from earlier in the dream

then appeared from nowhere, as often happens in a dream, and took a stool beside Felix.

"Felix, it's simply not professional to stop halfway through a Bach concerto and walk off the stage."

He turned to answer and Sally didn't want to hear another infuriating reply so chose to move closer to the lady in the sequinned dress playing the piano. Sipping the Sprite through a straw, she decided it tasted exactly like the real thing.

The pianist had a rich, husky voice and she played the piano beautifully but making her way across the club, through speech bubbles of chatter, Sally couldn't help but think the talent was wasted, even if the song was being sung in that slouchy, lounge style.

I saw a mouse!
Where?
There on the stair!
Where on the stair?
Right there!
A little mouse with clogs on.
Well I declare!
Going clip-clippity-clop on the stair.

Beyond the piano, Sally was drawn to the barley twist rope hanging between a line of chrome posts that cordoned off a quiet corner of the club. A sign attached to one of the posts confirmed the area to be for 'VIPs ONLY'. Beyond the rope, a lectern stood in front of a pair of red velvet curtains. Sally's interest was piqued by the illuminated box above the pelmet which displayed the word 'CASINO' and she was about to duck under the rope when Charles the doorman made an address from behind the lectern which took her by surprise.

"I'm sorry madam, but only VIP number elevens are allowed to enter the casino. May I ask if you are one?"

A raised eyebrow accentuated the question.

"I don't know. How do I become one?"

"You don't become one Madam, you're born one. May I check? It's Bennett isn't it, Sally Bennett?"

Charles opened a thick ledger book, switched on the reading lamp and began leafing through the pages. Sally assumed he was checking the list of members. Standing with her hands behind her back, patiently waiting for status to be clarified, she heard the rattle of a ball bouncing around a roulette wheel and people gambling beyond the curtains. The triumphant 'ooh's' counter balanced the downbeat 'argh's'.

"Ah yes, here we have it."

Charles looked up with his index finger pinned on proof of identity as though it were a mouse trapped by the tail.

"You are indeed a VIP Sally, and a most distinguished one at that. Lady luck awaits in that case."

Charles was about to part the curtains when a debilitating wave of tiredness swept through Sally's body bringing a halt to all further motion. Her exhausted brain, fatigued by the rigours of inventing a dream on the fly, with dialogue and characters and elaborate staging but with no script for guidance, was calling the night's performance a take! Sally raised the back of her hand to cover a weary yawn. Charles let the curtain drapes fall back into place, he knew only too well what was about to happen. A second yawn followed the first and the extraction process commenced with tinctures of Sally's presence dissipating in compounding increments. Her fifty per cent tint became a thirty, then a ten and soon

Sally's presence in The Market Square was little more than an opaque, colourless shadow and in short order, it became nothing at all. She wouldn't be breaking the bank that night.

Felix stayed at the bar an hour longer and enjoyed another three Sprites and four packets of Cheesy Wotsits before returning home to bed. The single bed in which he slept head to toe with his elder brother.

Chapter 4

Something happened

The following morning, with memories of the dream still vivid, Sally was disturbed to discover that the events from the night before seemed to have mistakenly registered themselves in her consciousness as *actual* occurrences. As though she really *had* been in that music room and in the Number 11 Club. The sugary taste of Sprite still tickled her tongue!

Something, no, *someone*, had made an indelible impression on Sally's brain and thoughts of Felix in his stupid bow tie, blowing smoke rings and eating Cheesy Wotsits raised her hackles. The source material for the first part of the dream, the singing lesson, was easy to identify. And the mice show? Ditto. That was all down to Mr Jinx!

But Felix? A boy I hardly know from school spending all that time in my head, smoking a cigar and drinking at a bar, while I was sleeping! Where had all that come from? Why did I give him such a major role in my dream?

She would never see Felix in the same light again.

And as for the violin playing, what was all that about?

Sally purposely avoided all proximity to Felix in school assembly and during the two lessons that followed. Half way through morning break, as she practised *Little Mix* dance steps with a friend, Felix walked over as bold as brass with a supercilious grin on his face.

"Hi Sally. How are you feeling this morning?"

This is odd. I've never really spoken to Felix but after appearing in my dream, he suddenly comes wandering over like he was my flippin' brother.

Felix's glasses sat at a wonky angle on the bridge of his nose and he poked them back into place with his finger. The friend skipped away to dance with another group.

"We had a great adventure in our dream didn't we? I knew you'd like the Number 11 Club!"

Had Sally been a cartoon character, this is the scene where she appears to run desperately through thin air before plummeting down into the deepest of canyons. Sally had no idea of how to reply to what she'd just heard so played the part of someone dumbstruck, and the role came naturally under the circumstances. She shot a furtive glance from side to side, someone might have overheard what Felix had just said.

"Are you feeling okay Felix? What club? I've no idea what you're talking about."

"Yes you do Sally. Our dream in The Market Square last night. Remember? With the giant mice? Then I took you to the Number 11 Club and you shouted at me because I was smoking a cigar."

Sally's knees buckled as she hit the canyon floor and a groundswell of panic rose like a cloud of dust.

Every Monday morning, the entire school was drilled on the actions to take regarding 'disturbing situations' and the words of warning rang out like an alarm bell.

If something should happen we know to be wrong. If someone is naughty or someone is cruel. At home, outside, be it family or friend. Always tell teacher because teacher knows best.

But what Felix had said, knowing all about her dream, didn't feel like one of those 'disturbing situations'. Mrs Broughton was talking to Miss Samaya just twenty metres away. Should she go and tell them about what had just happened? A *something* she knew to be wrong. Sally took a deep breath and agreed with the observation that she was safe enough in the middle of the playground, and besides, she was curious. Could Felix really have been there, experiencing the same dream at exactly the same time? Walking down that dark alleyway together? Or was he playing some kind of trick?

Whatever the explanation, the playing dumb wasn't working so Sally adopted the new strategy of 'shrugging it off'.

"Oh you're so funny, you really make me laugh."

This declaration, announced somewhat theatrically, was followed by a burst of forced laughter.

"You have the craziest ideas Felix, how does your brain think up things like that?"

Sally scanned the playground with a radar like glance, grabbed Felix by the elbow and pulled him sharply towards her, nose almost touching nose.

"How the heck do you know about my dream last night Felix?" she hissed.

"Because I was there, with you."

"Where?"

"Everywhere! In L'Ecole. In The Market Square. At the club. I was with you all the time. And I know you were there too."

"But you couldn't have been in my dream, that's impossible. That was my dream, in my head, while I was asleep in bed."

Felix gave Sally a half smile and shrugged.

"No, it doesn't work like that. I've been loads of times. I

know."

Hot breath fogged Felix's glasses such was the pressure of steam in Sally's boiler. She pushed him away.

"You . . . weirdo! That was definitely my dream and I want to know, how you know. I mean, I want to know how you knew. Look Felix, how the hell did you do that?"

"Do what?" asked Felix.

Sally wanted to throttle him there and then.

"How did you get into my dream?"

"It's called straddling. It's connected to the way you learn stuff in The Market Square. It's how I learnt to play the violin and speak English."

"Felix, you really need to explain that to me right now or I'm . . ."

Sally saw the checkmate move. There was still five minutes until the end of break. Pinching a fold of soft skin on the back of Felix's arm and maintaining meaningful pressure, she marched him from the playground, pushed through the double doors and checked the length of the corridor. The teachers were either in the staff room or on duty outside so the coast was clear. Sally steered Felix toward the music room with her fist now gripping the back of his sweater. Thankfully, the music room was empty.

"Go on, prove it" she said, shoving him free. Sally was nodding towards the only violin the school owned. It was lying in an open case with the bow alongside.

"But what if someone comes?"

"Felix! Show me."

"But I haven't got my music."

"Now Felix! Quickly, before the bell goes."

Sensing that Sally's patience was wafer thin, Felix

shrugged and said, "alright, but you can't tell anyone. It has to be our secret."

Felix gently positioned the violin beneath his chin, raised the bow, blinked twice as he looked Sally in the eye and the jagged opening notes of Bach's Partita in D minor for solo violin soared across the music room, through an open window and out into the playground.

Sally snatched the violin from Felix's hands, placed it back in the case with its bow and slammed down the lid.

"Meet me in the corner of the playground by the wall at lunchtime. We need to talk."

"Talk about what?"

"Are you doing this on purpose? Being totally stupid? I'm serious, you have to tell me what's going on. About the dream last night, both of us in the same place, how you learned to play the violin? How *I knew* you could play the violin. This isn't normal. It's totally amazing Felix. Like a miracle. How did we do that?"

"That's what happens in The Market Square. What you do in a dream becomes real when you wake up."

Sally's eyes were drawn to the upright piano to the left of the music teacher's desk.

"Shit" she said.

"Shit happens" said Felix, pushing his glasses back into place.

The sudden clang of a bell made Sally jump. Break was over but she had to find out.

It can't be. That's impossible!

Sally darted to the piano and stood with her outstretched fingers trembling above the keys.

So how do I start? What do I play? What happens now?

41

She turned to Felix for reassurance, or perhaps approval to proceed and then back to the piano. After closing her eyes she travelled back to the relevant sequence in the dream; to the part where the teacher with the cravat was explaining how to run your fingers across the piano keys while your eyes followed the notations on sheet music.

Surely that was all just a fantasy, an impression, a representation of playing. Like a game of make believe. Nobody could learn to play a piano just by dreaming about it.

Like water dripping from a tap, Sally's index finger plonked on middle 'C', her middle finger on 'D', third finger on 'E' and the floodgates opened on a reservoir of piano playing know-how. It seemed that having learned a little, Sally knew where to find the lot.

When the lunchtime bell brought morning lessons to an end, Sally dashed to the wall in the far corner of the playground where Felix was waiting as instructed.

During a fifteen minute interrogation, he was probed and questioned on everything he knew about shared dreams, learning to play instruments in L'Ecole and discovering the Number 11 Club. Of course, Felix was unable to give any sort of authoritative answer because he didn't understand the workings of The Market Square himself. However, he did talk with certainty about two funny men he'd met one night.

"One was short and chubby and the other was tall and thin" he said. "They told me there's dream energy and time energy and if you combine both of them, that's how you learn things quickly. It's called straddling. They said it would be better to keep my dreams in The Market Square a secret. I think you should as well."

Sally was no longer listening. She'd heard enough, or simply taken in all a ten-year-old could be expected to assimilate in terms of learning from dreams, being a number 11 and playing instruments without lessons.

Mrs Broughton took Sally to one side after a history test later that afternoon.

"Is everything okay Sally? You look very pale. You didn't raise your hand to answer a single question and that's not like you. You just stared out of the window like you were in a trance. I think you could be coming down with something. Ask Kay to take your temperature when you get home."

Always tell teacher because teacher knows best.

Mrs Broughton would certainly listen, but unless she'd also been to The Market Square, she wouldn't know how the term 'best' could be applied. Sally decided to follow Felix's advice and keep this particular *something* a secret.

Two weeks later, despite some of the high notes sounding like a fingernail scraping down a blackboard, Snow White received a standing ovation from a school hall filled with parents, pupils, teachers and her closest friend, a handsome prince.

During the months that followed, Sally and Felix became the talk of the staff room and openly referred to as the 'odd couple'. However, since they were head and shoulders above the rest of the class in terms of academic ability, it was a relationship to be encouraged; the girl who'd lost both parents enjoying the friendship of a boy whose family had lost everything. Best friends by day, and inseparable by night.

The repercussions of evening classes in L'Ecole rippled through the vicarage one night as Kay sat watching *University Challenge* on TV. Sally was sprawled on the rug at Kay's feet playing with Mr Jinx. Distracted? Absent minded? Either way, she should have known better than to respond to the following.

"And now your starter for ten."

Sally not only answered the starter for ten but also the three questions that followed, all of which related to opera. The answers were *Gilbert and Sullivan*, *Tosca* and *Madame Butterfly*, in that order. Fortunately, Kay was well into her bottle of red and through a haze of fuzzy logic presumed the answers were a result of the show being on repeat and praised Sally's powers of recall.

One morning, a week before the end of the final year of Junior School, Felix's chair was empty when the register was called. He didn't attend school that day, nor the day after or the day after that. Sally asked Mrs Broughton if Felix was ill and if so, when would he be back? She wanted to say goodbye before they all broke up for the summer holidays but Mrs Broughton said it was something she couldn't say too much about and reached for a tissue as tears brimmed over her eyelids.

"He won't be coming back Sally, I'm so sorry dear, there's been a terrible accident and Felix is no longer with us."

For ten consecutive nights, Sally waited for Felix on the steps of L'Ecole but he never turned up. The shared dreams were over, the curtain had fallen on their midnight matinees and Sally never saw Felix again.

Chapter 5

The warrior

Fourteen months later, with the summer holidays about to begin and thankfully, all the challenges and torment of a first year at secondary school over for six weeks, fate once again threw Sally a curveball.

Kay was standing by the fridge sipping a mug of coffee and chatting with Leanna. Leanna was the housekeeper, odd job person and Kay's irreplaceable Woman Friday. Sally was sitting at the kitchen table eating a lunch of fish fingers on toast.

"No Mr Jinx, you know you're not allowed to go on there."
Sally's white mouse broke house rules when it ran down her arm and scurried over the food plate.
"Sally love, for heaven's sake. How many times do I have to tell you? It's so unhygienic having a bloody animal running over the surfaces we eat on."
Sally gave Kay a hapless look.
"I didn't mean to let him do it. He just wants to explore everywhere today. He went missing in my room and I ended up finding him in one of my shoes and when I woke up this morning he was ... "
"Well that's just great. So where is he now?"
Sally turned back to the kitchen table. The mouse was nowhere to be seen.

"See, that's exactly what I mean, he just keeps going off on one. I think he needs a Mrs Jinx to keep him under control."

Kay laughed and poured the dregs of her coffee into the sink.

"I've got the awards dinner tonight so I'm off to the Trafford Centre to look for a sparkly dress. Do you want to come?"

"No, I'm okay thanks. I need to find Mr Jinx. He's going to be grounded for two days when I catch him."

Church properties in Victorian times were not constructed with half measures; three floors of spacious rooms with big boned furniture and more hidey holes than a Swiss cheese were a definite home advantage for a mouse on the run.

After twenty minutes of shifting and lifting and prodding and poking and a process of elimination, Sally stood on the threshold of the final place to look. She felt uncomfortable in the dining room and had left it last for that reason. The air carried a chill even with the heating on and damp mustiness was a permanent feature. When Kay threw dinner parties, guests preferred to eat and drink in front of the wood burning stove in the kitchen rather than by the grandiose fireplace in the room Kay referred to as 'Miss Haversham's boudoir'. On the chimney breast, the triptych of carved panels depicting a one-sided dust-up between natives throwing spears and demons raining down lightning bolts did little to warm the atmosphere. There was something about the panel that Sally found unsettling and she tried not to let it catch her eye as she entered the room on all fours like a lion cub on the hunt.

"Mr Jinx, you're in such trouble. There'll be no Tesco's

vintage cheddar for you tonight."

Sally's knobbly knees made the floorboards creak so she stopped stalking her prey and lowered her head to survey the world from mouse perspective, but Mr Jinx remained elusive. She clambered to her feet, walked over to the bay window and lifted the curtain drapes from the carpet. The damask fabric was thick and heavy like tapestry, and as folds fell back into place, dust particles raised by the disturbance swarmed like angry microbes in the sunlight. Sally was half-expecting Mr Jinx to sneeze but instead felt her hair crackle with static and then rise as though someone had brushed a party balloon on a sweater and was holding it to the back of her head. Something, or someone, had entered the room and the atmosphere was positively charged. Sally didn't feel threatened so held her ground, expecting the sensation to be fleeting like the rush of a draught from an open door, but the force wouldn't release its hold on her hair. She slowly turned to face the source and experienced a sensation she had no words to describe; her 'mind's eye' or a 'sixth sense' wouldn't do it justice. The presence in the room was that of a man standing to the right of the fireplace, facing up to Sally as she stood with her back to the bay window.

Her immediate and only impression was of a primitive being, a warrior, from some ancient time in history. A tall, broad shouldered figure with long matted hair and a stern expression on a face streaked with sweat and dirt. A round shield of beaten metal protected one arm and his torso was covered with a combination of upper body armour and some form of warrior's skirt defined by broad strips of thick leather hanging down over muscular thighs. His left hand clutched a spear, the point of which was almost touching the ceiling. On his feet he wore open toed sandals with the fastenings criss-crossing his muscular calves.

The confrontation between the two, a silent face off, continued for several seconds and it was odd to say the least! To be able to acknowledge a figure, to register details of their attire and physical aspect in an empty room, when by definition there was nobody in the room at all. Though the warrior projected a countenance of foreboding, Sally perceived no danger or physical threat. Rather, she sensed the invisible yet perceptible presence was simply making a protest about all the disturbance and wanted Sally to know it.

"Sorry for waking you up" she said, backing away and closing the dining room door quietly as she left.

In the hallway, a pink worm tail disappeared behind a plant pot and Mr Jinx's game was up.

Later that afternoon, Sally was curled up on the sofa with her iPad. She was searching the internet for details of the history of the vicarage, when Kay walked into the lounge chewing on a stick of celery and flopped down beside her.

"How was the run?"

"Great Sal. Did Ten K. Wilmslow and back. Hey, you can have that as my nickname. Ten Kay!"

Sally rolled her eyes.

"Yeh, it was really good. Just what I needed. Got all those toxins out of my system and now I'm so ready for tonight."

If Kay wasn't stressed with production deadlines and the pressures of work, she was stressed by all the jogging she had to do, in the little free time she had, in order to de-stress from said deadlines and pressures of work.

"Why, what's happening tonight?"

"I told you, it's the TV Awards dinner in Media City. I'm up for News Producer of the Year. I won't get it though! That lazy cow from ITV will win with that fake report about that other lazy cow."

Kay crunched away at the celery.

"Auntie Kay, just because everyone's not on a diet and surviving on coffee and raw vegetables doesn't mean ... "

"Okay, yeh. She's a good producer, and I agree, she's talented. I also know it's not politically correct to use derogatory terms nowadays. But she's still a lazy cow."

Sally started laughing.

"I need to go and get ready love. And Leanna's staying over cos I'll be back late."

Kay paused in front of a mirror to check her teeth for celery strands.

"Is this house haunted Auntie Kay? I mean, have you ever seen a ghost here? Like maybe in the dining room for example, it's always freezing in there and that wooden picture is pretty scary?"

"Don't be silly love, there's no such thing as ghosts. Besides, they wouldn't want to live in the same house as me. And that carved panel, I think I bought it at a car boot sale about five years ago. Probably got a 'Made in China' sticker on the back. Anyway, don't be late to bed love, tell Leanna to lock all the doors and make sure Mr Jinx stays incarcerated, I don't want a surprise under my pillow when I get home half sozzled at half two."

Sally heard Kay take the stairs two at a time, gazelle like, and returned to the Google search on her iPad.

She unearthed plenty of information about Christ Church

Cheadle including the starting time for Sunday mass and a new online streaming service, but nothing concerning the vicarage or strange happenings in a dining room; other than Kay Hope, a well known media personality had bought the property at an auction in 2006.

Placing the iPad to one side, Sally reflected on the possible nature of the phenomenon from earlier that afternoon. The more she thought about it however, the more she was drawn to the conclusion that her experience may have been nothing out of the ordinary at all. Probably just a trick of the light combined with cold air rising from the cellar and an overactive imagination. A final line of enquiry was worth pursuing to bring the matter to a close and Wikipedia was the starting point.

'History of Cheadle, England'.

'There has been human occupation in the area that is now Cheadle since prehistoric times. The earliest evidence is of burial mounds dating from the iron age, belonging to the Celts who occupied Britain. Later, the area was occupied by Brigantes, whose activity was discovered in the form of axe fragments.'

Cheadle didn't have much else to say for itself history wise, other than it was mentioned in the Domesday Book and men from the area fought in the Battle of Flodden.

'During the uprising of Bonnie Prince Charlie, his troops marched through Cheadle. Some remains have been found, including swords.'

Sally was looking for a bridge to connect her mental rendering of an ancient warrior to a vicarage in Cheadle.

Perhaps this battle at Flodden or the remains of Bonnie Prince Charlie's troops have something to do with it?

Sally clicked the link to the Battle of Flodden.

'The battle was fought in Branxton, in the county of Northumberland in Northern England on the 9th September 1513 between an invading Scots army and . . .'

Sally stopped at that point. The battle had taken place nowhere near Cheadle. And though it was possible soldiers had fought in Branxton and perhaps returned to Cheadle, where one of them may have died on the site of the vicarage, Sally had a feeling that soldiers in 1513, though over five hundred years ago, wouldn't look like savages with long, matted hair and carrying spears. She'd seen a picture of Bonnie Prince Charlie in a history book and seemed to recall him wearing something like a dress with a ruffle collar and a pair of white tights and lipstick.

Where did I read that bit about burial mounds and the iron age?

She flicked back through the search history.

'The earliest evidence is of burial mounds dating from the iron age, belonging to the Celts who occupied Britain.'

Sally had no idea who the Celts were, or Brigantes for that matter, so she clicked on Google images.

Two-seconds later, she was startled to be presented with an artist's representation, an illustration in full colour that clearly captured her warrior, or someone astonishingly like her perception of him, in actual physical form. It seemed a Celt, a member of a race of people that had existed a thousand years ago was residing in the dining room and perhaps it was his spirit that had confronted her earlier that afternoon.

In the way that someone online shopping for *this*, is also prompted to consider looking at *that*, Sally's thought processes followed a link back to a similar strange event years earlier. The boy and girl in the children's home had also been *there* yet *not there, sensed* more than *seen* and they were still stamped as indelible, glowing figures in her memory. She considered the possibility that a similar, embossed effect might also exist to define her warrior, to make *him* visible to the naked eye, albeit fleetingly, if only he could be illuminated in just the right way.

An idea for replicating the conditions in the children's home; replacing total darkness with a split second of light, was refined within a half an hour. Sally labelled the experiment she was planning to perform that evening as 'lamping.'

Leanna arrived at seven, Kay left in a taxi at eight and by nine the vicarage was cloaked in darkness. The bulb in the exterior light outside the dining room window had blown so that was a stroke of luck. Sally drew the curtains all the way round the bay window and made sure they overlapped to form a light-tight seal. She switched off the candle pendants on the wall, closed the door but as she stood in silence in the blacked-out room, somewhat self-consciously, she suddenly felt silly and fanciful about what she was planning to do. The experience in the children's home had made a lasting impression but in hindsight that may well have been nothing more than the remnant of a dream spilling over into the next morning or a hallucination while sleepwalking. She considered abandoning the lamping experiment in favour of watching TV with Leanna; but a propulsive force pushed her curiosity and the desire to try and replicate the phenomenon held sway.

The room was dark, but not pitch black; so not dark enough! Light from a distant street lamp was seeping from a narrow gap between the wall and the top of the curtains. Sally returned to the dining room with a bundle of towels and standing on tip-toe, on a chair, she was able to snuff it out. Now the room was almost ready, virtually pitch black. Sally tucked the edges of the curtains deep inside the recessed window and after that, she couldn't see the hand in front of her face.

"Perfect" she said, nodding approval at the total blackout and stubbing her toe on a chair leg as she fumbled for a light switch.

Sally returned to the lounge where Leanna was watching *'Call the Cleaners'*, the TV programme she described as "Mastermind, for people like me". Her attention didn't shift from the screen.

"You alright Sal?"

"Yeh. I'm good. Just to let you know, Mr Jinx has gone walk about again so if you hear a bit of banging, it's only me trying to flush him out."

"Okay, luv. Shut the door then."

Sally allowed herself fifteen minutes to go through the commotions of earlier in the afternoon, to follow her own noisy footsteps. Furniture was shifted with bangs and scrapes, the hall rug was given a vigorous shake and plant pots and vases repositioned. In the dining room, chairs were given a new seating plan, wine glasses in the dresser moved around like chess pieces, crockery was re-stacked and cutlery rattled in the drawer. The base of the triptych was pulled away from the wall and allowed to drop back with a thump loud enough to wake the dead.

When the prep work was complete, Sally took the heavy

duty flashlight from the cupboard under the stairs, changed the old batteries for new, removed her shoes and tiptoed back to the dining room. Before entering, she took mental bearings on the position of the dining table and the number of steps needed to reach 'x' marks the spot. The hall and landing lights were switched off. Sally slipped inside the dining room, silently closed the door and immersed herself in coal mine blackness. Slowly inching across the carpet she bit her lip and hoped a floorboard wouldn't creak. Once in position, the torch was readied with her thumb poised above the 'ON' button and the lens pointed directly ahead. Sally stood motionless for three minutes, hardly daring to breathe.

When the torch clicked 'ON'; as the raiding party of photons sent darkness scurrying from every corner of the room, Sally lamped her warrior. A not particularly fearsome warrior, for he held his ground no longer than the singular moment needed for his glowing essential features, his existence, his very being in that room to become fleetingly apparent.

Sally held on to the memory of the warrior as she climbed into bed and switched off the bedside light. Replicating her experience in the children's home was positive proof of something but it felt like another of those *somethings* about which Mrs Broughton, or even Kay for that matter, would be unable to give *best* advice.

Pulling the duvet under her chin Sally shrieked when she saw the luminous green hands and the glowing face hovering directly in front of her eyes.

Somehow, during the process of lamping the warrior, she'd also managed to lamp her watch.

Chapter 6

Fluorescence

"Sally. Are you awake? It's a big breakfast day!"

Kay was calling from the kitchen and the smell of fried bacon was tickling Sally's nose to confirm the fact.

"Yeh, coming down now, I'm starving."

As she checked on Mister Jinx and filled the water bottle clipped to his cage, an explanation for what she'd witnessed the previous night, terms to describe the revelation, the exposure, the end result, played hard to get. Was it a ghost or a spirit that she'd illuminated in the dining room? Sally associated the word 'ghost' with poltergeists and hauntings but there had been nothing ghostly about the warrior. The word 'spirit' she associated with energy, the residue of a past life, fast and fleeting, there and not there; it seemed a more appropriate label for the spectres, the apparition, she'd encountered. Spirit would do as a working title. The lamping of the warrior dispelled any lingering doubt that the sighting of the children in the home had been a figment of her imagination.

Fastening her watch strap brought to mind the glowing numerals and a comparison with the glowing detail of the 'spirits'. They weren't exactly the same, but appeared to possess very similar qualities.

Sally entered the kitchen as Kay, in slippers and dressing gown and with a tea towel over her shoulder, was serving breakfast. Leanna had emptied the fridge and was washing glass shelves and plastic trays in the sink.

"Sally darling" said Leanna without looking up, "you're not starving, people in Africa are starving. You're just very hungry."

"Quite right" said Kay as she carried two plates of sausage, egg, bacon and fried tomatoes to the table and plonked herself down on a chair. "My bloody head's pounding. I was listening to my body when it screamed for a full English but with that greasy sausage grinning at me, I can't face it. Now my body wants a full Manchester instead, coffee and a fag."

Leanna was tittering to herself as Kay reached for a pack of Marlboro Lights.

"Your Auntie Kay didn't get home until turned three this morning, the old trollop. And she had to make the walk of shame, trying to find a taxi in Salford at that time of the morning."

"Leanna, you can sod right off. That was no walk of shame. It was actually a stride of pride, because look, I had this for company."

From under the kitchen table, having reached down into a crumpled carrier bag, Kay retrieved what appeared to be a brick of glass engraved with a TV Awards logo and triumphantly placed it on the table with an emphatic thud.

"Producer of the year for news features. Now that's what I'm talking about."

Kay smiled and winked at Sally with a still bleary eye.

"Auntie Kay, you did it, bloody hell. Oops, sorry for swearing. Oh I'm so happy for you."

Sally rushed round the table to give Kay a congratulatory hug.

"I'm so pleased, fantastic, fantastic, you showed that lazy cow!"

"Yeh, it's about time real talent was recognised in this business, rather than all the . . . sycophancy. And that's not the word I really want to use Sally, but you're too young for the unedited version. You know what I'm saying though, don't you Leanna?"

Leanna turned from rinsing a cloth in the sink and with a look of acquiescence confirmed that she most certainly did.

Sally helped Leanna re-stock the fridge as Kay showered and dressed for work. She returned fifteen minutes later wearing a black business suit, her hair still damp, and gulped down cold coffee as she rummaged in a shoulder bag for her phone. Sally could smell vanilla in Kay's perfume. She loved her aunt's morning hustle and bustle routine; the way she could emerge from a cocoon of crumpled pyjamas and bed head and become a dynamic TV executive simply by changing into smart clothes and applying make-up. It was like living with Wonder Woman.

"Frank, you said you'd be here ten minutes ago. I've got that scripting meeting at ten so if I'm late, I'm dragging you in there on my behalf to apologise. Chop chop. Beep as you pull up onto the drive."

Normal service had resumed. Kay's working day had begun and war paint, the red lipstick and mascara, was being applied.

"Leanna, sorry, but there's a tap dripping in my en-suite and the shower door keeps jamming, can you put them on that plumbing list for Ted? And can you call someone about a wasp's nest? I think they'll find it in the roof outside my bedroom window, I've seen them flying around a hole and there were three dead ones on the carpet this morning."

Sally admired the fine art of applying lipstick while talking at the same time.

"What are you up to today Sal? And more to the point, what have you got planned for the next few weeks? You can't stay cooped up playing on your iPad all day. You need to be outdoors, in fresh air; that'll work wonders for your eczema. My schedule's chock-a-block for a fortnight but I told them, after that, I'm out of there until the end of August, we need a holiday. Invite some friends round Sal, go to the park, have a picnic. It's a lovely sunny day."

Kay was peering into a compact mirror and applying eye liner as she spoke.

"Mmm, that friend thing. It's not really coming together at this school."

Sally had loved junior school but secondary education was proving to be a different lesson in life altogether and the first year had been tough. Sally knew eczema was a common complaint, given her age and the trauma she'd been through. But it seemed all the kids in her class thought the untimely death of both parents and the unsightly skin condition were contagious afflictions and avoided her company like the plague.

Kay placed her hand on Sally's.

"Are they still doing that thing with their desks?"

"Yeh, they still make sure there's more space round mine than the others. And I do try and make friends and keep my eczema covered up but they still taunt me or ignore me. So I don't want to invite anyone round; we don't want another birthday situation."

The previous November, Sally invited children in her new class to celebrate her twelfth birthday. Kay booked two lanes at Super Bowl and a table for ten at Pizza Hut, but only two kids turned up. As the mothers chatted awkwardly, the children went through the formalities of bowling for ten minutes and then they all made excuses to leave early. The half-eaten cake was thrown in the bin a few days later.

"Don't worry, I'll be fine. I've got a new project to work on so I won't be bored. Two weeks will soon pass and then you said we're going to France."

Kay's driver beeped as he reversed the car up the drive.

"Auntie Kay, when I went to bed last night, I took my watch off in the dark and the numbers were glowing, how does it do that. I mean, what's that called?"

"It's called having a fluorescent watch. The face is made with a chemical that shines in the dark, something like that. Look it up on the internet. I've got to go, Frank's waiting and I'm running late."

Leanna went to wheel the bins down the drive ready for collection. Sally dashed upstairs to start the research for her project.

What makes the hands on a wrist watch glow?

Google's answer was succinct.

'The most common watch that glows in the dark is called a phosphorescent watch. Essentially the watch is coated in a paint which absorbs light and then re-emits it.'

What does phosphorescent mean?

'Light emitted by a substance without combustion or perceptible heat, in a similar manner to fluorescence but on a longer timescale.'

What is fluorescence?

'Fluorescence is the emission of light by a substance that

has absorbed light or other electromagnetic radiation. It is a form of luminescence.'

The research was off to a bad start. Sally needed a beginner's class not degree level information so she went back to basics on the meaning of the word, 'substance'.

'Substance is the material or matter, of which something is made. Substances are physical things that can be seen, touched or measured. They are made up of one or more elemental parts.'

Sally tried to weave the disparate strands of information together.

Lamping a watch face creates phosphorescence, because the watch absorbs torch light and then reflects it, no emits it, as a different kind of light, as luminescence. Lamping a spirit creates something that looks like phosphorescence, but is really fluorescence, because the glowing outline only lasts for a short time.

She still couldn't make anything of it, it was like knitting with spaghetti.

Sally lay back on the bed holding the iPad above her head and read the search results for a second time. This time, two lines in particular stood out.

'Fluorescence is the emission of light by a substance.'

'Substances are physical things that can be seen, touched or measured.'

She sat bolt upright.

Hold on! So if lamping creates a type of fluorescence, a fluorescence that can only be emitted by a substance, and since a substance is something that can be seen, touched or measured . . .

The penny dropped.

. . . that means the fluorescence from the warrior makes him

a substance — and if he's a substance, he can be touched and measured — so he's real. The spirit of the warrior was actually there, in the dining room, as something that still exists.

It would be no exaggeration to say the conclusion came like a bolt from the blue.

So the fluorescence comes from the part of a person that remains when they're no longer alive. And the same with the children in the home. Part of them was left behind and whatever it is, is real, a substance.

Sally placed her iPad down, rolled off the bed and walked over to the window. She could see the graveyard at the top of the church field and the gravestones all lined up in rows like soldiers parading outside their headquarters.

Maybe the warrior is in the dining room because he was buried in one of those mounds somewhere in the garden or under the house? Maybe he didn't move too far from where he used to live? Or the place he died?

Thoughts were running through Sally's brain faster than Mr Jinx in his exercise wheel.

The boy and the girl at the children's home didn't look like they were brother and sister. Maybe they became friends in the afterlife to keep each other company, or they both died at the children's home or somewhere near there, or the home was something else at the time? So if I've discovered three of these 'substances', maybe I can find more. A vicarage near a church with a graveyard would be a good hunting ground, don't you think, Mr Jinx?

Whiskers twitched to confirm that Sally's reasoning was sound.

Chapter 7

Seek and ye shall find

"Leannaaa"

Sally was yelling from the top of the stairs.

"I'm building a cinema in the attic. We want to watch Tom and Jerry on YouTube. In the dark!"

"Thought you did that in the basement yesterday?"

"Yeh, but I couldn't make it dark enough, I want it to be like Cineworld."

"Okay luv, be careful with Kay's things, you might need to move them to one side to make some space."

"Yeh. I am. And I need some bin bags to cover the skylight window and your little folding ladders. Have you got more sticky tape?"

Sally discovered four non-extinguished spirits residing in the attic of the vicarage. The first of them was Roger, a wiry seven-year-old boy who had been a sweep's apprentice over a century earlier. Encouraged to attain the highest levels in his work he became stuck in the chimney for the fireplace in the dining room and choked to death on soot and pigeon droppings. Roger had skulked in the attic since 1868, unhappy with his short life and poor career choice. However, since he did nothing but moan to himself, another century was expected to pass before his Outer Shell would hit the three ounce mark. The elderly lady by the name of Florence had been bludgeoned to death with a blunt object while placing a posy of wild flowers on the grave of her daughter Agnes. Agnes had bled to death during the birth of her first child, out of wedlock, in one of the farmworker's cottages that once backed on to the church field. Agnes waited in the attic for seven years until her mother finally arrived. Florence was now perilously close to the three ounce mark and clinging on to the last moments of afterlife. She didn't want to lose her daughter again but her shell was giving up the ghost while Agnes had at least sixty years to while away.

The fourth and final resident of the attic was Martin Dobson, a twenty-three-year old trainee vet who'd been knocked off his motorbike outside the vicarage by a pensioner who shouldn't have been driving on account of his cataracts. Martin had only been in the attic for a year and his shell was weighed down considerably by the pain of passing away well before his time.

Those early days of the summer holiday were filled with wonderful fun and Sally played hide and seek with the residents of the attic for hours on end, but not in the carefree manner of a Famous Five or Swallows and Amazons novel.

After lamping the living daylights out of the spirits on at least ten occasions, Sally started concocting experiments using home-made Heath Robinson like contraptions to catch one of them. The reasoning being, that if spirits were real, a substance that could be measured, then they could also be captured, because how else would you be able to measure one?

Sally tried to snare Agnes in garden netting covered in aluminium foil. Attempted to lock Roger in a cupboard lined with metallic gift-wrap paper. Then dressed herself in a suit of aluminium foil to try and grab Martin. Assuming that Florence wouldn't be so fast on her feet, Sally tried to restrain her with her bare hands and was convinced of a tingling sensation as Florence slipped through her fingers.

Google had been helpful in outlining the various methodologies suggested for snagging a spirit but despite following instructions down to the letter, Sally's goal remained tantalisingly out of reach. Even the metal box filled with graveyard soil, a five star recommendation on ghostcatcher. org, failed to do as advertised on the tin. So Sally considered a more scientific approach and conducted desk research into questions such as 'How to catch light?' and 'How to store fluorescence?' And the wildly optimistic, 'Is it possible to trap energy?'

Surprisingly, the answer to the latter, in a round about sort of way, was yes; in a microwave, but Sally had already tried that on Martin without success.

The questions were academic however, because a few days before Kay was due to start her break, with a driving holiday in France and Italy and a week in Cornwall on the itinerary, the four spirits residing in the attic handed in their notice and moved out.

Three sharp raps on the door designated as 'The Gateway. Residents Only' echoed around the Hall of Extinguished Spirits and Big Mac looked up from his ledger book, startled by the unscheduled arrival.

"Goodness me Mr Cake, that one's keen, I thought we'd finished for the day. Hurry along and let them in, they're about to wake the dead."

"Oh, very droll!" said Short Cake, rising from his desk and straightening his black tie. He then strode off to answer the door and disappeared behind the stack of gold bangles designated as the year of 2015.

Big Mac was frantically leafing through pages of forecast arrivals, searching for the clerical error, when he heard Short Cake proclaim, "it's Florence. Florence Mayweather."

Big Mac ran his chubby finger down a column of names and heard Short Cake beckon Florence to enter. The name of Florence Mayweather didn't appear to be on his list. Big Mac was about to double-check the spelling of the surname Mayweather, when he clearly heard Florence declare, in a bitter and protesting tone of voice, "she made our life 'ell she did, that bloody witch!"

This was followed by the sound of Short Cake closing the door, only for another series of short sharp raps to echo around the hall for a second time. Big Mac heard Short Cake once again open the 'Residents Only' door.

"Well" exclaimed Short Cake, taking a step back in surprise, "if it isn't Agnes. As in Agnes Mayweather, the daughter of ... "

He turned to Florence and then back to Agnes.

". . . the daughter of Florence Mayweather! Mother and daughter on the same day. What a coincidence! But Agnes, I don't think you're expected here for another sixty years?"

Agnes took a stride forward, eyes blazing and prodded Short Cake on the lapel of his jacket with a bony finger.

"You think I could stay there with that bloody lunatic knowing me mam was 'ere? Well you can think again."

"Err, Mr Mac" said Short Cake, his raised voice wavering in tone, "we have something of an issue here! A double booking. An early arrival. Can you come and clarify the matter, urgently?"

Irritated by the mistake in his accounting and the unseemly disturbance, Big Mac rose to his feet and slammed the ledger book shut. Then he opened the book to release his tie. Then he closed it again and waddled off to find out what in the name of The Powers That Be was going on. There had been no major disaster flagged in the traces, no exorcism, no lightning bolts directed at the vicarage, so there was no logical explanation for the arrival of both Mayweathers, at the same time, on the same day.

As Big Mac arrived at Short Cake's side, another fist pounded on the door and then Roger, the chimney sweep's apprentice burst in followed by Martin, the trainee vet.

"Can someone please tell me what is happening here?"

The exhausted and about to be extinguished spirits all turned to Big Mac.

"I'll tell you what's 'appened" said Agnes, pointing the same bony finger back in the vague direction from which she'd just travelled, "it's that bloody girl. She's what's 'appened!"

"She tried to trap me in a microwave and I had to use all my energy to escape" moaned Martin.

"She made me lose the will to live!" said Roger, mournfully.

Two hours later, with the columns in the ledger book now totalling zero, precisely as they should, Big Mac looked up from his desk.

"Mr Cake, would you care to divulge your take on the situation with Sally Bennett? I think it's probably time we brought her in for a little chat, don't you?"

Short Cake's gaunt features bore more than a passing resemblance to Florence Mayweather's. His impersonation was all the better for it.

"It's that bloody witch. She's what's 'appened! Let's 'ave her in shall we?"

Big Mac was still chuckling to himself as he pushed open the door designated 'Exit to Eternity' and toddled off to discuss outcomes and repercussions with The Powers That Be.

Chapter 8

Back off

Dusk was descending on The Market Square as Sally arrived in her favourite pyjamas; a pink pair in brushed cotton with a seahorse embroidered on the breast pocket. Lovely as they were, the pyjamas were not going to cut the mustard that night, because a Year 10 fashion show was in progress and Sally was most certainly *not*, dressed for the occasion. A bench by the Clock Tower offered a vantage point for viewing the catwalk running up the centre of The Market Square and far enough from the razzamatazz for Sally to stay anonymous. Even at that distance, she recognised many of the celebrities in the audience; familiar faces from gossip magazines and reality TV and influencers on Instagram.

Many of Sally's teachers had accepted their invitations and Rachel Tiffany Thomas, the ringleader of the gang targeting Sally at school had a front row seat. Other girls, most notably the clique of self-centred wannabes from two years above, were playing the part of fashion models strutting down the catwalk as though parading through Cheadle on a Saturday afternoon. Flashes from paparazzi cameras lit the scene in silent bursts of light. Even at her young age, Sally recognised the event as a visual metaphor for her suppressed emotions. This was a dream bearing a grudge.

She studied her tormentor-in-chief. Rachel Tiffany Thomas was puckering her bee sting lips, arranging locks of hair over heavily made-up eyes and sucking in her anorexic cheeks to gorge on selfies. Sally had the urge to go and slap her stupid, idiotic face. And she wouldn't get into trouble for it either; after all, this was only a dream. To see a stinging, red handprint superimposed on all that pink blusher and the teary look of shock, oh, that would be so satisfying. But Sally didn't have the malice for such a pointless act of retribution. The fashion show was just a foolish fantasy; the frustrations and torment of school, thinly veiled.

Back in The Market Square after such a long absence, she remembered Felix and the way he had been so kind and considerate in that final year of junior school; a true friend, by day and night. Looking back to L'Ecole, she recalled the time they'd pushed their desks together and held hands in the classroom. She could still picture the view from the window. The endless fields of beautiful red flowers balanced top heavy on slender green stems sashaying in the breeze.

I wonder if they're still there. There's only one way to find out.

Turning her back on the fashion show and heading down towards the far corner of The Market Square, Sally could see what appeared to be a passageway running alongside L'Ecole and presumed it would take her to the fields at the back. Drawing closer however, she did a double take. The passage was identical to the alley that led to the Number 11 Club; the same narrow, brick lined walkway but without the disturbing optical effects. The air was still and musty like the inside of an old wardrobe and equally uninviting. However, reassured by the fact she had come to no harm the last time, Sally set off. With arms raised either side, she was able to stay within touching distance of each wall; fully prepared to steady herself against a sudden, dizzying shift in perspective. Steady

69

progress continued for perhaps a hundred metres until a final step brought liberation into bright sunshine on the shoreline of a shimmering lake of crimson. The infusion of peppery cologne in the air made her nose itch.

Looking back over the wall, the creamy stone fascia of L'Ecole was visible at first floor level. Sally waved at the classroom window to acknowledge the memory of Felix then turned to wade into the poppy field. Her hands paddled through the waist deep flowers as though swimming through velvet. When a flash of light glinted on the horizon like a message in Morse code, she was forced to shade her eyes and squint. During a pause in the dot and dash of reflections, the hulking form of a white building came into view as if it were a ship adrift on the horizon. Sally could identify a series of broad steps leading up to a magnificent portico supported by stone columns and the signalling was courtesy of sunlight bouncing off windows in the wings extending away either side. At a distance, the structure resembled The National Gallery in London remembered from the time of her school visit. Sally was drawn to The Gateway as it was to her and with message received and understood, after taking only six steps forward she'd arrived.

Standing in shadow deep inside the colonnade, Sally considered the tarnished brass plaques above the two nondescript doors.

The plaque on the left announced: 'The Gateway. Visitors Only'.

The plaque on the right: 'The Gateway. Residents Only'.

As she reached out to the door on the left, before her hand could exert any pressure, the door swung slowly inwards which invited her to step inside.

When Sally laid eyes on the short, rotund man with the bald head and the black jacket and trousers walking towards her, the parallel was comical; he was Humpty Dumpty in a business suit.

"Good evening Miss Bennett, I'm so pleased you could join us. Welcome to The Gateway."

"Yes, welcome to our Hall of Extinguished Spirits" said the other man following in his wake; a tall, thin character also with a bald head and a smart black suit. He reminded Sally of a creepy butler from an episode of *Scooby Doo*. The man's words were accompanied by an overly formal bow and imperious sweep of the hand.

The tendons in Sally's neck strained as she tried to assimilate the extraordinary size and scale of the interior and the mind-boggling panorama. Her only frame of reference was a cathedral; but no cathedral had ever been constructed without an apparent limit on size. The procession of stained glass windows high above her head appeared to continue without end. As did the ineffable spectacle of huge mounds of gold jewellery. A million glittering bangles, the undulating dunes of a boundless golden desert, were biblical in both scale and portent. The bangles were literally spilling around Sally's feet all over the red marble floor. The stunning visual spectacle felt out of character with previous Market Square visits and beyond the realms of her imagination in the way that the visit to the Number 11 Club had been. A construct of pure creativity and without precedent. A dream without provenance.

Perhaps something like this happens whenever you walk

down one of those alleyways. You enter a different part of The Market Square. A new type of dream?

Sally was wide awake to the fact she was both overawed and ill at ease with the experience.

"Where am I?" she asked.

"Ladies and gentlemen, boys and girls, it's showtime," came the reply.

At the sound of Short Cake's clicking fingers, instant darkness flooded the cavernous hall as though a dam holding back midnight had burst. Then a second click summoned downlighting which illuminated Big Mac and Short Cake like a double act on stage. Aliens might well have been preparing to 'beam them up' when Short Cake coughed to clear his voice. The spotlight cast dark shadows under his protruding cheek bones projecting a sinister special effect.

"Allow me to answer your question Sally. My name is Short Cake, my colleague here is Big Mac and once again may I welcome you to our Hall of Extinguished Spirits."

This time, the second imperious sweep of the hand drew attention to nothing more than impenetrable blackness and not being able to see the point, Sally stood there looking confused.

Big Mac and Short Cake then began tap dancing. At least that that was the intention. Big Mac resembled an Emperor penguin waddling over ice with his stubby arms flapping like wings. Short Cake was jerking about like a demented marionette having a fit.

After several seconds of excruciating embarrassment, Short Cake disappeared from view as he stepped into the shadow between the downlighting and reappeared in Big Mac's personal space where he could be seen whispering and

72

remonstrating to his partner about something. When Short Cake clicked his fingers for the third time, the darkness gushed back to whence it came and the hall reverted to standard light setting.

This is like being on stage, right? In some incredible pantomime with these two acting stupid and getting things wrong on purpose.

Big Mac waddled over with his egg head nestling in his shirt collar and with a tip of the spoon smile cracking his face.

"Sorry about that Sally, I wanted something regal, a trumpet fanfare to herald your arrival in The Gateway, but my colleague had something showy, more Las Vegas in mind. Which clearly fell flat! I told him we have to rehearse but of course he never listens. Anyway, the theatrics are over for tonight thank goodness, so in answer to your question, think of this place as a Hall of Remembrance, a mausoleum, where the deceased are remembered with a personalised gold bangle instead of a tomb."

Big Mac picked two bangles from those spilling over the floor and gave one to Sally.

"You see, when a person dies, there are two routes that can be taken. For those whose spirit is completely exhausted, the only option is to climb our stairway to heaven. The Outer Shell that carried that person here, the last vestiges of their will to live, is *extinguished* and converted to three ounces of gold in the form of a bangle. The Residual, the part of the spirit that can never be extinguished, what you might call their soul, then departs The Gateway through the appropriate door, to join The Powers That Be."

"These bangles represent those that have 'lost the will to live' you might say."

"Indeed Mr Cake. But those that have *not* given up the ghost but are *nevertheless,* dead, like someone in an unforeseen car accident, well, they exist as a *non-extinguished* spirit until their Outer Shell falls to the three ounce mark."

"They shed weight by expending energy on ghostly goings on. Making things go bump in the night. Or skulk in attics for centuries until the excess weight eventually falls off by itself."

Big Mac took the bangle from Sally's hand and drew her attention to the inscription on the flattened inner face and passed it back.

"The personalisation is necessary for our records."

The lettering was tiny and not easy to read.

"It says ... Florence ... Mayweather ... I think. Eighteen fifteen. Until two thousand and seventeen."

"Indeed it does" said Big Mac. He then passed the second bangle to Sally. "Try and guess the connection?"

Sally jumped to the conclusion that this was her role in the show. To play the part of a contestant in a guessing game. The bangle was identical to the first. Same weight. Shiny and smooth. Once again she struggled to read the fine detail.

"This one says ... Agnes ... Agnes Mayweather. Eighteen thirty-five, until ... two thousand and seventeen. That's this year as well. Wait a minute."

Sally was puzzled.

"So if this is a kind of headstone, that means, er, Agnes was ... one hundred and eighty-two years old. And Florence was ... two hundred and two years old when she died. But how can that be? Nobody can live for two hundred and two years."

"Ah, but in some ways they can, because they did!" said Big Mac.

"Were they related, Agnes and Florence? The Mayweathers? I guess they must have been. Is that the connection?"

"Yes. And no" said Big Mac. "Yes they were related, mother and daughter actually, but no, that's not the connection I'm looking for."

"They both died this year, in two thousand and seventeen?"

"Getting warmer" said Short Cake.

Sally was looking for visual clues as her gaze tracked the line of hanging banners hundreds of years into the past.

"Is the connection, they were sent back to the spirit world because they died before their time, so they weighed more than three ounces and then they came back this year, because . . ."

"Much warmer"

Big Mac gave her a clue.

" . . . because someone gave them a bit of a workout? Yes, and prematurely as matter of fact. We weren't expecting Agnes for another sixty years."

Sally still couldn't see beyond the family name.

"Think closer to home," suggested Big Mac, "your home . . . and theirs."

Short Cake was waiting with an expectant smile as the two pennies dropped.

"Ohhhh, I've got it. They were both in the attic, together, at the vicarage. Florence and Agnes were two of the spirits I lamped with my torch?"

"Exactly. The mother and daughter you tried to snare with silver foil and nets and other paraphernalia. Avoiding those sorts of boobytraps consumes a fair amount of spirit energy and leads to unscheduled departures and arrivals.

"What Mr Mac is trying to say Sally, is that when you scare a spirit to death by forcing them to expend the excess energy in their Outer Shell, they arrive here sharpish. And when you create something of a stampede, like you did with the residents of the vicarage, well, we're not geared up for that level of unpredictability. We don't like a rush hour. So we brought you here to tell you in no uncertain terms to STOP DOING IT! You may well be a very special eleven Sally, like that miscreant Wilson Armitage, but that doesn't mean you can't have an *unforeseen* accident."

"In short Sally, you must cease your lamping activities forthwith, unless you also want to end up in an attic for a hundred years or more!"

Sally should have been intimidated by the act of being threatened, but her focus was elsewhere. She traced the inscriptions on the inside of the bangles with the tip of her finger. The names of two people who had died. Two members of the same family. A mother and daughter who had once been living and were now together again chasing seahorses through breaking waves on a beach with sand as white as sugar?

"Can I see, I mean, is it possible to touch the bangles for my mum and dad? I know they didn't return as spirits, they would have come to see me, given me a sign to say they were there."

Big Mac and Short Cake stood shoulder to shoulder, their hands behind their backs, wearing the same, emotionless expressions like the grim undertakers they were.

Big Mac then bobbed away like a buoy slipping its mooring and beckoned Sally to follow. Short Cake picked up a brush and began sweeping stray bangles back into the correct piles.

Behind the mound of bangles for '2015', beyond the executive-style desks with matching chairs and angle-poise lamps, Big Mac pointed to three doors set side by side in a brick wall.

Sally immediately understood the significance. She turned to Big Mac who nodded his consent and Sally walked to the door.

The 'Exit to Eternity. Residual Spirits Only'.

The door was tall and unusually narrow; a featureless, grey steel door; just wide enough for one soul travelling light with no earthly possessions. A nondescript threshold to an indescribable paradise. This was the door Sally's parents had passed through and the stairway to heaven was on the other side. She pressed her ear against the door and caressed the surface with her fingertips. There was no sound of crashing waves, no whinnying of seahorses, not a soul could be heard. Tears were welling as she turned to Big Mac.

"Were they happy when you saw them? Did they know I'd be okay? That I wouldn't make it difficult for Auntie Kay even though they'd left me behind.

Short Cake appeared from nowhere and pressed something cold into Sally's hand. She gasped at the sight of the gold bangle and a single tear ran down her cheek.

Sally slowly raised the bangle between thumb and forefinger and after reading the inscription her legs gave way. She slumped to the floor as though the puppeteer manipulating her life, the Christof character, had cut her strings.

Clare Bennett 1982 - 2015

Sally kissed the inscription and let her finger run slowly around the inside face, feeling the delicate tracery of the numbers and letters. Her hand passed easily through the bangle and she let it rest on her wrist.

"Love you Mum. I'll be with you soon."

"Ah, hem."

Short Cake pretended to cough and held out his open hand.

Sally slipped the bangle from her wrist, kissed the extinguished spirit of her mother for a second time and gave the bangle back.

"So," said Big Mac, steering Sally to the door designated as the 'Exit to The Market Square', "before we send you on your way, do remember our warning from earlier. Playing hide and seek with the spirit world can lead to terrible consequences. We'll be watching you!"

The following morning, Sally followed the foot worn trail through the church field, past the old tennis court and climbed the wall into the graveyard. For two hours she searched for the graves of a mother and daughter. When the church bell chimed out the eleventh hour, beneath a chestnut tree and hidden within a thicket of waist high nettles, she discovered the crooked, weathered headstone bearing their names.

Rest in Peace beloved Daughter.
Agnes Mayweather
1835 - 1873

Who waited in heaven for her beloved Mother.
Florence Mayweather
1815 - 1880

As Sally sat on the graveyard wall looking down the field towards the vicarage, she tried to picture the lives the two women had lived. The women she'd seen as iridescent outlines, a fleeting, luminous pencil sketch of pinafore dresses, lace trimmed aprons, ribboned bonnets and bitter faces ingrained with the worry lines of poverty. They were from a time of hardship, a peasant life she couldn't begin to imagine.

Placing a spray of dandelions and daisies on the headstone she apologised for being the cause of their premature departure.

A week later, Kay and Sally drove down to Dover for the start of their holiday touring France and Italy. Shortly after that, Sally's star stopped spinning out of control and disparate planets began to gravitate towards her orbit.

Towards the end of October, a few weeks before her thirteenth birthday, Sally was involved in a serious car accident outside Davenport train station.

As I mentioned earlier, this was a consequence of my shepherding of the flock and engendered a curious circle of life. The convex of Wilson's yang, locked perfectly with the concave of Sally's yin.

More to the point, they both ended up in Stockport Infirmary, which was *my* objective all along.

Chapter 9

Clan Montague

The day Vanessa Clarke was found rain-soaked and confused on a park bench overlooking the Ness Bridge, PC Simon Montague was on duty, drinking beer in the South Kessock Golf and Country Club with his dad.

Montague's father, a former policeman himself, and a high ranking one at that, had retired from the force years earlier with ambitions for his son to not only follow in his footsteps, but to travel further. Clan Montague had practically built Inverness so that allowed for a career path of privilege, the opening of normally closed doors and a different approach to policing altogether.

"Forget the day-to-day son, the petty details. You need to see the bigger picture. First I'll help you become Chief Commissioner for Scotland and after that, The Met. Then back to Edinburgh and Parliament. Leave it to me. It's all about succession planning and I have the contacts and influence to smooth the journey."

Montague's father tapped the side of his nose with his index finger.

"It's not what you know, it's who you know."

So, the following afternoon, doing the donkey work to find relatives of the deranged woman abandoned by the bridge, was not PC Montague's idea of a 'high flying' policeman's responsibility. A copy of bus station camera footage, which included images of Vanessa alighting the overnight coach from London had been placed on his desk with a post-it note from the Chief Super', asking him to go through it 'with a fine-tooth comb'. Had Montague followed instructions and applied some elementary policing nous, the case would have been solved that very day. The blonde woman reported missing in London, a fresh entry on the national missing person's register, was a dead ringer for the brunette stepping down from a coach in Inverness bus station. A coach that had just arrived from Victoria Station, which just happened to be in London! A fax to the Metropolitan police followed by a phone call to an anxious husband would have tied everything up with a non-slip knot; case closed, nothing to see here, move along now.

However, none of that happened and as a direct result of Montague's dereliction of duty, the true identity of Alice was never fully investigated, in fact, not pursued at all. Montague told the Chief Super' that even though he'd worked extra hours of his own time on the enquiry "no sir, there was nothing on the tapes from the bus or train station of any relevance."

Vanessa Clarke languished in the South Kessock Care Home as her child grew to adulthood and her husband's life fell to pieces. You could also argue that Montague senior's ambitions for his protege didn't proceed as anticipated either.

The private dinner with all the old boys with chevrons on their shoulders and medals on their chests should have been a relaxed evening of schmoozing with the top brass; the first in a series of adroitly planned moves that would propel PC Simon Montague quickly up the career ladder. But you didn't need to be a detective to see that Simon was dim-witted, clueless as a copper and socially inept and would never be more than a head scratching Mr Plod. When he eventually attained the rank of Assistant Chief Constable at the age of fifty-four, a year before he was due to be forced into retirement, the upgrade was seen as more of a fob than a promotion.

The photos of a young lad, the so-called, Mr Frank Spencer, seen waiting on a platform at Inverness train station, then leaving the car park of Piccadilly station at eleven-thirty at night, came as a pleasant surprise to ACC Montague. A gilt-edged chance, a golden opportunity to put the record straight. To tell the people of Inverness, and the bloody newspapers, that the tragedy of Vanessa Clarke was actually all down to this lad, and not *his* incompetence, as the papers were hinting! He'd heard what they were whispering around the station, but a new headline was going to change all that.

'North Caledonian Constabulary exonerated as dogged top copper solves seventeen-year-old mystery.'

"We checked the registration plates sir. The scooter belongs to a Wilson Armitage of 7 Midland Drive, Bramhall, Cheshire. Just turned eighteen and goes to the same college as Graham Clarke, Vanessa's son. The boys are best friends apparently."

Sergeant Jordan had done a thorough piece of investigative police work on Montague's behalf. Unwilling to accept that wrongdoing had played a part in the lad's visit to the care home, he'd nevertheless followed up on the suspicions of the duty manager and was surprised by his findings.

"Any previous?"

"Nothing I could uncover sir. Clean living lad with no toxic lifestyle. Mum works in a charity shop and Dad's some kind of energy research bod. Oh, and we got another match.

Armitage called the home from his mobile."

"Splendid Jordan, that's excellent work. You can leave those photos with me for now and I'll have a little think about our scooter boy. Perhaps it would be in the interests of the force to discover what he's been up to. Maybe we weren't so dilatory after all?"

Assistant Chief Constable Montague then slipped the telltale evidence into the top drawer of his desk, which was empty, except for a VHS video cassette containing security camera footage and a photo of Vanessa Clarke with blonde hair. Montague locked the drawer and put the key in his waistcoat pocket then reclined back in his executive policeman's chair and considered how to turn all of this to his advantage. The possibilities for headlines were endless.

Chapter 10

Dragnet

Wednesday 22nd November 2017

Daisy was reading a new book titled 'Why We Dream' written by the science journalist Alice Robb. With a pencil she was underlining the extracts she intended to read to Wilson as soon as he was able to stay awake for more than ten minutes.

'To the Mekeo of Papua New Guinea, the dream is an actual experience, not indistinguishable from waking reality.'

'For the Mekeo, the dream represents the night time action of the soul, which is liberated from the body in sleep.'

Wilson was propped up on pillows in his hospital bed and his upper body rose and fell almost imperceptibly with short, shallow breaths as he drifted in and out of sleep. For ten days his metabolism had been working overtime to recharge batteries and reboot systems and seven kilos of body weight had been consumed in the process. His skin had the semi-translucent, waxy quality of greaseproof paper and the contours of his jaw and cheekbones were sharply defined.

The previous day, the hospital hairdresser had cut Wilson's hair in the rough crop style he liked. Afterwards, though Daisy fought to block the unwanted and inappropriate visual simile from her mind, Wilson's emaciated body, in striped pyjamas a size too big, brought to mind an image of the holocaust.

The monitoring machine above his bed, measuring heartbeat and other vital signs was beeping reassuringly in a ward that contained just six beds, including that of Tom Rowlands, the other boy rescued from The Annexe by Daisy. Sally Bennett had left the ward six days earlier and was recuperating at home.

As Daisy closed the book and reached for the bag of crisps in her bag, a tall, middle aged man in a police officer's uniform quietly entered the ward. His manner was relaxed and friendly. Courteously he reassured Daisy that his visit was "nothing to worry about." He asked if, "a quiet word in the corridor outside would be possible?" and presented an ID card with the name, 'Sergeant Derek Jordan. North Caledonian Constabulary'.

"Miss Meadowcroft, isn't it? Daisy Meadowcroft? You're a friend of Wilson's I believe. Wilson Armitage. The lad you were sitting with back there in the ward."

Sergeant Jordan's craggy features, which included a full head of black hair greying at the temples, weather beaten skin and granite grey eyes could have been those of a character actor playing the archetypal, rugged Highlands' copper. Daisy perceived a principled man and though she had no idea why he was there, she was at ease in his presence.

"Yes, he's my friend, my boyfriend. He had an accident but he's getting better now. Can I help you with something?"

The sergeant's voice was as mellow as a fifty-year-old single malt.

"Aye, I understand the lad's been poorly and I'm happy to

see he's on the mend. I'm here to ask if you can spare a wee moment to answer a couple of questions on his behalf. Just to clear something up that I've been asked to take a look at. Ach, he's not in any trouble from what I can see, so don't be alarmed, but we've been given some information, up in Scotland, in Inverness. I was hoping you might be able to help."

Daisy felt her cheeks flush slightly as Sergeant Jordan pointed to the small waiting room he'd asked a nurse to keep free.

"Rather than stand out here in the corridor, can we talk in there? It's more private."

Sitting beside Daisy in a moulded plastic chair, he took a notebook and pencil from his top pocket.

"Hope you don't mind if I jot a few things down, I've a terrible memory, senior moments coming thick and fast, I'm planning to retire in a couple of years."

Daisy said nothing, her mouth too dry to lubricate her vocal chords.

"Miss Meadowcroft, I'll get straight to the point if I may. I'm sure you'll have read about this in the news because it concerns a friend of Wilson's. The lad's name is Graham Clarke but you know him as Teaps. A few weeks back, shortly before Wilson fell ill, a lady known as Alice, living in a care home in Inverness, was identified as a person reported missing seventeen years ago. To get to the point, this lady, Alice, turned out to be the mother of the friend, Graham. Do you know anything about this? Did Wilson say anything at the time? Ring any bells?"

Daisy blinked as something clamorous like Big Ben clanged inside her head.

Sergeant Jordan was used to people drying up during a conversation. It was not always a sign of guilt.

"Can I get you a glass of water, something to drink?"

"Please, if you don't mind, it's really hot in here."

Daisy was desperate to buy time, to work out where this conversation was going, to man the defences in the absence of Wilson, but the water dispenser with plastic cups was only a metre away in a corner of the room.

Daisy sipped the water as Sergeant Jordan settled back in his chair.

"While the discovery of Vanessa Clarke is a wonderful story, a miracle really, the problem is, miracles don't generally happen. And for that reason I'm wondering, and this is the curious bit, what Wilson was doing in a care home in South Kessock showing an interest in the plight of a resident by the name of Alice. This is the day before she was discovered to be Vanessa Clarke, the missing mother of his best friend. We have photos, mobile phone records, he definitely visited her, the question is why and how did he know she was there?"

"Yes, it was incredible for that lady to be found after all those years. Wilson's mum and the doctors think the delayed shock of it all had something to do with Wilson becoming ill."

Daisy's tongue was sticking to the roof of her mouth. She was struggling to speak and act innocent and think of alibis all at the same time.

Bloody hell Wilson, why were we so stupid? We never thought of the cameras. And you used your mobile phone to call the home!

She held her nerve.

Best say nothing for now. No comment!

"So you're saying Wilson was in Scotland the day before

Vanessa was found? Wow, what a coincidence that would be. Are you sure? The photos? Are you certain it's him?"

Daisy hoped her facial expression was capturing the look of someone innocent, surprised and lost for an explanation.

Sergeant Jordan took a folded sheet of paper from an inside pocket. It showed a series of pictures taken by security cameras during various stages of Wilson's trip.

"We have these clear images with date and time imprints. The receptionist and duty manager both recognised him. He called the home on his mobile the day before to make an appointment and said his dad had dementia. We've checked. He doesn't!"

"God, how weird. Yeh, I'm pretty sure his dad's not got dementia. Though he goes salmon fishing and hasn't caught anything for years, which is a bit odd, it must be said."

"It is indeed a puzzle, and unfortunately, with Wilson still receiving critical care, the doctors have refused our request to question him. They've asked us to wait another week before a formal interview can proceed so that's why I wanted to speak with you. To see if there was an innocent explanation that we might have overlooked, a reason for us not to have to come back. Like I said, I'm not sensing any major misdemeanour here, but I would like to get to the bottom of it. If Wilson's involved in a good way, through some amateur detective work to help his friend, it wouldn't surprise me if he didn't get a medal. We just want to know what he was up to. Anyway, thanks for your time. I'll be in touch with Wilson when he's feeling a little stronger. Goodbye Miss Meadowcroft."

Daisy sat in the waiting room for ten minutes mulling things over, searching for a plausible explanation, a safe house for two criminals on the run. Criminals who'd done a good thing, who'd solved a mystery, given a terrible tragedy a happy ending and performed a miracle rather than committed a crime. Unfortunately, nobody would ever believe them, nor could anybody ever be told the true story.

All I need is an explanation for how Wilson thought of a way to connect Alice with Vanessa. Something he stumbled upon that set the whole thing in motion.

Daisy's search for an explanation would have taken on more urgency, if she'd known that during her conversation with Sergeant Jordan, a conversation along similar lines was taking place between Wilson's father and Assistant Chief Constable Simon Montague.

"So let me get this straight. You seriously think I was instrumental in Vanessa Clarke's disappearance because we were having an extramarital affair and then I might possibly have accidentally assaulted her causing brain damage? So then I drove all the way up to Inverness, to abandon her in a place where she was completely unknown and Wilson, my son, the best friend of *her* son, who was only a baby at the time, is in on the act?"

Alex Armitage would have found the accusations hilarious, surreal, a prank, if it wasn't for the deadly serious look on the face of an Assistant Chief Constable sitting in the lounge of his house. Thankfully Gloria was out, working in the charity shop.

"And you say you have evidence, photographs, mobile phone records and so on, that seem to suggest Wilson was involved in the discovery of Vanessa Clarke, who, for all those years was known as Alice and lived in a care home near Inverness. Is that correct? You have mobile phone records and photographs?"

"Yes Mr Armitage, our initial findings clearly suggest that and you're beginning to repeat yourself. I always think it's suspicious when a person of interest does that."

Alex was becoming irritated by the self-satisfied, smug look on Montague's face.

"And because Wilson had only just been born when Vanessa disappeared, you think I must have been involved in her disappearance, had something to hide and eventually needed my son to get involved? For what reason? To bring everything out and into the open? To assuage my guilt? For Wilson to take the blame for something his father did all those years ago? That has to be the most stupid thing I've ever heard. None of this makes any sense."

"Mr Armitage, I . . . "

Montague wanted to speak again but Alex raised his hand as if to say "hold on a minute, this is like having a conversation with the village idiot."

"So after years of guilt and discovering somehow that Alice has actually lost her memory and can never speak of the past, can never tell the truth and point the finger at me, I persuade my son to go to the care home alone to set her free. Is that what you're suggesting and accusing us of?"

"Mr Armitage, hard facts don't lie."

"Please leave this house right now or I'm going to throw you out."

Montague wondered if he could arrest Alex for threatening to forcibly eject a police officer from a private residence. He wasn't sure if that was a crime and he certainly didn't want to take a chance filing an arrest report that would make him the laughing stock of the station. Alex escorted him to the door.

Montague turned to face Alex as he walked down the drive to a waiting car.

"The moment your son is able to speak, we'll get to the bottom of this. And if I discover there's a thread of any wrongdoing by you or your son, I'll find it and pull you both in with it. The North Caledonian Constabulary will leave no stone unturned to correct the tragedy that befell Mrs Clarke, mark my words Mr Armitage, mark my words."

"Yeh, right, now you mark *my* words mate. You lot should have been doing your job properly up there in Inverness seventeen years ago when she first went missing. Then we wouldn't be having this bloody conversation."

The parting shot stung Montague.

Alex closed the front door and exhaled a long, slow breath. When he punched the wall he felt a bone crack in his hand. He was angry with Wilson for the mess he'd got them both into with his foolish game of playing God. Angry that Gloria was going to have a nervous breakdown if the truth came out about how Wilson had really discovered the identity and location of Vanessa and angrier, because he'd told that bloody trumped up police officer he'd never met Vanessa Clarke. That was a lie. Vanessa had been his girlfriend for a couple of months but their relationship had ended well before she met Michael.

Later that evening, sipping drinks in the bar of the Midland Hotel, Montague outlined his plan for the following day to Sergeant Jordan.

"With experience, a good policeman develops a sixth sense Jordan and mine's telling me that Alex Armitage is hiding something. He knows more about this than he's letting on. And if the lad's girlfriend has refused to play ball, perhaps his other friends might have something to say? Go to the college tomorrow, speak with his teachers, ask around for anything suspicious, bad behaviour, petty crime. I'm off to Chester first thing to the private clinic where they're keeping Vanessa. I've arranged to meet her husband and son. I can't wait to see the look on their faces when I drop this bombshell."

Montague signalled to the waiter for another gin and tonic.

"But sir, are you sure? Mr Clarke and his son have been through a lot, should we be moving so quickly? This is quite a revelation and could cause problems with the friendship between the two boys, especially if the Armitage lad's a hero and there's a simple explanation."

"No Jordan, I'm certain a crime's been committed and it's my job to find those responsible. The shadow hanging over the force, over me, needs to be dispelled quickly. Conduct the interviews and tomorrow afternoon we'll head back north. You say it's a week before we can get to speak with the Armitage lad? Fine, we'll be ready!"

Montague crunched on the ice from the bottom of his glass.

"Oh, and go and pay the mother a visit. Armitage's wife. Let's leave no stone unturned."

Sergeant Jordan wanted to object to bringing Mrs Armitage into the enquiry without having spoken to Wilson first; the idea of talking to his schoolmates was bad enough. It all seemed unnecessarily disruptive, like they were two ogres who'd flown down to Stockport to ruin a fairytale. He decided to share his viewpoint in a less obvious way.

"Perhaps we should also try and have a word with Gladys's dad sir?"

"Gladys's dad? Who the hell's Gladys's dad?"

"He lives in South Kessock, on a dairy farm."

"And what's he got to do with anything?"

"Well, when I was a kid, the milk lady, Gladys, she used to call at the house every Saturday morning for the milk money. Remember those days? Blue tits used to peck away at the foil tops before we could bring the milk in. Buggers they were. Anyway, on this particular morning, my mother had gone shopping and left me the money. Gladys arrived late and I remember her looking flustered as she fiddled about for change in this big, leather wallet. I asked her if she was okay and do you know what she told me? She said, her dad had been up to his tricks again. He'd opened a gate to let all the cows into the wrong field and that's why she was late. She said she saw him do it. She also said that sometimes he unpegged clothes on the washing line just to let them fall in the mud so they'd have to be washed again. And she'd seen him do *that* as well. She was very matter of fact about it. Just accepted it. She was a tough, no-nonsense farmer's wife Gladys. She didn't have time for making things up. But the thing is, Gladys's dad had been dead for six years. My mother told me that when she came back from shopping."

"Jordan, are you trying to wind me up?"

"No sir, I was sort of joking. I suspect we may never get to the bottom of this Vanessa discovery and perhaps some mysteries are best left unexplained."

"Let's just focus on the living shall we Jordan?"

Montague liked to have the last word.

Chapter 11

The rise of Bradley Givens

It was Sigmund Freud who suggested we are all born with the instincts of Neanderthal men and how, during our formative years, parents, friends and teachers help iron out the feral creases to create well adjusted members of society. In the case of Bradley Givens however, a steam roller would have been hard pressed to smooth out his primeval fault lines. Like a new car built the day after a Bank Holiday he was always going to be a problem and looking back, I can't recall why we agreed to his eleven plus status in the first place. Perhaps we saw it as an opportunity for social engineering. A gamble on how The Market Square might straighten him out. Give me a child until he is seven and I will show you the man, that sort of concept; it was an abject failure though. We made a terrible error in allowing Bradley that degree of self empowerment. It was a blessing he despised and like a wild animal in a zoo, Bradley was always ready to pounce the moment the keeper turned his back.

Bradley's parents quickly discovered his evil streak. As a baby he'd scream incessantly with nerve shredding intensity, but then smile and gurgle when the light to his room came on and his parents' sleep had been disturbed. He would knock the food bowl from his high chair and the malice in his eyes would confirm he'd done it just for the hell of it! A scrapbook of childhood achievements would have captured the life and times of an *enfant terrible.*

'Bradley at seven, with frogs skewered on pointed sticks.'

'At nine, with starling chicks still warm from the nest suffocating in a glass jar.'

'At ten, with his collection of stolen mobile phones.'

'Bradley at eleven in a balaclava with a stolen bike and two hundred pounds in cash snatched at a cash point from a young mother with a baby in a push chair.'

Not that young Bradley needed the money. His father was a successful property developer and the family lived in a large house in Hale Barns, a postcode for Manchester's bees, wannabes and footballers. He was educated at a private school where academic ability came easily and placed him in the top tier in all the top sets. He excelled at rugby. Strong and thickset, Bradley loved tackling kids half his size and landing an upper-cut during the scrum. He would smirk as a child was led from the field with blood pouring from a broken nose.

Turning through the pages of his teenage years, Bradley's petty crime, the shoplifting, the bicycle thefts, quickly graduated to 'pass and grab' on hot-wired mopeds. Wallets, mobile phones and designer bags snatched on the move, provided the funds for expansion into 'passing off' fake brands: cosmetics, perfumes, trainers and the like. Burglary and breaking and entering were favourite subjects during his A-level years. You could say Bradley was born to it and always a step ahead of the police, as though inside information was an accomplice to his crimes.

When eight Rolex watches were stolen from a jeweller's shop in Alderley Edge, the police suspected an employee, or the owner himself. The culprit was Bradley of course. He'd seen the codes for the burglar alarm and the night safe and knew how to disable the surveillance cameras online. This information was readily available in The Market Square if you knew where to look. Though no one was formally charged, the lady who'd worked in the shop for twenty-seven years was made redundant three months after the break-in.

It was on the day of the drugs heist that Bradley Givens finally came of age. That was the moment he recognised the full potential of an amazing business opportunity; a franchise for a new kind of criminal activity with a modus operandi uniquely suited to him. It also marked the first, fully accredited instance of collateral damage and that's what finally brought Bradley and his misdemeanours to our attention.

By the age of seventeen, Bradley had cultivated a business relationship with Banger, a foot soldier in the crime syndicate controlling drugs in their part of south Manchester. (Banger was also the fence for Bradley's knock-off and stolen goods and did a reasonable job of laundering it in the car parks of local pubs.)

Bradley suspected that Banger's flat was also a safe house where wholesale quantities of dope were broken down into retail size bags. So one night, in the shadow of the Clock Tower, Bradley closed his eyes, painted the perfect portrait of a young thug with a distinctive tattoo on his neck and pulled him into The Market Square. Banger was sitting on a bench seat opposite when Bradley walked over and placed a hand on his shoulder.

After sifting through the memory traces of years of neglect, domestic violence, poor schooling, the lack of a father figure and a litany of missed opportunities to smooth out the wrinkles in Banger's life, Bradley tuned into the recent past. A sequence of images portrayed in easy to follow steps, how a kilo of hashish was deposited every Monday night in a litter bin by a bus stop in Wythenshawe. Bradley identified a one minute window of opportunity in which to beat Banger to it. Four nights later he was concealed by bushes, forty metres from the bus stop, watching and waiting for the drug drop to play out for real.

Bradley was clad in black with a scarf over his nose and mouth and the peak of a baseball cap shading his eyes. A stolen mountain bike, the getaway vehicle, lay waiting at his feet. At nine thirty precisely, a Mercedes hatchback pulled to a halt alongside the kerb. A passenger climbed out, dropped a KFC family bucket and a Coke cup in a litter bin, the passenger returned to the car and the car drove away. At the same time, the door to a ninth floor flat in the block opposite opened and Banger stepped out. His face was shrouded by a grey hoodie as he walked along the balcony with a bounce in his step and his hands in his pockets. As the pixie point of his hood dropped down into the stairwell, Bradley emerged from the bushes, sprinted to the litter bin, retrieved the KFC bucket and dashed back to the bushes. He stuffed the brick of hashish in a backpack and sped away on the bike down the footpath that led into the park. At a safe distance, hidden behind a hedge, Bradley removed the scarf and turned to see Banger speaking on his phone and remonstrating about something with his arm in the air. Then the arm plunged deep into the litter bin to retrieve nothing more than a red cup with a Coke logo on the side.

Two nights later, Banger crawled into the A&E department

of Wythenshawe General Hospital with a broken leg and facial injuries. The collateral damage arrived later when Banger's long-suffering and completely innocent girlfriend decided she'd finally had enough and left to live with her mum in a similar flat, on the other side of Wythenshawe. Unfortunately, the crime syndicate saw this as proof of the girlfriend's complicity in the theft of the hashish and so she too ended up in Wythenshawe Hospital with bruises all over her body. A few days into her convalescence, a nurse confirmed the miscarriage of a foetus she wasn't even aware she was carrying.

Chapter 12

There's an art to it

"It's a Basquiat, a bloody big one, painted at the end of eighty-seven and with plenty of provenance. It was on the wall of his studio when he gave an interview to *The Sunday Times* just before he snuffed it, and it's been in four or five exhibitions since then. I've got three of the catalogues here on my desk."

"There'll certainly be an appetite for it Bradley. I'm thinking our Arab friend or the twins in Shanghai, the one with the villa in Geneva. Sounds perfect for his lounge overlooking the lake."

"Yeh, it's framed and glazed to museum standard and signed and dated on the back. It's about a metre square. Weighs a bloody ton. George Michael made a telephone bid when it was last up for sale at Sotheby's but Lord and Lady La-de-da, the toffs down the road, bagged it for their private collection. And six months ago, I bagged it from them! It was hanging in the hallway in their flat. I didn't leave a calling card so the law still think it's an inside job for the insurance; an upperclass stitch-up. But the painting's here, I'm looking at it leaning against my wall."

Bradley Givens was in his study speaking on a burner phone to Marcus Blakely, the well respected proprietor of The Dollthorpe Gallery in Mayfair and a lesser spotted dealer in stolen art. Bradley was slouched back in a chair with his legs crossed on the surface of an antique desk and the metal segs on the heels of his size twelve, hand-made cowboy boots were gouging deep tracks in the rosewood inlay. The Sheraton Partners chair and the matching desk were perks of the job. Exhibits 'A' and 'B' in a case against the adage that crime does not pay.

"What are you asking for that particular piece Bradley?"

Blakely's plummy accent was as fake as the fruit in a photographer's prop room.

"A similar one went for three million at Christie's last year so I reckon on the black, you're asking three hundred for me, four fifty with your commission."

"Funds transfer at point of sale and directly to the Cayman's I presume?"

"Yeh, the blonde will drive down with it tomorrow. She'll ring you when she's round the back of your place, needs to be in and out, about two thirty. Be ready!"

"No need to worry, I'll be waiting."

"Oh, and while I've got you on the blower Marcus, there's another thing."

"Go on."

"There was a second Basquiat in that apartment. I'm thinking of going back for it tomorrow afternoon now the dust has settled and the place is open to the public again. They're bloody idiots. Only upgraded the door lock. We'd get a premium for a pair, right? One for each Shanghai twin?"

"Double the returns without a doubt."

"Put the word out then, we have a pair, I'll call you when it's done. The blonde will still be down tomorrow with this one though."

"Splendid, speak later then."

The untraceable call ended.

Bradley threw the phone in a drawer, hitched his XL chino's over the folds of his burgeoning backside and walked over to the abstract painting resting against the oak panelled wall of his study. He tilted his head and released a dismissive grunt.

"Bloody thing looks better upside down."

Bradley Givens' open access to The Market Square had served him well. He was thirty-seven years old, single and extremely wealthy by virtue of the proceeds from his nefarious activities. He lived with his girlfriend Lena, termed 'the blonde', at The Maltings, a faux Edwardian gentleman's residence set in five acres of land near Tarporley village in Cheshire. Bradley had acquired it without the need for a mortgage and threatened to disclose his solicitor's marital infidelities if a bank in the Cayman Islands was ever referenced as the source of the funds.

Over the years, Bradley Givens had chalked up over ten thousand hours clocking in and out of The Market Square and so it came about, as the axiom clearly states, that a tipping point was reached. A tipping point that involved the attention and intervention of Balthazar Smith.

Chapter 13

The man in the Havana

Wednesday 22nd November 2017

247 Chapel Street is a building at a crossroads, quite literally. The four storey property sits at the junction of Quay Street and Chapel Street; a wolf whistle from the fashionable Spinningfields district and within staggering distance of the Rover's Return on Coronation Street.

In recent years, 247 has begun to feel like the last man standing; a stubby old tooth in the smile of gleaming progress. Noisy neighbours and families of giants have moved into the area. Blocks of towering concrete, the shoebox homes for workers in tech start-ups and the gig economy are shooting up and creeping in on all four sides and their eagerness to squeeze out the elderly citizen in their midst is almost palpable.

Built in 1870 for mixed office use, 247 Chapel Street has Grade II listed status on account of the front elevation, which according to Salford Planning Department, 'incorporates fine architectural features of the Victorian era, including sandstone scrollwork and gingerbread'. Frog-eyed gargoyles, their chiselled features disfigured by acid rain, glare down on visitors from the cornice at first floor level. Four, foot-worn steps lead up to the original, solid oak entrance doors. To the right, three name plates, barely legible beneath layers of traffic grime identify the commercial occupants as follows:

Balthazar Smith. Dealer in coins and antiquities.
Ground Floor.

The Manchester Lepidopterist Society.
Floor One.

The Savants' Club.
Floor 3b.

Balthazar Smith's private apartment occupies the second floor. As the address suggests, 247 Chapel Street is open all hours but has never entertained any of Manchester's lepidopterists or any savants for that matter, well, perhaps one or two of the latter.

As he emerged from Salford Central train station, Balthazar turned left at the lights on Chapel Street and with a purposeful stride began the one kilometre walk to his office; through the midst of what can only be described as a giant building site. The cold nip in an east wind bit through the layers of his raincoat and tailored suit and the dusty slipstream of a passing bus tried to lift the Panama hat from his head. A watery sun bathed the burgeoning, new-build apartment blocks in lukewarm light.

Pressing on, the rapid-fire thump of bed rock under the hammer, the nasally grunt of bulldozers, whirring motors on swinging tower cranes and the clangs and bangs and all the shouting and yelling reminded Balthazar of the Lego movie. Stepping to one side to allow a gang of workers in Hi-Vis jackets and hard hats full use of the pavement, he was almost expecting a chorus of 'Everything is Awesome' instead of the

103

"cheers buddy". The sun's reflection bounced off plate glass windows like a flaming pinball as Balthazar strolled along in brogues as polished as his manners.

The custom made case he was carrying contained a Teknetics T2 metal detector and the instrument had lived up to its reputation as 'the best in the world for finding relics and coins'. Three King George III solid gold sovereigns sat heavy like loose change in one pocket of his raincoat. An Anglo-Saxon gold amulet was safely wrapped in tissue in the other. The treasure trove would fetch over twenty-thousand pounds, more than enough to keep the office going for the next three months. Balthazar arrived at his destination, pressed the entrance buzzer and waited. He peered up at the security camera and pulled a face. The door swung open and he stepped inside.

In the 1890s, the ground floor of 247 Chapel Street was the banking hall for Williams Deacon's Bank. The capacious space still possessed many of the original features including the marble mosaic floor, a walk-in safe, a glass pyramid atrium with decorative wrought ironwork and oak panel wainscoting around all four walls. The old world met the new on a loft style, mezzanine floor of steel beams and reclaimed bricks built in the 1990s. Balthazar turned right on entering the banking hall, pushed through an oak door with a leaded glass window and entered the room described in faded lettering as the 'Manager's Office'.

The mahogany desk with a leather inlay surface creased with age appeared very much at home. As did the marble fireplace with a grate and a chimney in working order. Demands from the bank for arrears, elegantly written with fountain pen ink on cartridge paper and dating back over a century, were framed as a set and graced the chimney breast. A pair of Italian design sofas and a matching coffee table were arranged by the fire on antique pine floorboards blemished with knots like liver spots. On the surface of the desk, the front covers of two newspapers were awaiting Balthazar's attention.

The headline on the *Manchester Evening News* read: 'The Invisible Man strikes again'.

The sub-headline: 'Wealthy widow dies from heart attack after daylight robbery'.

The headline on the *Stockport Advertiser* read: 'Two miracles in a week' and pictured Teaps with both parents outside a private hospital somewhere near Chester.

A second, smaller photo showed Wilson grinning from his bed in Stockport Infirmary.

Balthazar draped his raincoat on a rack of deer antlers mounted on the wall then fished the treasure trove from the pockets. He was unwrapping the amulet as his two assistants, Mark and James, entered the office drinking coffee. James handed a third mug to Balthazar.

Mark and James lived in a flat in the basement of the building and were Balthazar's trusted lieutenants. They'd chosen a civil union rather than marriage. Mark was forty-seven and the elder by four years, which may explain a tendency to hector his partner on occasions. Mark had an unkempt mop of curly black hair and a careworn face like a clown's without make-up. His stocky frame carried the paunch of too many restaurant meals and too little exercise. Strenuous activity was limited to dancing to Northern Soul music in the clubs of the gay village on a Friday night.

In comparison, James was a Jack Spratt and carried not an ounce of fat. He seldom smiled so the corners of his mouth, through lack of practice, had seized on a drooping crescent shape that gave him the air of someone permanently crestfallen. When asked a question or an opinion he would often scratch his pate of thinning, close-cropped hair as if to dig out a reply. This was always a red flag for Mark's hectoring and stoked much laughter and an obvious comparison when they were out with friends. The couple's dress sense, always in step with the current fashions, made them appear to be younger than their years. Their nicknames were Stan and Ollie.

Mark and James were number elevens and undertook a variety of administrative duties for Balthazar's office. Balthazar was a turbo charged eleven and for want of an official title, a roving ambassador, a trouble shooter, a Mr 'Fix It', for The Powers That Be.

James was blind as result of an accident about which only Balthazar and Mark knew the details.

"Morning chief" said Mark, casting his eye over the treasure trove on the desk, "fruitful, by the looks of it?"

Mark placed a coin in James's hand and with a thumb and forefinger James read the relief lettering like Braille.

"Ah, a twenty-two carat Sovereign! King George. Very nice! Where did you get it?"

Balthazar was happy to tell the story.

"The coins were under the seventh green at a golf club in Bury. I had to dig those up last night, without using a torch and it was bloody freezing. I left more than a pitch mark unfortunately. The green now breaks to the right over a speed bump like crazy golf."

The corners of James's mouth did rise perceptibly at that.

"They were stolen ninety years ago from a dealer in Bolton, well before the golf course was built. The burglar buried them in what was a farmer's field at the time, waited three months before going back to retrieve them but lost his bearings. He spent five nights digging before being arrested for trespass and criminal damage on account of all the giant mole hills and eventually confessed to the theft. I found an article with decent photos in the Evening News archive at the Central Library and traced his past to get the full story. He was a rubbish burglar. He stole the amulet from Bury Museum and had no idea what it was worth, so stashed it behind a loose brick in the vestry of Bury Parish Church. Then he was nicked for the coins, served a few years in Strangeways prison and forgot all about the amulet. The lord works in mysterious ways."

Balthazar took a cloth from a drawer and began to polish one of the coins.

"Nice aren't they?"

"They'll make a pretty penny" said James, flipping his coin in the air.

"Anyway, take some pictures, get a valuation from a couple of our dealer friends and bang it all on the website."

Balthazar paused to sip his coffee.

"The good thing is, we'll be back in the black for a while so can you put the metal detector in the safe for now Mark. And thank goodness. I'm getting a bit too old for all that digging around in darkness at midnight. So, what's on the agenda for today then?"

Balthazar's attention was drawn to the cover stories on both of the newspapers.

"The priority is the Invisible Man" said Mark, pointing to the *Manchester Evening News*. "Bradley Givens, our public enemy number one. We reckon he's accumulated ten million quid in the last two years alone."

Mark continued with the briefing as Balthazar scanned through the report.

"And he's showing no signs of stopping despite a couple of hefty warnings from The Gateway. And as always, it's the collateral damage that's the major issue."

"What's his method?" asked Balthazar, pushing back from the desk and clasping his hands behind his head.

"It's not rocket science. He scans the society pages in upmarket magazines. You know, the ones with photos of the great and good at a posh ball or a charity fundraiser and then he targets their expensive jewellery and watches; but that's just the day job. In his spare time, for a hobby, he goes after paintings, collectibles, antique furniture and luxury vehicles."

Mark tapped the photo of the elderly woman smiling on the cover of the paper.

"This lady was on the board of Age Concern. Hubby was a director at Boddington's Brewery and passed away about five years ago. Givens must have cooked up some reason for a meeting, a fundraising idea I would imagine, so it was easy to pull her into The Market Square after that. He then sifts through her memory traces until he reaches the one where she enters the code in the strongbox hidden in the back of a cupboard. James has double-checked this upstairs by the way. So in broad daylight the next afternoon, he turns up in disguise pretending to be from the council with some story about mice infestation. The lady lived in a farmhouse near Bowden, it's a Thursday afternoon and Givens knows the housekeeper takes that afternoon off. So then he ties her up and walks out with ten grand in cash, a box full of diamond jewellery bought by her husband, and also the family heirlooms she'd inherited. The aftershock killed her. Oh, and Givens thinks it's funny to leave his 'Invisible Man' calling card at the crime scene."

James continued with the next chapter. A chapter only he has the privileges to see, courtesy of the Savants' Club on the top floor.

"But the body count doesn't end at one. As Givens is driving through Altrincham, doing forty in a thirty zone, rushing to get the jewellery to his fence, he causes a midwife driving in the opposite direction to curse the bloke in the Landcruiser for going too fast. She can see the back of Bradley's car in the rearview mirror and tries to read the number plate. So her eyes are not on the road when a four-year-old girl, crossing a zebra with her mum, realises she's dropped her sweets, pulls her hand free and dashes back to get them. The girl will be in a wheelchair for the rest of her life and the midwife took a fatal overdose when she found out. There are going to be lots of repercussions in a number of maternity wards because that midwife, who still had a long career ahead of her, is no longer around. Bradley's charge sheet is longer than your arm."

"What's the verdict from the top floor?" Balthazar asked.

Only James could answer because Mark never entered 3b, the current of energy coursing through the room was so intense it made him nauseous.

"We've been asked to terminate Bradley Givens with extreme prejudice and if the girlfriend is collateral damage, so be it. She's no angel. East European mafia connections and a CV that includes drug trafficking and modern day slavery."

"Who's ready for action?"

"The High Brown Fritillary, a couple of big ones emerged last week and they're good to go" said Mark.

Balthazar turned to James."What's the strategy?"

"He's planning to steal a painting from a stately home tomorrow. Our intervention leads to a police chase and Bradley is terminated in the car crash. A policeman is injured unfortunately, but from what I see he retires early on a full pension. It all looks nice and clean."

"What are the odds?"

"Pretty much guaranteed to happen, so a safe bet, but there is one cloud on the horizon. The future traces following Bradley's demise are not settling and there's interference from a number eleven by the name of Wilson Armitage. Mark, can you show Balthazar the story in the paper."

Balthazar read the story in the *Stockport Advertiser* which suggested Teaps had been blessed with two miracles in quick succession: the discovery of his missing mother and the best friend coming out of a coma.

"Mmmm, well let's solve one problem at a time shall we? Let's get the Bradley issue sorted."

Mark and James left Balthazar's office through a second door leading to the stairwell that served the rest of the building. On reaching the landing on the first floor they entered the premises of the Manchester Lepidopterist Society. It wasn't an office as such, the open plan space was more of an incubating room, a warm and humid nature reserve specially created for members of the society. Scores of butterflies were captive behind glass panels in an artificial ecosystem that resembled the Insect House at a zoo. Some were fluttering around excitedly while others were perched on the stems of foliage, clapping their wings like children anticipating a treat, or assassins anticipating a mission. Mark slid back a glass panel, took a fine mesh net and located the two High Browns. The flash of tiger stripes on orange offered little camouflage in the jungle of green and the butterflies volunteered their services readily. Once inside the net, pairs of antennae twitched as though messages were being exchanged. With the lightest touch, Mark pinched the tip of the gossamer sails with his fingers, raised a sash window and set the mission in motion. The beautiful insects raced away in haphazard, erratic flight, as though playing tag while connected by invisible elastic thread.

James climbed the next four flights of stairs alone and entered the quarters of 'The Savants' Club' on the top floor. Savant business was always conducted in complete darkness and that was never an issue, for it was James and only James who conducted the business anyway.

Chapter 14

Flight of the butterflies

Wednesday 22nd November 2017

The High Brown Fritillary is Britain's most endangered butterfly and as the insects took a bearing south along the course of the A56, they were also Britain's most dangerous.

On the outskirts of Cheadle they flew over a vicarage with a crenelated turret and weathervanes on the roof. Inside the house, a thirteen-year-old girl lay on her bed reading a textbook. Her guardian, Auntie Kay, had just entered the room and was sitting beside her.

"Is everything all right love?"

"Uh huh, I'm good, feeling much better thanks. And look, this scar on my arm has almost gone."

The fine pink line with needle pricks either side resembled a zip and could have been the work of a tailor rather than a surgeon.

"Ha yeh, they've stitched you back together very nicely. You'll hardly be able to see that in a month's time."

Kay paused for a moment as she lined up a batch of sentences in the correct order and brushed stray hair from Sally's eyes. The locks fought back with static and stubbornly fell back into place.

"What are we going to do about school then? They rang me at work yesterday and wanted to know when you're planning to go back?"

Sally didn't look up from her book.

"I spoke to Dr Giurgus at the medical centre and he told me it would help your recovery in lots of ways if you went back to school as soon as possible. Back to a normal routine. The moment you feel up to it."

Sally replied but still didn't look up from her book.

"I don't want to go back to school."

Kay had been anticipating something like this.

"But love, you have to go back to school. You'll fall behind with your education. There's no other option."

"Well, I was already miles in front so it'll give everyone else a chance to catch up then."

"Sally you don't mean that. What about your friends, they'll be happy to see you back in school?"

"What friends Auntie Kay? You mean the kids we didn't invite to my birthday party last week because we knew they wouldn't turn up? The ones who avoid me like the plague, who pour orange juice in my bag, steal my books and stand staring with their backs against the corridor walls whenever I walk past like I was a leper? Those friends? Oh yeh, they're really missing me. Course they are."

Sally closed the book.

"Anyway, I've decided to self educate and work from home for the next few years."

Kay half laughed, not certain if Sally was half joking.

"It's true. Look, I've started already."

Sally showed Kay the front cover.

'GCSE AQA Computer Science. Syllabus Revision and Practice'

"It's not difficult. And I can work much better from home."

Kay realised Sally was fully serious and began to bristle.

"But Sally love, you know that's totally out of the question. Not only will we have all kinds of trouble with the school, that half-wit director of social services will go mental again."

"I'm sure you'll be able to handle that" said Sally dismissively.

"Sally I know you've had . . . Look, I understand how difficult these past couple of years have been for you. To lose your mum like that – and I still weep for my sister most days let me tell you – then to lose your dad so soon after and then the car accident. I know it's been traumatic, just horrible, horrible, but I'm only trying to help. To do the right thing."

"Then let me stay away from school and teach myself."

"Sally that's not going to happen. You have to go back to school and you know it. And what's more, you're acting like a child . . . "

"But I am a child."

"Stop that right now, you're just being a petulant teenager. You know I can't change what has happened, because it's happened, so we just have to get on with things and deal with the future in a positive way, together."

"But I am Auntie Kay, I really am. I think I'm being super positive."

Kay's cup had runneth over, she'd heard enough.

"Look, you stay cooped up here all the time, with no mates, you never go out, live like a bloody hermit and never show any gratitude for me trying to help, providing you with a home or show the slightest bit of sympathy for the fact that I lost my sister as well. You know you can be so stubborn and cold sometimes Sally. Cold and emotionless! Even uncaring. You didn't cry once at any of the funerals and just carried on as though nothing much was happening. There's only one family photo in your room. It's as though you don't seem to care about anything or anyone anymore, just yourself. I'm doing my best for you Sally, I really am, but all this is too much for me."

Kay buried her face in her hands, retracted her claws and began to sob.

Sally placed the book on the bedside table, wrapped her arms around her aunt and the embrace lasted for a minute or two.

"Don't cry Auntie Kay. If it will make you happy, I'll go back to school after Christmas. It's almost the end of term so no point in going back now."

Sally passed a tissue to Kay who responded with a weak smile and blew her nose.

"I've been thinking about things a lot since the accident and I want to tell you something."

Kay was now wiping away smudges of mascara.

"But there's one condition. You can't ask any questions until I've finished."

"Okay" said Kay, relieved the loggerheads moment had passed – for the time being anyway.

"When I was little, like five years old, I used to have these amazing dreams that were so real I was always sad when I woke up the next morning. You know, when I realised the new bike I'd been riding all night wasn't in the garage."

Sally chuckled at her foolishness.

"I loved the dreams involving Mum best of all though, cos she was in lots of them and they always involved a fantastic adventure or a holiday somewhere. And there's this one particular dream, a recurring dream that I'll remember

115

forever. We were at the seaside and there were all these beautiful, multi-coloured seahorses. They had wavy golden hair and long eyelashes and wore lipstick and me and Mum were pretend mermaids and the seahorses would take us for rides in this bubbly warm green sea like a jacuzzi."

Kay reached for Sally's hand.

"That's such a lovely image to remember your mum by Sally, it really is."

The next morning, at breakfast time, I'd look at Mum and try to see something in her face, to give me a special smile to show that we'd shared the seahorse dream together; but she never did. I could have asked her I suppose, I didn't say anything because I thought she'd think I was being silly.

Sally paused for a moment and her pupils appeared to dilate, as though focusing on the best part.

"The day before Mum died, when there was just me with her in the hospital, she asked me if I could keep a promise. She said it was a very strange promise that I had to lock away in my heart. So of course I said yes. And do you know what Mum told me Auntie Kay?"

Kay shook her head, for how could she possibly have known?

"Mum told me never to forget all the dreams of us riding on seahorses together."

Kay gasped and for a second struggled to catch her breath.

"Mum had been there with me Auntie Kay. We'd been sharing those dreams all along. It's incredible isn't it?"

"Oh Sally, that is so wonderful, so magical. Such a lovely way to remember your mum. Like a fairytale."

"I know, but it's not a fairytale at all. It's not something I've invented to bring back nice thoughts about Mum. Because

116

Mum also told me that soon after she dies, Dad would die as well and I was not to be too upset because after that I was going to join them both and then we'd *all* play on the seahorses together."

The blood drained from Kay's face.

"Mum also said that I would come here to live with you. That's why I'm telling you this and breaking my promise to keep the secret, because if I go to school or not, it won't make any difference. When I saw Mum that night in the children's home, I think it was a message to tell me that both her and Dad are waiting for me and something is going to happen soon that can't be changed. It started when I met Felix and we went to this place in our dreams called The Market Square. And just before our holiday in France, a few months ago, I had an even stranger dream in which these two very odd men told me I would have an accident. And I did. Then after the accident, when I stopped being unconscious, I saw them in a dream again and also the person who saved my life when I was trapped under the car. All these things are connected Auntie Kay. I need to speak to Wilson, the boy who was in the same ward with me. I feel like I'm meant to, expected to. If he's still in Stockport Infirmary can I go and see him tomorrow? I think he was the one who saved my life."

The higher mental functions of Kay's brain were incapable of processing information by this point so the primitive part, the part that deals with knee jerk reactions, provided the answer. In other words, Kay wasn't thinking properly when she said. "If you think it will help love, and make you feel better to talk to someone closer to your own age, of course you can."

117

An hour later, while Kay was on the phone confirming the visiting times with Stockport Infirmary, the High Brown Fritillary butterflies were making adjustments for a crosswind and setting a final course for the stately home of Lord and Lady Delbury. The Dee estuary at high tide shimmered on the horizon as the sun slipped into the sea like a butter biscuit being dunked. The grounds of the private hospital in which Vanessa Clarke was being cared for were also visible twenty miles to the left.

Three significant things will happen tomorrow: Montague will meet with Michael and Graham Clarke. Sally will meet with Wilson and Daisy. And Bradley Givens will meet his comeuppance. As I write, these events are woven into the filigree of the foreseeable future but beyond that, for the days to follow, the weather looks to be murky and unsettled. A strengthening wind is disturbing the tracery of destiny. James believes a tornado is coming and that's bad news, because it's difficult to escape the path of a tornado when you can't predict where the twister will go.

Chapter 15

This may come as a shock

Thursday 23rd November 2017

Montague flashed his ID card in cursory fashion at the girl behind the reception desk of the Chester Trauma and Rehabilitation Centre.

"I'm here to see Mr Michael Clark; his wife Vanessa has been here for a month or so, the lady who . . . well, you should know the circumstances, my secretary called to arrange an interview and a meeting room. I'm Assistant Chief Constable Simon Montague from the North Caledonian Constabulary. Can you let them know I'm here?"

The receptionist nodded obligingly as she checked the details on her laptop.

"Mr Clarke and his son are in consulting room 1B. They're waiting for you sir. Down the corridor and the last door on the right."

Montague tucked the ID card back in his wallet and strode off with confident purpose, he could hardly wait to break the good news.

When Montague entered the room, Teaps and Michael were sitting at an oval table in a small meeting room that overlooked manicured lawns and neat flower beds. A cafetiére of fresh coffee stood on a tray with milk, cups and biscuits. They stood nervously to attention as Montague entered the room. Both father and son were fearful that a dark shadow was about to be cast by the new light in their lives, the happiness dimmed in some way. Michael stood tall, broad shouldered and clean shaven and Teaps appeared to have acquired greater stature. As though the return of his mother had revitalised and nourished an inner self and he'd finally blossomed after years of harsh winters.

"Please sit down," said Montague, helping himself to coffee and biscuits. The notion that refreshments could be for all present company didn't enter his head. He removed his flat topped hat, sat down opposite Teaps, opened his briefcase and placed a manilla folder on the table.

"So how can we help you officer? We've not been told anything about why you're here."

After being informed of the request for a police interview, Michael had been bracing himself for further revelations regarding his wife. It had to be something serious for a senior policeman to travel four hundred miles all the way from Inverness to discuss.

"Well, as you know Mr Clarke, I'm Assistant Chief Constable Simon Montague from the North Caledonian Constabulary. We cover the Highland's region that includes Inverness and you won't be surprised therefore, if I tell you this is a rather sensitive matter concerning your wife. Before I go on though, may I ask if she's on the mend, on the road to recovery?"

Michael's hands were trembling as he lifted them from the table and wiped his palms on his trousers.

"Unfortunately no! We're not expecting miracles, we're just elated to have found her after all these years. The therapy is focused on improving her recollection of the present.

Everything before the stroke has gone. It's difficult for her emotionally to comprehend who we are and where she is. It's not surprising really."

"And how are you son, over the moon I expect?"

"Yes, I'm happy we finally discovered what happened and she's back with us. But it's hard to think about all those years that were wasted and the fact nobody cared who she was or investigated her disappearance properly. If only people had looked harder at the beginning, that's the toughest part to deal with."

Montague wondered whether father and son had read the allegations of police failings in the newspaper. Was the lad now sticking the knife in?

"And you say she has absolutely no recollection of what happened, how she travelled to Inverness or why?"

"No, those memories have all gone."

"In that case, I may be able to shed some light."

Montague placed his hand on the folder.

"Before I present you with information you may find disturbing, can I ask for the moment that you keep this conversation strictly confidential?"

Michael had no idea of where this was leading or what the hell could be in the folder. Teaps sipped a glass of water.

"The day before Alice was identified as the missing person Vanessa Clarke, a seventeen-year-old male visited the care home. Initially there appeared to be nothing suspicious about this, the lad was representing a family seeking a care home for a relation with dementia. True, it was unusual that he was alone and relatively young for such a responsibility, but there's no crime in that. However, as the duty manager at South Kessock was showing the lad around the place she sensed an unusually high level of interest in Alice. Almost as though he was there to find her, to check her circumstances, Celia couldn't put her finger on her intuition at the time. Later that day, when the written note was discovered in Alice's room and her true identity revealed, Celia put two and two together and sensed the visitor from the previous day, this lad, could have had something to do with it. My sergeant initially scoffed at the notion, but I was intrigued and as a senior police officer, I felt it was my duty to pursue the matter."

Montague opened the folder and methodically placed four black and white photographs in a row in front of Teaps and his father.

"Do either of you recognise this person?"

Teaps looked at each of the images and with a finger slowly pulled one closer. He stared in disbelief at the familiar face of his good friend sitting on a bench on a railway platform. The date and time generated by the camera ran across the top of the page 'Inverness Station. Ptfm 3. 15:40 31.10.2017'.

Teaps looked up with a puzzled expression on his face.

"Yeh, this is my best mate, he's called Wilson Armitage. We go to the same college."

Teaps's father then leant forward, studied the slightly fuzzy yet unmistakable images and turned to his son.

"You're right, that's Wilson."

"To be exact, it is a Mr Wilson Armitage of Midland Drive, Bramhall. He used his mobile phone the day before to make the appointment with the care home and three of the staff, including Celia Green, plus a taxi driver all recognise him. Any ideas what he was doing there? Has he been behaving strangely or said something that stands out as unusual over the past few weeks?"

Michael and Teaps were both speechless.

"Yes, I'm sure this revelation must come as quite a shock."

Teaps gathered the four photos together and brought them closer to his face to be certain his eyes weren't playing tricks. Once convinced, he gently placed the irrefutable evidence back down on the table and for a few seconds refused to utter words that were about to incriminate a trusted friend.

"A few weeks before Mum was found, Wilson asked me about her. I thought nothing of it at the time. He just wanted to know the facts about her disappearance. We were talking about all kinds of stuff actually, about PlayStation games and girlfriends but then weeks later, the day after Mum was found . . . " Teaps's voice quivered as his throat tightened, "he asked me what I thought about her being alone in *that room* and would she *get her memory back*? And I thought it was strange that he could have known those things, like where she was and what was wrong with her."

Teaps turned to his father as his face flushed and his eyes watered.

"He was my friend Dad, my best friend. What was he doing? And why did he never tell me if he knew where Mum was?"

"Look son, whatever it is, we'll get to the bottom of it. There's obviously been some terrible mistake, a misunderstanding about the facts."

Michael didn't have any other words with which to placate his son *and* explain the photos.

Montague was keen to hurry the conversation along.

"On the face of it, there appears to be no wrongdoing, no criminality that is on the part of this Armitage lad. But I'll get to the bottom of it mark my words, it's just a matter of following the trail and piecing together the facts. I suspect the father had the major part to play. Wilson Armitage was just a baby at the time of your wife's disappearance and although he's now become a person of interest after the fact, perhaps as some kind of accomplice, I believe it's the father that holds the key. Do either of you know Alex Armitage?"

Michael couldn't understand how a door had opened to bring Alex Armitage into the conversation.

"Wait a minute Constable Montague."

"Assistant Chief Constable Montague, if you don't mind."

"Sorry, yes, Assistant Chief Constable, hold on, you've lost me. You think Alex Armitage played a part in the disappearance of my wife in Inverness seventeen years ago? How? Why? For what reason would he do that? The doctors have told us she suffered a stroke. How could Alex have given her a stroke?"

"Maybe it wasn't a stroke. Perhaps it was a blow to the head that caused a stroke . . . after an argument possibly? We're just soft thinking at the moment and exploring avenues of enquiry."

Teaps wanted to leave the room and run from the accusations. His emotions were trapped in a claustrophobic lift plummeting downwards as feelings of panic were rising. A cold sweat had broken out over his father's forehead.

"But why would Alex have taken my wife to Inverness of all places?"

"That's what we're going to find out Mr Clarke, with good old-fashioned detective work."

Michael shook his head in disbelief. Something about the policeman's manner and the self-satisfied smirk struck him as out of kilter with the gravity of the revelations. The whole thing was bizarre, surreal, like a game of make-believe or Cluedo. Wilson on a station platform with a train ticket. Alex in Inverness with the lead piping.

"Can I see your identity card again please?"

Montague handed it over to Michael and the face in the photo carried the same smug expression.

"I don't know what to say, none of this makes sense. Surely there's a logical explanation. Perhaps Wilson was in Inverness for a university interview or to visit a friend or a relation."

"Yes, that's possible, Mr Clarke, but it wouldn't explain why he was also in the South Kessock Care Home showing an interest in your wife the day before she was identified as Alice. Perhaps Alex was also there, pulling strings in the background somewhere?"

"But Alex didn't know my . . . "

Michael Clarke's voice trailed away. He turned to his son as words at the back of his throat congealed to form something distasteful.

"When I met Vanessa, she'd just ended a relationship with her previous boyfriend, and that boyfriend was Alex Armitage!"

During the flight back to Inverness, Montague listened as Sergeant Jordan summarised his findings.

"None of the teachers had a bad word to say about Wilson or his relationship with Graham Clarke; nor did any of the students that knew them, and there were plenty, they're both popular lads!"

"What did Armitage's wife have to say?"

"I didn't manage to track her down sir. When I called at the house nobody was home so a neighbour gave me details of the charity shop where she worked but it was closed when I got there."

Which was a barefaced lie, because Sergeant Jordan had made no effort whatsoever to contact Gloria.

If truth be told, all he'd done was spend the best part of a day putting ridiculous questions to teachers and college kids who thought he'd completely lost the plot.

"Not sure we've got enough to charge them at the moment, but keep digging sergeant. Check every record you can find for Vanessa Clarke in the six months before she disappeared, bank statements, tax returns, medical history. Michael reckons Vanessa and Armitage were only in a relationship for a few months but there's a bad smell about this case and my nose is telling me it's all about to hit the fan for Armitage and son."

ACC Montague pressed a button to fully recline his seat, much to the annoyance of the person behind and then pulled the peak of his hat down over his eyes. He was more than satisfied with the direction his enquiries were taking.

Chapter 16

Kindred spirits

Thursday 23rd November 2017

A phone call from Kay to Stockport Infirmary confirmed that Wilson was allowed non-family visitors between twelve and two but only three people were permitted by his bedside at any one time.

After enquiring at the reception desk, Sally was directed "up two flights of stairs, a right turn down the corridor, or you can take the lift over there to Ward 7."

Two floors above, Wilson was eating his fifth energy bar of the day and Alex, Gloria and Daisy were at his bedside. In the space of just twenty-four hours his appearance had improved markedly. On the litmus scale of health, the colour in his cheeks was no longer an insipid creamy white, now it was more of a mottled pink and his pyjama jacket no longer resembled a striped throw covering spindly furniture. With every banana and milkshake he was gaining weight and his sunken features filling out. Gloria was describing an amusing incident from the previous day in which a lady in the shop put her handbag down, only for an elderly customer to then pick up the bag and try to buy it. Wilson's laugh turned into a cough.

Alex would have dearly loved to share the happiness in the moment; to enjoy Gloria's relief that her son was on the mend, to replace her worry lines with those of laughter.

Wilson was returning to something like his old self in a ward for people getting better, but now a policeman was waiting in the wings to step in and spoil his recovery. Alex desperately needed a word with Wilson, alone.

On the other side of the bed, Daisy was also wearing a false smile. She wondered if Alex and Gloria knew about the police officer investigating Wilson's trip to South Kessock.

"Anyway love" said Gloria, "that's brought you fully up to speed with all the news from the outside world. Your sisters told me to say hello and keep getting better. They promised to come and see you as soon as they can."

"Well I can hardly wait for that" said Wilson rolling his eyes. "When I spoke to them on FaceTime the other day they asked me to be a model in their fashion show cos I looked so thin. They said their clothes would look great on me. Can you believe that?"

Gloria started chuckling. "You know they were only joking. But I'm happy to see grumpy old Wilson is back to being his usual self."

Daisy was feeling through the blanket for Wilson's toes to tickle his foot. "Think I preferred the other one to be honest, the quiet, docile Wilson. He was no trouble at all."

"Okay, well just so you know, the doctor said I'll be good to go next week. Daisy will you get off, you know that's really irritating and not funnyyyy, stop it. I've asked him if I can stay for a month of peace and quiet with no visitors."

"Wilson, that's a terrible thing to say. You're improving far too quickly for my liking."

"Yeh. I'm going to buy him a 'get well slowly' card in that case" said Daisy.

"Okay, joking time over. I'm ready to get out of this mad

house."

The background noise in Ward 7 had slowly been rising as conversations around the various beds competed to be heard. Three children were playing hide and seek and one toddler was trying to lose herself in the drapes of the divider curtain gathered behind Wilson's bed.

A noise alarm must have sounded somewhere, because a nurse entered the ward, clapped her hands and politely but firmly told everyone to lower their voices and to keep children under control "with no more running around!"

"About time" said Wilson, sinking back into the pillow and closing his eyes.

Daisy smiled and turned to watch the nurse leave the ward. It was then she was startled by the face of the girl who had been permanently in the back of her mind since the day Wilson emerged from his coma. With her heart suddenly pounding, Daisy rose from her seat and tried to sound as casual as could be.

"Oh look Wilson, I think you might have a new visitor. It's Sally, the girl who was in the ICU at the same time as you. I'm just gonna go and say hello."

Sally was reluctant to enter the ward because of the three people rule.

As Daisy walked over she almost broke into a run, for she had no intention of letting Sally escape without an explanation this time.

"Who's that?" asked Alex.

"Not sure" said Wilson, forcing himself higher up the bed. "I kind of recognise her, but I can't remember from where."

"Listen love" said Gloria, gathering her handbag and coat, "we've been here for an hour and you're only allowed three visitors, so Dad and I are going to head home. You're looking so much better today son, much improved, I can't begin to tell you how happy I am. I'll give the ward a call later this afternoon to confirm arrangements for taking you home. I'm sure there'll be some instructions about resting and diet. We have to do things properly now and not take shortcuts like the first time you were ill. If we'd been more careful maybe none of this would have happened."

"Sounds like a plan Mum."

Gloria kissed Wilson's forehead.

"Take it easy son" said Alex, patting his shoulder. Wilson noticed the bruising and the swollen knuckle. "Your mum's working tomorrow afternoon so I'll probably call in by myself, I've not been able to get a word in edgeways today. It would be good to catch up."

Wilson read between the lines and knew his father wasn't expecting a reply. The source of the bruising would have to wait for the 'catch up'.

In the corridor, Gloria and Alex were introduced to Sally and after a brief conversation Gloria finally turned and waved goodbye. Daisy ushered Sally back into the ward and made sure they sat down with the minimum of space between their chairs. Daisy didn't bother with introductions as she grabbed Sally's hand and sighed with relief. The questions she was desperate to ask were tearing free from their bindings and Sally wouldn't be allowed to disappear this time without facing them.

"Sally, I'm so pleased you're here. I really am. I didn't have time to thank you on the day everything happened and the day after you'd been moved to another ward. Then when I tried to find you, they told me you'd gone home and wouldn't give me your address. How did you know Wilson was in the white room? And about The Gateway and the bangles? And what made you think I could go and find him?"

Wilson was now sitting bolt upright and none of what he'd just heard made any sense whatsoever.

"Wilson saved my life, and I was meant to save his" was all Sally said by way of reply.

"Whoa," said Wilson, "time out".

Daisy's questions had clearly made sense to Sally.

Daisy reached out to Wilson with her free hand.

"I've not had chance to tell you about everything that happened. It was Sally who told me you were in a white room, in The Gateway, and without her help I would never have found you and brought you back."

"Double whoa," said Wilson flopping back into his pillows, "Daisy, you're going to have to go back to the beginning and explain all of this very slowly and very, very clearly."

So over the course of ten minutes, as Wilson lay still and silent in bed, with the look of disbelief on his face growing into one of astonishment, Daisy explained the sequence of events and the dreams that transpired while he was in his so called, 'persistent vegetative state'.

"And that's what happened Wilson. I've not had chance to tell you because you've either been sleeping or you've had other visitors."

"So you think I was sort of being held against my will by Big Mac and Short Cake, or because of a bet that was connected with your grandmother returning the bangles?"

"Yeh, I do Wilson. I'm sure of it."

Wilson couldn't help but see the funny side.

"I'd love to have been in that wild west dream, sounded awesome."

He paused for a moment.

"So let me get this straight, you were the girl trapped under the car outside the station. The girl who was in the same ward as me?"

Sally nodded. "I was moved onto another floor the day after you came out of your coma."

"In that case, thanks for saving my life and I have to say, you look a lot better than you did the last time I saw you."

"Mmm, my leg still aches sometimes, but you can't really see where I had the stitches anymore. The scars on my shoulder and on my arm are quite long though."

"Yeh, you do tend to come off worse if you pick a fight with a car."

"Kay said I have to double-check both ways when I cross the road in future."

"Or maybe wear a suit of armour?"

"Ha, yeh, that's a much better idea."

Wilson could tell from the distracted look on Sally's face, and the way she was perched nervously on the edge of her seat that there was more to come; further revelations possibly. Sally was tugging at a loose thread on her bobble hat, making the hole bigger. She seemed hesitant and uncertain when she finally spoke.

"I hope you don't mind me coming here and I don't want to waste your time; you're both going to think I'm mad, cos this sounds crazy even to me."

Sally then addressed Wilson directly.

"Nobody told me it was you who saved my life Wilson, I

saw it when I was in the white room. I saw you come out of Davenport train station and come running to help."

Daisy was thankful the patient in the next bed had gone for a coffee with his wife and the conversation wasn't being overheard.

"How do you mean, you saw what Wilson did?"

"I saw him take off his coat and roll under the car and give instructions to the policeman. I saw everything. I was in the white room standing next to Wilson and when I touched his hand I saw these moving images of how he saved my life. Then Big Mac, the short round one, came to me and said I was getting better and didn't have to stay in the white room anymore. So I followed him through the hall with the gold bangles and then I was back in The Market Square. That's why I spoke aloud to Auntie Kay about the experience, the dream, or whatever it was. I described it in a way you'd immediately understand when you were sitting at Wilson's bedside, and you'd hear me and go and find him."

"But why did you think I would be able to do that, to rescue Wilson?"

"Because the first time I went to the hall with all the gold bangles ..."

"You mean The Gateway?" Wilson wanted to be certain they were talking about the same place.

"Yes, The Gateway. Where Big Mac and the other one work. It was during the summer. They told me off for shining torches and doing lamping experiments that made spirits use up their energy. They said I was as bad as Wilson Armitage. So when I was starting to get better and I recognised your face in the bed next to mine and your clipboard said your name was Wilson Armitage, I assumed you'd also been to The Gateway.

And I guessed that Daisy might have been there as well and if she found the white room she might be able to rescue you. But the weird thing is, how could I have heard your name from Big Mac? I mean, how could I have known that you existed before I'd even seen you in the hospital? A person whose name I heard in a dream, who I'd never met, turns out to be the person who saves my life. I think Big Mac told me your name in advance, for a reason."

Sally dropped her head and she returned to picking the hole in her bobble hat.

Wilson and Daisy looked at each other, trying to read what was going on in the other's mind. Daisy placed her hand on Sally's to stop the hole from getting bigger.

"Sally, we don't think you're crazy. Everything you've told us we understand."

"And there's something else."

Sally took a deep breath in readiness for the most troubling part of the confession.

"Two years ago, just before my mum died, she told me Dad was also going to die and I'd go to live with Auntie Kay. And all that has happened. I also found out that me and Mum had been sharing dreams so I think she'd been to The Market Square as well. When I went to live with Auntie Kay, I had a vision in which Mum was still alive and on a beach. She was inviting me to join her and laughing like she was telling me to hurry up and get a move on. I think my life is leading me to her and she's expecting me. I'm on a conveyor belt I can't get off and it's all out of my control like *The Truman Show*. All this was meant to happen and you're both involved because the journey has now brought me here, but I don't know how everything fits together Wilson."

Wilson nodded, but had no idea why. It was a reflex action to his name being mentioned. He was transfixed by what he was hearing.

"That's why I don't really want to go back to school. There's no point. I tried to talk to Auntie Kay about this but she got upset and angry. That's why I came here, I thought you might understand or feel something similar, some kind of . . . connection."

The confession over, Sally returned to picking the loose thread.

Wilson's response came as a big surprise to Daisy.

"We need to go back to The Gateway. To speak to Big Mac and Short Cake. Sounds to me like something's going on here and as usual they're behind it."

"Wilson no! Absolutely not! You promised. We promised. We agreed we'd never go back to The Market Square. If I ever see those two again I'll kill them, and I mean it!"

"Daisy don't be so melodramatic. No harm has ever come to us in The Market Square or in The Gateway! It's the corridor leading to Ward 3B that we need to avoid. And besides, you can't actually kill someone in a dream. Big Mac and Short Cake are not real."

"No? Well they nearly killed you Wilson and one of their evil mates broke my finger and tried to push me under a bus! Remember?"

"Mmmm. Fair point. So what do we do?"

The question was answered when a doctor conducting his rounds entered the ward and brought the conversation to a premature end.

"Look, it's time for me to go now, but thanks for listening. Auntie Kay is waiting in the car park. If you think of anything that might . . . "

"Sally, wait, we can't speak anymore today but I've got an idea. Why don't we meet again in the next few days, just you and me? I'll tell you all we know about The Market Square and The Gateway and see if our experiences are similar and try to understand where they overlap. Let Wilson and me think about what you've told us and see if we can read anything into it, that was quite a lot to take in. Not your normal chit chat by a hospital bed."

Sally smiled, relieved that she had been taken seriously, that her hunch hadn't been completely foolish.

"Let me have your mobile number Sally. Where do you live?"

"Cheadle. With Auntie Kay."

"Okay, I'll text you. We can meet somewhere in Cheadle, after school maybe."

"I don't go to school at the moment."

"Okay. Sorry, yeh, you said."

Daisy didn't find the appropriate moment in which to tell Wilson about the visit from Sergeant Jordan and that was probably just as well. Sally's disclosures had been more than enough for one day and when they left his bedside, Wilson's eyes were closed.

Chapter 17

Night mission

Evening of Thursday 23rd November 2017

Delbury Hall & Gardens is well sign-posted to the east of Tarporley and open to the public for ten months of the year. The stately home of Lord and Lady Delbury is famous for its arboretum and prize winning collection of rare orchids. Guided tours of the main house are offered every Monday afternoon and a new extension to the building overlooking the visitor's car park houses the gift shop, the estate office and the luxury apartment of the Delbury family. By late November, the gardens are no longer embroidered with a tapestry of colours and the trees, draped in autumnal swatches of russet, umber and ochre are shedding layers and dressing down for the threadbare look of winter.

At ten minutes to closing time on the last visiting day of the year, it was not unusual for the grounds to be cloaked in darkness and the visitor's car park to be almost empty. The black van with false number plates parked to the left of the gift shop and close to the door that led to the private apartment, *was* unusual. The vehicle's engine was running and a thickset man in the driver's seat was counting down the minutes to 5.30 p.m.

Bradley Givens had never set foot in the Delbury Hall apartment but knew the layout like the back of his hand. Esther Gifford, the lady who ran the gift shop, had given him a guided tour courtesy of The Market Square. Bradley Givens possessed a photographic memory for faces and places; an invaluable asset in his line of work.

The previous night, several hours after speaking to Marcus Blakely about the existence of a second Basquiat painting, Bradley was cast as an Aunt Sally in a satirical dream about a County Show in which the cobbled surface of The Market Square resembled the parkland grounds of a country estate. Bradley wasn't interested in the allegory and had long since given up trying to fathom the rhyme and reason behind the machinations of The Market Square. The scattering of pole marquees with red and white striped canvas tops could well have been lifted from the medieval days of King Arthur. The sweet scent of freshly cut grass hung in the air like mother nature's perfume. Lengths of bunting with triangles of fluttering flags crisscrossed The Market Square like washing lines. Bradley sniggered at what he supposed was a visual metaphor for the jousting about to begin. He walked over to a bench seat, lit a cigarette and filled his lungs with a slow draw.

Twenty metres away, the nearest marquee was identified by a pennant fixed on a king pole as 'Turner's Country Clothing'. The marquee for 'Frazer's Farm Produce' stood to the left with 'Sculptures by Chain Saw' on the right. Beyond that stood the 'County Cheese Emporium' and another marquee offering pottery demonstrations and one selling homemade ice cream and then jams and pickled produce and so on. Morris dancers wearing smock shirts and white bonnets of knotted handkerchief and with bell pads on their shins, were hopping around the base of the Clock Tower shaking tambourines and bashing wooden sticks together. The Clock Tower itself, was dressed in a flimsy skirt of ribbons and somehow appeared embarrassed to be playing the role of a makeshift Maypole. It was as though the dream was fulfilling its mandate to be a dream but in the most perfunctory manner; killing time, as it waited for the audience of one to leave the theatre. Bradley's cursory glance took in the low budget production as he flicked ash from the tip of his cigarette.

From the direction of L'Ecole or from nowhere in particular, as often happens in a dream, a gruff voice yelled 'pull' and the crack of two shotgun blasts in quick succession gave rise to the 'phut' of a clay pigeon disintegrating. This must have been the signal to open the entrance gates, because the site of the County Show quickly began to fill with all manner of folk, young and old, male and female; like herds of lovat sheep all following the country code of flat cap, waxed jacket and green wellies. Bradley flicked more ash from the tip of his cigarette with a dismissive grunt. He hated the Cheshire set, their pretence and fake pastoral aesthetic. The irony in the dream was poking Bradley firmly in the ribs and he got the point.

The County Show was left to play in the background as the night shift started and Bradley reached into his mind for the tools of the trade.

His composition began with emerald green eyes blinking in response to an unusual question about the arboretum. The highlights in the auburn hair were a result of winter sun flooding through the gift shop window. Next came the red lips giving directions to the Orchid Room and the slender wrist and the index finger tipped with nail varnish pointing the way. The milky wash of complexion, the chiaroscuro folds in the fabric of a blouse and the study in comportment brought the painting to life. Finally, a palette knife smudge of eye shadow and a single bristle stroke for the eyelids were the finishing touch like a signature bottom right. Bradley's portrait of Esther Gifford was a masterpiece of realism. When the artist opened his eyes, the lady in the grey silk blouse and pink wool skirt was as conspicuous as a sheep in a field of tweed.

"Morning darlin" said Bradley, he was keen to get down to business and ignored Esther's reply.

Fingers as fat as Cumberland sausages clamped hard on her shoulder and Bradley felt the tingle run up his arm as all motion in The Market Square ceased. The Morris dancers, with arms in the air and feet raised mid-step, froze in motion against a mask of toffee wrapper yellow like insects stuck on flypaper. Roundels of red, purple and green bloomed like droplets of ink on the surface of water and then floated free, moving forwards, growing in size and acquiring definition. They soon resembled giant, shiny baubles from a Christmas tree. Clearly visible on the convex surface of each was an action sequence like a home video. A red bauble reflected a clip of Esther Gifford preparing breakfast for her husband. Bradley ignored the scenes of domestic life advancing on the cluster of baubles behind and moved his attention to the green bauble on the far left, depicting Esther serving a customer in the gift shop.

That's more like it.

Bradley's focus caused the green bauble to shift position, to change lanes and move into his direct line of sight. Neighbouring baubles all tuned to the same channel. Esther opening the gift shop. Esther stocktaking. On a yellow bauble, one scenario portrayed Esther counting out the day's takings and this caused Bradley's eyes to dart from one adjacent bauble to another as though playing a computer game; he was looking for a very specific event but couldn't seem to bring that particular action sequence into view. He switched back to the yellow bauble. It floated silently by and popped like a soap bubble but the roundels bringing up the rear were now picking up the story. He was getting closer. Esther Gifford locking the gift shop and speaking to Mr Ennis the security guard. Mr Ennis setting off on his rounds as Esther makes for the entrance to Lord Delbury's private apartment.

Here we go.

Bradley took a small step forward, eager to get a closer look.

This is it.

Esther tapping in the new eight digit code for the entry lock. Six. Six. Six. Three. Three. Two. One. Four.

Looks like they've reverted back to only changing the code on a monthly basis.

Esther entering a vestibule.

Now opening a drawer and depositing the day's takings for banking tomorrow.

Peanuts. Not worth bothering with!

Bradley shifted his focus to a new bauble advancing with the next instalment.

Esther entering a new set of digits into a second keypad.

Three. Three. Two. One. Eight. Six. *Got that.*

Esther opening the door to the private apartment. *Excellent.*

Okay, she's walking down the corridor. Peering into each room. Checking all is as it should be.

There's the second Basquiat painting. Looks slightly

bigger than the other one. That patch of discoloured wallpaper next to it isn't lying.

That's right, good girl, a last check in each room.

She's closing the door. Re-entering the same sequence.

Three. Three. Two. One. Eight. Six.

Esther paused to hear the tamper proof, six barrel door mechanism slide home and the alarm beep as it clocked on for duty.

Later, Bradley stood by the Clock Tower chain smoking as he waited for the 'dream sleep' phase of his night to pass. He considered trudging up to the top of The Market Square where steam powered farm machinery looked to be drawing a large crowd, but since he'd acquired all the knowledge he needed from this particular dream, he was impatient for the night to end. It was green for go for the following afternoon.

Hunched down low in the seat of the stolen van, Bradley's eyes followed Esther Gifford as she emerged from the gift shop carrying a green drawstring bag and quickly walked the twenty-five metres to the apartment. She tapped a code into a keypad, entered the vestibule and pulled the front door closed behind her. Bradley set the timer on his watch. Three minutes later Esther emerged and keyed in the code for a second time to lock the door. She was no longer carrying the cash bag. After checking the entrance was firmly shut, Esther walked across the car park to the driveway leading up to Delbury Hall itself, where bang on time, her husband was waiting in his car to take her home. Ennis was ushering a group of Japanese tourists out of the main building. After locking the front doors, he strolled up the drive to the gatehouse for his after-closing mug of tea. The Japanese tourists in two rental cars and a man in a baseball cap in a black van drove past him as they followed the exit signs on their way out. The rental cars turned left at the gates onto the main road and headed north in the direction of Manchester. The black van turned right at the main road but after three hundred metres abruptly turned sharp right again through an open gate and over a cattle grid. With the headlights off and steering blind, Bradley drove slowly to keep the van within the furrow of tractor tracks. After performing a bumpy three-point turn over rutted ground, he re-aligned the vehicle facing back to the gate and switched the engine off. Bradley removed the baseball cap and pulled a black balaclava over his head. He was dressed in black boots, black denim jeans and a black polo neck sweater. His business suit in other words. Through the gaps in a thicket of bushes and beyond a barbed wire fence, Bradley could clearly see the car park from moments earlier. It was illuminated by the sodium orange glow from a security lamp above the entrance to the gift shop. Curiously, for that time of year, two huge moths were playing tag in the fuzzy corona of light.

With the double doors at the back of the van open in readiness for a quick getaway, Bradley used secateurs to open a man size gap between two rhododendron bushes. He snipped a two metre section from the barbed wire fence with wire cutters and before crossing the car park crouched for five minutes to be certain the coast was clear. He checked his watch, Ennis would be sipping tea for another ten minutes with his focus on a crossword puzzle and not the security cameras. Keeping low, hugging the ground, Bradley's bulky figure moved surprisingly quickly across the car park. At the entrance to the private apartment he keyed in the code.

Six. Six. Six. Three. Three. Two. One. Four.

Beep. Buzz.

Abracadabra!

The door clicked open.

In the vestibule, he faced the second door that led to the private residence of the Delbury family. Bradley brought to mind Esther tapping out a six note sequence and his fingers copied the movement.

Three. Three. Two. One. Eight. Six.

When the confirmatory tone fell silent, the keypad bulb switched from red to green and he was in.

With a small Maglite torch clamped between his teeth, Bradley moved with purpose down the hallway, his head dipping and twisting from side to side like a bear on the scent of a meal. The second Basquiat was where it was supposed to be, hanging alongside the space vacated by its stolen sibling and exactly as portrayed in The Market Square. Rubber gloved hands silently lifted the artwork from its fittings like a sportsman lifting a cup and as Bradley turned to make off with his booby trapped trophy, the shutter in a micro-camera clicked open and the video recording began. The shrieking alarm was ear piercing in the narrow hallway. Bradley clamped the bulky painting under his arm, turned and ran; out of the apartment, out of the vestibule and out into the cold night air. A second alarm, even louder than the first was yelling from somewhere outside the gift shop as though relaying a baton of sound to a team member with bigger lungs. This screaming for attention followed Bradley as he laboured across the car park and while struggling to locate the gap in the bushes, security cameras had ample time to point out the guilty party. The Basquiat was placed on the floor of the van and covered

144

with a rug. The doors were slammed shut and with all lights blazing, Bradley sped down the tractor tracks, through the gate and out onto the public road. Rubber gripped tarmac with a sudden screech as the van raced away in the direction of The Maltings. Ennis was standing outside his lodge by the exit gates and saw the black vehicle zoom off into the night. He'd also seen the camera images that had automatically fired off a request for urgent assistance. As every police vehicle within an eight mile radius followed GPS directions to pre-determined roadblock locations, the drawstrings of a dragnet were about to be pulled tight.

Bradley angrily tore off the balaclava with a free hand.

"Shit, shit and double shit." His fist bounced off the steering wheel three times as if to emphasise his misfortune or careless planning. There was no sign of a flashing blue light in the rearview mirror as he turned off the main road and into the short cut of a narrow country lane. Bradley pushed the accelerator pedal fully to the floor, he needed to get home and the van off the road asap.

Ten minutes later, the lantern lights mounted either side of the entrance to The Maltings curved into view a mile ahead. The road became arrow flight straight as home sweet home loomed large. Streetlights a hundred metres apart bounced beams from the bonnet as though drawing and then pushing the van onwards toward safety. Bradley's palms were clammy, beads of sweat surfaced on his forehead and ran stinging into his eyes. He checked the mirror again, still no blue-flashing lights, then he fished out the gate remote in the tray between the front seats. Four streetlights away from sanctuary, from safety, he thought he'd made it, by the skin of his teeth. Then something big and angry with fluttering felt wings lunged at his face. He tried to brush the bloody thing away without looking from the road but that only made the huge butterfly more persistent. It ran across the bridge of his nose and Bradley could feel hairy spidery legs and something prickly touch his eyeball. Panicked by the thought of a sting, he took both hands from the wheel and tried to cup the insect with his hands. The van was travelling at seventy miles per hour as the butterfly escaped and settled on the rim of the steering wheel. Bradley raised his hand in order to smash it to pulp once and for all but the High Brown was too agile and danced away as the misguided slap caused the van to veer sharply to the left. As Bradley slammed on the brake, the van hit something solid on the side of the road and an air bag exploded in his face.

Bradley fought his way out from behind the wheel and heard a crunch underfoot. Fragments of coloured glass sparkling like gemstones were strewn over the road, along with the remnants of a smashed wing mirror and parts of a bumper. The lamppost was still standing but at a drunken slant and its light shone down at a woozy angle as though seeing stars. The turn into the driveway for The Maltings was tangibly close; just eighty metres away. Bradley was caught in two minds.

Grab the painting and make it home on foot.

Or try and start the van and drive. Or push the van if you have to, you need to get the bloody thing off the road.

The decision became irrelevant as the sound of a police car siren and blue strobing lights came into view through trees less than half a mile away.

Bradley stepped away from the van and into the middle of the road to wave the police car down. The other hand was used to shield his eyes against the increasing glare of the approaching headlights. His face painted a picture of relief and innocence as the police car pulled to a halt. Bradley turned and pointed to the van, playing the role of a hapless driver in an unfortunate accident seeking assistance. He couldn't see if he was gesticulating blindly at one, two, or more occupants in the police car.

The solitary policeman was having none of it and clicked his radio to network broadcast.

"All units, to all units, this is car 346. Have one black van and a single male occupant in an RTA. Repeat, in an RTA. No other vehicles involved. White male, six foot plus and stocky. Fits description of suspect in the break-in at Delbury Hall. Over."

"Roger that 346, GPS from your vehicle noted. Support en route. ETA six minutes. Over."

The policeman dipped his lights, switched the car engine off, grabbed the torch on the passenger seat and stepped from his car. One hand was clamped on the baton by his side as he shone the torch at a driver mumbling about a deer jumping out in front of his vehicle. The policeman shone the torch at the damaged van and the beam slowly brushed over the debris in the road. Bradley could see the dark shape of the policeman in the sweep of torchlight and didn't hesitate to take his chance. He covered the ten metres with the speed of a wing-back and hit the policeman with a tackle that would have downed a prop forward. Stumbling back to his feet, the policeman fumbled with the canister of Mace on his utility belt but the uppercut from Bradley's fist was as clinical as instant chloroform and knocked him out cold.

Bradley ran the eighty metres to his drive and for a big

bloke, the time of seventeen-seconds, adrenalin assisted, was impressive. He stormed into the house with the emergency escape plan clearly laid out in his mind. First he extracted the duffle bag containing three hundred thousand pounds in used notes and two fake passports from the void above the ceiling in his study. Then he changed clothes and grabbed the keys for the Porsche 911 with the full tank of fuel in the garage. Like the van, the 911 was a stolen vehicle and with the same number plates as an identical Porsche owned by a Mr J Howard of Bristol. Bradley owned a passport, a NI number and a driving licence in the name of this Mr J Howard and all with the same address. The Market Square didn't follow the dictates of the Data Protection Act.

As the electric gates to The Maltings silently swung back, the 911 nosed out. The policeman came charging from nowhere and grabbed the door handle with one hand while shouting at the radio held in the other.

"Suspect leaving property in a black Porsche 911. Repeat, suspect now in black Porsche."

Bradley pushed the accelerator pedal to the floor. The long arm of the law is no match for the power of four hundred horses and the policeman permanently damaged his neck as he was jerked off his feet and sent spinning across tarmac. (The injury will result in his early retirement and a lifetime pension as mentioned by James in Balthazar's office.)

Bradley's emergency plan didn't include his getaway car being identified so he had to think fast. The emergency protocol called for an early morning channel crossing at Dover then lying low in Nice for a few months while slowly building a new operational base on the French Riviera. Think of it as an overseas posting for a successful businessman, or an occupational hazard. The car was a problem however, because it was now a top trump on every traffic officers most wanted list and Bradley needed to ditch it fast. As he sped along a minor road heading for the A51 and the junction with the M6 south, Bradley switched off his headlights. Then he quickly turned them back on again. It was suicidal to drive that fast in the pitch black. He picked up the burner phone and with his eyes flitting from phone to road and hoping a police helicopter wasn't tracking him from above, he called the blonde.

"Lena, the party's cancelled for this weekend. Where are you?"

She heard the agitation in Bradley's voice and recognised the meaning in the message.

"Nearly back, twenty miles from Sandbach services. The trip was good."

"Okay, wait on the northbound side, park in a bay as you enter the car park and stay in the car. I'll be there in twenty minutes and I'll walk over to your side. You've got your provisions in the boot right?"

"I'm not a bloody idiot Bradley."

"Right, twenty minutes. See you there."

Bradley switched off the phone and never heard Lena say, "be careful."

An illuminated sign was fast approaching.

I think that's the stop sign at the T-junction with the A49.

Blue lights then appeared in the rearview mirror like fireflies. The bloodhounds had picked up his trail but they were some way off in the distance. Bradley floored the accelerator pedal and the Porsche leapt forward like a greyhound leaving a trap. The white centre spacings on the road became one continuous line. The illuminated sign was growing larger by the second as Bradley resisted the urge to break until the last moment and that's when the second High Brown launched its attack.

"What the Hell? Not another one of those bloody things?"

Fluttering wings violently slapped his face and a furry caterpillar body brushed his lips and nose. Bradley instinctively and repeatedly swatted at the insect but it was too nimble for clumsy reactions. A final angry whack missed the butterfly completely and caused an explosion of pain as Bradley's thumb pushed his eyeball back into its socket. That was the self-inflicted killer blow. Bradley stood on the brake pedal with the illuminated sign now less than a car's length away. Pads gripped discs with carbon claws and the back wheels locked as the engine heavy rear chose to race neck and neck with the bonnet. Indifferent to the laws of friction regarding rubber on tarmac, the 911 acquired the grace of an ice skater and glided serenely across the junction, onto the A49 and into the path of the petrol tanker that had left Stanlow Oil Refinery forty minutes earlier. The forty ton buffalo hit the fleet-footed cheetah head on and flattened it like a game hunter's rug.

Bradley came round with a strange feeling, a weird sensation that the night's events, the theft of the painting, the car chase and the accident had all been part of a terrible dream. A nightmare from which he'd escaped, thankfully, prior to returning to the comfort and safety of a warm bed. On opening his eyes however, he found himself facing two narrow doors both of which were painted grey. A second strange feeling suggested only the door on the right would open for him.

Chapter 18

If and only

Friday 24th November 2017

"Wow! What an adventure Bradley!"

Short Cake was clapping his hands and smiling like a toddler on seeing a kitten for the first time.

"Now that's what you call going out with a bang."

Big Mac gave Bradley a thumbs up and a warm smile and then inverted both to the polar opposite.

Bradley peered across the cavernous hall and over the dunes of glittering golden bangles. Nothing had changed much since that summons six months' earlier. He'd ignored all the warnings of course and now his pigeon had finally come home to roost. Bradley thought of Lena and wondered if she'd still be waiting at Sandbach services as the ambulance and the fire engines with cutting gear raced up the M6? Would she follow them to a roadblock manned by police officers in yellow jackets? Would she duck under the cordon of tape, fight off the efforts at restraint, frantic with tears and grief? It didn't really matter. It was of no consequence anymore. Nothing mattered now. And besides, Bradley was fairly certain Lena wouldn't be doing any of those things. More likely, she'd have raced back to The Maltings to fill her car with all the small valuables she could lay her mitts on and then scarpered.

He wasn't angry or bitter about the savage turn of events. Strangely, he felt calm. As if wrapped in a shroud of heavenly bliss. A sensation of peace and tranquility was coursing through his body as though the effects of a powerful sedative were kicking in.

"You can't say you weren't warned Bradley" said Big Mac, closing the door behind the new arrival. "We told you in no uncertain terms what would happen. Such a shame. You had so much potential. Anyway, what's done is done. Come along now, we need to complete the paperwork."

Short Cake weighed him up with the calculating eye of a livestock dealer. Bradley Givens was big, very big and in prime condition.

Definitely more than three ounces left on that one.

Bradley followed sheepishly in Big Mac's footsteps as all new arrivals do, having seen their life flash before their eyes. This retrospective is always accepted with a weary sort of resignation by those on a one-way ticket through The Gateway. Short Cake referred to the sedative as 'the time to move on' drug.

Big Mac shifted his executive chair forward and opened the ledger book on his desk. He pointed at a plastic chair by way of instructing Bradley to also take a seat. Short Cake took residence at his desk, adjusted his tie and sat back with his hands behind his head.

"Now then Bradley," said Big Mac without looking up. The nib of his fountain pen was poised above a page. "Can we start with your date of birth? Mmm? Oh, silly me, I already know that."

Big Mac scribbled away mumbling to himself.

"Tenth of the ninth, nineteen eighty-one."

He looked up.

"And today's date?"

"Ah, no need to reply, I know that as well."

"Twenty fourth of the eleventh, two thousand and seventeen."

"And the cause of passing away?"

Big Mac's raised eyebrows emphasised the question and while waiting for an answer, the pen twirled around his fingers like the sail on a windmill.

Bradley Givens was indifferent as to how his demise should be termed and shrugged his shoulders.

"A car accident I suppose? But you already know that, right? I hit the brakes too hard or too late and the car skidded into an HGV or something. Don't remember too much about it to be honest, it all happened so fast. Heard a bang and that was it."

Bradley smashed the knuckles of his fists together by way of illustration.

"I'm not sure that adequately captures the gist of it" said Short Cake disdainfully. He reflected on matters for a moment longer then addressed his colleague.

"I think Bradley's epitaph should read 'terminated with extreme prejudice', as opposed to 'traffic collision'. I think that spells out the facts with greater . . . perspicacity, don't you Mr Mac?"

"Indeed I do" said Big Mac, immediately putting pen to paper and making a meal of the entry. Terminated . . . with . . . extreme . . . prejudice."

Bradley let the words sink into his soul for a few moments.

"Terminated with prejudice by who? By the lorry driver? How was he prejudiced? It was an accident and completely my fault, self-inflicted. I was driving too fast, trying to get away from the police."

"Yes" said Short Cake, miles ahead in seeing the full and absolute truth in Bradley's observation.

"Quite correct Bradley, it *was* self-inflicted. All of it. And you are indeed the architect of your own downfall. That's also true. But I'm afraid you were not the executioner."

Bradley wasn't following and really couldn't have cared less.

"Look . . . Whatever! We can discuss the semantics all day, but to be honest, I'd like to get this over and done with as soon as. I'm keen to get a move on. Can't wait to see what's happening through the Exit to Eternity."

"What do you think?" asked Big Mac, once again addressing his colleague.

"He's well over," said Short Cake, "a good two ounces at least to burn off."

Big Mac placed his pen on the table and cleared his throat.

"Mr Givens. How can I put this? Your case is one of those tricky ones that comes along every now and again. You see, I'm also of the opinion that you're far too heavy for the Exit to Eternity but unfortunately, given your Curriculum Vitae, we can't offer you a ticket back to the Spirit World either. You're what we call, a bad 'un Bradley. So, I'm afraid you're going to have to lose those extra ounces elsewhere."

Short Cake picked up the conversation.

"What my colleague is trying to say Bradley, is that those terminated with extreme prejudice, must, by definition, be denied the privilege of extending their presence on Earth in spirit form. They must face the aftermath of their actions. Fall at the feet of their victims and beg for mercy. And the midwife, one of your more recent casualties, well, she can't wait to get her hands on you."

154

"What's that supposed to mean? What bloody midwife?"

"The one who saw you in her rearview mirror as you raced away from that jewellery robbery. The lady who took her eyes off the road at precisely the wrong moment. As a direct result of your selfish behavioural choices Bradley, a little girl was paralysed and many lives with huge potential will never emerge from a maternity ward."

Big Mac ran his finger down a column in the book.

"According to the latest figures, updated just last night in fact, your family tree of fatal repercussions has branched out to touch over two thousand poor souls. That's quite a number of followers you've built there Bradley. Excellent on Twitter. But in here, it's absolutely atrocious."

Big Mac slammed the book shut and walked to the front of his desk.

"So there's really no alternative, you're going to be expending all your excess energy, your quite considerable Outer Shell, *in there*."

Big Mac pointed to the hole in the wall a few metres to the right of the three exit doors behind his desk. The hole had been roughly knocked through brickwork leaving a jagged black opening like a missing piece in a jigsaw puzzle. While this was being brought to his attention, Bradley heard banging noises and muffled shouting from somewhere deep inside the hole. Then a voice screamed in agony, as though a builder working on the floor below had suffered a workplace injury.

"It's payback time" said Short Cake, smiling and rubbing his hands together in a gleeful manner.

Incarceration in purgatory with a regime of extreme pain for eons would come as a shock even to someone catatonically high on the 'time to move on' drug. As reality finally dawned,

Bradley acquired the hangdog look of a condemned man.

"You orchestrated it all didn't you? Beginning with the accident with the van? It was all planned to bring me here, before my time. You actually . . . murdered me, on purpose, for some kind of . . . retribution!"

"Three skulls in a row and jackpot" said Short Cake, enjoying the look of horror slowly creeping across Bradley's face as a High Brown Fritillary butterfly fluttered into view and perched on his shoulder. The upright orange wings with leopard spots slowly flexed open and closed sending a 'V' sign, a 'V' for victory. The second High Brown was preening itself on Big Mac's shoulder.

Bradley sprung from his chair as though an electric current had just surged through it.

"That's how you did it, you distracted me with those bloody moths when I was driving too fast. And all because I didn't follow your warnings."

"Yes, unfortunately that is completely true! But you can't say you didn't have it coming Bradley. You were disciplined so many times and now it really is time to face the music." Big Mac took a step forward as Short Cake padded menacingly out from behind his desk.

Bradley grabbed the chair by the backrest and jabbed out the legs to fend off Short Cake.

"Oh no, this isn't right, you two must take some responsibility as well. You made me a number eleven. Gave me access to The Market Square. I was just a pawn in your gambling games. It's not down to me. You knew all along this would happen."

"That's correct," said Big Mac. His voice was cold and calculating. Short Cake was drawing closer. They were positioning themselves for a well-rehearsed pincer movement.

"You had ample opportunity to heed our warnings Mr Givens. To change tracks. To stick to the straight and narrow. To follow the path of righteousness. You had choices Bradley! But you chose the path of evil."

"The bad 'un is about to pay a visit to *Abbadon*" said Short Cake. He pulled back his thin colourless lips to reveal a mouthful of teeth and his eyes rolled back like a shark about to bite.

In the living world, Bradley would have been the firm favourite in a fight with Big Mac and Short Cake. He could have taken one with each hand. But he wasn't in that world anymore and no longer the physical threat he used to be. He was dead and about to be tossed into purgatory, into a torture chamber, for an undisclosed period of time. The defensive moves for that sort of tight spot don't come naturally, but funnily enough they did, because in addition to his plastic chair, Bradley still possessed those most valuable of weapons, the primeval instincts he'd been born with.

Big Mac and Short Cake lunged for an arm each but Bradley fended them off by stabbing out the chair legs and taking a step backwards. When they surged for a second time, Bradley darted through the gap, clambered over Short Cake's desk and made for the exit. Short Cake, fittingly attired in all black, tried desperately to bring him down with an illegal rugby tackle, but Bradley shook off the neck hold and powered his bulk over the try line and out into The Market Square.

Bradley Givens had side-stepped the clutches of the undertakers for The Powers That Be and by escaping through the door labelled 'Exit for Non-Extinguished Spirits' not only had he avoided his comeuppance, he'd acquired the fully justified appellation of 'rogue spirit'.

Chapter 19

The bad news keeps coming

Friday 24th November 2017

And the day started off so well.

"In terms of your body returning to normal Wilson, the olfactory organs are on the last page of the re-boot manual so when you start to recognise flavours again, you'll be well on the road to recovery."

Wilson's taste buds blossomed as he was eating breakfast. He told the auxiliary nurse that the taste of "soldiers dipped in egg were almost to die for" and chuckled to himself.

Wilson spent most of the morning drifting in and out of sleep as the conversation with Sally played on repeat in the back of his mind. Irregular shaped questions would surface like flotsam on a troubled sea. Questions like, what are the chances of a car accident victim and the lad that saved her both being number elevens and the rescue act being reciprocated? Incalculable in the real world, but in The Market Square, a safe bet. But why?

Five minutes into visiting time, Wilson woke with a start to find Daisy and Alex seated either side of the bed. Daisy was picking at a burr of skin on the side of a fingernail. Alex was playing with his wedding ring. They appeared to be lost in thought, preoccupied, troubled even.

Wilson raised himself higher up the bed and rubbed his eyes.

"Sorry folks, I must have nodded off for five minutes. Why didn't you wake me up?"

"Morning son."

"It's okay, we've literally just arrived."

Wilson plumped the pillows into a comfier position.

"So why the long faces? I am getting better you know."

Daisy shot a glance at Alex before she spoke.

"Have you heard anything from Teaps? Have you had any contact with him?"

"No? Why, is he okay? Has something happened to his mum? You both look like . . . "

"No son, as far as we know, Vanessa's fine, she's still undergoing rehabilitation in Chester. The thing is . . . I mean, it's just that the police have been to see us. They've been asking questions."

Alex paused, he was reluctant to release words that would set like concrete once poured into the conversation.

"The police know about your involvement son. They have photos from the train station in Inverness and in Manchester; a taxi driver remembers taking you to the home and a manager confirmed she showed you round the day before. And Teaps knows about it. Michael called me last night to say the police had been to see them both in Chester. Teaps is coming to see you this morning."

Each slug of news hit Wilson in the face like paintballs and stung on impact.

He massaged his face with his hands to try and wipe away the allegations and then ran them through his hair and kind of laughed as his face turned red.

"Mmmm, we never thought of that did we?"

"No, and they have your mobile phone records, and probably mine, from the time you were on the train."

Wilson thought for a moment and then shrugged the revelations off, as though the matter could simply be swept under the carpet.

"So. We'll just tell them it was the result of internet searches, amateur detective work and a hunch combined with a lucky guess."

Wilson wanted to reassure Daisy and his father that although the situation was awkward they would find a way to explain things, but he could see they sensed the false bravado.

"Look, I didn't do anything bad. I'm not a criminal, I didn't commit a crime. Daisy and I solved a mystery, gave a tragedy a happy ending. Teaps will be coming to say thanks won't he? I'll tell him I got a phone call, on WhatsApp, from someone who told me they'd discovered what happened to Vanessa, but they couldn't reveal their identity. That might be enough. All he wants to hear. Like I received an anonymous tip-off. Better still, a Snapchat message!"

Wilson considered the off-the-cuff explanation from a few angles and at first glance it looked plausible, until a chasm opened. An anonymous informer would be hard for Teaps to accept.

'So why didn't they contact me Wilson? She was my mum. Why would they choose you? A complete stranger!'

'I've no idea mate.'

The rift was widening.

'And why did they wait for seventeen years Wilson? Why didn't they get in touch sooner?'

'And why did you want to go alone? To be the hero? To

claim all the glory?'

The expressions on two faces told Wilson the Snapchat defence would never placate Teaps or satisfy the police. Alex and Daisy had pulled at a similar thread during a conversation in the hospital café earlier and the unknown informant alibi had unravelled fairly quickly.

"Look" said Wilson. "If I stick with my story, there's nothing the police can do. Teaps might be angry, mystified, and not speak to me for a few weeks, but he'll get over it. Besides, we can't go back and do things in a different way. It's too late. What's done is done! And we, I, haven't committed a crime."

Wilson nodded to himself to solemnly confirm his defence statement was a true and accurate description of events, but unfortunately, he'd not heard the full charge sheet.

"Yes, but they're not really after you son. You're just an innocent accomplice, a fall guy. It's me they're after."

"What? What are you going on about Dad? That doesn't make any sense."

"Wilson, the police are not just interested in how or why Vanessa came to be found, what they also want to know is what happened to her in the first place. How she ended up in Scotland? How she travelled there? Who abandoned her and for what reason? The doctors say she had a stroke, but they can't be certain. So that raises a possibility something else happened seventeen years ago, a criminal act and Vanessa was the victim! That's where the policeman who interviewed me yesterday is going with this. His theory is that I did something to Vanessa just before she went missing. It couldn't have been you son, you were just a baby. But he suspects I felt remorseful, overcome with guilt, and thinking enough time had passed and

161

the truth would never come out, I used you to finally reveal where she was. That's what they're thinking. And although none of it's true, this Montague idiot is determined to invent a crime to fit the evidence."

"But how could they connect you with Vanessa dad, you didn't even know her and Teaps wasn't even my mate when I was a year old? I don't see the connection. I'll stick to my story that I got an anonymous message, a Snapchat that quickly disappeared, like they do, with no trace, and the message told me where to find Vanessa."

"Tell him Alex" said Daisy.

"Tell me what?"

"The problem is Wilson, I did know Vanessa. She was my girlfriend for a few months just before I met your mum and Vanessa met Michael. We all sort of knew each other at the time, through friends of friends."

"So the police think what? That because you knew Vanessa, went out a couple of times and it came to nothing, you were so angry, you conjured up a brain seizure, made her lose her memory and then drove up to Scotland and left her there?"

Wilson was starting to believe his first line of defence wasn't so flimsy after all.

"I know it's ridiculous, but when you hear it from a policeman, they have this way of making everything sound real. Like there's a possibility I could've done those things. When they put you on the spot you can't think straight. I made a mistake. I told the policeman, Montague, that I'd never met Vanessa. But Michael knows I went out with her and he'll have told Montague."

"But why would Michael do that Dad? Why would he

drop you in it? Mix you up in something you haven't done?"

"Because I would do the same thing if I were in his shoes. I'd be bloody angry that my wife had disappeared for seventeen years and that someone had known where she was all along. I'd want to find out who was behind it and I wouldn't care where I got the information from."

"Your dad's right Wilson, you have to look at it from their viewpoint. *We* know what happened, the real truth, but as they see it, with no other explanation for you being in the care home, it all looks suspicious."

"So why haven't the police come here to speak to me about it?"

"They plan to son, the moment the doctor says you're well enough. They'll probably visit you at home, sometime next week. At the moment, they'll be digging away at our backgrounds and texts and phone calls and looking to see what still exists of Vanessa's past – her old phone records, bank statements and medical stuff – anything they can find to link us together at the time she went missing."

"So if Teaps knows all about this, when did you say he was coming to see me?"

"Later this morning son, Michael didn't say an exact time when he called me last night."

"If Teaps thinks I had something to do with his mum being found, and he's seen the photos like you said, I imagine he'll be here as soon as he can."

Wilson sunk deeper into the pillows as he remembered a conversation that had jarred with Teaps the day after his mother was found, when he almost let the cat out of the bag.

'What did you think when you saw her in that room Teaps?'
'How did you know she was in a room Wilson?'

Chapter 20

Look me in the eye

Friday 24th November 2017

"If Graham arrives early son, it's probably for the best if I'm not here. Besides, I've a train to catch later and a stack of reports to read for a meeting in London tomorrow. Say hello from me will you and pass on my best wishes? And as for the problem, well there's nothing we can do to change things, so just let the future run its course for now and we'll see what happens."

Alex said his goodbyes and departed. Wilson asked Daisy if she was okay to stay.

"Daisy, I know this is all my fault. If I hadn't insisted on doing something good and finding Vanessa in the first place you and Dad wouldn't be involved in this mess."

"Wilson, it's not your fault. I was the one who said do something good, not you."

"Well, if you're going to put it like that, come to think of it, it is all your bloody fault."

Wilson was grinning, more at the ridiculousness of the situation than the need to lift the mood. Daisy rose from her chair to give him a hug.

"I've missed you Wilson. This is the first time you've been awake properly in ages and just when I thought everything was going good there's another problem to deal with."

Wilson felt the hug grow stronger.

"Don't do anything like that again. You promised me we'd be like ordinary people. I want that. I just want everything to be normal from now on." Her voice trailed off.

Wilson placed his hand on Daisy's arm and turned his head so they were face to face. Strands of hair were sticking to a tear track on her cheek. Every shade of brown sparkled in her eyes. They kissed noses, Eskimo style.

"We're partners in crime now Daisy, you and me, so we have to stick together no matter what."

Daisy rose from Wilson's side and wiped her eyes with the back of her hand.

"You can't always joke things away. I was being serious. I had to rescue you from a dream that was trying to kill you."

"I know, I'm sorry, and you're right. I promise, no more Market Square. We did an incredible thing and this police investigation will blow over. I'm leaving the hospital in a few days, I'll rest at home for a week or two, then back to college for end of term and then Christmas to enjoy. Presents under the tree, watch *Elf* on TV, eat turkey and mince pies, nothing more normal than that is there?"

Daisy chose not to reply and her bottom lip trembled as she returned to the burr on the side of her finger.

"Come on, let's go and get a drink in the café. We can see reception from there and watch out for Teaps. I can't wait to see him and I know it's gonna be a bit awkward, but let's do this."

Wilson pulled back the sheets with a sense of purpose and in slippers and dressing gown walked down the corridor towards the lift with Daisy. His legs felt stiff and hollow, as if completing the final stage of a marathon journey; which in some respects, they were.

"3B's not down here is it Daisy? I seem to remember us taking a walk like this before."

They ordered two cups of coffee, two energy bars for Wilson and selected the table with the best view of reception. Doctor Khan saw Wilson enter the café and came over soon after he'd sat down.

"It's good to see you up and about Wilson, and I have to say you're looking remarkably well, all things considered."

"Yeh, over these last couple of days I've felt quite a bit better, more energised."

"I've been keeping an eye on your notes. I find it astonishing that you came through your illness unscathed. No after effects? Loss of faculties? Restrictions on movement? Inability to concentrate?"

"No, I feel good, really good."

"May I?"

Doctor Khan was asking permission to shine a penlight in Wilson's eyes. He was still not convinced of a total recovery with no aftereffects.

"People who emerge quickly from a coma, like you Wilson, often find they've left something behind in terms of physical or mental function. Or, in rare cases they come back with a new facet to their personality or a new skill, like being able to do long division in their head, something they didn't have before. Trauma can alter the brain's circuitry."

Wilson's eyes appeared to be working fine.

"I'm not saying that will apply to you Wilson, but don't hesitate to get back in touch if you experience anything . . . unusual."

Doctor Khan patted Wilson on the shoulder. "I'm really

pleased to see you doing so well."

Wilson clocked Teaps approaching the reception desk a few minutes later.

"Daisy he's here. Look, the guy with a ponytail, wearing the white shirt."

"I know, you brought him into The Market Square and I've seen him on TV. He's sort of famous remember? Sit there, I'll go and grab him before they send him up to the ward."

Wilson followed Daisy's progress as she waltzed around tables and chairs in her Doc Martens' boots. He was reminded of the night they drank magnums of Champagne in the Blackpool Tower Ballroom to celebrate the liberation of Vanessa, never thinking for one minute it would lead to this.

Daisy returned with Teaps close behind.

The greeting was hardwired. A high five, a fist bump, the spidery thing with the fingers and then they hugged like long-lost brothers. The palm slap at the end became a clumsy, arm wrestling mock trial of strength that Wilson couldn't possibly have won.

They were both grinning from ear to ear as the female referee stepped in to pull them apart.

"Teaps, you look great. Bigger and different somehow."

"And you look exactly the same Wilson, but thinner."

Though the smile was wide and genuine, Teaps was wary, he was already conducting a quality assessment on a once best friend. Appraising the mate on one hand, with the incriminating photos on the other.

Teaps said thanks but no thanks to Daisy's offer of a drink as they sat back down at the table.

"I can't stay long. Dad's waiting in the car park. It's the first time I've been away from Mum for more than a couple of hours so I want to get back soon. Make sure she doesn't disappear again."

Teaps paused as that last leaden sentence fell to the floor and fractured the ground between them. Making light of things was a throwback to a former friendship and old habits die hard. He quickly kicked the words out from under his feet.

"So you're the mysterious Daisy then. It's great to finally meet you. You know, I didn't believe Wilson when he told me where you met, something about a dream and a drama class, I thought he was winding me up. But it seems you do exist after all. Not sure what you see in him though."

The fracture was closing.

"Steady on mate, you've only been here a minute. Give the other lads a chance. Besides, Daisy's clever, there's no way she'll be interested in becoming one of your groupies."

"I am here you know, and I can make my own decisions. So how many other girls will I be competing with then?"

"Daisy stop! He's not that bright, he'll think you're being serious."

"But I am being serious Wilson, what makes you think I'm not?"

Daisy nudged her seat closer to Teaps who winked at Wilson in return.

The divide had closed.

Twenty minutes passed as questions and answers were patted back and forth across the table like a video game of pong.

"So what caused the sudden illness Wilson? Is it likely to

happen again? Bloody lucky you were in a hospital at the time. You're going to be okay though?"

"Does your mum recognise you and your dad? How much does she remember of the old days? When will you be taking her home? Where are you going to live, not back in that flat, surely?"

The prognosis for Vanessa was not positive but Daisy sensed only unbridled happiness in Teaps's voice as he spoke about his mother. His euphoria allayed any lingering doubt that they'd done the right thing.

"Who can say what the future holds? Anything can happen. More of your mum's old memories might return with time, you know, with the familiarity of you both being back in her life. And if not, you can try and replace them with fantastic new ones. Anything is possible if you want it enough."

Teaps acknowledged Daisy's positive thinking then checked the time on his phone. The moment to address the real business of the day couldn't be avoided any longer and in recognition of the fact, Wilson shifted awkwardly in his seat.

"It's been great to see you Wilson, it really has, and meeting you Daisy, really enjoyed it. But before I go mate we have to talk about the main reason I'm here, the policeman from Scotland who came to see me and Dad. I know you're not a hundred per cent, so I feel bad for raising this while you're still in hospital, but you have to tell me what you were doing in Inverness? What made you go all that way to a care home in the middle of Scotland? This wasn't someone playing amateur detective cos Dad tried that years ago. You brought Mum back from the dead as far as I'm concerned Wilson. How did you do that? How did you know she was there?"

Teaps sat opposite his best friend and coolly stared him

down with a look that sought only the truth. A full and frank explanation that would restore trust. It was nothing more than he deserved.

"She was in that place for seventeen years Wilson, why didn't you tell me what you knew? Why didn't you ask me to go with you? And why didn't you go sooner?"

"Teaps, look, I didn't know it would be her. And I went as soon as I got the anonymous text or the Snapchat message, I don't remember. I don't have it anymore so I can't show you but . . . "

Teaps needed something far more substantial, with certainty.

"You've had all this time to think and you still don't know which it was? A text or a Snapchat? A text message which you would've had to delete, so there'll be a record? Or a Snapchat for which there's no record, but you can't remember which, or exactly what it said, because it isn't important. Even though it sent you all the way up to Inverness by yourself. You then check the home out on my behalf, keep everything secret like a game and then come back with your bloody fingers crossed having left a cryptic bloody clue in my mum's lap. Oh, but it's not important to tell me or my dad! No, the people who most needed to know. The person who also happens to be your best bloody mate. Just leave a little note and hope for the best. And you did all that because of what?"

"Look Teaps, I know it sounds . . . hard to believe, but that's exactly what happened. Maybe I could have handled it better, I agree, but I wasn't sure and why would I lie? And your Mum's back after seventeen years, so that's the main thing isn't it? Does it really matter how I found out?"

Teaps stood up and pushed his chair back. There

was nothing more to discuss, no point in continuing the conversation. Customers on adjacent tables were aware of a confrontation looming.

"So that's the story is it? A secret message from the fairies? Or from your dad, because that seems more likely. Anyway, whatever bullshit you two have been up to it will all come out now that the police are investigating."

Teaps placed both hands flat on the table and leant forward, his face just a few inches from Wilson's.

"Listen pal. If I find out you let Mum stay in that place a minute longer than she needed to, you're gonna have a big problem, and not just with the police!"

Teaps turned and stormed off, scattering chairs in his wake.

An hour later, Wilson received the following text message from Teaps.

'Just spoke to the police about your lame Snapchat excuse. They don't believe it and neither do I.'

Wilson forwarded the message to his father and Daisy.

Chapter 21

Quantum flapdoodle

Monday 27th November 2017

Gloria was vacuuming the carpet in Wilson's bedroom and singing to herself as a key turned in the front door. Alex was home after two days in London.

"Gloria, I'm back."

"Be down in a minute, just have to put fresh sheets on Wilson's bed and change the pillowcase and then I'm done. Can you put the kettle on?"

Alex offloaded his overnight bag and satchel and draped his jacket over the newel post at the foot of the stairs.

"What do you want, coffee or tea?"

"Tea! I'm spitting feathers!"

"Gloria, have you been up there all afternoon waiting for me to come home just to crack that joke?"

From the tang of pine scented polish, Alex concluded his wife had been cleaning the house in happy anticipation of Wilson's arrival and her joke was a further sign of a joyous mood. Beneath the gleaming surfaces however, a grubby secret was waiting to be exposed and his stomach lurched at the prospect of having to tarnish everything.

Alex was stirring the drinks when Gloria entered the kitchen in a t-shirt, sweatpants and trainers. Her face was flushed and sticky with perspiration and Alex asked if cleaning had become an Olympic sport.

Gloria laughed, sipped her tea and leant back against the fridge. Alex took a perch on the edge of the kitchen table.

"No, it's just with Wilson coming out of hospital tomorrow I want everything to be perfect for when he walks in the house. Plus, the girls are back next Saturday and with Christmas on the horizon. Actually, I think I just had a lot of nervous energy and stress balls to get out of my system."

"Or is it nest building, for the baby coming out of hospital?"

"Ha, yes! Nest building, I suppose so. I'm just pleased things are finally getting straight. It's been a tough few weeks. I don't ever want to go through anything like that again."

Gloria was touched by the parallel with nest building.

"He needs to be home, nice and safe with his family."

Alex rose to take the mug from his wife and wrapped her in his arms.

He kissed Gloria's forehead and ran his fingers through her ponytail.

"I just want him better Alex."

"I know, I know love, I want exactly the same as you."

Gloria's tears trickled into the crook of his neck.

The conversation about the police would have to wait until later.

Alex prepared the evening meal as Gloria showered and changed. He could hear her singing above the soft whirr of a hairdryer. As he sliced garlic, fried the mince and brought spaghetti to the boil he was dreading having to shatter the homecoming party mood. The issue had to be confronted that night, before Montague with his smarmy, stupid insinuations came walking up the path to the front door. Besides, Wilson wasn't in real trouble, he hadn't hurt anyone and he wasn't going to be poorly again, so things weren't that bad.

On the train back from London Alex decided he would support Wilson's story, however unlikely it sounded. Gloria would just have to accept it and then they could all move on.

"You look tired Alex. You've got dark shadows under your eyes. Did you have a heavy night while you were away?"

Gloria had finished her meal and was questioning Alex over a glass of red wine.

"I wish! No, I think I'm just mentally tired more than anything else. I've got quite a bit on my mind at the moment. Work stuff and other things."

"Why what's happening at work? I thought you liked this new government advisor role?"

"Yeh, the advisory stuff is interesting and straight forward enough. It's not hard to gather evidence to reassure MPs they're not about to die from brain tumours caused by mobile phone masts. It's the research stuff that's the real challenge. The quantum world moves very quickly and I'm not as young as I used to be. These PhD students are so smart nowadays, I have to ask them to speak in the language of physics I can actually understand."

"Come on Alex, it can't be that bad. I think you're just showing your usual self-deprecation. So come on, tell me what was so important that you had to be in London over the weekend, hey, but in layman's terms?"

Alex set his wine glass on the table.

"In layman's terms? Wow. Gloria what I do doesn't come with layman's terms! And making the world of quantum energy complicated is an unwritten law. Richard Feynman, this brilliant mathematician, said that anyone who thinks they understand the quantum world obviously doesn't. So that's the sort of bi-polar science I have to deal with nowadays."

"Quantum as in *Quantum of Solace*?"

"Exactly, yes. As in the movie."

Gloria was feeling relaxed, well into her second glass of wine and in a carefree mood. Alex was preparing himself to broach the big issue.

"So is your boss called Q or M or something like that?"

Alex looked at his wife in wonderment.

"Gloria, you never cease to amaze me. How did you get from me advising committees on energy matters to me being James Bond?"

But there was no holding Gloria back, she was off on one.

"It's funny, I never saw my husband as the special agent type. Alex Armitage. Licensed to kill. Cos I remember when we first met. What was the nickname they gave you when you worked at BT? Shaggy? That was it, Shaggy. Because of your hair and your cargo pants and the t-shirts and the laid-back approach. I remember now. It's all coming back to me. Shaggy. Licensed to chill."

"Gloria, I think you've had too much wine. And I wouldn't mind, but your wordplay is not even funny . . . "

"Okay Shaggy, so tell me why you're laughing then? Err, I mean Alex. Sorry, I'll stop. You're right, I was just joking. So come on tell me more about the quantum flapdoodle, seriously, I'm interested."

Alex rolled his eyes. The conversation was heading in completely the wrong direction. He'd have to jump off at the next convenient junction, just as soon as he could stop Gloria in her tracks.

"Alright, in layman's terms okay. So let's go back to the word quantum. In physics, a quantum is the minimum amount of any physical entity involved in an interaction. Think of it as a piece of energy. Quantum theory suggests that energy, an electron for example, can be both a particle, like a ping pong ball and also a wave, like a wave breaking on a beach. So if the ping pong ball is also a wave, in theory, it can be in two or more places on the beach at the same time, because if the wave crashes everywhere along a beach then so does the ping pong ball. The basic thing to grasp Gloria, is that energy can be in two places at the same time. Got it?"

"Yeh. Keep things easy to understand, just like that."

"For two days, and I'm sorry for being away over the weekend, I was on a panel of experts at the Department of Neuroscience at University College assessing the merits of a proposal for an experiment. The human brain uses a lot of energy, in neurotransmitters and synapses and so on. And in the brain, at molecular level, quantum rules apply. So, these research students want to try and determine if mental energy can appear in two places simultaneously. They have a hypothesis that could form a basis for understanding telepathy. How two people can think the same thing at the same time and I had to sign off the research grant."

"Did the experiment work?"

"It's very early days, but I think it looks promising as a hypothesis and I'm recommending the project should continue to be funded. An interesting extrapolation, a follow-on hypothesis for the future, is that two people can also share the same dream at the same time. And why not? It's only like telepathy while you sleep."

"Mmm, that sounds really fascinating when you think

about it. Actually, it reminds me of the conversation we had in the Yang Sing restaurant on Wilson's eighteenth, about baby spiders being able to spin a web because they share the same instructions with other spiders. I think Wilson called it the WiFi of nature? Something like that."

"Yes, the subjects I'm involved in are all part of the same ball park, the dangers of magnetic fields around electric car batteries, 5G transmitters that affect bird migrations and so on. Anyway, that gives you a flavour. The reason I don't talk about the research work is because most of it will lead nowhere or it's pseudoscience or just downright daft."

The appropriate moment for Alex to alight had arrived.

"Funnily enough, that reminds me, there's something else equally mind-bending that I've been wanting to speak to you about that also involves Wilson, but this is true."

Gloria's heart skipped a beat.

"Is it something the doctors have told you, privately?"

"No, nothing like that. Nothing to do with Wilson's health."

"Alex my heart just fluttered. I thought you were going to tell me he . . . "

"No Gloria, this doesn't concern Wilson's well-being. He's fine. He'll be home tomorrow. It's just that he's got himself into a spot of bother and it involves the police."

Gloria could solve that problem instantly.

"If the tax has run out on his scooter or it's the insurance, I can pay it first thing in the morning! He's not been able to do it because he was in hospital. Surely he won't be in trouble for that?"

"No Gloria, it's nothing to do with the Vespa. It's something else. A bit more serious than that and I don't really

177

"know how to tell you."

"Alex, just tell me. Quickly. Please. You're scaring me."

"It was Wilson who discovered Vanessa Clarke in Scotland."

"Who's Vanessa Cla . . . ? What? *The* Vanessa Clarke. You mean Graham's mother? Teaps? His mother? The lady in the news missing for all those years?"

"Yes. Wilson went to Inverness in secret and found her."

"Alex, are you teasing me, playing a game, because if you are this is not the appropriate subject matter. You can't make a joke about something like that."

"I wish I was, but I'm totally serious. And the police know it was him and want to find out how he came to be involved."

"Alex, that doesn't make any sense." Gloria shook her head. "Go back to the beginning and tell me again."

"Remember a few weeks ago, at the end of October when you went to stay with your sister Rita and I was working away. It was just for one night."

"She'd slipped a disc and I left fish pie in the oven and a note for Wilson."

"Yeh, well the next morning, Wilson took a train to Inverness, to a care home for people with dementia and found Vanessa there. He knew who Alice really was. He left a note to reveal her true identity then caught the train back and arrived home late that night. You were in bed and Wilson initially said he'd been out with Hoover, but that wasn't true. So then I got the full story."

"That's not possible Alex! How would our son know that? He never met Vanessa and besides Wilson was just a baby when she went missing."

"He said he got a Snapchat message with the information

from someone who didn't want to reveal their identity. So he went to see if it could be true. The police want to ask him some questions as soon as he comes home from hospital. They don't believe the Snapchat story."

"But why didn't he just go and tell Graham or better still, his dad? Or us?"

"I don't know love."

"So he's not done anything wrong. He helped Teaps to find his mum. It's an incredible thing, to do that, to solve that mystery all by himself. So why are the police involved?"

"Because they think someone else could have known her whereabouts and they kept it a secret for years."

"But that couldn't be anything to do with Wilson. He was a baby."

"I know. You're missing the point. They don't believe his Snapchat alibi. They think he was just a messenger boy, the gullible accomplice for the evil genius who was really behind her disappearance."

"And who's that?"

"Me Gloria! They think I'm involved! I'm not James Bond I'm Doctor Evil."

"Alex, I swear if I find ... "

"I'm being totally serious. And it all sounds so ridiculous I want to laugh. But I'm telling the truth."

"But what connection do you have with Vanessa Clarke?"

"I don't have any connection, but the police think I assaulted her and abducted her and took her all the way to Inverness with a brain injury."

"Alex, can you pinch me please, I think I'm on another planet or you've spiked my wine. Why on earth would you do that? You only went out with her for a few weeks and soon after you two split up I remember seeing her in a bar in Manchester and she looked fine. She was off her head in fact, dancing on a table and Michael was with her. More likely that Michael did the abducting don't you think?"

"Hold on. You knew Vanessa was my girlfriend?"

"Of course I bloody did Alex. And I made my move for you as soon as I heard it was over. It was me that asked you out. Oh you won't remember that, men never do."

"Blimey! That's a relief. I was dreading having to tell you I went out with Vanessa, but you knew all along. I've aged a year in a week."

"Alex, you even act like Shaggy sometimes, but that's not the point. How could Wilson have received that Snapchat message?"

"I don't know, I'm just telling you what he told me. What other explanation could there be?"

"More quantum flapdoodle?"

"No Gloria, even quantum theory can't explain this."

"And there's nothing on his phone, no incoming number, nothing backed up anywhere?"

"Old data files don't exist with Snapchat. There's only the text messages sent between Wilson and Daisy the day he travelled to Scotland on the train."

"Oh, here we go. So Daisy was involved was she? Well that's just great! Why is it, that ever since that girl has been involved with our son, we've stumbled from one catastrophe to another?"

Chapter 22

The genie is out of the bottle

Monday 27th November 2017

The police officer from the Art and Antiques Unit took one look around The Maltings, realised he was hopelessly out of his depth and called in three experts from Sotheby's Manchester office.

By 7 p.m. that evening, an inventory of valuables compiled from the lounge alone filled three A4 pages and all of it reported stolen at one time or another; including the 60" high definition TV and the Bang and Olufsen surround sound system to go with it. Some items on the list had even been stolen from Sotheby's themselves during a midnight raid on a high security storage depot in Crewe. The thief had left a calling card with the name, 'The Invisible Man'.

1 x Persian Hunting Carpet
2 x Daum Crystal Chandeliers
2 x Tiffany Lamps
1 x Japanese Ivory Netsuke
1 x Faberge Azov Egg
1 x Rubens Agate Vase
1 x Swiss Singing Bird Box
1 x Cellini Salt Cellar

Bradley's home was an Aladdin's cave of antiques, art,

jewellery, historical artefacts, ancient manuscripts, prized collectibles and all acquired via the showrooms of The Market Square.

The Cheshire Constabulary didn't have an evidence room large enough to store everything being catalogued, so eight policemen teamed in pairs on a six hour rota were assigned to guard the property until a secure location could be found.

"Our view is that it's worth somewhere in the region of seven to eight million in total. And that's a conservative estimate" said the expert from Sotheby's.

The spectacular demise of Bradley Givens made headline news and inside information, suggesting The Maltings contained more treasures than 'Tutankhamun's tomb,' drew the media like Howard Carter to Luxor. To be first to snap the all important photographic evidence was too good an opportunity to miss. A live broadcast by BBC North West from outside the entrance gates described Bradley as the highly secretive, super-thief who liked to keep himself to himself. It was lacklustre coverage of a treasure trove of a story. Pictures of the interior were needed to make it a goldmine for the tabloid press.

A reporter from *The Sun*, with a fat bundle of notes in his pocket was hoping to have a word with one of the policeman and hopefully buy five minutes inside, just as soon as the BBC cameras buggered off.

At around 9.30 p.m., the two PCs patrolling the premises were in the kitchen of The Maltings taking a short break over mugs of soup from a flask. Both policemen lived in the area. Pran was of Bengali heritage, married to a pharmacist and lived in Congleton with a two-year-old son. Dev's family were originally from Pakistan but he was born in Llandudno and lived with his parents in Holmes Chapel.

"So how do you think he managed to pull off all these thefts by himself Pran? He must've had a team to help him, surely?"

"Sarge says not. He says they collected over thirty of the invisible man calling cards over the last few years, mostly from south Manchester and Cheshire and whenever he was picked up on a camera, he was always by himself; disguised in black combat gear, this big stocky bloke, but they never got close to catching him. The getaway vehicles were always on false plates and he changed the van after each job. There's two more in the garage apparently. That's where the Sotheby's people have locked all the small valuables, all the jewellery and gold watches and pocket sized stuff. They don't trust us coppers. CID took all the cash and a pair of Purdey shotguns."

"Typical, eh?"

Pran whistled as he looked around the kitchen. "This room alone is bigger than my bloody flat. Twice as big in fact. And they say crime doesn't pay? I'd have to work a year just to buy that fridge. It's almost big enough to walk inside."

"Yeh, well it's not much use to him now is it? None of it is; the antiques and the paintings, all for nothing. He died of greed and I'm pleased it'll all go back to the rightful owners. Most of it was insured apparently, that's why he was seen as a bit of a charming villain. Leading the police on a merry dance with his calling cards, robbing from the rich and giving the insurance companies a headache. Nobody was injured, no violence, nobody really lost out. Just the insurance companies."

"Mmm, I'm not really sure about that." Dev looked at his

watch. "Last half hour coming up then we're done for the night. We need to complete the shift report before we hand over to the next lot so I'll walk round the outside of the house and double check everything for a final time. You check all the windows and doors on the inside?"

"So where are those photos they left us? We're supposed to sign them on the back to say each room looked exactly as it was supposed to at the end of the shift. With everything in its place and nothing missing!"

Dev was tugging the handles of the garage doors to be certain they were securely locked when he heard a whistle and turned to look down the drive. The line of sunken lights illuminated the tarmac like a runway. Someone was waving from outside the small side gate to the left of the main entrance.

"Sorry to trouble you officer, I'm Tim Geary of *The Sun* newspaper. I work on the North West news desk. Tim passed a business card between the wrought iron swirls of the metalwork. This is Andy, my photographer. Can you tell us what it looks like in there? We've heard it's an Aladdin's cave. Valuable antiques, jewellery, paintings in every room. Is it really that spectacular? Would make a great story. We just need a couple of interior pictures. Any chance?"

Dev opened the gate and passed the card back to *The Sun* reporter.

"Look lads, you know that sort of permission won't come from my rank. You're gonna have to come back tomorrow when the Chief Super is here. He's giving a press interview in the morning."

Dev was about to suggest the reporter was wasting his time standing out there all night in the freezing cold, when he heard a whistle and turned back to see Pran standing outside the house and waving.

"Dev. Quick. You need to come and help me take it down."

Dev marched back up the drive to see what all the fuss was about. Pran was standing outside the front door holding the A4 sheets bearing colour photos of all the room interiors. A wide angle picture of Bradley's study was printed on the top sheet.

"I know you're winding me up mate, wanted to make me jump, and I bloody did, but seriously we've got to put everything back in place."

"What you talking about Pran?"

"That joke pyramid you've built in the office, the study, the one with the big fancy desk."

"Are you losing the plot mate? What bloody pyramid? I haven't touched a thing."

Dev's quizzical facial expression wasn't what Pran had been expecting.

"You'd better follow me then. Looks like we've got a major problem. There's someone in the house."

In his haste to rush back up the drive, Dev had forgotten to shut the side-gate so Tim the reporter interpreted this as an open invitation to enter. He told Andy the photographer to nip up the drive and take shots from the outside, through the windows.

The door to the study was closed and Pran held Dev back to show him the A4 sheet once again.

"This is a photo of what the room on the other side of this door should look like, right? The study. Take a look at it."

Dev was familiar with the layout and contents, the antique desk and chair, museum stuff, fancy lamps, ornate rug, loads of different ornaments.

"Yeh. So what? I was in there half an hour ago looking at the pottery in that glass cabinet."

"So beyond that door, in that study, it looked like that photo, half an hour ago?"

"Yeh. Exactly like that. Why? What's happened?"

"Well, it doesn't look like that now."

Pran pushed the door open and they entered the room.

There was more than a moment's silence as Dev attempted to make head-scratching sense of a pyramid *inside* Tutankhamun's tomb!

"Shit," said Dev, "who the Jeff could have done that? And without us hearing them?"

"I've just told you, there's someone in the house and they're doing this for a laugh."

The Sheraton Partners chair was standing on the Sheraton Partners desk, a hatstand was balanced on the chair and the Persian rug had then been draped over everything like a cloak. A collection of porcelain figurines were arranged on the desk top like worshippers huddled together in a nativity scene.

"Come on, help me take it all down before something falls and smashes. Then we need to check every room, try and get in the loft, check all the windows are locked again, look in the wardrobes and under the beds. Someone's here, perhaps the girlfriend is still in the place. Maybe there's a panic room or a cellar."

Using the photo for reference, the police officers quickly

186

returned every item back to its starting position, switched off the lights, closed the study door and with batons and torches in hand went to arrest the culprits.

"Dev, we need to start at the top and make our way down. Let's work as a pair so we don't miss anything. And bring the photos for all the rooms, we need to make sure nothing else has gone walkabout."

There was indeed a loft, but the layer of dust covering the floorboards like fingerprint powder was evidence that no one had been up there for years. All five bedrooms were equally unoccupied with no one hiding under a bed or in a wardrobe. Every window remained securely bolted from the inside; the same with the outside doors. Whoever was in the house was still there and not perturbed by two police officers repeatedly threatening arrest for trespass. Pran even checked inside the fridge.

As the police car carrying the two officers for the next rota pulled up outside, Pran and Dev were standing in the entrance hall, they'd been through the house with forensic precision. There was not a soul in The Maltings, other than themselves.

"Do you think it could have been kids messing about, hoping they could nick something."

"So why didn't they take anything? Why build a bloody statue and then just bugger off? And how did they get in?"

"No idea, Dev. I don't get it."

"Look mate, the night lads are here now. Go and check the study again for a final time, sign the photos and I'll go and tell 'em to watch out for kids or an intruder larking about."

"Roger that."

Dev went to open the front door to greet his colleagues

and was raising his hand to the latch when he heard his partner say, "Dev, I've got some bad news for you mate, those kids are still here. They've built the pyramid again!"

Dev swung back the main entrance gates of The Maltings; they'd been switched over to manual operation. Pran drove past, wound down his car window and stopped before pulling out onto the main road.

"Cheers Dev. See you at four tomorrow. We'll catch the little sods next time."

"Yeh, enjoy the rest of your evening, what's left of it."

As Pran drove away, the reporter from *The Sun* and his photographer approached Dev.

"That looked like a bit of a strange how do you do" said the reporter.

"No idea what you're talking about."

"The furniture in that room, all piled up like that."

Dev turned to confront the pair as the realisation dawned.

"So it was you two. I should have known. How'd you get in? I can arrest you for trespass. Oh shit, it was me, I left the gate open didn't I? When I gave you back your card."

"No, it wasn't us. And Andy didn't go inside the house, so it wasn't really trespassing. And we didn't see any little sods. But we did see this! Actually, Andy's camera did, when he fired the flash through the windows. I'm guessing it shows Bradley's office."

The still image portrayed on the camera's viewing screen wasn't brilliant, it was underexposed in terms of light balance, but self-explanatory nevertheless. It showed the inside of the study, with the chair on the desk, the hatstand on the chair and a Persian rug suspended in mid-air like a flying dust sheet;

or a magic carpet. There was also the faint, glowing stencil of a figure with their arms raised to the heavens standing beneath. As though a sparkler in dextrous hands had sketched the ghostly form of Bradley Givens on a Bonfire Night sky.

Chapter 23

When Daisy met Sally

Tuesday 28th November 2017

Leanna was planning to go to John Lewis to buy a Nespresso coffee machine, so it was no problem to drop Sally off at Barney's Coffee Shop in the centre of Cheadle village. Sally had arranged to meet Daisy at 11.30 a.m.

They ordered cappuccinos, found a free sofa in the lounge space downstairs and when sitting comfortably, Daisy asked Sally to repeat everything she'd said at Wilson's bedside right from the beginning. Including all the finer details relating to the process of lamping the spirits in the attic of the vicarage; the repercussions as far as Big Mac and Short Cake were concerned; the curious incidents regarding her mother both before and after she died and everything Sally could remember about being in the white room with Wilson.

Over two more cappuccinos, Daisy then shared relevant details of her life and her experiences in The Market Square, going back to a time well before the night she met Wilson in Sampson's Motorcycle Workshop. She also brought her up-to-date with the story of Vanessa Clarke.

The Venn diagram of the conversations overlapped on the subject of being bullied at school.

"There was one particular girl I remember called Janet Soames. She didn't even try to conceal her bullying; she was just a thug, plain and simple. She broke my nose once with a hockey stick in the changing room when we were getting ready to play, and I know she did it on purpose. Didn't even say she was sorry."

Daisy ran Sally's finger down the ridge of her nose. Sally laughed. There was barely a lump.

"So in The Market Square one night, when I was still angry cos she'd thrown my trainers in the bins at the back of school or smashed my phone, something like that, I closed my eyes and started to think about all the things I'd like to do to pay her back. And when I opened my eyes she was there, as if by magic, right in front of me! I couldn't believe it. Janet Soames was right there and I feel so bad for doing this now, but Sally, I have never slapped anyone across the face that hard in my entire life. She was crying, with this big red slap mark on her cheek, but do you know what, I didn't enjoy doing it. I felt sorry for her and guilty."

"Yeh, I know the feeling, I wanted to do the same thing to Rachel Tiffany Thomas a few months ago. But I didn't do it. I couldn't."

"Then you're a better person than me because I really whacked her. And I feel even worse about it now, because I recently found out she was being abused by her brother at home and that's probably why she was so nasty. If I'd rested my hand on her shoulder I might have been able to help, to see what was happening in her life. That's how Wilson and I discovered what happened to Vanessa. I pulled her into The Market Square, put my hand on her shoulder and we saw the past. The Market Square comes to a standstill when you do that and these coloured baubles appear. They showed images of Vanessa's life like home movies and we saw what happened to her. We can't tell that to the police, obviously, which is why Wilson and his dad are in trouble, they don't believe someone sent Wilson a Snapchat."

"Do the people you pull in know they're in The Market Square?"

"No, I don't think so. Wilson pulled two friends into The Market Square one time and neither of them could remember it the next day."

"Have you ever tried to do it with someone who might not be alive anymore?"

"Gosh, I've never tried so I don't know. Looking back to a specific moment in time, back through a life, like I did with Janet and Vanessa, involves straddling two types of energy. Dream energy to pull them into The Market Square combined with time energy, the energy left by every moment in the past. I don't know if you can do that with someone who's not alive. That's a strange thing to ask."

"Maybe. Or maybe I was meant to ask it? I want to know what happened to a friend. This boy called Felix I knew at junior school. I think he might have died."

"Sally, some things are best left a secret. You can't always put them back in the box. Trust me. It makes me shudder just thinking about what Wilson and I did."

"You helped a missing lady be with her family again. That's an incredible thing to do."

"But you can't control what happens afterwards, like the police then becoming involved and Teaps falling out with Wilson. You can't control the aftereffects."

"But what if those things were meant to happen? You know, like you were meant to go and find Vanessa. Like you didn't choose to do it. You only think you did. That's what I feel is happening with me."

"Yeh, I've been thinking about what you told us last week, about the feeling your life is building up to something, but I don't think you can predict what that will be in advance. Sally you can't see the future because it hasn't been created yet."

"Mmm, maybe, but now I'm beginning to think that whatever happened to Felix could also be connected. That he has a part to play. Why else would he come in and out of my life so quickly like a character in *The Truman Show*?"

The conversation had to end at that point because Leanna had found them, "gossiping like a pair of washer women on the front step," as she later described to Kay. Leanna had agreed to collect Sally on her way back from John Lewis.

"Sally, are you ready luv? I know I'm a bit early."

"Yes, don't worry. This is Daisy, the friend I told you about."

"Hello love, nice to meet you. How's your boyfriend coming along? Sally said he'll be out of hospital soon."

"Yes, he's coming out this afternoon actually. He's still not totally recovered but much better than he was."

"Oh, well that's good. Wish him all the best from me won't you."

"Thanks, I will."

Daisy turned to Sally.

"I'll give you a call, let's meet for coffee again. I enjoyed today."

"Me too."

Daisy paid the bill and left to catch the Macclesfield train. Sally said she would wait on the sofa while Leanna nipped to the loo. The person sitting at the table opposite was hidden behind a tabloid newspaper. Sally could see the front page and the headline grabbed her interest.

'Brad's back from the grave!'

The sub headline was also intriguing.

'Ghost of criminal mastermind caught on camera.'

And the grainy photo beneath, taking up two-thirds of the page, was a total revelation.

Sally stepped forward to take a closer look.

It was a black and white picture of the inside of a room with furniture piled precariously on a desk and what appeared to be a blanket or a rug was being thrown over the furniture. The person doing the throwing wasn't really in focus, only a fuzzy outline, like the glow from a spirit after being lamped.

Sally asked Leanna if they could stop at a newsagents on the way home, she wanted to buy a magazine and a copy of *The Sun*.

The newspaper was lying front cover up on the kitchen table when Kay came home from work and she passed her observations to Leanna immediately.

"What's *The Beano* doing on the table? Thought you only read the *Daily Mail*?"

"I didn't buy it, Sally did."

"I wanted to know more about the story on the front Auntie Kay. They say it's a picture of a phantom moving furniture around in a house. Looks really weird."

Kay was biting into an apple as she picked up the paper and skimmed over the story.

"Yeh I heard about this. The sister of a lad in the accounts department is the girlfriend of one of the policemen. She said it really happened. Apparently!"

194

Kay tossed the paper back on the table.

"Looks like fake news with a retouched picture to me. You can even see where they've added the glow layer in photoshop. Right, what's for tea, I'm starving."

"Auntie Kay, you're not starving, you're just very hungry. Only people in Africa are starving."

Chapter 24

Welcome home

Tuesday 28th November 2017

Alex didn't recognise the number flashing on his mobile and afterwards wished he'd not taken the call. It was Montague and without pleasantries he got straight to the point!

"We spoke to reception at the hospital earlier Mr Armitage and I understand your son will be home later this afternoon. Is that correct?"

Alex swore under his breath, he really didn't need this.

"I'm going to pick him up around six."

"In that case we'd like to conduct the interview at your home address this evening; shall we say seven-thirty? We're booked on the flight down to Manchester at five."

"You know you're wasting your time don't you?"

"I think I'll be the judge of that Mr Armitage."

"Is it really so important to fly down the very day Wilson leaves hospital? Can't it wait a week?"

"No, I'm afraid it can't. Too many days were lost by Vanessa in the care home and I'd prefer not to waste any more."

"Look, alright, I admit it, I lied to you when I said I'd never met Vanessa. We had a relationship for a couple of months. But it was over when she met Michael and then I met Gloria around the same time. I don't know why I didn't tell you the truth. I was only trying to protect my wife. Turns out she knew about Vanessa and me anyway."

196

"And your point is what, Mr Armitage?"

Oh for God's sake.

"My point is, our relationship had been over for a considerable amount of time before Vanessa disappeared. Surely Michael, her husband, would be a better person to waste your time with?"

"So why is *your* son at the centre of this?"

"All Wilson did was receive a Snapchat message with details of where Vanessa could be found."

"Mr Armitage, I'm not prepared to conduct investigations over the phone. I'll formally interview Wilson at seven-thirty this evening and it's important you're there. I have information you and your wife may find, how can I put this, disturbing, let's say."

Gloria insisted on travelling to the hospital with Alex. She wanted to thank all the nursing staff and double-check Wilson had packed all his belongings, particularly the new pyjamas she'd bought from Selfridges.

Driving back through the centre of Stockport on the return leg, the neon light from the 'Santa on ice' themed illuminations and the strings of coloured bulbs between lamp posts failed to lift the sombre mood in the car. Thoughts were on the other visitor flying down from the North. Gloria tried to spread good cheer by pulling verbal crackers. First with Wilson, when she asked if Hoover had missed a marketing opportunity by not developing a missing stocking website. Then with Alex, by asking if Santa used quantum energy to deliver all the gifts to all the children at the same time. And then she pulled crackers with herself by talking about the

Bratz Doll stocking fillers she'd bought for Kate and Megan. What should have been a joyous homecoming, a Champagne moment, remained distinctly flat!

Montague and Sergeant Jordan were waiting as Alex pulled into the drive.

Wilson sat between his parents on the sofa. Good cop, bad cop, took the easy chairs. Montague let his sergeant open the proceedings.

"So you say you received a Snapchat message, which said what exactly son? And when did you receive it?"

"The day before I went to the care home, in the morning, very early in the morning. It just pinged onto my phone. It said something like, 'you'll find Vanessa Clarke in a care home in South Kessock in Scotland'. That was all. Then it disappeared, like Snapchat messages do. It took me a while to find the place on Google Maps because I thought the message said South Keswick, which is in the Lake District, but then after playing with the letters I found it."

"But why didn't you tell someone? Your best friend would have been the obvious choice?"

"And say what? Teaps, I just got a random message to say your mum's been stuck in Scotland for seventeen years, fancy going up there to rescue her? How could I do that? The message could have been a wind-up; so that's why I chose to go alone. I told my girlfriend Daisy I was going, she's the only one who knew. So when I found out Alice really was Vanessa, I left the note and sent a text to Daisy to say it was true."

Gloria rolled her eyes at each mention of Daisy's name.

"I'd like to give you the benefit of the doubt son, but it

does seem awfully far-fetched, hard to believe, a message like that arriving out of the blue. And why leave the note?"

"Because I couldn't save the Snapchat. Like you said, it just arrived out the blue, hard to believe. I wanted to avoid sitting here doing what I'm doing now. What do you want me to say Sergeant Jordan? That I dreamt Vanessa was in Scotland and in the dream I saw what happened so I . . . "

Montague wasn't about to allow any more benefit of the doubt.

"What you should say young man is, 'I'm sorry for not taking a serious situation more seriously.'"

Montague then turned to Alex.

"Mr Armitage, can I ask . . . " Gloria rushed to her husband's defence.

"Alex has admitted he knew Vanessa, but that was much earlier, over a year before. At the time she went missing Vanessa was married to Michael, had a baby and her own business. There must be an explanation other than it was Alex just because his son received a message!"

"Yes, there are other possibilities, but Wilson is slap bang in the middle of every one. Indisputable evidence of involvement. So my approach is to start at the centre and then work my way out and the first step leads directly to the father. Or even the mother, possibly?"

Gloria stared at Montague with a look of incredulity.

"Me? How on earth could I have left Vanessa abandoned in Scotland? I was probably working the day she disappeared, or pregnant with Wilson, probably both!"

"Mr Armitage, would you have a diary from that time?"

"No, of course not. It was seventeen years ago for goodness sake. I've no idea what I was doing on a particular day seventeen years ago. Nobody keeps records for that long."

"Ah, but that's where you're wrong, because there are some records that go back that far. Medical records for example. And our enquiries have uncovered something very interesting. Would you care to explain Sergeant Jordan?"

Sergeant Jordan appeared reluctant to follow orders but then reached for his notebook and cleared his throat before speaking.

"According to a credit card statement we have on file, Vanessa used her Visa card to pay for the services of a private hospital in Wilmslow a week before she went missing. The clinic won't give details of a patient's history without the disclosure of information notice I've applied for but . . . "

Montague was keen to get to the heart of the matter and cut across his sergeant for the second time.

"Are you aware of any reason why Vanessa would visit a private clinic Mr Armitage? To keep a medical matter private from her husband, possibly?"

"No, I've no idea."

Montague sat forward in his chair as though it were the cliff hanging moment in a soap opera just before the adverts come on.

"Well I have a theory Mr Armitage, and it goes like this."

"I believe your relationship continued with Vanessa Clarke after you both married different partners. I suspect Vanessa became pregnant with your child and I think the records from the clinic will show she had an abortion. I put it to you that you fought with her about that abortion and somehow she was gravely injured."

It would have been laughable had Montague not been so serious. Gloria's look of incredulity was turning to one of pity.

"You are a complete idiot" Wilson muttered under his breath.

With much sympathy, Sergeant Jordan noted the three faces staring straight ahead. All bore open-mouthed, shocked expressions that didn't appear to carry any evidence of guilt. In fact, Gloria didn't appear to be breathing. Alex felt like a character in a comedy farce being staged in his own lounge.

"So what happened then? Dad drove her from London to Inverness? Why Inverness?"

"That's a good question Wilson! Mr Armitage, did you work in Scotland around that time? The year two thousand?"

"Very possibly, I was working for BT then. We were repairing glitches relating to the millennium bug. I was in charge of national data networks and router centres and literally crisscrossing the UK every week."

"Could you have visited Inverness?"

"Of course, there was major hub there, and in Glasgow, Edinburgh and Aberdeen and also in Southampton, Bristol and other major cities."

"Was there one in London?"

"Yes, obviously."

"So, at the time Vanessa went missing in London, only to be discovered the next day in Inverness, by your own admission, you were crisscrossing the UK every week and often travelling to London and Scotland? I'd call that a suspect who is able to hide in plain sight Mr Armitage!"

Alex turned to Gloria, his eyes appealing for help, his hand reaching out like a man sinking in quicksand, a man who can feel trust slipping through his fingers as each accusation drags him down.

"So we have a motive and we have a means. I'd say we're

starting to build a compelling case here Sergeant Jordan."

Sergeant Jordan looked as though he was about to say something but thought better of it and returned his notebook to his pocket.

"Can you let my Sergeant know more about your work schedules from around that time Mr Armitage? Perhaps BT still keep old project information, meetings you might have attended . . . "

Sergeant Jordan had heard enough.

"Simply put, if you can prove you were working in Bristol on the day Vanessa went missing, that would be handy and put an end to it. Here's a card with my email address. If you can send me the name of your boss at the time or the office you were based at, I can contact BT on your behalf. I'll ask them to move quickly, to get this over and done with and the sooner the better in my opinion."

Montague rose to his feet with a scowl on his face. *He* wanted the last word.

"Please don't make any plans to travel too far from Greater Manchester in the next few weeks Mr Armitage. You and your son are both suspects in a criminal investigation. I'm going to ask a magistrate to allow me to confiscate your passports tomorrow."

Gloria didn't shift from her position on the sofa for fifteen minutes. This wasn't the start to Christmas she'd been planning.

Chapter 25

Scene: Balthazar's apartment

Evening of Tuesday 28th November 2017

The future looked off beat and out of step as Balthazar led Mark and James into his apartment. The syncopated rhythm of jazz playing in the background made the ideal mood music.

Balthazar was an avid collector of Blue Note vinyl and the Technics deck and bulky Wharfedale speakers from the '70s were his guilty pleasure. The interior of the apartment was worthy of a feature in a magazine. An artistic abode of shabby chic from the days when shabby chic was the look of an eclectic lifestyle rather than a euphemism for shoddy taste. A list of contents for *this* room would have included totems from a life dedicated to the service of The Powers That Be rather than stolen goods. Every keepsake a medal for services rendered.

The plasma screen TV on the chimney breast flickered with mute life as ice cubes plopped with a fizz into three scotch and sodas. At the press of a button, flames leapt from fake logs in a grate like dancing sprites. The artificial fire wasn't Balthazar's style, but he'd grown tired of carrying kindling and sacks of seasoned firewood up three flights of stairs. A battered Victorian armchair with some of the stuffing knocked out of it, *was* his style. The chair and other furniture items in the apartment had been bequeathed to Balthazar in his younger days, by the family of the man with the bronze statue in The Market Square, the Mr Ludlow or Mr Abingdon, but that's a story for another time.

Balthazar passed drinks to Mark and James who were seated on a red leather Chesterfield creased with age lines. Balthazar took the armchair.

Mark handed Balthazar a copy of *The Sun* newspaper. Imminent chaos looked to be an odds-on possibility.

"Yeh, I've heard. It's a mess! The story was on the news earlier, looks like the media are camped outside the place waiting for another sign of the afterlife."

Balthazar sipped his drink and tapped his fingers to an irregular beat. He'd been in similar situations before and the interventions required at this early stage were never clear. Besides, this mission would be directed by a decision-maker way above *his* pay grade and involve a different species of butterfly altogether.

"One thing's for certain, if he continues building statues out of furniture, he won't be doing it for very long" suggested Mark.

"Short Cake said he was well over three ounces, off the scale in fact. I expect he felt he still had a lot to live for and not happy about the termination" said James. "All the relevant traces are vacillating and refusing to settle so at the moment they're finding it hard to pick an ideal outcome. Big Mac said it was like fighting a grass fire in a hurricane. But you're right, he'll soon run out of steam if he maintains that work rate."

"It's the hurricane we need to get to grips with first" said Balthazar, "once the wind stops blowing, the forsaken will stamp out their own small patches of fire, they always do. For now though, all we can do is sit tight and wait for the intervention to reveal itself."

Mark's doubtful expression and the fact that his drink remained untouched suggested something had been overlooked.

"Go on, spit it out then" said Balthazar.

Mark took a deep breath and then slowly exhaled. Displaced air is often a sign of a storm on its way.

"Balthazar, what if, and this is only a what if. What if, now that he's got everyone's attention, Bradley's next performance only requires the bare minimum in terms of expending energy? He doesn't need to create another major spectacle. With all those TV cameras outside the place the merest manifestation of paranormal activity will make him front page news again."

"I know that Bradley Givens was blessed with elevated eleven status Mark, and he's smart, but . . . ?"

"It's not just that he's smart Balthazar, it's the fact that he's also smarting, that's the problem. I think he's going to have some fun with this. I don't believe he intends to lie low, put it that way."

Chapter 26

Curry sauce

Wednesday 29th November 2017, 1.30 a.m.

Daisy was killing time on the steps of L'Ecole with her legs folded up against her chest and her chin resting on her knees. The funfair dream was playing a repeat performance with the giant bats and catapult gliders and all the same faced people. Sally stood out like a window dresser surrounded by mannequins as she came running over the stone cobbles.

"Daisy, wow, what a brilliant surprise, what are you doing here?" Sally sat down on the step below. "I thought you said you were never coming back to The Market Square?"

"Yeh, that was my intention, but when I fell asleep last night I was thinking about you and your friend Felix and the next thing, I'm here. I've either been brought against my will or after speaking to you yesterday, I'm supposed to be here. I dunno, I had a funny feeling you'd turn up though. Better not tell Wilson. He'll go spare!"

"Well I'm glad you came. All the identical people were looking at me like I was some kind of freak!"

"Ha, don't worry, they stop staring after a while. Hey, since we're here, I've got to tell you, there are some awesome rides. We'll try them later if you like. The Ten Mile Drop is amazing, but I wouldn't really call it a ride, it's more like sky diving without a parachute."

"Cool. If we have time I'd like to try them all, but first can we do the thing you told me about yesterday, you know, to try and pull Felix into this dream?"

"Yeh, I'm thinking that's probably why I'm here. I'm meant to be involved somehow, and against my better judgement! Where do you want to try, on these steps?"

"No, let's go down to the music room. I think I'll be able to remember Felix better in there."

"I don't remember where the music room is."

"It's in the basement."

The elderly lady in the office confirmed the directions without looking up from her typewriter.

"Along the corridor and down the flight of stairs at the end. But there are no classes today."

"That's alright, we've arranged to meet a friend. We'll only be a few minutes."

"Off you go then, the light switch is on the right as you go through the double doors. Turn them off before you come back up, we've been asked to be mindful of our carbon footprint."

They were still laughing at the weirdness of being urged to be energy efficient in a dream as Daisy flicked the switch and fluorescent tubes juddered into life.

The music studio was exactly as Sally remembered. Four empty chairs faced the conductor's lectern in the middle of the stage to the left. The grand piano with the lid up dominated the centre of the room. Instruments on stands with amplifiers and speakers connected by snaking cables were everywhere and the recording booth and the mixing desk were to the right.

"This is impressive, so different from my flute lesson

days" said Daisy.

"It's where I saw Felix the first night I came here. He was playing the violin on the stage."

Sally located the exact spot.

"I was standing right here and Felix was in that first chair and he came over and spoke to me."

"Okay, so here's what you need to do. Close your eyes and from your memories of Felix create a perfect match. The colour of his hair, his eyes, the shape of his nose and mouth, everything is important. Bring to mind all the small details, create an exact copy and focus on it for two minutes."

Sally repeated the instructions to herself and then closed her eyes.

"I've got it."

"You'll know when he's here. You feel something hatch inside your head like an egg and the image kind of comes to life."

Daisy wasn't certain that last instruction was particularly helpful or accurate.

Sally did what was asked and gathered all the ingredients she needed to make a Felix, as though following the recipe for a person with chocolate coloured hair and caramel coloured skin. The hundreds and thousands of freckles on the bridge of a nose and the sticky tape repairs to a pair of glasses were the icing on the cake.

Sally focused on the image for two minutes then three minutes. For a full four minutes she held fast to her lifelike render of Felix and didn't let him wander from her mind's eye, but no eggs cracked open.

Eventually came the tap on the shoulder.

"I think you can stop now, Felix isn't coming."

Sally scanned the empty music room, she even walked over to the stage to see if the static in her hair would register the presence of Felix as it had the warrior.

"I did everything just as you said."

"I'm sorry Sally, I don't know what else to say. And I can't try and do it for you because I've no idea what Felix looks like."

"Well, he's got dark skin, his hair is short and curly and . . . "

"Sally, that's never gonna work. I can't picture someone I've never seen! And even if you do describe him as best you can, I'm just as likely to pull in Kanye West as I am Felix."

"So does this mean that Felix really is dead? That's why he's not here?"

"Probably. I mean, he might still . . . exist, if that's the right word, as a non-extinguished spirit, but perhaps spirits can't enter The Market Square or their energy is wrong. Who knows? To be honest, I'm not really sure what I'm doing here myself."

Sally walked over to the piano, sat at the stool and closed her eyes. A stream of notes flowed out through her fingers and the melancholic chords of the Ariana Grande song washed her picture of Felix away.

Daisy couldn't recall why she'd plumped for flute lessons rather than the piano. There was a warmth and richness to the sound of a piano, an expansive quality, with every note both expressive and resonant. Perhaps Sally could introduce her to the basics? Daisy was about to suggest exactly that when a better idea came to mind. The idea she was meant to conceive.

"Sally, stop! I need to ask you something. I know you wanted to bring Felix here to discover what happened to him. So what if we try again, but with someone who knew Felix, that you also know, and we bring them here and find out that way. Did you meet his parents?"

Sally rose from the piano stool and walked back to Daisy.

"No, I never met them. He had an older brother but I don't know what he looks like either."

"What about someone from school?"

"There's Mrs Broughton. She was our form teacher at junior school; she's the person that told me Felix wouldn't be coming back to school; and she was upset."

"So that means Mrs Broughton might know what happened to Felix. Or knows someone who does?"

Sally's eyelids were scrunched together before Daisy had even finished the sentence and two minutes later, her old form teacher dressed in a white blouse and a pleated skirt was standing near the door to the recording booth tapping her fingers on a snare drum.

Sally couldn't stop smiling as Daisy led her across the music room.

"Hi Mrs Broughton, how are you? You don't know me, but do you remember my friend Sally? Sally Bennett? You were her teacher in junior school?"

Mrs Broughton's crescent smile almost stretched from one hoop earring to the other.

"Of course I do. You know Sally, I was only thinking about you the other day. How are you enjoying secondary school?"

The question and the circumstances under which it was being asked stumped Sally for a second.

Daisy whispered in her ear. "Ask if she still remembers Felix and if she does, place your hand on her shoulder. We might not have much time left."

"Mrs Broughton, do you remember Felix? The boy who stopped coming to school? When I asked about him you wouldn't tell me what happened."

"Goodness, I've taught quite a number of ... "

The smile waned.

"Oh Sally, that poor boy, he was your best friend. It was two years ago wasn't it, at the end of term? Yes, I remember it vividly he ... "

Daisy grabbed Sally's hand and placed it firmly on Mrs Broughton's shoulder.

Time stood still as the tragedy of Felix, as witnessed by his form teacher, was revealed by the cadre of coloured baubles advancing to offer their testimony.

Mrs Broughton parking her car in a side street. Opening the car boot and lifting out a bouquet of flowers. The white card with a handwritten message clipped to cellophane. Mrs Broughton walking back to a junction with a major road, turning right, and then walking along a row of sorry looking shops in a cheerless precinct. The final shop, a Chinese takeaway with a Day-Glo poster in the window offering chips and curry sauce for a pound. Mrs Broughton reading the sign above the 'Wang Fu Takeaway'. Then the right turn that leads to the front door of the flat above the takeaway. A door in need of paint with a cracked glass panel repaired with sticky tape. A teddy bear, with wet and matted fur and wearing Felix's broken spectacles sits on the stone step. A wreath with a message from Mrs Hill, the headmistress, also leans against the door. Mrs Broughton gently placing her bouquet down between the two and adjusting the card to make it visible for any passerby who might happen to stop and read.

'Dear Felix
In the short time you were with us you touched our hearts
with your love of life, your thirst for knowledge and your inner
beauty. And the best smile in the world. You were a favourite of
mine. Rest in peace Felix.
All my love.
Mrs Broughton x'

Daisy lifted Sally's arm from Mrs Broughton's shoulder.

"Sally, I'm so sorry, this is so, so sad. I told you not to go looking for secrets in this place. Nothing good happens here. Only things that go on to make you upset."

Sally wasn't listening. She was picturing Felix opening that door, climbing a dingy staircase, entering a poky flat.

"No, I wanted to see it. To see where he lived."

Sally closed her eyes, made a wish, vowed a promise and said a silent goodbye to Felix.

"Thanks Daisy. Thanks for showing me, for making this possible."

"What do you think happened to him?"

"I don't think he died because he was ill or had an accident cos he would have wanted me to visit him in hospital. He said his dad broke his glasses and used to hit his mum, so a fight with his dad maybe? Or he was attacked in the street by a racist, someone who didn't like Felix's family because they were from Somalia. I'm not sure I want to know. I'd like to go and place my own flowers on the step though. Some red poppies; I think Felix would like that. Daisy what was the name of the road on the row of shops. It was on one of the first baubles, when Mrs Broughton turns the corner."

"Park Road. I remembered the name because it didn't look like a park sort of area. It must be fairly near to your junior school though. Did Felix walk to school?"

"Yes, he did. And he was always tired when he arrived because he said it took half an hour. Maybe he was targeted by a gang when they saw him walking to school? If I could see one of the gang, I could bring them here and . . . "

"Sally, stop. I know where you're going with this and it's a non-starter. You can't start forcing the future to take a particular direction. Things are meant to be the way they are for a reason and it's not for us to change them. Once you start influencing stuff like we did with Vanessa, there's no escape. Everything snow balls out of control. You understand what I'm saying don't you?"

"Yeh, but it's upsetting to think how I . . . "

"Sally, please, stop. Put all the things you've seen tonight in a box and lock them away. This place messes with your head. You have to try and be . . . normal! Wake up tomorrow, be upset, cry for as long as you like . . . "

"I'm not going to cry; cos I'm actually happy. Happy that Felix is in a much better place now. I'd like to leave some flowers. I promised myself I would. Can you remember the name of the Chinese?"

"Okay good, that's better, a normal thing to do. It was something like Wang Fu or Wung Fu. I'll go with you if you like."

Sally wrapped her hands round Daisy's waist and gave her a hug.

"Thanks. Thanks for helping me, for showing me this. Can we go in the morning?"

213

"Err, sure, why not? I'll skip college. I won't miss much; everyone's more focused on Christmas now anyway. I'll work out where the takeaway is and I'll text you in the morning with the address and the time to meet. Will you be okay to travel there by yourself?"

"I'll be fine. I could even ask Leanna to take me. Could Wilson come as well?"

"Mmm! I'm not really sure about that. I don't think he's well enough just yet. Besides, I spoke to him on the phone and there's a big problem developing. The police are convinced his dad had something to do with Vanessa's disappearance and since Wilson can't tell them the truth, they're making up all kinds of ridiculous accusations. Plus, his mum thinks I'm a bad influence, so no, I don't think Wilson will be able to go with us."

Chapter 27

Up to his tricks

Wednesday 29th November 2017, 3.30 a.m.

The huddle of news reporters and curious locals gathered outside The Maltings began to melt away as rain turned to sleet. The wind chill factor and a change to the security rota, during which a departing policeman confirmed 'nothing out of the ordinary' had happened during his six-hour shift, was enough to persuade even the hardiest believer in paranormal activity that a warm bed was the more sensible place to be. Tim Geary and Andy agreed to stick it out for another hour. As did the mate of Tim's from an online news platform. Standing under umbrellas and looking up at a house with all the lights on, they occasionally saw the black uniform of a policeman pass by a window.

The audience outside the gates had little to do other than stamp their feet, blow warm breath on crossed fingers and hope for something newsworthy to happen.

At 4.30 a.m. The Maltings suffered a power cut and all the lights in the house went out. It must have been a blown fuse or a trip switch issue as opposed to a problem at the sub-station, because the recessed lights bordering the driveway were still shining. The reporters could see torch beams bouncing around the interior of the house as the occupants searched for a fuse box. The policemen soon found what they were looking for because within a minute the lights in the kitchen came back on. Three pendant lights hanging above a breakfast bar were clearly visible through the big window on the ground floor.

There was definitely a fault with the wiring though, or a problem with an appliance, for a few moments later the kitchen circuit tripped for a second time and the house plunged back into darkness. Then a single bulb, visible through a frilly shade hanging from a ceiling rose in an upstairs room suddenly came on and after three-seconds, that also went out. Tim looked at Andy and Tim's mate started laughing.

The kitchen lights came on and went off again.

"They just need to find the master switch. Not the ones for each individual room."

Tim pressed 'record' on his phone camera just for the fun of it. Perhaps there would be a story after all. A comedy of errors involving dopey police officers.

The front door of The Maltings burst open and torch beams came sweeping out in the hands of two hapless policemen. They walked over the lawn, away from the house and turned to gaze back.

Visible through the huge arched window directly above the front door, a chandelier with candle lights hanging above a curving staircase came to life, and died just as quickly. This was followed by the lights in the kitchen. On then off. Then a wall light in the porch flickered on, and off. All four lights, each in a different location in the house followed the same sequence of illumination, on and off, in rotation.

At first there was a distinct pause between the sequence of light bursts, as though someone was following step by step instructions for rebooting the system.

Kitchen on. Kitchen off. Upstairs on. Upstairs off.

And so on.

Kitchen. Upstairs. Kitchen. Hallway. Porch. Pause.

Kitchen. Upstairs. Kitchen. Hallway. Porch. Pause.

Kitchen. Upstairs. Kitchen. Hallway. Porch. Pause.

The electrician found his rhythm and the on and off sequences increased in tempo.

Kitchen. Upstairs. Kitchen. Hallway. Porch. Pause.

Kitchen. Upstairs. Kitchen. Hallway. Porch. Pause.

The two policemen took steps back, well away from The Maltings, further out onto the lawn. The house was tripping the light fantastic.

Kitchen. Upstairs. Kitchen. Hallway. Porch. Pause.

Kitchen. Upstairs. Kitchen. Hallway. Porch. Pause.

Kitchen. Upstairs. Kitchen. Hallway. Porch. Pause.

Andy whispered to Tim.

"It's a message."

"A message? What do you mean? Like Morse code?"

"No! The lights are flashing in time with a tune. Listen and watch."

"Down. Up. Down. Up. Down. Stop"

"Down. Up. Down. Up. Down. Stop"

"It's from the movie, *Close Encounters of the Third Kind*, when the aliens send the signal."

"Duh! Dah! Duh! Dah! Duh!"

"So you think aliens are making the lights go on and off?"

"No Tim, you bloody idiot. It's someone having a laugh. There's someone else in there flicking the switches in a fuse box, another policeman. They're playing with us because I got that photo yesterday and it was a front cover story."

"Clever! Clever sods. They knew we'd be the last to leave so they've waited until now to put a show on just for us."

Andy whistled to catch the attention of the two officers transfixed by the entertainment and gave a thumbs-up when one of them turned.

"Nice one lads! Like it. The aliens are coming. Get it. It's funny." Andy had to yell because the officers were about fifty metres away. "You can tell whoever you've got in there playing on the fuse box they can stop now. We're going home."

One of the policeman shouted back.

"There's nobody in the house mate. The fuses and trip switches are all in the garage and we don't have keys for the garage doors. We haven't got a clue what's going on."

Tim Geary's report made the second edition of *The Sun* later that morning but the video from a phone camera, instantly uploaded to myriad websites, was halfway round the world before the print media had got its boots on. The video, of a house with lights that could turn on and off by themselves, first went viral and then turned virulent, infecting people with all kinds of notions regarding spirituality, religion, the paranormal and the supernatural. The believers began gathering in increasing numbers within the hour outside *Bradley's Believe It or Not,* Cheshire's latest tourist attraction.

Chapter 28

Strangers in the night

Wednesday 29th November 2017, 4.30 a.m.

The girl was sitting on floorboards with her back pressed hard against a door in order to keep someone or something out of the room. The panelled door and its architrave frame were of antique pine and heavily knotted. The room was in an old house, Victorian most likely, because of the high ceiling with its deep, plaster cornice and the ornate moulding of the skirting board. Wilson wasn't aware of other features in the room because the dream was focused only on the girl, the door and the side of a deep wardrobe which also occupied his field of view.

There was an unusual quality to the light. It was composed of grainy particulates, as though darkness had been separated into constituent parts and sooty granules of pure night were suspended in a medium of clear air. The dream didn't supply personal details, such as the colour of the girl's hair or the shape of her face. Her upper body was nothing more than a vague, homogenous grey mass. The dream supplied an image of her legs though. They were long and slender schoolgirl's legs. Knee length white socks were pulled up tight and she wore summer term sandals with buckles on the sides. A red patch of inflamed skin could be seen just above the knee. Both legs were fully extended and the sandals were angled sharply forward, her feet stretching out to touch the base of the wardrobe. The girl needed greater purchase, to force both feet against something solid but her toes fell tantalisingly short. Wilson stepped forward with the intention of helping the girl; to jam *his* legs hard against the wardrobe; to brace *his* back and keep the door firmly shut.

As he dropped to one knee and twisted into a sitting position, side by side with the girl, from somewhere threateningly close there came a vicious snarl, as if a wolf or ferocious dog were defending a meal. It was so sudden and disturbing that Wilson's initial response was to run. There was a possibility the snarl had come from the girl, from the featureless face at his side and an attack was about to follow, but he didn't sense the presence of danger in the room. Wilson's legs were outstretched with both feet wedged firmly against the base of the wardrobe and his hands were palm down on the floor by his side. A shadow passed across the space between door and floor and the creature on the other side began sniffing at the narrow gap. Wilson felt the base of the door flex inwards against his back as the animal pushed from the other side and then a solid thump from something angry hit the base of his spine. Then it was all over. The augury passed as the emulsified light dispersed. The girl, the door and the wardrobe dissolved into the night and the dream shape-shifted.

Wilson was standing by a pair of lift doors in the long, narrow lobby of an iconic building such as the Ritz Hotel or the Empire State Building. There were six lifts in total, three on either side. The interior decor, which featured floor to ceiling smoked glass mirrors, wall coverings with sunburst patterns, geometric shapes in the red carpet and a Clarice

Cliff vase filled with poppies standing on a black lacquered table suggested the art deco era.

Numbers denoting each floor stretched from 1 to 122 and ran in a line on an illuminated panel above the lift doors. This was quite an expanse of figures to fit in a two metre space but the dream created the impression without difficulty. A flash of green light in a perspex push button told Wilson his lift had arrived. The burnished copper doors parted and Wilson stepped into the lift. There was a man inside wearing a Great Gatsby style suit with a trilby hat angled low over his eyes and he was pressing every floor button repeatedly with a finger ingrained with dirt. The stranger had no need to look up and acknowledge Wilson nor the need for a specific floor it seemed. The lift was slow and took forever to reach the top, and then just as long to come back down again. A bell tinkled to denote the passing of each floor.

"Teacher says every time a bell rings, an angel gets his wings."

Wilson was aware the man had made the statement for his benefit.

The man continued pressing buttons with his back turned and this journey to nowhere continued until the dream ended.

When Wilson woke the next morning, the dream with the girl struck him as both bizarre and interesting and he was convinced that a true meaning would reveal itself in time. The elevator sequence didn't induce any remarkable insight other than the lift had failed to stop on any of the floors and the sound of the tinkling bell was still ringing in his ears.

Alex was on the phone speaking to Sergeant Jordan and

Gloria was ironing in the dining room when Wilson came down for breakfast. While taking a shower, he'd heard his parents arguing and sensed a charged atmosphere and unanswered questions hanging in the air. It was like playing *Whack-a-Mole*. Knock down one problem with the explanation of a Snapchat message then up pops another problem needing a different fictitious explanation.

As he poured milk over a bowl of cornflakes, Wilson evaluated the pros and cons of telling his mother the truth, the whole truth and nothing but the truth, leaving his dad completely out of the picture of course. But the cons won before he'd even reached for the sugar.

Alex entered the kitchen when the call was over.

"That was Sergeant Jordan. They didn't fly back to Inverness last night."

"And?"

"I told him I couldn't find anything in my old files. They only go back to two thousand and eight so Sergeant Jordan said he'd contact BT. He strikes me as being on our side in all this madness. I told him to ask human resources if they can check what work was going on in Inverness at the time. If the main exchanges were being upgraded to fibre networks, there's a chance I could have been there. I'm going to ask the bank for credit card and bank statements to see if they show anything."

"I checked online Dad, the banks only keep them for seven years. But I was thinking, what if we check all the old photos and the videos you backed up on DVD, maybe we can find something that matches the date Vanessa went missing. We might have been on holiday or spending a day at the zoo?"

"Your mum thought of that. She was up at six going through it all."

Wilson continued spooning down cornflakes.

"Don't worry Dad, if this goes really pear shaped, I can soon find out where you were on that date."

"How?"

"You know how. In the same way I discovered what happened to Vanessa."

"Wilson, don't even think about doing that."

Gloria strode into the kitchen with a stack of folded tea towels and put them in a drawer.

"I've asked Megan and Kate not to come home to see you this week Wilson. They're really busy with an end-of-year show and besides, they'll be finishing for Christmas soon. I'd like to keep them well away from this police business."

"Gloria, I told you before. I'm not involved in this . . . police business, no matter what Montague tries to dig up. And Wilson's telling the truth! Why won't you believe your own son?"

"I do believe him Alex, cos maybe that Snapchat message came from you."

Alex gasped and began laughing out loud as Gloria stormed off.

"Gloria. That is the most ridiculous . . . "

"Dad, stop! The only way to sort this out is for *me* to sort it out. I'm sticking with my Snapchat story and all I have to do is find you an alibi. I'll do it tonight when you're asleep, you'll not even know I've been there. I'm making Mum a cup of tea. Do you want one?"

"Son, I mean it. Don't go there!"

Gloria was in the lounge fixing a zip in a skirt when Wilson placed the mug of tea on a side table. Her bifocals were defying gravity on the tip of her nose. The TV was on with the volume muted.

"Mum, I'm sorry. You're right, I made a mistake. I should have told Teaps about the message. But my reasoning was, what if I'd mentioned it and he'd gone all the way to Scotland and Vanessa wasn't even there?"

Gloria raised her head to bring Wilson into focus.

"Why didn't you tell me what you were doing? I would have understood. I wouldn't have been able to explain it, but I would have supported you and been on your side. Right now, I don't know who or what to believe."

Wilson reached for the TV remote and turned up the volume.

Gloria returned to her needlework as she spoke.

"That story has been on the local news all morning. This video is supposed to show a ghost playing tricks in a house near Tarporley. Apparently the owner died recently in a car crash and they're saying it's his poltergeist they've caught on camera. All sorts of people have been chipping in with their opinions, a psychologist, someone from the local council and a vicar who's an expert in exorcisms. The world's going crazy."

The video, taken at night, captured footage of lights in a house being turned on and off in the same sequence repeatedly. The image was a little blurred and shaky as it zoomed-in on the two policemen standing on a front lawn. They turned to the camera and shrugged, as if to say, "What the hell's going on here then?"

Chapter 29

A flower for Felix

Wednesday 29th November 2017, 11.35 a.m.

The Wang Fu takeaway stands on the corner of Park Road and Grange Road in Gatley, a ten minute drive from the centre of Cheadle. Sally was standing by Leanna's car clutching a bouquet of poppies when Daisy arrived. Leanna sat in the driver's seat reading a magazine.

"Hi Sally, sorry I'm a bit late. Have you been waiting long?"

"No. We've just arrived, it only took a few minutes in the car."

"Those flowers are lovely, I love poppies."

"Me too. The florist said she didn't normally sell them at this time of year. So I was lucky. They remind me of Felix. We used to watch them swaying in the fields behind L'Ecole. I don't know what message to write on this though."

Sally unclipped the blank message card.

"Write what you feel. It's not an exam."

"Ha, yeh, you're right, but it's difficult to say what I want to say in words. Felix was my best friend and then suddenly, like my mum and dad, he died. So I suppose I think of him in a similar way. It's like I told you and Wilson. I don't think my parents have gone forever. And I feel I'll see Felix again. How do I write that?"

"I don't think you need to Sally. The flowers alone say everything. If Felix can see them from wherever he is, I think he'll understand."

Sally found the pen in her pocket and wrote, 'I won't forget you Felix. x' on the card and clipped it back on the cellophane wrapping. She was about to place the bouquet on the stone step when the door was jerked open from the inside and a Chinese woman carrying a mop and bucket stepped out. She eyed the two girls suspiciously and then saw the bouquet. Daisy quickly took the cue.

"We only heard about Felix yesterday. We don't really know what happened and we don't want to trouble anyone. My friend just wanted to leave these flowers, in remembrance."

"Okay. But don't put your flowers here, they'll be stolen in two minutes. Waste of money. Put them in the flat. I go for more hot water from my kitchen and back in a few minutes. You can go up."

"Can you tell us what happened to him?"

"Old story now, and not nice. I don't want to think about it. Terrible! And in my flat!"

"Did Felix die here? Upstairs in the flat?" Sally was pointing to the narrow staircase beyond the open door as she asked the questions.

"I hear a big fight with father and two boys and small one needs ambulance, but arrive too slow. Then police take family somewhere else. My sister moving into the flat next week, so I clean. It's okay. You can go up."

Sally didn't need to be told twice and dashed up the stairs.

Daisy spoke with Leanna to reassure her all was okay and rushed back to catch up with Sally.

Though the studio flat was sparsely furnished with a mismatch of secondhand furniture it was clean and smelled

226

lemon detergent fresh. The window in the lounge-cum-kitchen offered a view down Park Road from directly above the takeaway. A partially open door revealed a toilet and the corner of a shower cubicle. Through a second open door Daisy could see the corner of a bed frame and a bare mattress. Sally was on her knees resting the bouquet of flowers against the third door. She was smiling as she took three steps back, turned to Daisy, and said "he was here."

"Who? Who was here?"

"Felix! He was here when I walked in. Standing over there!"

Sally pointed towards a sink unit and a freestanding gas cooker with a three ring hob.

"I didn't see him like you can see me. But I felt him, I felt his presence, he was watching the moment I walked in. It was like he'd been waiting."

"What? You felt the presence of Felix?"

"Yes, he was here in the flat when I entered. I don't feel him now but he was definitely here."

Daisy was momentarily lost for words.

Sally pointed to the window. "If we block out all the light we might be able to see him with the torch on my phone. Just like I did with the people in the attic."

Daisy knew there was absolutely no possibility of that happening, the Chinese lady would be back in a couple of minutes.

"Sally how do you . . . ?"

"I just sensed he was here! In the daylight you can't see their glow but for a split second when a light comes on in a dark room they become visible and fluorescent. I call it lamping, I think they always stay near their last known address."

Daisy surveyed the room and opened her mind to the possibility of being in the presence of Felix.

"I don't sense anything . . . I mean, nothing is giving me the chills or making my hair stand on end . . ."

"No, I can't either now. He's gone I think. We have to move the furniture around. That might bring him back."

"Sally we can't do that."

Two voices were rising up the stairwell. Leanna was outside the front door talking to the Chinese lady.

"Come on, we have to leave now."

Sally reluctantly turned back to the flowers, to say a final farewell to Felix. The bouquet had fallen over so she returned to place it in the upright position. Daisy was looking on as stems were gathered with one hand and the top-heavy crowns cradled in the other. Sally inhaled deeply as though taking in the scent and slowly released her breath.

"I just smelt Felix. I could smell his school jumper mixed in with the flowers. He moved the bouquet on purpose, I didn't place it on the floor like that. It was his way of telling me he's still here."

Daisy walked over to the sink unit and stood in the patch of space that had supposedly been inhabited by Felix when Sally entered a minute earlier.

"Are you here Felix?" she asked quietly and self-consciously.

Sally placed the flowers against the door and crossed the room to stand by Daisy's side.

"Look Felix. Sally's here! Your friend from school. Can you see her?"

Sally's hand slipped inside Daisy's.

"She came here to say goodbye. She misses you Felix. If

you can hear me. If you can see Sally, can you let us know?"

Daisy suspected she was letting her imagination get the better of her sensibilities, but what the heck.

"If you still have energy left in your spirit Felix, can you use a little of it right now. Show . . . "

A metallic note rang out somewhere beneath or behind the sink, as though a plumber had tapped a pipe with a spanner. Sally's grip tightened.

"Was that you Felix?"

A second knock came from the same place. Then a third, and a fourth. Too startled to speak, Daisy pulled open the door in the sink unit and looked inside. And a fifth spanner tap. The noise wasn't coming from under the sink, but Daisy was getting close. The noise was coming from behind the cooker. And a sixth.

"Sally, grab the other side of this and help me pull it away from the wall. It sounds like the noise is coming from the back of here somewhere."

The bulky appliance was heavy and stubborn, but by twisting and rocking it from side to side they managed to shift it six inches from the wall. The knocking stopped.

The rear of the cooker was filthy; it hadn't been cleaned in years and the wall was coated with the sticky yellow residue of spent cooking oil. The smell turned Daisy's stomach. As they peered from either side into the six inch gap, there was nothing to see other than grease-caked workings and each other's face.

"Wait."

Sally dropped to one knee, placed her cheek against the side of the cooker and began reaching underneath for the edge of something she could see sticking out.

"I can't quite reach. I need to get my shoulder in, then I'll be able to get it."

"Get what?" Daisy went round to Sally's side and edged the cooker another inch away from the wall.

"Nearly . . . I can touch it . . . but . . . just need to grab that corner and . . . got it!"

Sally slowly extracted her shoulder and then her arm. The sleeve of her duffle coat was coated with a layer of yellow grease but her hand was clutching a hidden treasure. She triumphantly passed the photograph to Daisy. It was the head and shoulders school portrait of a timid and sensitive looking boy. A refugee from Somalia, smiling at a camera in a school shirt and tie and with teeth gleaming like polished opals. His hair was the colour of dark chocolate and his skin, the twin tones of caramel and butterscotch.

"That's Felix."

"But what's this doing under the cooker? How did his photo get there?"

"I think Felix put it there before he died. Or after he died maybe. He wanted us to find it."

Three sharp knocks on the pipe brought astonishment and then laughter.

"I told you Felix was funny."

"Sally. Daisy. Are you both okay up there?" It was Leanna shouting from the foot of the stairs.

"Err, yeh, yeh, we're fine. We're coming down now."

"Sally, quick. Help me get this thing back in the right place. And mind your fingers on the back. It's bloody disgusting."

Leanna said it was no problem to drop Daisy at the train station in Cheadle and they'd been travelling for five minutes when the conversation took an unusual turn.

"There was another weird incident at that haunted house last night Sally, you know, the one in the paper. All the lights were switching on and off by themselves and someone filmed it on a phone. There's no explanation because the house was empty. You can see the video on YouTube, thousands of people have been watching it."

"What's that Leanna?" Daisy was in the back of the car and reached for her phone immediately.

"It's the second night that something strange has happened at The Maltings. It's like the building is possessed. Nobody can explain it."

"Whose house is it?"

"The owner was called Bradley Givens. Some criminal mastermind known as the Invisible Man. They called him that because the police couldn't catch him. He died in a horrible car crash two nights ago and since then strange things have been happening in his house."

"How do you spell Givens? G...I...V...E...N...S?"

"Yes."

"Got it" said Daisy.

"They're saying it's Bradley sending a message from beyond the grave and that something might happen again tonight."

"Can we go there Leanna and watch?"

"Good heavens Sally, no! Gives me goosebumps just thinking about it. You won't get me within ten miles of that place."

Chapter 30

How was your day?

Wednesday 29th November 2017, 7.45 p.m.

"Tell me again what you were doing, I didn't understand the text message. Why were you in a flat above a Chinese takeaway in Gatley this morning?"

Wilson was speaking with Daisy on the phone, resting on his bed, trying to recuperate and take it easy just as matron Gloria had ordered.

"I was with Sally. She pulled one of her teachers into The Market Square and that's how we found out what happened to her friend Felix. The boy who died."

"We found out. What do you mean *we* found out?"

"I showed her how to do it. Like I did with you."

"Daisy I thought we'd agreed not to go back. You were adamant about wanting a normal life, the typical girlfriend and boyfriend routine, don't you remember our little pact? One last good thing and then stop. Oh and by the way, I have to tell you, that last good thing we did, well it's like the gift that never stops giving!"

"It wasn't my intention, but sitting on the steps outside L'Ecole it's as though I was meant to be there, to play a part in Sally's story and be involved in what happens next."

"And you think the spirit of Sally's friend, Felix, was there in the flat?"

"Yes, definitely, making a banging noise. He made us

laugh. It was . . . surreal. And then Felix sort of steered us to his school photo hidden underneath an oven."

"Surreal! That's more like surreal to the power of . . . tell me all that again!"

"So you really believe you were meant to go there, with Sally, to find the photo?"

"Yeh, I do. She wouldn't have been able to move the cooker without me. Or find the flat in the first place. Or know how to pull in Felix. I think I have a purpose in Sally's story, on this path she says she's taking, this conveyor belt she said she's on."

"And finding the photo is also part of that?"

"Obviously! We were meant to find it."

"And Felix's involvement? Felix being killed by his . . . "

"Maybe he's also connected as well. Felix introduced Sally to The Market Square and became her best friend. Sally said she can sense non-extinguished spirits and I believe her, because Felix then revealed his presence and led us to the photo. I know I'm describing a lot of small, different steps Wilson, but they all seem to be joining up to move in the same direction."

"Hold on a sec Daisy, my mum's shouting something."

Wilson returned a few seconds later. "Sorry about that."

"How is your mum?"

"Like a hedgehog, you know, when you try and touch one how they curl up into a ball to protect themselves. Mention the name Vanessa, Teaps, the police or Snapchat and she becomes all defensive and prickly. She seems willing to accept my explanation, probably not a hundred per cent, but she's definitely got it in for Dad. I'm sure deep down she doesn't really believe he's involved, it's just that Montague has a good

233

way of connecting unconnected things. Like he's desperate to find someone, anyone to blame. Mum's also still associating you with bad news. But I'm working on that. I think this will all blow over once the police find there's nothing to support their daft allegations."

"Wilson, if we could turn back time, would you do it again?"

"Yep, for sure! But with hindsight, I think I should have sent a real Snapchat to Teaps and kept well away from Inverness."

"If and only Wilson. Two small words, but when you put them together the most powerful in the English language."

"Bloody hell Daisy, where did that come from?"

"It's one of my dad's favourite phrases. Hey, I meant to ask, have you heard anything from Teaps?"

"No, he's not answering my messages. Hoover and none of the other lads are communicating with me either, I think they've found me guilty in my absence. I'm sure we'll get back to normal soon though, even Teaps will eventually have to accept the explanation."

"I hope so Wilson. I've missed you these last few days. I wanted to be there when you came out of hospital."

"I know. I'm missing you as well. I'm running out of magazines with sticky pages and half eaten bunches of grapes."

"Oh very funny! You need to be careful what you say to me Wilson. I'm probably stronger than you at the moment."

"Yeh, but in a week you won't be. Mum says I'm eating her out of house and home. The doctor recommends short walks but nothing strenuous for a month, so after that, bring it on."

"Hey Wilson, this is going to be our first Christmas together. What would you like from Santa?"

"How much money have you got?"

Chapter 31

Punch drunk

Wednesday 29th November 2017, 8.50 p.m.

As Wilson and Daisy compiled their wish list, a list which consisted of little more than a desire to enjoy Christmas dinner together but with a question mark over whose house, Kay had almost polished off the bottle of red. Sally was playing chess on her iPad and on television, the BBC news channel was anticipating the next episode of the Bradley Givens' show.

"What a joke! Sally look at this. Have you seen how many people are outside that bloody house in Tarporley? There's a crowd of hundreds. This is just brilliant. Keep it going until Christmas Day and what a story that'll be. Oh look, they've sent Tony Chapman to cover it. Sal, turn up the volume will you love, the zapper's next to your leg?"

The anchorwoman in the BBC studio in Salford was talking to Tony Chapman reporting live from outside the gates of The Maltings and Kay was right, over five hundred people had gathered there.

"Yes Diana, I would certainly describe this as a festival atmosphere. Something like the crowds in Albert Square waiting for the lights to be switched on. We've even got our own Christmas market."

The cameraman scanned to the right and zoomed in on a food vendor selling roasted chestnuts. The clutch of people visible over Tony Chapman's shoulder were pouring shots from a hip flask and raising their glasses with a smile as if to say 'cheers' to friends back home.

"Tony, can you confirm if police officers are still on patrol inside The Maltings?"

Viewers could see the front elevation of the house picked out by the lights along the driveway but the interior itself was in darkness.

"No Diana, the house is empty. It was checked this afternoon by a team with thermal cameras and they couldn't find a living soul, if you'll forgive the pun. The doors and windows are all locked and there's a team of policemen on a guard duty rota outside. Cheshire constabulary has copped a fair amount of ridicule over the last twenty-four hours so now it seems they're taking things more seriously."

"So are you anticipating another close encounter this evening?"

"Funny you should say that. This crowd is certainly hoping for another inexplicable occurrence. You know, it's quite incredible. Apart from the hundreds of people here, who all seem to be using this as an excuse for an early Christmas party, this . . . spectacle, as I speak to you right now, is also being streamed to thousands more via social media."

"Looks like it's going to be a long night Tony."

"Yes Diana. WHOA! Get away from me!"

That was the moment a terror-stricken response to being assaulted live on television was captured on camera. Video footage that would make global headlines the next morning. Footage of Tony Chapman, an experienced BBC reporter seemingly being attacked by an imperceptible assailant. By an invisible man. The shocking reaction of someone who, without a right to reply or a means of escape, was being repeatedly punched with a fist that no one could see. Neither Tony nor the cameraman filming the episode knew where the next vicious jab was coming from. As the reporter tried in vain to protect himself with nothing more than a microphone, his head would snap back one way then the other as he reeled from indefensible blow after blow. Blood began pouring from his nose and a nasty gash ripped open an eyebrow like a studio special effect.

"No! Get away!"

He'd spin round, trying to thwart the attack now coming from a different direction.

"Stop! Get back! Get off! Help me someone. Get it away from me."

But get what away from where? Tony gave the impression of trying to box his own shadow, a shadow that was floating like a butterfly, stinging like a bee and always out of reach. As Tony crumpled to the ground the live broadcast was pulled and a weather report brought Diana a much needed moment of respite.

If this was fake news it made great TV. The only problem Kay could envisage was the graphic violence being aired so close to the 9.00 p.m. watershed. And for the life of her, she couldn't work out who was likely to be behind the stunt, or the point of.

"Was that real Auntie Kay?"

"Course not love. It was a wind up. Like those TV shows, what were they called?"

"*Jackass*?"

"Yes, *Jackass*! A load of nonsense created for ratings and advertising money."

"It looked real to me. Did you see his face? He was bleeding and terrified. Something tore the sleeve off his coat."

"No, it was just good acting and make-up and special effects; his sleeve was probably attached to a nylon line that was too thin to see on TV."

BBC security people ferried Tony Chapman to hospital where X-rays showed a fractured cheekbone and jaw. They then whisked him away in an unmarked vehicle to an unspecified location for a debrief and an exclusive interview. Tony's fifteen minutes of fame had arrived.

Chapter 32

The only way is up

Thursday 29th November 2017, 2.15 a.m.

The corridor was long and straight with no discernible features. The walls were white, the ceiling was white, the floor was white and all surfaces were finished in the same, smooth-faced, plastic material. The corridor was brightly lit but the source of illumination was not apparent. Daisy didn't turn to see what lay behind, she knew there'd be nothing there. This was the start and nothing had come before. After walking for thirty metres, she reached a junction with the option to turn left or right. There was no signpost to suggest which should be taken. She turned left.

The corridor was long and straight with no discernible features. The walls were white, the ceiling was white, the floor was white and all surfaces were finished in the same, smooth-faced, plastic material. After walking for twenty metres, she reached a junction with the option to turn left or right. There was no signpost to suggest which should be taken. She turned right. Then right again. Then left, then another left and this aimless wandering proceeded for quite some time until she took the next right turn and walked headlong into someone coming the other way.

"Whoa Wilson! Bloody hell. I nearly jumped out of my skin."

"Yeh, and I could say the same to you."

"Where the hell are we?"

"I don't know. I've been stuck in this maze for ages. I can't find a way out. There are no doors. Just a left turn or a right. I've been going round in circles."

"Are we in The Market Square?"

"I presume so. They know we'll never come back willingly so maybe it's in disguise and this . . . labyrinth serves some obscure purpose. Either way, I guess we're here for a reason!"

"Yes, and that's exactly how I felt last night sitting on the steps of L'Ecole, knowing full well that Sally was going to show up. I'm getting really hacked off with this. Why won't they leave us alone?"

"If Big Mac and Short Cake are playing with us like lab rats, then refusing to go along with their maze experiment is fine by me. We have to stage a protest, take a stance, show them we want to move on and leave all this madness in the past. As far as I'm concerned, we can stand right here until the dream ends."

Wilson wrapped his arms around Daisy and gave her a hug, partly to hide the bemused grin on his face which would have been a red rag to a bull. He nuzzled his face in her hair and breathed in the scent of vanilla and almonds from the shampoo.

The strikers on the picket line remained resolute for a little over two minutes until Daisy whispered to Wilson.

"It's a bit daft this, don't you think? Just standing here, waiting for a dream to end?"

"Yeh, I was about to say the same thing. Shall we go and find out what's going on?"

"Okay, but which direction do we take? We could end up

wandering around aimlessly all night. And I know it's only a dream, but this never-ending tunnel thing is starting to spook me out."

"If Big Mac has brought us here on purpose, then this charade will lead to something, trust me. We just have to play his silly game. To make an effort to solve the puzzle and find the way out, they're probably betting on it."

Before following the corridor down a turn to the right, Wilson used the black rubber sole of his slipper to scrape a directional arrow on the wall.

"Let's mark here as the start."

Twenty minutes later, they had run out of virgin territory and black arrows pointed in every direction including upwards. Smiley face emojis had also begun to appear. Sliding his foot back into the slipper, Wilson began laughing and shaking his head.

"Daisy we're so stupid to rely on this process of elimination and being methodical. There's no way they'd make it that easy for us to find a way out. We have to find a less obvious solution. We've got to think more laterally!"

Daisy banged on the wall with the side of her fist. The dull thud was the sign of a solid, permanent construction rather than temporary partitioning and the smooth, matt surface revealed no cracks or joints to indicate an escape hatch or a hidden door. Wilson considered the ceiling. It was too high to touch, but only by a few inches.

"Daisy come here a sec. I'm going to lift you up. Put your foot in my hands and steady yourself against the wall, see if you can touch the ceiling. Perhaps it's false. Are you ready?"

Daisy's foot found the stirrup of interlocking fingers as

Wilson braced himself for the lift.

"Yep! Wait. No! Wilson you're not supposed to do anything strenuous remember?"

"Yes, but this is a dream. I'm not *really* lifting you up."

"Mmm, not sure about that! Let me lift you up. You try and touch the ceiling, you're taller."

"Go on then, if you insist. I'm all for equality. One, two, three, lift."

The ceiling was indeed a *false* ceiling. Not false as in suspended, but *false* as in, not actually there. The appearance of a ceiling had been created with an optical illusion.

Wilson accidentally stood on Daisy's head as his fingers found the top of the wall and he pulled himself through a trick of the light and onto a ridge about half a metre wide. The surface of the ridge consisted of raised dimples that ran in pairs along its length creating the impression of a wall made from giant Lego bricks. Finding his balance, Wilson slowly stood upright and observed the full extent of the maze. A maze of white walled corridors covered The Market Square and he followed the various pathways and turns like Pac Man until a gap in the perimeter became apparent.

"I can see a way out Daisy, it's over there, opposite The Bank. Follow the sound of my voice as I walk along or do you want me to pull you up? There's a great view of the Clock Tower from here."

"Wilson I'm beginning to feel claustrophobic and possibly going snow blind so can you just get a move on."

"Ha ha ha. Okay! Follow me. Right at the next turn."

Wilson scampered along the wall like a squirrel on a fence

and paused to steady himself only twice. Daisy followed the sound of his footsteps.

"Don't worry, I'll catch you if you fall."

"Think that's supposed to be my line Daisy."

Wilson hung by his fingertips for a moment before dropping to the ground. Stepping out of the maze and onto the paving stones bordering The Market Square they stood facing the entrance to The Bank, the 'office in town' for Big Mac and Short Cake.

"I thought as much, that's why the exit is here. They'll be on the first floor, come on, let's get to the bottom of all this."

Daisy was a step ahead and already reading the note pinned to the front door.

'Sorry, but we grew tired of waiting.
When you do eventually find your way out of the Magic Maze,
please come to the Number 11 Club. Top of The Market Square
after Sampson's. Then turn left at the alley and keep on until
morning. Regards, Peter'

"Who's Peter?"

"Peter Pan, that's his famous saying. Turn left at the stars and keep on until morning. I guess it's Big Mac and Short Cake's way of trying to . . . make light of things."

"Mmm, well I can't guarantee I'll be making light of things when I see them."

Wilson could see the swinging sign for Sampson's at some distance along the pavement. The last time he saw it, the sign was smashed in splinters around his feet and he was almost beheaded by a falling roof tile. Daisy had a different memory.

Of running faster than the speed of her dream into Sampson's Workshop only for Sampson to keep asking "can I help you?" like a bloody robot.

"Come on Wilson. Let's keep going."

They hurried past the butchers, the bakers and the candlestick makers and along the frontage of chocolate box cottages with hanging baskets overflowing with flowers. The white perimeter wall of the maze ran alongside on the right, like a Berlin Wall, segregating one part of The Market Square from another.

When they reached Sampson's, a notice with the words *'Gone Fishing'* was hanging in the window and the front door was locked. They peered through the window at a row of motorbikes with lots of gleaming chrome.

"Wilson, do you think Mark will let me have a go on a Harley Davidson? There's a fantastic one over there next to a Vespa like yours."

"I'm sure he would, but we're not planning on coming back remember? And besides, what if you woke up and the bloody thing was parked next to your bed the next morning? Your dad would have a fit. Not to mention all the Hell's Angels that'd come looking for it."

The thought of another gold bangle scenario on a bigger scale made Daisy shudder.

"Yeh, and I'd never get it down the stairs anyway."

Opposite the entrance to the alleyway, the wall of the maze had been vandalised with spray paint graffiti. Wilson wondered if there was a message to be deciphered in the symbols and tags, a gang threat for those who had ventured beyond their own patch. But when he read the words 'Clapton is God' it was obvious the work had been created by the street artist known only as Short Cake.

"Wilson is it me, or has the perspective in this passageway gone a bit warped?" Daisy was peering down the alley and tilting her head from side to side. "I think I'm looking into an Ames Room. You know, one of those illusions where you take three steps and then you have to crawl because the ceiling is only a metre off the ground?"

"Yeh, this rat run is probably another part of the maze, a continuation of the puzzle."

"And what about all the graffiti? Do you think it's safe? Looks a bit dodgy and gloomy down there. I can't see any sign of a club and look Wilson, this alley's stretching out now, growing longer and thinner, like it goes on for miles."

Daisy's eyes were struggling to find a focal point in the shifting perspectives but Wilson could see past the mind games.

"There's only one way to find out. Come on."

Daisy was muttering to herself as she hurried to catch up. "This is one bizarre dream."

On reaching a point where the distance travelled, based on the pinprick spot of light behind them, appeared to be the same as the distance still to be covered, in other words, halfway down the passageway, they were presented with a nondescript door with a glowing neon sign above. The Number 11 Club had arrived.

"Wow, look at this . . . came out of nowhere. Three steps earlier there was nothing and then suddenly, we're here."

"It doesn't look like much of a club Wilson. The 'hole in

the wall' would have been a more appropriate name. I like the bouncing dice logo though."

Wilson stepped forwards and banged on the door three times with the side of his fist.

They waited for longer than should have been necessary, given they'd been directed to the Number 11 Club in the first place, so Daisy gave it her impatient best with two solid raps.

Wilson was about to knock for a third time when a vision panel slid open and a pair of unusually large eyes peered out and then down at the new guests. The hatch slid shut and after a series of mechanical clunks, Charles pulled back the door.

"So sorry to have kept you waiting Mr Armitage, Miss Meadowcroft. I had to check if you'd been invited to our special event this evening – as indeed you have!"

Charles offered the same smile and the sweep of a hand that had once beckoned Sally and Felix into the premises.

"Come on, let's get to the bottom of this nonsense." Daisy barged past Charles pulling Wilson in her wake and it took a few moments for his eyes to adjust to the subdued lighting of the foyer and to gather a first impression.

"May I take the stole madam?"

The woman's voice drew Wilson's attention to a cloakroom attendant wearing a white blouse and a chunky pearl necklace. She was talking to a customer, a second lady, who was also standing at the counter but with her back to him. This lady was wearing a black sequinned dress which clung to her figure so tightly she must have been poured into it. The lady stood tall and shapely in stiletto heeled shoes and there was a shawl of black fur draped loosely across her shoulders. Wilson couldn't see Daisy anywhere in the foyer so it felt odd to then hear her voice.

"Wilsonnn! What just happened here?"

The lady in the sequinned dress with hair pinned up in an Audrey Hepburn style turned round and somehow, that lady had become Daisy. Or the other way round.

"Bloody hell! How did you do that?"

Daisy was admiring her figure in a full-length mirror and smoothing out imaginary lines in the dress.

"You look incredible! That dress has changed your . . . shape."

"Wilson, I was always this shape, you haven't had your eyes open properly."

"You look incredible."

"You just said that, and besides, you don't look too bad yourself. Apart from the messed up hair and the spots on your chin."

Wilson's black leather shoes were as comfy as slippers as he stepped in front of the mirror to admire the tailored suit, crisp white shirt and silk tie. Gold cufflinks in the shape of bouncing dice were a classy touch from whoever oversaw the wardrobe department.

The pair stood side by side, both amazed and delighted with the instant makeover. Daisy was smiling at Wilson's reflection with lips full and ruby red and her eyes held a seductive allure.

"Bewitching, that's the word that springs to mind Daisy. You look positively bewitching."

"I don't think you know what that word means Wilson. Or the implications of being bewitched!"

"Probably not, but it sounds like the perfect word to describe you at this particular moment."

Daisy was checking her teeth for signs of lipstick smudge

as Wilson took her hand.

"I think we might like this club."

Charles pulled the velvet curtains to one side.

"I think that's all the boxes ticked regarding our dress code. I do hope you enjoy your evening, Mr Armitage, Miss Meadowcroft. Would you like to follow me."

As Charles led them across the club to the only free table, an audible hush descended as all eyes followed the new arrivals. Charles helped Daisy take her seat.

"May I take an order for drinks madam? The house cocktail is highly recommended. The Number 11 Highball."

"Oh yeh, I definitely want to try one of those."

"What's in the recipe?" Wilson asked.

"Vodka, Gin and Grenadine in equal measures with a dash of Sprite."

"Okay, in that case, I'll have a Martini please with an olive, and shaken not stirred."

"That is a most excellent choice sir."

There was a glint of gold tooth as Charles smiled with pirate charm. "Enjoy the entertainment."

As Charles walked over to the bar, the background noise of music and conversation returned to its former level.

Daisy drew closer to Wilson and lowered her voice.

"What's going on? Are we supposed to just sit here and wait for something to happen?"

"Search me. But I think everyone here was expecting us."

Daisy continued to whisper, her mind made up after assessing the calibre of the clientele.

"I think this is the sort of club where the glamorous super rich hang out in Monaco or Las Vegas."

A waiter arrived with the drinks and a ramekin of nibbles and since these were nothing more than Cheesy Wotsits, Wilson was amused by the reference to the super rich.

Daisy sipped the Highball and a red imprint of her lips was franked on the rim of the glass as she placed it back on the table. The rays of light from the facets on a huge gemstone were targeted at Wilson's eyes on purpose.

"Do you think this ring is real or one of those cheap Zirconia copies?"

"Zirconia in my opinion, but my Rolex is real."

Wilson extended his arm to reveal the gold watch on his wrist.

"Wow, yeh, that does look real. So what time is it?"

"Err, eleven minutes past eleven. Wait, hold on . . . look, there's only eleven hours on this watch and they're all the number eleven, there's no other time. It's always going to be eleven minutes to, or eleven minutes past . . . eleven."

"I might be wrong Wilson but I don't actually think Rolex make one of those. Make sure it's not on your wrist when you go back to bed though."

Wilson unclasped the watch and slipped it into his jacket pocket.

Daisy had just ordered a second Highball and was bordering on tipsy when the pianist waited for polite applause to subside before speaking with a husky voice into a microphone.

"Thank you ladies and gentlemen, that's very kind, thank you, thank you. As you know, we have two distinguished guests with us this evening and I want to let you in on a secret. One of this fabulous couple also happens to be a wonderful musician. I think with just a little encouragement they might be persuaded to join me for a duet."

Wilson rolled his eyes, he couldn't see the point in what was about to follow. The dream seemed to be idling without a purpose and going absolutely nowhere. It felt as though they'd turned up to the wrong party and the host was too polite to ask them to leave.

Surely we've not been brought to The Market Square just for this. I only played bass guitar for that one night with The Girl Guides, hardly makes me a wonderful musician. Don't call me up on stage, please.

"So I do hope you'll join me with an appreciative round of applause for . . . Daisy Meadowcroft."

Daisy was up and off, striding round tables, smiling and saying thanks for the whistles and cheers and all the hand clapping before it dawned on Wilson that he'd been eclipsed. The pianist gave Daisy a hug and whispered something. Daisy looked sensational in the headline act dress. The starburst sparkles from sequins reflected in her eyes and smile.

"Would everybody love to hear Daisy Meadowcroft play jazz flute?"

The whoops of encouragement continued as Daisy self-consciously addressed the audience.

"Okay, I guess I could play a little ditty, but I'm not prepared."

The moment he heard those words, Wilson saw where the segue was leading and broke into a grin. Daisy was in a parody of her favourite movie, *The Legend of Ron Burgundy,* and she knew every line.

"I'm really not prepared for this at all."

A flute was thrust into her hands and she turned to the pianist.

"East Harlem Shakedown. E Flat. Come on sister, let's take that piano for a walk."

Daisy emulated a complete beginner by playing a handful of random notes which the pianist tried to follow, as happens in the movie, but then it all came together.

"We got it now. It's all right. We're babymakin'."

Big Mac and Short Cake appeared midway through the performance and solemnly took a seat either side of Wilson. (Daisy had reached the part which involves playing her flute while stepping from table to table crushing cocktail glasses underfoot.) Without any form of greeting or a preamble in terms of chit chat, Short Cake clicked his fingers and the dream shape-shifted. White smoke from what could have been a dry ice machine drifted across the Number 11 Club smothering sound and vision in a dense, creeping mist. For a few seconds Wilson was completely enveloped but as the fogginess drifted away, the air cleared and the dream finally revealed its true purpose. Daisy and Wilson had been at the right party after all.

They were still in the Number 11 Club but the seating plan had changed. They were now at a table in a dimly lit corner adjacent to an area cordoned off with thick rope hanging between chrome posts. Behind a lamplit lectern, above a pair of velvet curtains, a box sign illuminated the word 'CASINO'.

Wilson was back in the pyjamas and slippers he'd been wearing earlier in the maze and Daisy was in her towelling shorts and vest. She looked vulnerable and half naked seated with Big Mac and Short Cake like mute bookends either side, but apart from that, normal service had resumed. Music,

251

laughter, milling waiters, everything was business as usual in the Number 11 Club. The sound of lady luck at play, dice bouncing down a table and the 'oohs' and 'aarghs' of winners and losers, permeated through the velvet curtains. Wilson removed his pyjama top to reveal a white t-shirt and passed the jacket to Daisy who slipped it on, fastened all the buttons and rolled the sleeves up. She was as sober as a judge despite the Highball and didn't hold back with the summing-up.

"Okay you two, so what exactly is the purpose of all this? And don't talk in riddles like you normally do! Wilson and I said we'd never return after our last little adventure yet I've been brought back twice now, against my will, and I know you two are behind it."

"Up to mischief, you might say. Making us escape from your Magic Maze, leaving cryptic messages" As he spoke, Wilson checked the pockets of his pyjama bottoms for a stowaway Rolex.

"So come on, spit it out before I give my hockey teachers a call" said Daisy.

Big Mac was the first to reply.

"That really won't be necessary. We'd like to call a truce. To let bygones be bygones."

"To be one big happy family."

Daisy scowled at Short Cake. She didn't feel comfortable in his presence even with the pyjama jacket buttoned up and was immediately irritated by his perpetually annoying way of chipping in with banal comments and finishing sentences.

"So why are we here, spending half the night in a dream that makes no sense whatsoever? And more to the point, why are we back in pyjamas?"

"You are about to be introduced to an important person

who asked to meet the *real* you and the reason we brought you here is for you to meet *that* person."

Big Mac and Short Cake rose from their seats and Daisy and Wilson were asked to follow. It seemed the layers of artifice had been peeled from the dream and now they were being led to the heart of the matter. The charade was coming to an end.

"So who is this mystery person then?"

"Come along. He'll be waiting and time is slipping away."

Big Mac then ushered Wilson and Daisy through the cordoned off space to where Charles was holding back the black velvet curtains on the threshold of the 'CASINO'.

Daisy's gasp was longer and louder than Wilson's and she held her hand to her mouth, not for the sake of good manners, but as a reflex action to the shock of being visually stunned. For a minute both were speechless; the new setting for the dream was simply too incredible for words. Eventually Daisy managed to string two together.

"What ... the ... !"

"This," said Big Mac, "is The Citadel of Angels."

"Isn't it heavenly?" added Short Cake.

"Heavenly?" Wilson and Daisy replied in unison and with the same measure of astonishment.

The stage set was so extraordinary, so magnificent, that Daisy hadn't thought through the implications of her next question.

"Are we in heaven, did we die in our sleep?"

Big Mac chuckled. "No Daisy, you're both safe and sound in bed dreaming about this wonderful moment."

"I don't get it" said Wilson. He was overwhelmed by the

sheer, breathtaking grandeur of the vision. It was as though The Market Square was merely the domain of ordinary folk, while this place, *this* place was where the jet-set lived. A casino that made the swankiest joint in Las Vegas look like a penny arcade on Blackpool promenade.

"It's like that Shard building in London, but turned inside out. There must be hundreds of floors up there and I can't see the top."

Wilson's head was tilted as far back as his neck would allow.

"And look, everything is made from glass. Glass floors, glass ceilings, even the escalators and the roulette tables are made of clear glass. I think I can see clouds at the very top, the sky is definitely being sky-scraped."

"Tell Wilson how many floors we actually have Mr Cake."

"As of yesterday we had one hundred and twenty-two years and fourteen days worth of floors!"

Daisy followed the zig zag inclines of the escalators as they rose in a never-ending 'z' shape upwards.

"But there are no escalators coming back down."

"There's no need for one to come down Daisy. Angels never come down; they win their wings on this floor then fly up to the next year, and so on, and eventually fly away."

Daisy cast her eyes over 'this floor' but the words didn't do justice to what she was observing. There had to be thousands of roulette tables occupying the space because the rows were endless and 'this floor' had no discernible outer walls, glass or otherwise, just acres of gambling space. At the foot of each table stood a single player and no croupiers were present.

Short Cake felt the need to clarify his point.

"The angels don't actually fly, like a bird!"

His flapping arm movements were not necessary.

"That's just a metaphor. They take the escalator, it's much easier. They start their apprenticeship here, on the ground floor so to speak, with responsibility for a single newborn life. If they navigate year one successfully, the apprentice is promoted to full guardian angel status and they fly up to the next floor, to the next level of problem-solving, to protect year two of life and then year three and so on. And we all know problems get bigger as the kids get older."

"So everyone out there, standing around those roulette tables is learning to be a guardian angel?"

"You bet they are Daisy! They may inadvertently take their eye off the ball of course; an unforeseen accident, a moment of negligence. When your number's up, your number's up, as they say."

The sinews in Short Cake's neck stretched taut like steel cable as he admired the architectural splendour of the structure towering above. "There's no glass ceiling for an angel."

"So if this is the ground floor, for apprentice angels, are the people playing at these tables spirits from The Gateway who passed through the Exit to Eternity?"

"Yes Daisy, before they move on to the happy ever-after of heaven, they can play guardian angel in a competition to fly the highest. Some choose not to participate of course, those dead set against gambling for example, so those spirits are free to push back the boundaries of the universe, or hang out in the Number 11, or visit paradise or whatever rocks their boat in terms of heaven. It's quite the rite of passage."

"So why does everyone look so . . . "

"Like they've just stepped from the pages of a catalogue?"

suggested Big Mac.

"Yeh, I suppose so. They all look so . . . ordinary!"

"That's because we have a code that not only applies to dress, it also applies to physical appearance. There's no need for piercings, green hair or tattoos when you're learning the ropes. Our apprentice angels must choose their avatar from our manual of conformity."

"One size fits all on this floor" added Short Cake.

Big Mac checked his wristwatch. Wilson had another question.

"So what happens when someone dies naturally, of old age say, on the eighty year floor. What happens to their guardian angel then?"

"It's game over! They retire and go and push back the boundaries of the universe or whatever rocks their boat in terms of heaven."

"Indeed, Mr Cake. For heaven is a big place to explore in the circle of afterlife."

Big Mac checked his wristwatch for a second time.

"We really must get a move on. Your presence will be fading soon. It's nearly eleven minutes past eleven."

"And lucky it's not the eleventh day of the eleventh month, because that would have been so not relevant!"

Short Cake chortled at his fatuous aside and rocked on his heels.

Big Mac waddled off towards the glass escalator as Wilson and Daisy followed with Short Cake bringing up the rear.

Walking down the avenue of roulette tables, Wilson couldn't help but notice the lack of an actual roulette wheel and the sounds of gambling from earlier. At the head of each table, instead of the spinning wheel of numbers and the bouncing ball, a glass dome had taken its place. A dome filled with clouds and presenting something like the view one might see from the window of an aeroplane. Daisy caught up with Big Mac and tapped him on the shoulder as they continued walking.

"How do they gamble and bet? They don't have any chips, just a collection of toy models?"

Big Mac raised his voice for the benefit of Wilson as he pointed to the right.

"Each table presents certain scenarios that can arise in the first year of life. The scenarios appear in the glass domes as obstacles to be overcome, problems to be solved. My colleague refers to the domes as the windows on the world."

As he hurried to keep within earshot of Big Mac, Wilson studied the tables to the right and left. They were covered in green baize and in the middle, a grid of numberless squares created a checkerboard pattern of black and red. Instead of coloured chips, one solitary square on each table was covered with a toy model. A die-cast metal car on one table, a washing machine from a doll's house on another and a fireman the size of a toy soldier on the next.

Big Mac now pointed to the left.

"When the ill wind blows, as it is here . . . "

The soupy smoke contents of that particular dome were stirring and thickening. Wilson and Daisy hurried by. On the next table the dome appeared less foggy and the view was settling into focus.

". . . the need for an intervention will be revealed, as it is here."

Wilson pulled up. The image had congealed to portray a real life moving image of baby in a cot or a Moses basket. The baby was red faced with tears streaming down its cheeks. The open mouth appeared to be screaming in silence. The apprentice angel at the foot of the table, a nondescript character dressed in corduroy trousers and a polo neck sweater was toying with figures and models as though they were chips of differing values. He was holding a child's life in one hand and weighing the odds of a successful intervention with the other. The man selected a small white vehicle, an ambulance with a red cross painted on the roof, and rolled it across the green baize of the table. It stopped on a red square. Then the man scooped up a pair of dice, shook them in his hand and sent them ricocheting down the table. They kicked along the baize surface with the bouncing motion of rugby balls.

The man caught Wilson's eye.

"That's my last ambulance. But I've still got a nurse and a doctor left for other emergencies." He selected the appropriate figurines and held them up for Wilson to see.

"You can't have enough medical personnel to hand when you're babysitting. I lost my last toddler to meningitis and had to start all over again. And the poor little chap was only a day away from his first birthday. Another twenty-four hours and I'd have earned my wings. Minimum bet, one life. Yes! Look at the dice, a three and a two makes thirty-two red."

Wilson stepped forwards for a closer look at the image of the distressed toddler inside the glass dome. The emergency was being attended to. A pair of hands poking out from green and white Hi-Vis sleeves could be seen reaching into the cot to comfort the child.

The would-be guardian angel clenched both fists and smiled with joy.

"Hallelujah, my medical professional is saving the day.

Only another thirty-seven days to go and I'm moving on up. Wish me luck won't you."

"Wilson! Come on!"

Daisy was standing at the foot of the glass escalator with Big Mac and Short Cake by her side. As Wilson hurried to cover the distance, he saw Big Mac turn and step down into a stairwell.

Short Cake was waiting to escort them in the same direction.

"Been quite a night hasn't it? But the best is yet to come. Chop chop."

Wilson and Daisy followed him down a flight of ordinary, non-glass stairs to a plain grey door set in a non-glass wall that good reason suggested would lead to a maintenance room or an office.

Short Cake stopped at the door.

"Oh, one thing I forgot to tell you. The angels that fly to the top of The Citadel, those who take the greatest care, well, they receive a special honour. They get to play the high stakes game in here." Short Cake opened the door to a room that was clearly someone's private space for there was nothing transparent about the interior.

Daisy instantly felt the plush, deep pile carpet underfoot. Wilson noticed the crystal chandelier above a single gaming table then the burgundy wallpaper with its lustrous, gold embossed pattern and a drinks trolley in the shape of a globe hinged open on the equator. They both saw the figure preparing the drinks. Big Mac and Short Cake stood to attention on his right, with their hands behind their backs like valets in service of a dignitary. The figure was tall and broad shouldered. He wore a blue, pinstripe suit, cut in a loose, old fashioned style, with a black shirt and tie and the brim of his trilby hat was pulled down at an angle to cover his eyes. The gaming table had a glass dome just like the others, a window on the world filled with swirling clouds, but this table was bigger, double the size of the others and dominated the room. The man in the suit turned from the trolley with two tumblers in one hand and a single tumbler in the other.

"Please, take a seat, I hope you don't mind scotch and soda?"

Wilson recognised something familiar in the sound of his voice.

The man placed two drinks on the edge of the table in front of two stools and walked round to the other side. There was also something familiar in his gait. He took his stool as Wilson and Daisy took theirs.

The man sipped his drink and continued to avoid eye contact.

Daisy nudged Wilson.

"Do you think any of this will make sense tomorrow? It's all completely bizarre."

"Search me. I'm pretty sure this is going to be the big finale though."

The bubbles in the soda water popped on Daisy's tongue.

"Cheers" she motioned to the man in the hat.

"Cheers" he replied, without looking up.

Two models stood on red squares in the middle of the table. One was a hangman's gallows, ten inches in height and clumsily constructed from balsa wood like a schoolboy's history project. The second model was of Westminster Abbey or a replica of some equally majestic cathedral that might have been bought from a souvenir shop.

Cradling a drink on the green baize surface, even at a distance of three metres, it was hard to miss the man's large hands. They were dirty and oil stained and the crescents of grime beneath each fingernail were incompatible with the smart suit, shirt and tie. Wilson sensed the man was play acting and being theatrical to create an atmosphere, building up to a crescendo that surely was only minutes away.

The realisation came with a Snap! First, a matching pair for the suit and the trilby hat and the recollection of a lift in a totemic building and a finger repeatedly pressing buttons. Of going up and down and going nowhere. Then, the recognition of a mechanic's grimy hands and a voice trumped by an all too familiar way of walking.

"Couldn't we have just met you in the workshop? It would have been so much easier."

Mark Sampson slowly raised his head and pushed back the brim of the trilby.

"Aww, I was so enjoying that Wilson, playing the man of mystery."

"Bloody hell, Mark! I should have known from the state of those hands. And I should have put a brick through your window for acting like a robot when I really needed help! Come on Wilson, let's go. Or pinch me at least so I can wake up. This is all just completely stupid."

Wilson placed his hand on Daisy's to hold her back, the dream had still to run its course. There couldn't be much more to follow yet something was still missing. Information to be imparted. A secret to be disclosed. Whenever Big Mac and Short Cake were on stage, there was always a segment of arcane dialogue or a hidden message to take back to bed. For some reason however, the creepy couple were staying tight-lipped, not speaking unless spoken to and Mark Sampson was obviously the reason. They appeared to be in awe of his presence. Wilson put the question to Big Mac.

"Is Mark your boss? And by that, I mean a *really* big boss?"

Big Mac nodded, his hands still clasped behind his back.

"Is he one of The Powers That Be?"

"Indeed! Mr Armitage, you don't miss a thing" said Short Cake.

"So, at last, we've discovered one of the mystical Powers That Be. And I thought you were just a mechanic who helped me fix the Vespa."

Sampson leant over the table and interlocked the fingers of his hands like a canal lock closing.

"The semantics of who, or what I am, are not important right now. And Daisy, I apologise for the inconvenience of not assisting you in your search for Wilson. House rules I'm afraid. Though I have to say, the idea of recruiting those two hockey teachers was a genius move. It was packed in here that night and virtually nobody saw it. A colleague of mine won a fortune. Only hypothetically of course, because we don't have need for money. Pride is what's really at stake. And the chance to knock me off the top floor of course."

Daisy stifled the beginnings of a yawn and missed the significance in the words.

"Wilson, Daisy, I can see that you'll be leaving soon, so let me quickly tell you why I brought you here. Suffice to say, we have a major problem and believe it or not, a phenomenon that goes by the name of social media is to blame. Before Twitter and Facebook and the like, we always found a way of pouring water on our fires. Social media however, has the ability to spread flames like a bush fire. Stamp out a spark here and a thousand ignite somewhere else. We've never had to deal with word of mouth supported by live pictures before and it's a powerful dynamic. According to the traces in my looking glass here, certain matters are about to spiral out of control. Aspects of the future are in the grip of err . . . let's call it a tornado. The near horizon is very disturbed and we can't see what's coming along next because no one can predict where a twister will go."

Daisy released a second yawn and though this proved contagious, Wilson wanted to remain anchored in the room and gripped the seat of his stool.

"Why are you telling us this Mark? What can we do about the future . . . about a tornado?"

"All I can present are the two models in front of you. A symbol of belief in the happy ever after and a short cut to take you there. If I disclose more, my colleagues will accuse me of cheating."

Daisy pushed herself from the stool, now she really had heard enough.

"So even in the face of what you're saying is an impending disaster, you're still playing gambling games?"

"Of course, we must, there is no other way to control outcomes! But I suspect when this is all over we may have to change the house rules, on account of social media. Otherwise our game will soon be up."

"But how are we involved in this? Why did you bring Wilson and me here?"

"Because in looking at the traces of the future, the only intervention that appears capable of calming the storm involves you two. You always appear near the epicentre of the action. So it's a safe bet you're about to play a big part in said intervention!"

Daisy could feel herself fading from the room but had one final question.

"Does any of this involve Sally Bennett . . . or her friend Felix?"

Sampson sipped his drink.

"We've seen his presence, albeit fleetingly and that of Sally Bennett much more so."

Daisy heard Sampson's reply, but as he continued to speak, she was no longer by Wilson's side.

"And there's another interesting aspect to all of this Wilson."

"And I presume you're about to tell me Mark?"

"It's the side bet."

"What's the side bet?"

"The side bet regarding the policemen from Inverness of course. The repercussions from your Vanessa rescue mission are still rippling across this table and attracting plenty of interest. It's what we call an accumulator. You help me Wilson, and the wager is then multiplied by me helping you. It's like placing a bet on a bet, a double down, a mega gamble."

When Wilson woke the next morning, he rolled over on to his favourite side in readiness for dissecting the night's dream and something sharp scraped his chest. He patted the front of his pyjama jacket, searching for the jagged edge of a damaged button but felt something in the breast pocket instead. It was someone's business card, blank on the reverse, but on the front it carried the following details.

Balthazar Smith
Dealer in coins and antiquities
Ground Floor, 247 Chapel Street, Manchester M3 5EP

Chapter 33

What a wus

Thursday 30th November 2017, 8.05 a.m.

"Listen, cos I'm not going to say it again. This business card was not in my pocket when I went to bed. I've never met anyone called Balthazar Smith and I've never been to his antique shop. This was placed on me by Mark Sampson or Big Mac last night!"

Daisy finally accepted the unpalatable truth of another artefact escaping the confines of a dream. It was just after eight in the morning and the conversation concerning the previous night's events had been galloping off in every direction for ten minutes.

"So if it's not bad enough we spend the night talking to one of The Powers That Be about a mystery mission to halt a tornado, we also wake up with another bangle scenario in the form of a calling card. Wilson, this is so messed up. We agreed to avoid The Market Square and all we do is get sucked in deeper."

"Yes, it seems that way, and there's something else, something Mark Sampson said after you left."

"Oh Wilson, I really don't to want hear it. What? Go on, tell me!"

"There's also a side bet involving me and my dad."

"A side bet, what's that supposed to mean?"

"As I understand it, they're still betting on the outcomes

from us finding Vanessa; what the police are going to do next, what will happen to Dad, the 'repercussions' to use Mark's words."

"Oh for crying out loud, this is never going to end. Our lives are not our own. I told you I wasn't comfortable with playing God and now some God like character is blackmailing us for doing just that. If I wrote this story down Wilson nobody would believe it!"

"Mmmm, think that goes without saying Daisy. I guess I need to go and see this Balthazar person as soon as possible."

"But I thought you were supposed to stay at home and rest."

"How can I rest with all this going on? I need to find out what we're being asked to do and the fact that Dad's involved makes it all the more urgent. It's Thursday today so Mum will be working in the shop this afternoon and Dad's home. I'm gonna persuade him to take me to this Chapel Street address. Which means I'll also have to tell him about what happened last night."

"Wilson, that will just make him angrier with me for getting us into this mess."

"Daisy, you didn't do anything, I was the one who decided to find Vanessa and he knows that. I'll call you later this afternoon when I get back. Have you got college today?"

"Yeh, but I don't need to be in until eleven."

"Speak later then."

Gloria was buttering toast and Wilson was eating porridge when the front doorbell rang. Alex was in the lounge watching the morning news on television and rose to his feet. Through the lounge window he saw the police car parked outside the house.

The neighbours will be having a field day.

"Morning Sergeant Jordan."

"Morning Alex, mind if I come in? I need to have a word with you in private if that's possible."

"Er, sure, yes, come in."

Gloria placed the knife down, eyes and ears on full alert like a rabbit when a hawk flies over.

Alex led Sergeant Jordan into the lounge and closed the door. As their conversation commenced, only muffled tones were audible in the kitchen. After five minutes Alex came out looking pale and sheepish.

"I've got to go with Sergeant Jordan love, they've got some new information. Apparently a record of my expenses from BT shows I could have been in Inverness when Vanessa went missing. Montague wants an explanation, he's waiting over at Cheadle Police station. Don't worry. It's nothing."

As Alex went to peck his wife on the cheek he sensed the volcano about to erupt.

"Gloria, no! Don't go there. Nothing you can say will change this. Just let me go and answer their questions. I've nothing to hide and Sergeant Jordan knows that. It's just Montague trying to kick up trouble. I'll be back within the hour."

Three hours later, Sergeant Jordan's car pulled up outside the house and he wasn't accompanied by Alex.

"Is your mother in Wilson?"

"Yes, we're bringing the Christmas decorations down from the loft."

"I need to speak to her. There's been a serious development."

"But there's no way Dad was involved in . . . "

"I know son, I know. This is something else. I really do need to speak to your mother."

Gloria sat on the edge of the sofa wringing her hands and shot an anxious glance at Wilson as the policeman took a seat in the lounge.

"I've got some good news and I'm afraid some rather . . . not so good news."

"Sergeant Jordan, why are you back here without my husband?"

"I'll come to that as quickly as I can, but the good news is we don't think he abducted Vanessa Clarke. The medical records from the hospital in Wilmslow came back and showed that Mrs Clarke paid for private tests because she was concerned about constant headaches. To get to the point, I spoke to a consultant who told me her brain scan revealed irregularities associated with seizures that needed urgent investigation. When I asked if it were possible for someone to have a seizure and in a confused state travel to Scotland, the consultant said similar things had been known to happen. I'm going to pass this information over to Vanessa's husband, he may not have been aware of her illness."

"So if that proves Alex didn't harm Vanessa, where is he?"

"That's the not so good news I'm afraid. He's been arrested!"

Gloria gasped and struggled for breath as though winded by a punch in the stomach.

"For what reason? He's got nothing to do with Vanessa going missing. This is so stupid it's almost bordering on lunacy."

"I agree with you Wilson, but your father hasn't been arrested for that, he was arrested for assaulting a police officer. He thumped Montague in the interview room, and when I say thumped, I'm using Montague's word because it was actually more of a push that caught him off balance. Montague twisted his wrist as he reached out to steady himself and insisted on an X-ray. That was just before I received the news about Vanessa's illness."

Though Wilson's laughter took a while to gain momentum, it eventually brought a smile to Sergeant Jordan. Gloria's expression was one of incredulity.

"Aye, there's a funny side to it all right. Your husband managed to stay calm for an hour of trumped-up nonsense and then he lost it, just for a second. But it's also serious. If Montague wants to go to town with this, your husband, even with an unblemished past could be in a fair amount of trouble."

The jovial undercurrent had developed a nasty rip.

"Come on, you don't get into trouble for pushing a police officer who's obviously trying to stitch you up for something you haven't done. With no evidence to prove anything."

"Aye, but according to the information we received from BT yesterday, there was a tiny possibility your dad could have been in the Inverness area. We have an expenses claim form that shows he bought fuel at a motorway services near Carlisle and at a petrol station in Glasgow and he stayed at a hotel in Perth. And while none of the transaction dates coincide with the day Vanessa was found by the bridge, or the days either side for that matter, ACC Montague suggested that Alex might have fiddled the dates of his expenses to cover his tracks. That's when the push happened and Montague made a meal of it by staggering back."

"Can I go and see my husband?"

"I'm afraid not Mrs Armitage. He's being held in the cells at Cheadle for now. The desk officer is booking Alex and I'm afraid assaulting a policeman is taken more seriously than handbags outside the pub."

"But surely there has to be a lawyer present, someone who'll explain that Dad was provoked and . . . "

"Son, between you and me, the whole thing's embarrassing and should have never reached this point. Montague has taken it upon himself to try and exonerate the force for its alleged failings in the Vanessa case. His failings if truth be told, because only Montague worked on the case and from the missing person's reports alone, he should have been able to connect Abandoned Alice with Vanessa. The problem is, Montague is aware of this and wants to shift the blame, so you being recognised in South Kessock has come as a godsend. He's asked that Alex be kept in jail overnight pending further investigation. What the desk officer will see on the charge sheet is a suspected abductor who used his son to help cover his tracks and then assaulted an Assistant Chief Constable in a police station."

Gloria began rocking on the edge of the sofa. She knew a sting in the tale was coming, it was a recurring phenomenon.

"I checked the guidelines earlier. On conviction of assaulting a police officer contrary to section 89 of the Police Act 1996, Alex could face a sentence of up to 6 months' imprisonment and a fine of £5,000. That would be the worse case scenario."

Chapter 34

News comes thick and fast

Thursday 30th November 2017, 1.30 p.m.

As Wilson was saying goodbye to Sergeant Jordan, Gloria was already on the phone to Cheadle Police Station. The desk officer confirmed that Alex would remain in custody overnight pending the results of blood tests which "will be back early tomorrow morning."

"Blood tests. Why does my husband need blood tests?"

"We need to check for the presence of drugs in his system. If he was under the influence at the time of the assault that will make things a lot more serious."

The desk officer then gave Gloria the phone number of the duty solicitor.

"Please contact her Mrs Armitage, she'll explain the procedures going forward."

Gloria ended the call and her head and shoulders dropped under the weight of shame.

"Wilson, what am I going to tell your sisters?"

'Call me asap. Major problem. Too much to send by text.'

Daisy responded to Wilson's message fifteen minutes later.

"Sorry, I was in a pottery class halfway through glazing a bowl. What's happened?"

"Where are you now?"

"I'm outside, at the back of college. It's okay, no one can hear me."

"There's been a change of plan, I can't go and see this Balthazar character this afternoon. Dad can't take me, he's been arrested. Daisy shush! Please, just listen. He's been arrested because Montague was winding him up and he lost it for a second and pushed him over. It's all being sorted out but the point is, I can't get into Manchester. Mum's not going to the shop this afternoon and she'll have a fit if I suddenly disappear on the Vespa without an explanation. She'll think something's going on with me and Dad that we're not telling her about. Plus, she's really down at the moment. I can't leave her. You'll have to go instead."

Wilson swatted away Daisy's protests and questions as they came flying out of his mobile phone like angry wasps.

"Yes Daisy, I'm sorry, but you definitely have to do it this afternoon."

"Just tell them you have a doctor's appointment or toothache."

"Yes, I'm sure you'll be home in time to see your brother and his kids."

"No, there's no phone number on the card."

"I'll text you the address and attach a photo of the card."

"No, I've no idea why Mark Sampson said he could see the presence of Sally in all of this."

"Okay, I agree, I'll call Sally and speak to her about last night. Maybe she can recognise a connection like you say."

"Text her number to me and text Sally to say I'll be calling. Ask her what time is good and then text me back. And call me tonight when you get home."

"Yes, I do think this will all work itself out."

The duty solicitor returned Gloria's phone calls just after three. Alex was being detained overnight, there was no possibility of visiting and he'd be released before lunchtime the next day subject to the blood tests. The case would come up before magistrates towards the end of January and yes, according to the sentencing guidelines, there was a chance that Alex could go to jail. That was all she could say at that moment.

Wilson received a text from Daisy at three-thirty to confirm she was on the train and just five minutes from Manchester city centre. The text also included Sally's mobile number and an instruction for Wilson to call her at four-thirty.

Montague's right arm, from fingertips to elbow, was encased in fresh plaster and cradled in a sling. The nurse who set the cast queried the need for such a cumbersome dressing when X-rays suggested an elastic bandage would be more than sufficient, but Montague insisted on the full monty. The stark white cast against his smart black tunic would make a dramatic image to accompany the statement he was about to release. The story was uploaded to the home page of the *Inverness Herald* website at four-fifteen.

SENIOR POLICEMAN ASSAULTED BY SUSPECT IN VANESSA CLARKE CASE.

In a remarkable turn of events, Assistant Chief Constable Simon Montague of the North Caledonian Constabulary was seriously injured this afternoon by a forty-five-year-old male at a police station in Greater Manchester. ACC Montague was questioning the man over his suspected involvement in the abduction of 'Alice the Abandoned' when he was the victim of an unprovoked attack. Alice became a local celebrity two months ago when she was identified as Vanessa Clarke, a Manchester based business woman who went missing under suspicious circumstances seventeen years ago. The male suspect is believed to have been involved in a relationship with Vanessa Clarke at the time of her disappearance. When questioned by reporters earlier this afternoon, ACC Montague said he would continue leading the operation which had shifted focus from Inverness to the Stockport area of Greater Manchester.

The article was accompanied by a photo of ACC Montague looking heroic and resolute with his plaster cast the focal point.

The home page was updated twenty minutes later following the receipt of 'further information from an undisclosed source'. The revised copy confirmed that the male suspect was thought to be Alex Armitage, a computer networks expert and government adviser from Stockport, whose son attended Stockport College with Graham Clarke, the son of Vanessa Clarke. Alex Armitage was allegedly having an extra marital affair with Vanessa Clarke at the time of her disappearance.

Trolls were storming the walls of Facebook within minutes of the new revelations being reported.

At four-thirty, Wilson rang Sally as arranged. She was waiting for the call in her bedroom and answered on the first ring.

"Hi Sally, it's Wilson. Daisy told you I was going to call, right?"

"Hi, yes she did. You okay?"

"Yeh, I'm fine. And you?"

"Good thanks. Daisy said you wanted to speak about a dream, it sounded very weird."

"Yes, this one was really odd, even by Market Square standards, like a different category of dream."

"She said you went to the Number 11 Club and met one of The Powers That Be in a casino with angels and Felix and I were mentioned."

"Yeh, you could put it like that. It was all over the place and seemed to go on forever. Like running in a race with no finish line."

Wilson ran out of words at that point as a feeling of uncertainty descended. He was suddenly having second thoughts about the wisdom of the call and not sure where to begin. Discussing angels and heaven and a casino made of glass suddenly didn't seem to make sense in the cold light of an informal chat with a virtual stranger! The conversation's content was about to become so bizarre he was conscious of the fact that any importance might only exist because he was about to talk it into being. In essence, he was about to ask Sally to help him weld sense from incompatible bits of nonsense.

It isn't too late to walk away from this Wilson.

Momentarily daydreaming, as can happen while waiting for a sense of purpose and direction to return, Wilson saw himself standing on the springboard above the diving pool at Stockport Leisure Centre.

"Did Daisy tell you what Mark Sampson told us? That a storm was looming and that we were both in the middle of it. That only *we* could calm the impending storm."

"Yes, she told me that."

Wilson bounced once on the springboard.

"You were also mentioned in the dream and your school friend Felix. The boy in the photo you found with Daisy."

"The spirit of Felix led us to the hidden photo. That was meant to happen."

Wilson dived in.

"Sally, remember when you said you thought your life was on a conveyor belt, on a journey that you had to take, and you felt there was some kind of overlap that connected us? Do you think what happened in that flat, and what Mark Sampson told us last night, could be connected to the same journey? Two parts of your destiny that are tangled with Daisy and me? I know what I'm saying sounds a bit of a jumble, but do you get where I'm coming from?"

Wilson came up for air as Sally considered how to answer the questions with some degree of certainty. Even the early evidence of a connection, the car accident and the quid pro quo of the white room revelation was beginning to feel like two distinct moments of serendipity rather than fate arranging ducks in a row. Then Wilson latched on to something equally strange, but unarguably tangible, and instead of trying to corral flighty happenings like passing clouds, he nailed them to the ground with a stake.

"Did Daisy tell you I woke up this morning with a business card in my pocket that wasn't there when I went to bed?"

"Yes, she said it was for an antique dealer."

"Correct. But I'm not sure that what he does is relevant. It's the fact that someone in The Market Square thought it sufficiently important to defy every law of science, as if by magic, and point me in the direction of a stranger in a building in Manchester. It's a clue, a message for the next step in the journey. A signpost that says we have to go and meet this

Balthazar character."

"Daisy told me your dad's involved, that he was mentioned in the dream as well."

"That's the other thing. Sampson said Dad was a bet on the side and now he's been arrested."

"What? Your dad's been arrested?"

"Yeh, it happened a few hours ago. He was arrested for assaulting the policeman trying to blame him for Vanessa's disappearance. And of course he can't tell anyone the truth, so he has to stay in a police cell overnight. Sally, somewhere under the surface all these parts are connected. It's like an itch from an amputated limb. You can't see where it's coming from, but you still feel it's there."

There wasn't much left to say after that for there was only one conclusion to draw. The conversation had merely reinforced what Sally had been saying all along. Their futures *were* inexplicably linked and neither he, nor Sally, had the slightest notion why. Wilson promised to call the next day with feedback on Daisy's visit to Balthazar Smith.

When the call ended, Wilson sat in silence with a grudging acceptance that something tumultuous was on the way. The comfort zone that he and Daisy were trying to inhabit, if such a place existed, was about to be invaded once again.

He lay back on his bed and stared at the ceiling. Not that he was actually looking at the ceiling, he was wondering why he now had the image of a lifesaving buoy in his head. The red and white striped life preserver you often see mounted in a frame by the side of a swimming pool. The lifebuoy you throw to someone when they're in danger of drowning.

Chapter 35

Eye of the storm

Thursday 30th November 2017, 4.15 p.m.

As the Macclesfield train pulled into Piccadilly station, Daisy checked the route planner on her phone and decided to walk to 247 Chapel Street rather than take the tram. Taking the tram would have been much quicker with hindsight, because navigating the city centre and the Christmas markets had something of the video game about it. *Avoid the woman pushing the double buggy, overtake those dawdlers on the inside, check phone again, cross the road here, oops, sorry, didn't see you on the bike, slip through this chicane of bodies, wait, now go, speed up, slow down, swerve.* The streets were packed with people. Pixie Lott was in town to switch on the lights in Albert Square and no one had told Daisy's phone.

Turning left at the end of Bridge Street with 247 Chapel Street standing just three hundred metres away, Daisy slowed her pace almost to a standstill. On the train twenty minutes earlier she was merely a soldier doing her duty and following orders without question.

"Go and speak to this mysterious Balthazar character Private Meadowcroft. Obtain information in double quick time and report back."

"Yes sir, Captain Wilson! I'm on my way."

Now, with the target in sight, Daisy realised the directive

could have been ill-conceived, the purpose of the mission was unclear and waiting for a set of traffic lights to change she found herself in no-woman's-land.

So what am I supposed to do when I get there? What's Wilson expecting me to say?

"Yes, I know you're only a dealer in rare coins Mr Smith, but are you sure you can't also solve this mystery? It involves angels, a girl I hardly know, The Market Square and Wilson's dad who's been arrested by the police. How did I come to have your card? Oh, that's easy to explain, someone who only exists in a dream and repairs motorbikes put it in my boyfriend's pocket while he was fast asleep in bed!"

Funnily enough, Daisy saw the comical side to her situation just as Wilson was grudgingly accepting his. The lights turned green, Daisy crossed the junction at Trinity Way and arrived at the four storey facade of the old bank building. On a chilly November afternoon, the golden hues of the weathered sandstone seemed to radiate a peculiar sort of welcoming warmth, as though the building was glowing with benign contentment and comfortable in its dotage.

Daisy checked the details on the nameplate then pressed the buzzer for the office on the ground floor. The photo of the business card was her secret password and raison d'être in the event of interrogation. Daisy heard footsteps followed by a bolt sliding to one side. The man who opened the door was of medium height and chubby, with a mop of hair so curly and black it could have been a dressing-up wig. He was smartly dressed in a lime-green Ralph Lauren polo shirt, grey trousers and tan loafers with tassels.

"Hi, can I help you?" the man asked.

"Er, yes I hope so. My name's Daisy Meadowcroft, you

don't know me but I think I'm supposed to show you this." Daisy stepped forwards and held up her phone so the man could read the details on the card.

"That was quick," he said, "we weren't expecting you until tomorrow. Are you here by yourself?"

"Yes, Wilson couldn't make it. His father had a . . . "

"Yes, James told me about that earlier. Well, come on in, Balthazar's in his office, he'll be delighted to meet you."

Daisy glanced up and down Chapel Street with the hope that someone was watching. Somebody who would be able to say at a later date that they definitely saw the missing girl in the bobble hat enter the building on Chapel Street. Never to be seen again.

"It's okay Daisy, you're amongst friends here. I'm Mark, I work for Balthazar. Come in, I'm letting all the heat out. This place is never warm at the best of times."

Daisy climbed the steps and there was no going back as Mark bolted the door behind her.

"Can I get you a coffee, tea, hot toddy? It's bloody cold out there. Where have you travelled from?"

Daisy followed Mark through a pair of glass swing doors and into the former banking hall. She mumbled answers to his questions and paused to admire the distinctive architectural features and the striking, loft-style mezzanine floor. Mark tapped lightly on the door to the Manager's Office and a voice replied in good humour.

"You never normally knock before you enter, so I presume our visitor has arrived."

Mark smiled, opened the door and ushered Daisy inside.

Any lingering feelings of anxiety were dispelled when Daisy saw the welcoming smile coming from the other side of the desk.

Whoa! It's George Clooney's brother.

"This is Daisy, I'm going to make her a cappuccino, do you want one?"

"No, I'm all right thanks. James made me one at lunchtime and I'm still buzzing from that."

Mark closed the door as Balthazar walked round the desk to greet Daisy with a soft and easy handshake.

"Goodness me, your hands are frozen. Come on, let's get you warmed up."

Balthazar suggested Daisy sit at the end of the sofa nearest the fire. She took in her surroundings as she removed her trench coat. The orange glow from embers in the grate made the room feel cosy. Daisy was beginning to warm to the mission.

"So was this once the bank manager's office?"

"Yes, a hundred years ago you might have been in this very room asking me for a loan."

Balthazar pointed to the chimney breast.

"We framed some of the old letters we found when we converted the cellar. Three pounds and sixpence to buy a sewing machine. Things like that. Fascinating! This is the original fireplace and still in working order!"

Balthazar crouched down to stoke the fire with a poker.

"So Wilson found my card I gather. And then sent you to do the real work did he?"

Daisy was on Balthazar's wavelength instantly.

"It tends to work like that with Wilson. He says he's the brain and I'm the brawn. So then I usually hit him."

Balthazar was laughing as Mark returned with Daisy's coffee.

"I've given James a shout. He's on his way down."

James entered the room through the door that led to the stairwell and the other floors. He moved carefully with slow and measured steps and felt for a seat on the sofa opposite Daisy using outstretched arms. When he looked across and smiled in her general direction, Daisy could see the colour in his eyes was missing, the irises had faded away, as though bleached by excessive sunlight.

"How much has been disclosed?"

Balthazar's question was directed at James.

"They had the tour of the Number 11 Club and The Citadel and Sampson presented two artefacts."

"Death and religion?"

"Yes. Those outcomes were already evident so were deemed acceptable. Nothing more was revealed and I believe they're not aware?"

"And the side bet?"

James nodded to no one in particular. "Yes, that was also disclosed."

Mark took a seat next to Daisy on one sofa. Balthazar joined James on the other. Daisy noticed the coils of dark hair on Balthazar's forearm and the gold Rolex watch as he rested his arm on a cushion with his shirt cuffs doubled back. His hands looked strong with the sun dried skin of a yachtsman. The finger nails were manicured. This man was no motorbike mechanic!

Balthazar adjusted his seating position in a way that said it was time to address the subject matter.

"Allow me to get straight to the point if I may. We have a problem Daisy and it's growing by the hour. It's alright if I call you Daisy isn't it?"

"Yes, absolutely" she said without having to think.

I mean come on, who's likely to say no to George Clooney's brother and a voice as charming as that?

"Before I get to the problem, I was thinking a short primer might be helpful."

James dipped his head, guru like, as though acknowledging an undeniable truth.

"Daisy, the reason you're here today and able to sit and listen to what I'm about to say, without running out of that door screaming about the madness inside your head, is because you are a number eleven. And a number eleven's brain is different. It has a special enzyme, one of the Eicosanoids to use the scientific name, that inhibits adverse reactions. In other words, it gives you auto-immunity against being driven up the wall by The Market Square and knowing what the place is capable of. Not only have you experienced The Market Square, you accept it as a real entity, a place that actually exists. This enzyme is the cognitive stabiliser that every number eleven needs to function normally."

Daisy reached for her coffee. She needed to stay alert and stabilised and remember everything for a report that was likely to grip Captain Wilson from the very first page.

"Number elevens were created with the sole purpose of disrupting the linear path of the future. They add an unpredictable and necessary spice to life. A middle ground between a world of murderous chaos, as in *Lord of the Flies*, and a world of pleasant predictability, as in the early days of The Garden of Eden. Have you read the book *Lord of the Flies*?"

Daisy said she hadn't.

284

"Well, in *Lord of the Flies*, a group of schoolboys are marooned on an island and because there are no adults around to supervise them, their primeval instincts surface and they turn into savages. The point being, that without rules and a means to enforce them, civilisation always descends into anarchy. The flip side is The Garden of Eden; a failed experiment by The Powers That Be, where the groundhog days of a perfect life bored everyone to death, quite literally. So The Powers That Be introduced e-numbers, the number elevens, into the mix. The number elevens disrupt the preordained order of things and add unpredictability to life. And with the introduction of these, 'wild cards', the betting on outcomes began."

Balthazar paused momentarily as Daisy sipped her drink.

"Every now and then, a number eleven with 'heightened' abilities, a chilli pepper you might say, is added to give an extra kick to proceedings. As happened with you and Wilson and the unforeseen gold bangles incident. Or the flavour repeats, as with the ongoing Vanessa related difficulties. It all makes for wonderfully unpredictable outcomes.

"The problem is, every so often, a chilli pepper grows from a bad seed and causes a kind of indigestion; outcomes that are unpalatable and impossible to stomach. When this happens, the only response is to reach for an antacid tablet, an antidote. The Powers That Be always have an antidote prepared in the medicine cabinet and the underlying directive in last night's dream Daisy, is for you and Wilson to deliver that antidote and remedy a poisonous situation."

There was nothing wrong with Daisy's hearing, the serious expression on Balthazar's face said as such. This was no joke.

Daisy paused for a moment, as though applying self-censorship to what she was about to say.

"Look, I don't want to sound rude, but to be honest with you, this feels like I'm listening to Mark Sampson talking in riddles again. Apart from the enzyme news, which is good to know, and I suppose does explain why Wilson and I are not in a padded cell, you've still not explained why Wilson was given your card. Can you tell me in plain English exactly what you want us to do? Is this all about that tornado?"

James answered the question as though reading from a legal contract.

"You were sent here, to be reassured by me, that Mark Sampson was correct. The artefacts you were shown on the gaming table are reference points for your navigation."

"Oh, thanks, that's made everything much clearer."

"Your journey started the night you met Wilson and for Wilson, it began beneath the wheels of a car outside Davenport train station when he saved the life of a young girl. You've been chosen, whether you like it or not."

"Chosen for what? That's what I don't understand James. Nobody seems to be getting to the point." Daisy turned to Balthazar. She was afraid she'd leave the building with absolutely nothing to take back to HQ, other than a cryptic request to fix a stomach upset.

"Balthazar, why can't you just tell me what Wilson and I are expected to do?"

"For one simple reason. We can't be seen to be exerting an influence on what happens next by suggesting a particular path. To do so would determine outcomes and invalidate the odds. We can't allow insider dealing to materially influence a true course, we can only offer our support once a decision has been made. That's all I can tell you Daisy. I'm sorry if I have added to your confusion but may I say that if I could have solved this problem myself, I would have done so, I assure you."

Balthazar walked with Daisy out onto Chapel Street.
"I know this must be confusing . . . "
"Balthazar, is there a time scale, I mean, a date by which Wilson and I are supposed to go and deliver this . . . antidote; is it needed soon?"
"You're already en route Daisy, that's why you're here. James has seen the future traces and the twister has arrived. We don't know the course it will take but we expect you to be somewhere in its path."

Making her way across the city centre and up to Piccadilly station, Daisy found herself dawdling. The first days of Christmas are a magical time to be in a big city and Daisy was happy to be anonymous, inconspicuous, drinking in the bucks fizz start of the festive season. She envied the carefree people in the pubs and bars with their after-work drinks and party plans and shopping lists and happy chatter. Looking through the window of Sam's Chop House, a young couple sipping glasses of hot glühwein were so close to the stereotype on her wish list, she would have signed transfer forms for her and Wilson there and then.

After calling into Waterstones to buy an advent calendar for her brother's children, Daisy picked up her walking pace, left her escapism dawdling behind and hurried to catch the next train back to Macclesfield. She was running late.

Back at 247 Chapel Street, Balthazar was sipping an early evening drink and reflecting on the meeting with Daisy. The filigree of life and its fine tracery of implications never failed to amaze him. How a Brimstone butterfly fluttering through an open car window can alter the course of a girl's life in a direction determined on the day she was born. How a prescription for an antidote can be written before all the symptoms are known. How a delivery note can be signed before the consignment has even left the distribution depot. He would never fully understand how that back-dating thing worked.

One day, when he takes his place at the gaming tables of The Citadel of Angels, Balthazar will understand. Until then, the stabiliser, the presence of the rare enzyme will cosset all concerns and a second scotch and soda will most certainly hit the spot.

Chapter 36

Two storms actually

Thursday 30th November 2017, 6.25 p.m.

The platform was packed with people like crackers in a box so Daisy was lucky to find a window seat on the train. A fat bloke with beery breath took the seat next to her and began reading the *Metro*. If Daisy had been able to see the front page headline she might have remembered the name of Bradley Givens from the conversation in the car with Sally and Leanna. The fat bloke nodded off ten minutes later and started snoring. Daisy gave him a nudge to free her arm and took her phone and headphones from her bag. As she clicked 'play' on a Spotify playlist, a message arrived on her screen with a ping.

'I hope your boyfriend's dad rots in hell for what he did to Vanessa Clarke. For seventeen years, that would be good!!!!'

The message was supported by a smiley face emoji and a thumbs up!

What the . . . ?

Daisy was alarmed, shocked and puzzled all at the same time. Although Alex hadn't done anything to rot in hell for, in the eyes of this anonymous texter, he most certainly had! Someone who knew her, her mobile number anyway, must have found out about the police investigation and jumped to an awfully incorrect conclusion. And how many other people were being misguided? The world of social media could be a very small place. A phone call on a packed train was out of the question so Daisy forwarded a message to Wilson with a request to 'text back, can't speak on the train, and where the **** has this message come from?'

Five replies came back like a flurry of newsfeed updates.

'I know, I've twenty messages just like it. Some worse! Inverness newspaper has story about Dad attacking Montague because he was a suspect in the Vanessa enquiry.'

'Story also on *Stockport Advertiser* and *Metro* websites and all round college on Twitter and Facebook.'

'Teaps sent me a message. Said it wasn't him or Michael who told the media. He thinks it was Montague. They spoke earlier. Montague said the real truth will be flushed out.'

'What a mess. Mum going mental.'

'We need to talk about Balthazar as well. How did it go? Was he expecting a visitor?'

'Wilson, too much to say by text. I'll write everything down later and send by email. Once you've read it we can speak. Better to write it, want to make sure I tell you everything. Will send to Sally also. It's true, we're all in this together!!!'

'Yeh, reached that conclusion with Sally earlier. Mum's gone to see her sister, needs her personal space, away from me! She's super upset.'

'Don't worry, we'll sort this, and when it's over, we're getting drunk on glühwein in Albert Square.'

'Albert Square or Market Square?'

'ALBERT!!!!'

Daisy then texted Sally to say she was going to send her an email and asked for the address.

With no phone, shoelaces, watch, wedding ring or a belt for his trousers, Alex was indeed in a strange place, mentally and physically. The police station cell was harshly lit by a single, unforgiving bulb and a wafer thin mattress covered a sheet of plate steel bolted to the wall. There was a loo with no seat and a sink with no soap, or a hand towel. The floor and walls and the ceiling were tiled as one hermetically sealed unit. There were no bars through which one could reach out for help; only a solid metal door with a hatch for food delivery and hourly observation. The only positive that Alex could see, which came during a wave of emotion bordering on hysteria, was the credential for ticking the box *'Get Arrested'* on the poster of *'fifty things to do before you die'* pinned on Wilson's bedroom door.

Alex's mood brightened a little as the young PC who'd brought his evening meal opened the door and stepped to one side to let Sergeant Jordan enter.

The disconsolate look on Alex's face made the perfect pairing with the downcast expression on Sergeant Jordan's.

Throw in calamitous, disastrous, grim and lamentable and you'd have the perfect hand for a game of Unhappy Families.

"I'm sorry Alex, I tried to pull a few strings to get the blood tests back early, to get you released today, but Montague stepped in and insisted standard procedures be followed, carefully and slowly."

"Hmm! I don't suppose Montague has ever had a blood test has he?"

"Not sure what you're getting at Alex, why would he need one."

"To determine if he's a complete idiot or not?"

Sergeant Jordan chuckled at the suggestion.

"Mmmm, if only that test had existed seventeen years ago. But you struck a senior police officer Alex, in a police station, that never goes down well with the bobbies. The desk officer agreed to Montague's pressure, they want to teach you a lesson."

For some reason, Alex wasn't surprised. This was Montague's parting shot before he scuttled back up to Inverness empty handed.

"We've nothing on you Alex, we never did in all honesty, but Montague can defend his motives. He'll state he was just doing his job with good old-fashioned coppering; following a legitimate line of enquiry when he discovered incriminating expenses receipts."

"So now I get a criminal record and automatically lose my job as a government advisor for something I didn't do. For being pushed into a situation I should never have been in."

Alex was wishing he could turn back time, start the day again, sidestep that moment of madness.

"As if I could have fiddled my expenses all those years ago.

Fiddle the dates mind, not the bloody amounts. Just the dates! And I bet I was never anywhere near Inverness that month. I may have been in Perth, but Perth's over a hundred miles from Inverness."

"Alex you need to calm down. Getting worked up is not going to help matters, or your blood pressure."

"So what happens now?"

"They have to release you before lunchtime tomorrow. Your lawyer was going berserk about the request for a blood test without a reason to justify it. She tried, but it was too late to ask a grown-up to overturn Montague's decision."

"Yeh, and if I'd known, I'd have brought my bloody toothbrush."

"I'm sorry Alex, but there's another thing, and that's why I'm here. Someone's leaked a story to the press about the assault on Montague. Your name's been mentioned not only regarding the assault, but as a suspect in the case of Vanessa Clarke. There's a photo of Montague coming out of hospital like some kind of hero with his arm in plaster."

"His arm in plaster? An assault? I only pushed him because he said I cheated on my expenses and he stumbled back in instalments. You were there. Why don't you say something?"

"Alex, he's an ACC. I'm only a sergeant, and nearing retirement. I can't risk taking him on. Look, let's see how this pans out. You'll have your say in court, tell the truth about what happened, how you were provoked, the magistrates will hear the recordings on tape. There's never been any real evidence against you and under oath I'll have to tell the truth. I know there's the possibility of a few months in prison, but in reality, it will be just a fine and community service, I'm sure. I'll write a letter of support if it looks like you'll lose your job."

Anaesthetic takes a moment or two to kick-in, so only then did Alex feel a numbness, as the full implications, the aftereffects of being outed in the press, coursed through his veins.

"Oh no. I need to speak to Gloria urgently. I have to tell her about the story in the paper. It'll be all over social media by now. I don't want her friends and the neighbours and Kate and Megan to find out before she does."

Locked in a prison cell, even the stabiliser was struggling to give immunity to the feeling of being handcuffed to a warped reality.

"Montague won't let you make another call but I spoke to your wife earlier, just after the story broke. She was upset at first but relieved when I promised you'd be home in the morning. I'm off back to Inverness tonight, on the nine-thirty flight with Montague. If you need me for anything she has my number. I'm sorry for darkening your doorstep Alex, I truly am."

The sergeant extended his hand and Alex shook it, he had no issues with this particular officer. Jordan maintained his grip for longer than can be considered polite and didn't let go as his granite grey eyes made enquiries.

"Can I ask you something Alex? Man-to-man. Off the record. Something that won't leave this cell?"

Alex nodded.

"*Did you,* have any part to play in Vanessa's disappearance? I'd like to know the truth, just between you and me."

"No sergeant, I honestly didn't know she was in South Kessock and I had nothing to do with her going missing."

"So you believe your son *really* received an anonymous tip-off? This, Snapchat message?"

Alex felt a bloom of sweat spread across his palms like the telltale response to a lie detector question. Could Jordan be trusted? Was this a ploy? A trap to snare Wilson with his confession? Or was the sergeant simply looking for confirmation that miracles do sometimes happen? Alex took him at face value.

"No Sergeant, there was no Snapchat, but there was a message, a different kind of message which actually came from Vanessa herself, in a way I can't explain."

The pressure around Alex's hand increased by a just noticeable difference.

"Is Wilson different Alex? I mean, does the lad have special talents, skills that ordinary people, people like me, will never be able to understand?"

"You could say that!"

Sergeant Jordan turned to ask Alex a final question as the young PC opened the door from the outside.

"And does the son take after the father?"

Alex nodded.

"Yeh, he's always doing things he regrets."

As a traffic officer drove ACC Montague and Sergeant Jordan down the M56 towards Manchester Airport with blue lights flashing at Montague's request, Sergeant Jordan was peering up at the clear, night sky; marvelling at the twinkling stars and the mysteries of the universe and how truth can often be stranger than fiction.

Perhaps the discovery of Vanessa Clarke was down to Gladys's dad after all. I should listen to my gut instincts more often.

Chapter 37

Swallow after reading

Thursday 30th November 2017, 7.25 p.m.

Daisy's elder brother Ellis and his children, Patrick aged seven and Ellen aged four, were in the hallway donning coats and scarves and preparing to leave when Daisy arrived home.

"Sorry Ellis, I had to go into Manchester to do a favour for a friend. The traffic and all the crowds for the lights being switched on meant it took much longer than I thought."

Ellis could see his sister was flustered about being late so there was no need to apologise as he explained to Ellen that gloves were not mittens, they had five separate fingers just like her hand.

"Make it up to us by coming over with Mum and Dad next week. It's Ellen's dressing up night at pre-school."

Ellen looked up at Daisy.

"And I'm going to be the wicked witch and turn you into a frog with my wand."

Ellen then realised she would never do such a thing and reached out to hug Daisy around the top of her legs. "I'm not a real witch Auntie Daisy. I'm only pretending."

"Oh, what a relief! You had me worried for a moment. In that case, you can have this early Christmas present."

"Look Daddy, Daisy's given us a Christmas window card like the one last year. Does it have chocolates inside?"

"You'll find out in the morning when you open the first

296

window."

Daisy was smiling as she turned to her brother.

"Are you still busy Ellis?"

"Yeh, I'm fully booked with work and it all needs to be finished before Christmas. Got a full house to decorate tomorrow and over the weekend. How's college going?"

"It's good, but things are easing off now, everyone's more interested in parties and planning their holiday."

"If only! Anyway, let's have a proper catch up next week."

Hugs and kisses were passed around like cups of good cheer and after waving until the car was out of sight, Daisy and her parents returned to the lounge.

"There's macaroni cheese in the oven love."

"You got my text to say I'd be late didn't you Mum?"

"Yeh, wasn't a problem. The macaroni might be a bit crisp though. I'm just glad you made it back to see Ellis and the kids. They were just about to leave and would have been so disappointed not to have seen you. Those kids never stop talking about their Auntie Daisy."

"Yeh, I tried to get back as quickly as I could. You should have seen all the traffic for Pixie Lott."

"Wild horses wouldn't drag me into Manchester at this time of year."

Daisy burst out laughing.

"Dad, you don't say much, but when you do, it's always deep and meaningful."

"Bah humbug."

Daisy ate the macaroni cheese and though she wasn't particularly hungry, it felt good, comforting, to be immersed in normal, family life. Later that evening, neighbours called round for a game of Scrabble. Lifting the lid on her laptop, she could hear them downstairs in the lounge, arguing about the validity of one of her father's invented words.

This is the report that was forwarded by email to Wilson and Sally a short while later.

Met with Balthazar - looks like a movie star. Swoon! Also met his assistants Mark and James – both nice as well, think they're partners. Not sure if they were expecting you Wilson but thought I was a day early. They knew about the police and the side bet with Alex. No idea how any of that is possible! They also knew we'd seen the two models, the church and the hangman gallows on Sampson's table!

Now brace yourselves. I'm trying to make gobbledygook not sound like gobbledygook!

Balthazar said when elevens with 'heightened abilities' (like chilli peppers) get together, they combine to make unpredictable flavours, hence the bangles incident. And sometimes, when an eleven comes from a bad seed, they can bring about a poisonous situation. And he said that it was up to us to reach for the medicine cabinet and deliver an antidote???

At one point he went off on a tangent talking about how elevens have a special enzyme in the brain that allows us to cope without going mad. (Er, my enzyme, the 'stabiliser,' isn't working cos I feel like I'm going mad writing all this.)

Balthazar said we had to work things out for ourselves, choose the direction we wanted to take and he could only help once a decision had been made. He couldn't be seen to be influencing outcomes with insider dealing. Something like that.

So, in my opinion, the toys on Sampson's table point the way, like clues. Oh, and this all started when you and I met Wilson, and you rescued Sally under the car. We're involved whether we like it or not.

I asked if there was a timescale and Balthazar seemed to think things will happen quickly. He made it sound like the future was already on its way. All very similar to what Mark Sampson said. I think they were saying they can help once we've worked out what to do. But do what?

Have a think what the reference to delivering an antidote could mean. (Calming the storm? That's what Sampson said. Think back to The Citadel dream Wilson, perhaps there are clues we missed.) Let's all sleep on it and discuss together on the phone in the morning. Can we have a FaceTime meeting with three people? Think so? Too knackered to do more tonight. Need to escape for an hour. Going to play scrabble downstairs. Share your thoughts tomorrow, however crazy they may be. Actually, they need to be crazy!

Daisy

P.S. Sorry for being ungrammatical, wanted to write it all down as I remembered.

Sally texted to say FaceTime would be good. Wilson suggested they speak at nine-thirty and Sally and Daisy replied with a thumbs up. Wilson and Sally then read Daisy's gobbledygook summary of the meeting with Balthazar Smith for a second time.

Chapter 38

Oh my lord

Thursday 30th November 2017, 9.00 p.m.

Leanna was struggling to complete her sudoku puzzle. Sally was reading the contents of Daisy's email for a third time and Kay was in an armchair, in her dressing gown warming her feet in front of the fire. They were together in the lounge, the TV was on and the nine o'clock news had just started.

"Good evening, this is Bundu Amagayou at the BBC. And the headlines tonight . . . "

"Brexit negotiators are at loggerheads as both sides claim minutes from meetings are being leaked by whistleblowers."

" . . . fresh accusations emerge regarding the alleged predatory behaviour of Harvey Weinstein."

" . . . and after paranormal activity is captured on camera at a property in Cheshire, we'll be joining Kimberley Charlton for a live update."

"UK Brexit negotiators have today accused . . . "

"Told you it would be the third feature story."
Leanna didn't bother to look up from her sudoku.
"No one was debating it with you Kay."
"This will all turn out to be a hoax, I'm certain of it."
"A hoax. For what reason?"
"To demonstrate how easy it is to fool people with fake

news. Serious journalists are sick and tired of all the poison being spread on social media and to be honest, it's dangerous. Politicians use it to spread lies like butter. Russia uses it to influence elections in other countries. I think someone's doing this to make a point."

"Seems like a complicated way to make a point if you ask me." Leanna remained focused on the puzzle. "And they've gone to an awful lot of trouble with all the special effects and the flashing lights and a reporter having a fight with himself."

"Yes, but it won't just be one person, there'll be a team of people behind it."

"I still don't get the point."

"Leanna it's obvious. They're doing this to make a name for themselves. Hoping to win a journalism award for a fake story that exposes how easy it is to create fake stories. Something along those lines. The one thing I can say with certainty though, is that nothing will happen in that house tonight. They've made their protest."

There ended the gospel according to Kay.

"He was once the king of Hollywood but tonight, Harvey Weinstein is facing . . . "

Kay placed her wineglass on the coffee table. "I need to nip to the loo before it starts."

Leanna had finally cracked the puzzle and numbers were going down like nine pins.

"Sally, I'll say one thing for your Auntie Kay, she has an opinion on everything and doesn't mind letting you know about it."

All were sitting comfortably when the third feature story

began.

"For three consecutive nights, strange phenomena, caught on camera at a mansion in Cheshire, have set the world of conspiracy theorists alight. Some are calling the paranormal activity proof of the afterlife, but rather than a message from the great beyond, could there be a more down to earth explanation? We're going live to Kimberley Charlton in Tarporley. Good evening Kimberley."

It must have been bitterly cold outside The Maltings because Kimberley was wearing a cossack style fur hat, her nose and cheeks were bright red and you could see her breath when she spoke.

"Hi Bundu, good to be with you."

"Kimberley can you briefly give us some background to this story."

"Yes, I'm standing outside a large, executive style home near the village of Tarporley here in Cheshire's stockbroker belt."

The front elevation of The Maltings was clearly visible over Kimberley's shoulder by virtue of the lights running up the drive.

"Look Sally, she's trying to stop herself from laughing. If Tony Chapman really did get beaten up by an invisible man last night, she wouldn't be standing there looking so relaxed. She'd be terrified. I told you it's all a hoax. And Kimberley Charlton is probably . . . "

"Auntie Kay, shhh, I'm listening."

"Five days ago, the owner of this house, Bradley Givens, died in car crash after allegedly stealing a valuable painting from Delbury Hall, just a few miles down the road from here.

Mr Givens is thought to have been the mastermind behind a string of thefts involving artworks and notoriously taunted police by leaving a calling card in the name of 'the invisible man'. A sort of catch me if you can challenge. The night after his death, a newspaper photographer took this photo."

Kimberley held the image up for the cameraman and pointed out the apparition that many believed was Bradley Givens sending a message from beyond the grave. An apparition in the form of a ghostly figure throwing a rug over furniture as though it were a dustcover.

"The following night, the house staged an inexplicable light show as this footage, caught on camera, shows."

The video clip of the flashing lights incident is accompanied by the verbal description of *The Sun* reporter who was recording it at the time.

The camera switches back to focus on the head and shoulders of Kimberley.

"Then last night, a crowd of hundreds standing here outside the gates, not to mention all those watching the news at home, were witness to a physical assault on my colleague Tony Chapman. His injuries required hospital treatment yet those in close proximity to Tony described the perpetrator as invisible, the invisible man perhaps?"

"So Kimberley, is a close encounter of the third kind expected tonight?"

"Ha, I'm apprehensive but I should be safe. There are some rather burly security men with me just in case."

"I can see there's a sizeable audience behind you there."

"Yes! People have been flocking here all day. It's become the destination for something of an exodus. A clarion call for those with every type of religious and spiritual belief. I've spoken to people of every faith, from the orthodox to the unorthodox. I even met one chap who'd driven up from Sussex to represent Opus Dei. He told me he'd thrashed his car to get here as quickly as he could, tongue in cheek of course, so that tells you there's also something of the outdoor theatre about all of this."

The cameraman scanned over the heads of the crowds behind Kimberley and the messages on the placards in the foreground were clearly visible.

'Give us another sign'

'Show us the afterlife. Show us the way'

'You can't say you weren't warned'

The cameraman, who was clearly a Manchester United fan, made a point of zooming in on the placard of one particular zealot which simply stated 'Cantona is King'.

"Kimberley, it seems the invisible man has developed a touch of stage fright. Could there be a more down to earth explanation for these phenomena?"

Kay leant forward and increased the sound volume with the remote. "Here we go Sal, this is the moment. This is where she'll say it's all a hoax to expose fake news."

"Yes Bundu. I had a phone number for the ghostbusters to hand but thankfully, I don't think we'll be needing it tonight."

Kimberley was still laughing at her own joke when she was hit in the face with such force even the TV viewers could hear the crack of her nose being broken. The invisible fist then smashed the lens of the camera and the editor was forced to switch to a second cameraman filming the house. His camera captured sensational footage of a driveway light exploding, then a second, then a third and the trail of destruction led all the way up the drive. The bulbs in two porch lights shattered, the front door flew open as though caught in a hurricane and then interior lights began to switch on and off with a mind of their own.

Kitchen. Upstairs. Kitchen. Hallway. Porch. Pause.
Kitchen. Upstairs. Kitchen. Hallway. Porch. Pause.
Kitchen. Upstairs. Kitchen. Hallway. Porch. Pause.
Duh. Dah. Duh. Dah. Duh.

The placard bearer's prayer had been answered in the most dramatic and extravagant fashion. A man with underlying health issues died from a heart attack during the melee that ensued between the believers drawn to the miraculous and the horrified fleeing the dangerous.

Kay's face was white, as though she'd just seen a ghost, which of course, in a way, she had.

"That wasn't supposed to happen. Was it?" Leanna was confused by what she'd just witnessed. By the way it contradicted everything Kay had been so certain about.

"Auntie Kay, her nose was smashed by something, I saw the blood. That wasn't fake."

"Sally, can you go and get my phone please? It's charging on the kitchen table."

Kay rang a colleague on the news desk in Media City and ended the call a few minutes later after receiving irrefutable answers to her questions.

In a zombie-like state she continued to stare blankly at the screen even though Leanna had switched the television off.

"Auntie Kay, that wasn't fake news was it?"

"No love. They're waiting for the ambulance to arrive. They think Kimberley's got concussion, a broken jaw, a broken nose and her front teeth were knocked out. The security men said there was nobody standing within a metre of her."

"What's going on Kay? What have we just seen?" There was a tremble of fright in Leanna's voice.

Kay was sobering up in record time.

"If your eyes are working like mine Leanna, I'd say we've just seen a dead person advertising the existence of the afterlife live on TV."

"Why would the invisible man want to do that, to hit somebody again?"

Kay had to think deeply to give Sally a reply. What sounded like a straightforward enquiry was loaded with ramifications she'd never had to contemplate before. It was as though Sally had invented a new type of question.

"Who knows love? He's certainly got the attention of the entire world from tonight. The religious, the atheists, the agnostics. It's going to make everyone believe in another realm of existence after we die. I'm struggling to make sense of it Sally."

"Are people going to kill themselves Kay? Those with nothing to live for might take a chance on the other side being a better option, now they're certain there's another place to go."

It was at that moment, that Kay fully grasped the staggering implications of what Bradley Givens had achieved.

"You're right Leanna. If you've nothing to live for, the lonely, the terminally ill, the war weary, why wouldn't you choose to move on? This is proof God exists – or proof of a place beyond the grave at the very least. It's going to cause a tsunami Leanna, a tsunami of theism. An unnatural disaster!"

Sally didn't need to read Daisy's email for a fourth time.

Chapter 39

Please turn off your phones

Friday 1st December 2017, 6.30 a.m.

Aftershocks from an evangelical earthquake were registering in every corner of the globe as Kay arrived for an emergency meeting with the news division and the regional director of BBC North West. Fear was evident in the grave expression and the worry lines creasing her forehead. Wars, famine, plague, terrorism, revolutions, Kay thought she'd covered it all; but this was on a different scale altogether, up there with an alien invasion or an asteroid on a collision course. Kay knew the meeting would be pointless. This wasn't a news story; a question of how to report yet another catastrophe; which camera angles cover all the different viewpoints. This was a metaphysical tipping point for all seven billion souls on earth and the church would be writing the headlines not the media.

Wilson had been awake since four-thirty, Daisy since five and Sally hadn't slept all night. Vapour trails crossed in cyberspace as emails flew from one to another. By six, Sally had control of air traffic, three flight paths were aligned as one and all incoming messages were landing with the same subject line: Bradley Givens.

A plan was required. A plan to snuff out a tornado. To extinguish the twister in the guise of a rogue spirit. To administer the antidote to a poisonous chilli pepper. Mankind was not prepared for the infection being spread by Bradley Givens, Mark Sampson had said as much. Maybe not in those words, but the portents from the models on his gaming table were as clear as the nightmare that had clarified in his window on the world. Daisy was adamant about the need to consult with Balthazar. Wilson was exhausted, his head spinning, he needed sleep. They all did! A rendezvous at eleven on FaceTime was agreed.

Kay's emergency meeting was descending into chaos. Of the seven people in attendance, four maintained the view that the incidents outside The Maltings were misguided stunts, orchestrated by publicity seekers sending discarnate messages about faith and spirituality. Someone with a twisted sense of humour called the stunts an 'immaculate conception'.

"Or what about extreme fundamentalists trying to send some archaic message to coincide with the first day of Christmas?"

"But Frank, you saw what everyone else saw live on TV last night. So you're saying a group of religious nutters have developed a new weapon, an invisible fist that can smash someone's teeth in. My niece saw what happened. That was no stunt. Kimberley couldn't have broken her own nose and she had security people on all four sides."

Kay had woken with a start during the middle of the night convinced the world as she knew it was about to end, but the people around the table were simply sticking their heads in the sand hoping the issue would go away. In her opinion, Bradley's spirit, a ghost, had been caught on camera for four consecutive nights, for the first time ever, for all the world to see and she was not prepared to side with the abstainers.

"Look this isn't an episode of Haunted House. Kimberley is in hospital with real injuries. You saw the bulbs on the drive exploding. Tim Geary at *The Sun* just tweeted that there was no power to the house and yet the lights inside continued flashing for half an hour. How do you explain that?"

"How do *you* explain it Kay?"

As the regional director, Frank had taken his usual position and was sitting on the fence.

"Look Frank, I know what I'm willing to accept goes against every atheist principle in the book, I have a science degree for goodness sake. But there's an awful lot of people in the world that don't give a toss about algebra and Boyle's Law because they believe in a different law, the law that states when we die we go to heaven. Whichever heaven that happens to be. It doesn't matter which faith you follow, Christian, Muslim, Hindu, the point is, those people who believe there's a stairway to heaven are vindicated by this. They'll claim this as concrete proof. And my point is, why not? Why couldn't it be true? The thousands who flock to St Peter's Square or walk to Mecca or are guided by the Koran, they all believe in their own particular brand of God. Well, maybe he just rocked up and said hello to all of them from Tarporley. If it's not a stunt, not fake news, and I don't believe it is, there's no other explanation, no matter how mind-blowing the reality of it may be. Anyway Frank, if you think what we all saw was an episode of *Jackass*, why did you bring us here at this ridiculous hour?"

"Because reports had started to arrive of an elderly couple in Warrington taking their own lives and leaving a suicide note to say, 'they were joining Bradley Givens on the other side!' There was an emergency cabinet meeting last night but the government have pulled back from commenting. They've chosen not to make a statement and are praying for it to stop I would imagine. Worst-case scenario, it'll be a permanent number one in the Top Ten of conspiracy theories. Or, in my opinion, it's an elaborate hoax that went too far. The police are going to enforce a perimeter around the property. No reporters, camera crews, general public, wise men bearing gifts, nobody will be within a mile of that property tonight. If this show really is the work of a spirit from another dimension of existence, he won't be breathing the oxygen of publicity tonight."

Kay was annoyed.

"Frank, Goebbels once said that if you told a lie enough times, people would believe it. So he made up stories about how the Jews were destroying German society and brought about the holocaust. A holocaust the allies wouldn't accept until they saw it with their own eyes. Frank, you're not opening your eyes! Spirit or not, the masses are going to put their faith in this and the couple in Warrington are just the start."

The meeting was over as far as Kay was concerned and she left Frank's office with an over the shoulder remark about an ostrich with its head in the sand. She needed to get closer to the news story of the century, of all centuries, and it was happening literally on her front doorstep.

Three hours later, Gloria was trying to hold back tears and retain her dignity as she remonstrated with the member of the board of trustees responsible for the Cheadle charity shop.

"But Alex hasn't been charged with anything to do with

Vanessa Clarke. It was all a misunderstanding."

"Mrs Armitage, your husband assaulted a policeman in Cheadle police station. The shop you manage is in the centre of Cheadle. I've spoken on the phone to the trustees this morning and they agree unanimously. Until this matter is resolved or it all blows over, we think it best if you step back from . . ."

"But that shop is my life. I opened the shop, I found the premises, I've put ten years into it. Everyone in Cheadle knows me from that shop."

"Exactly Mrs Armitage, that's the point, everyone in Cheadle knows you, and they also know your husband was arrested and is also linked to a missing person who is also the mother of your son's best friend. People will be talking about you and that isn't acceptable to the charity. I'm sorry, but you are suspended from work until further notice. Without pay!"

"But I don't take any pay, I don't even claim expenses to travel there. I know the other shop managers do but I never have."

"I'm sorry Mrs Armitage, there's nothing more to say. Goodbye."

Gloria threw the phone down the hallway shortly after the conversation ended.

Alex stood on the battery when he opened the front door later that morning. Then he saw the battery cover and the damaged phone on the floor. The trail of destruction led to the kitchen where Gloria was wiping tears from her eyes.

"What's happened love?" He placed the pieces of phone on the table and reached for Gloria's hand but she snatched it away.

"Don't touch me."

"Gloria, what's happened? Why is the phone in pieces all over the hall?"

Gloria glared at her husband then her face crumpled and squeezed out more tears.

"I've been fired from the shop."

Despair was manifest in the wretched contortion of her mouth.

"Gloria. Love. Why?" Alex reached out once more for his wife's hand.

"Because of you Alex, because of what you did. You hit a policeman."

"Oh, for crying out loud. I only pushed him. And I'd do it again. He was virtually asking for it, goading me on purpose."

The muscles in Alex's forearms tensed and his fists clenched.

"Where's Wilson, I need to have a word with that son of mine?"

"He's upstairs in his room."

Alex checked his watch.

"It's bloody lunchtime."

"I let him sleep."

Alex stormed off. "This is getting ridiculous. It's out of hand."

Gloria heard Alex thumping up the stairs.

"Wilson. You and I need to have one of our little chats."

All was quiet for a minute and then Alex came back and stood in the kitchen doorway.

"He's not in his room Gloria. He left this note."

Dear Mum.

Don't be worried about me. I have to go out and not sure when I'll be back. I think I know who sent me the message, the Snapchat about Vanessa. I can't clear things up if I'm stuck in the house. This will help Dad. And Mum, I know you're worried and you want me to get better, but I have to get to the bottom of something. I'll send you a message later. Love Wilson.

"I just checked, his Vespa keys are not on the hook."

Chapter 40

On the road again

Friday 1st December 2017, 11.30 a.m.

The garage door dropped silently back into the closed position. Wilson then pushed the Vespa for a hundred metres, zipped up his parka, swung the rucksack over his shoulder, locked the clasp on his helmet and kick-started the scooter. It fired up first time thankfully and he pulled away from the kerb. Cheadle was four miles away and Sally's address was in his phone. As the Vespa climbed the hill out of Bramhall village, with each bend, each stretch of road, Wilson knew the role he was about to play in the unfolding drama was being chiselled into the present on the runes of the future. He was convinced his complicity in what lay ahead was non-negotiable and every second brought it closer. There was no turning back.

He pulled onto a garage forecourt just outside the centre of Cheadle and sent a text to Sally.

'I'm at the petrol station, round the corner. Exactly where you said. Bring a warm jacket.'

Sally was wearing black Ugg boots, green leggings and a tartan duffle coat as she hurried across the tarmac. Wilson raised the Vespa seat to retrieve a spare helmet. Sally gathered her hair and he helped pull the helmet down over her head.

"Ouch." Wilson's hand recoiled at the crack of static.

"Jesus Sally, does your hair always do that? You could power a small town with all that electricity."

"Yeh, always, and it's been getting worse these last few days."

The exchange of looks said everything that needed to be said.

"Button up your coat, we need to get going, Daisy will be waiting. Have you been on a scooter before?"

"No. What do I have to do?"

"Climb up behind me. And hold on tight."

Sally had to shout over the engine noise as the Vespa pulled off the forecourt.

"Wilson did you bring your bag?"

Wilson's helmet bobbed up and down and he took his hand off the accelerator to raise a thumb. The rucksack was clamped between his legs.

Wilson followed the A34 all the way into the centre of Manchester, through Chinatown and Spinningfields and jacked-up the Vespa in an empty parking space at the rear of 247 Chapel Street. Then he rang Daisy who said she was two minutes away. Wilson took Sally's helmet and locked it back under the seat.

"What did you tell your Auntie Kay?"

"She wasn't home but I left a note. I said I was going to meet Daisy and I'd be back at teatime."

"Okay. Come on let's go."

Daisy was walking to meet them from the opposite direction as they turned the corner. They met halfway, outside the double doors with the grimy name plate.

Balthazar Smith. Dealer in coins and antiquities.
Ground Floor

The Manchester Lepidopterist Society.
Floor One

The Savants' Club.
Floor 3b

Wilson stepped back to take in the four floors as Daisy had done the previous day.

"Interesting building! Looks a bit out of place with all of these new flats. I think Hoover's sister rents one around here somewhere."

"Wait until you see inside. It's really cool."

Daisy stepped up to press the buzzer for the ground floor and while waiting for a response, she gave Sally a hug.

"You okay?"

"Yeh. I'm good. Nervous, cos I hope we're right, but good as well, because it feels like the journey is starting to have a purpose, like it's really beginning, if that makes sense?"

Daisy gave Sally a second hug and a reassuring smile that was for joint benefit; she was also harbouring a thought that the conclusion they'd reached could be embarrassingly wrong.

"Wilson's scooter's great!"

"You're lucky. He's never taken me for a ride on it. What did you tell Kay?"

"She's at work and it's Leanna's day off, so I left a note to say I was meeting you because Leanna sometimes calls round to see if I'm okay. Did you bring your bag?"

"Yes, it's here." Daisy twisted her shoulder to show the

overnight bag.

Mark opened the door and ushered all three inside.

The Manager's Office was too small for six people so Balthazar led them up to the mezzanine floor with its executive style table and high back, swivel chairs. Mark and James joined them moments later and Balthazar made the introductions.

"So," he said, lifting his arms to the ceiling and peering upwards, "the stars have aligned and the moment has arrived."

James nodded. His milky white eyes though blind to the present, had seen the coming together as foretold on the third floor.

Balthazar continued. "I presume Daisy has brought you up to speed following our get together yesterday?"

Sally and Wilson both said she had.

"Excellent, so no need to read the minutes of the last meeting."

Wilson agreed with Daisy's reference to Balthazar as George Clooney's brother.

Friendly face, tall, athletic looking, early fifties maybe. The casual clothes are obviously expensive. Genuine smile. Super relaxed. I once had a Rolex like that.

Daisy removed her coat, took a seat, tucked loose strands of hair behind her ears and got straight to the point.

"We know why we were sent here Balthazar. Why Wilson woke up with your card. Sally worked it out."

"We have to tell you our plan and then you can help us make it happen?" said Sally.

"That's correct."

Sally reached for Daisy's hand under the table.

318

"We have to extinguish the spirit of Bradley Givens."

"Also correct."

Balthazar smiled and appeared relieved, as though a difficult task, that of identifying a business strategy, had been agreed by the board with unexpected haste. Sally continued.

"The three of us must decide how we're going to do it and then you can help us."

Balthazar brought his hands together to form a dome with his fingers and nodded. As fingertips bounced off one another it was clear to Wilson he was waiting for a final part of the strategy to be confirmed.

"But you can't give us any advice, because if we follow your suggestions that means what happens in the future will have been determined by you. Like the observer effect. Nothing can be measured in pure terms, because the person doing the measuring has an influence on the measurement simply by being there. So the result can never be true."

Wilson's statement ticked the remaining box.

"Exactly! And I must say, that is pretty impressive given the sparsity of guidance!"

The corners of James's lips curled upwards. He was also impressed by the speed with which the code in the cryptic messages had been cracked. They'd got it in a nutshell.

Sally and Daisy shared a congratulatory smile and released each other's hand as Balthazar shifted the conversation into a new gear.

"I think at this point, it would be useful for you to know the background to the life and times of Bradley Givens. Mark can you take our guests through the relevant chapters."

Mark cleared his voice and over the course of twenty minutes presented all the information considered relevant and permissible. Daisy had no doubts that Bradley Givens had gotten exactly what was coming to him. Now they had to complete the job by fully extinguishing his fire.

"So we have to find a way to stop the spirit of Bradley Givens from continuing to expose the existence of the afterlife and bringing about catastrophic . . . repercussions. That's what the models on Mark Sampson's table, the church and the hangman's gallows, represented."

"Correct" said James "and for us to avoid steering your decisions and influencing outcomes, best not to ask too many questions like why or how."

James folded his arms and waited for the conversation to continue.

This time, Daisy spoke up.

"If Bradley's building pyramids from furniture, switching lights on and off and punching people, surely, he'll use up his excess energy fairly quickly? He can't keep this going for a hundred years?"

This was the same point Mark had raised in Balthazar's apartment.

"Bradley is clever. He knows the best way to make an example of himself is via social media. Text messages are one thing, but link a short video to a tweet and you create a viral blockbuster and irrefutable evidence of the hereafter. It's what millions of people have been praying for and Bradley has given them a sign. Anyone struggling with this life, will become a 'follower,' a devout convert. Putting on a light show in a house with no mains power and assaulting reporters with an invisible fist certainly makes the world take notice. So now we're all listening, Bradley doesn't need to yell anymore, he can sit back, conserve his energy and perform a minor miracle every now and again just to keep his account active."

Wilson agreed with Balthazar. "He's going to carry on until we stop him. After all, isn't that why we're here, on this journey? It's meant to happen. Bradley's light won't go out until we put it out, because we're the ones destined to do it."

"So why is he doing this Balthazar?" Sally raised her hand before asking the question then quickly realised she wasn't in school.

"For revenge! Pure and simple! When The Powers That Be realised the Bradley experiment had failed and their warnings ignored, we were instructed to despatch butterfly assassins to bring about his demise. Bradley views that as an act of murder and now wants to get his own back. It's not the first time an incident like this has arisen, we've had many rogue spirits over the centuries, though I must admit, none as social media savvy as Bradley Givens."

"But did he not realise the pain and . . . "

" . . . suffering, caused by exploiting the gifts bestowed by The Powers That Be? No Daisy, that simply didn't register. He was innately evil in life and in death there's still no goodness in his soul."

Given that a methodology for extinguishing a fully grown rogue spirit still needed formulating, something totally unexpected happened next. Sally stood up, took her coat from the back of the chair and said she had to go!

"Kay will be home soon. I'm supposed to be there when she arrives. Daisy you have to come with me. Mark you have to drive. And Wilson, you have to stay here."

Sally buttoned up her coat and delivered the words in an emotionless monotone as though it was an immutable directive and sacrosanct. She stood waiting for her instructions to be followed. It was as though she'd made a move in chess that hadn't been seen before.

Balthazar nodded at Mark. Daisy shook the look of astonishment from her face and obeyed orders.

"Daisy you don't need your coat or bag. Mark brings you back."

Daisy let her bag fall to the floor as she glanced at Balthazar.

"It's happening" said James. He'd maintained an upright, straight-backed position throughout the conversation and his glassy eyes were staring into empty space.

Balthazar reached out and patted his shoulder.

"We're there now James, you can log off for the afternoon, thanks, you've done well."

Mark kissed James on the forehead. "See you later." Then he motioned to Sally and Daisy.

"All right then, let's get Sally home to her Auntie Kay."

Wilson asked Daisy if she was okay about leaving.

"Yeh, I'm good. Nervous, uncertain, on-edge, terrified and probably insane, but apart from that, I'm fine."

Mark was laughing as he led the way down the metal staircase.

"Join the club Daisy, join the club."

Mark's vehicle was a people carrier with tinted windows and an electric side door.

"I feel like a celebrity, like a *Spice Girl* about to be ferried to a VIP party" said Daisy, looking over her shoulder for the seatbelt.

"Which *Spice Girl*?" asked Sally.

"Mad Spice" said Daisy, clicking the clasp into place.

"Mark, if you take us to the centre of Cheadle, Sally can direct you to where she lives from there."

"No problem!"

Mark eased the car into the traffic and slipped on the headphones connected to the car's music system. Better he didn't hear the conversation coming from the back.

As they followed the A34 out of the city centre, Daisy experienced a sense of foreboding. A mood change that left her feeling anxious and disorientated; as though it had suddenly dawned on her that she was lost in a foreign place.

Sally stared straight ahead without speaking until the car approached Cheadle village when her voice broke the silence.

"Something is going to happen to Wilson tonight. It's not something bad, but afterwards he won't be the same person."

"What? What are you talking about? What's going to happen? Sally, you're worrying me."

Sally continued. Her voice had the matter of fact tone of a virtual assistant.

"Don't worry. It's going to be a good thing. I saw this car journey as well."

"How? When did you see this?"

"Last night, when I couldn't sleep. I saw the red light again and I was on Wilson's scooter and we were hurtling along. People on the pavement passed by walking ten times faster than normal. It felt like time was racing towards the future. I saw everything that's happened today before it happened. I could have kept my hand down when I asked that question before, cos I knew you'd all find it funny, but I wanted to keep everything exactly as it was supposed to be. And this is the really weird part. The film showing the future stopped on the word stopped, which is the word stopped, that I just said. I think this is where my involvement ends."

Sally turned side on to face Daisy.

"From tonight, you and Wilson take over. I have brought you to this moment, as I was supposed to, since the day I was hit by that car. Now you have to do the rest."

After dropping Sally at the entrance to the vicarage, Mark felt Daisy tap him on the shoulder.

"Mark, we need to get back as quickly as we can. I think Wilson might be in some kind of trouble!"

Chapter 41

3b

Friday 1st December 2017, 5.00 p.m.

Balthazar excused himself to shower and change and left Wilson and James talking on the mezzanine floor.

"My father was a doctor and my mother a dentist. I was never ill. Never had a filling."

James opened his mouth to reveal perfect teeth which had the intended consequence of making Wilson laugh out loud.

"I discovered I was a number eleven on my third visit to The Market Square. I was sixteen at the time. Do you know what The Market Square is Wilson?"

"I think so; it's a place where the energy from dreams converges with the energy from actions of the past. It sounds pretty weird admitting that. Because you only go there in a dream, you sort of accept the place as a figment of the imagination, but it's real. I couldn't have woken up with Balthazar's card in my pocket and all the other things that have happened if The Market Square wasn't an actual place. Though don't ask me to explain The Gateway or The Citadel of Angels or who Big Mac and Short Cake are."

"I haven't been to The Citadel and The Gateway only once, on my eighteenth, but I communicate with Big Mac and Short Cake on the top floor sometimes."

"Can you tell me what happened to your sight? I don't

mean to . . . "

"That's okay. It was a self-inflicted accident many years ago. My irises and retinas burned out when they were overloaded with visual data. Too much information you might say, and the surge of energy was so strong that even closing my eyes made no difference."

"How? What were the circumstances?"

"Remember how you walked towards Ward 3B in Stockport Infirmary and into a wall of energy? Well, something similar happened to me."

Wilson shuddered at the memory and was startled by the fact that James knew about the episode. Then he saw the blindingly obvious in the earlier reference to Big Mac on the top floor.

"There's one here in this building isn't there? That's why the top floor's called 3b, like it says on the nameplate outside?"

"Yes, Balthazar does like his little jokes."

"Whoa."

Wilson pushed himself away from the table as a primitive defence mechanism kicked in, something like the instinct to step back on a station platform when a train thunders through. And since the chair's casters were well lubricated, Wilson nearly toppled off the edge of the mezzanine floor. James then heard another "whoa" as Wilson applied the brakes with his feet.

"You've got a Ward 3B energy funnel running through this building? On the top floor?"

"Yep, we most certainly do."

Wilson dug in his heels and pulled himself back to the table. "I'll give the guided tour a miss if that's alright with you."

"I didn't lose my sight here though, that happened in

a different 3B. I was retrieving an artefact, under similar circumstances to you actually, and all the electrical charge in my body was neutralised. I was in a coma for five weeks and when I recovered, my eyes had been so badly damaged I was left permanently blind. Anyway, to cut a long story short, I woke up with Balthazar's business card under my pillow and came here to meet him. He told me the energy flow in this building wouldn't be a problem and I trusted him. I entered 3b, I still remember that moment like it was yesterday, and it was like I could feel the energy from every 'polaroid moment of time', to use Big Mac's term, passing through me. And when I turned around I could also see the photos yet to be taken. That's when I realised that in losing my sight, I'd found a new ability. I could track the past to the present and follow it forwards into the future, I could see in the dark."

"Is that why you work for Balthazar? Because on the top floor you sense things that help with the work he does?"

"Yes, in 3b I can grab a snapshot of the future and then trace its timeline all the way back to the present. Then after an intervention, the despatch of a butterfly for example, I appraise the outcome and report back on the possible repercussions."

"James, I'm so sorry you lost your sight."

"It's okay. It was a long time ago and I'm used to it now. Being able to take a glimpse of the future more than compensates."

"That's amazing. Really, really incredible. I don't suppose there's any chance of the lottery numbers for tomorrow night is there?"

"Sure Wilson, but then I'd be able to see how unhappy all the money will make you, so trust me, you don't want those numbers."

"Hah hah hah, okay, good point. Not sure I can get my head round that."

"It's like playing Tetris. Think of every future moment as a brick falling into place. When the bricks are at the top of the screen you have plenty of time to shift them around. But then there's this last minute rush when everything locks into place and forms the present and it's too late to change anything. In 3b I can see how making an intervention to shift a forthcoming moment to a new position will change the here and now."

Wilson could visualise the analogy.

Perhaps dropping a handwritten note in Vanessa's lap was the equivalent of a Tetris brick dropping in an unintended slot. Everything thereafter had stacked up in the wrong way.

"I'm guessing it was a last minute change of plan that brought Daisy here instead of you?"

"Yeh, Dad shoved a policeman in Cheadle police station and that messed things up."

"Like I said, the far horizon is easier to manage because you have more time to play with possibilities. Outcomes from impromptu, last-minute actions like your father's, create consequences that are too close to call."

Balthazar was speaking on his mobile phone and finishing the call as he came up the steps of the mezzanine floor. The citrus zest of cologne tickled Wilson's nose.

"That was Mark. He'll be back here with Daisy in five minutes. They dropped off Sally with no problem."

Balthazar pushed back on his chair. Practice made perfect because he stopped short of the edge, put his hands behind his head and stretched out his legs. Curiously, the green Ralph

Lauren socks were similar to a repatriated pair in Wilson's sock drawer.

"Sorry James, I didn't mean to interrupt."

"We were talking about 3b and the background to me working here."

Balthazar picked up the story.

"Yes, I enquired about the building the day after Big Mac told me the top floor held a corridor of convergence. Had to cash in a hoard of Roman coins to buy the place from the previous owners; they ran an internet business here, something to do with hotels. I don't often go up to the top floor. Brings me out in a migraine if I go any higher than my apartment."

"Balthazar, what are we? Daisy, me, you, James, Sally, we're some kind of . . . freaks, right?"

"Freakish, but certainly not freaks. Far from it! Do you know what all number elevens have in common?"

"Something to do with numerology? A special enzyme? The Market Square?"

"Yes, all of that, but with a twist of the savant!"

Wilson paused to dust down a definition of savant.

"You mean like Stephen Wiltshire, the boy who took a helicopter ride over London and drew the view perfectly from memory?"

"Yes, Stephen was able to recreate that panorama days later because his brain could still access all the visual information collected during the flight. It's like you being able to . . . "

"Fly a helicopter?"

"Exactly! You've had flying lessons in your dreams and still have access to that information should the need arise. Where the information is stored, the location of the data room, be it in a photographic memory or in The Market Square, is not the point, it's just energy and energy can never be destroyed only . . . "

" . . . changed from one form into another?"

"Ha, yes, correct Einstein. The important point is that anyone can exhibit savant like abilities if they have access to the data room. Have you heard about Foreign Language Syndrome? It's when someone suffers a head injury and they wake up from a coma able to speak a different language?"

"Yeh, Mum once told me about a boy in America who was injured playing football and woke up speaking Spanish."

"Exactly, but that newly acquired skill didn't last long did it?"

"No, the boy went back to normal after a few weeks."

"Right, so the blow to the head was the key to temporarily entering the data room, to opening a door on his potential to speak Spanish. A potential that was always there. But when the recovery process brought back his brain's old operating system, the entrance to the data room closed again.

"Kim Peek is a particular favourite of mine. His brain was perfectly normal on the surface but the neural connectivity inside was uniquely different. This explained why he was able to do amazing things like memorise all the words in twelve thousand books. It didn't take a blow to the head to unlock his data room, he was born with it permanently open. It's amazing to think that every 'normal' person has the potential to speak a foreign language without lessons, to be a Kim Peek, all it takes is some electrical rewiring. Have you seen *Rain Man*?"

Wilson nodded. "I'm an excellent driver!"

"Well, the story of *Rain Man* is based on Kim Peek."

"So if every human brain has savant potential, how, why

has it been locked away?"

Balthazar pulled his chair towards the table and drew closer to Wilson.

"Because extraordinary talent is first envied then outlawed. Acquiring knowledge without the need for lessons is the sign of a witch and so purges and inquisitions were the bane of savant life for millennia."

James knew Balthazar was about to move onto indigenous Australians and their songlines and dreaming tracks and a whole world tour of savant phenomenon.

"Use the screen grab analogy Balthazar."

"Yes, sorry Wilson, I'm waffling on. To answer your question. One day I pressed two commands on my laptop at the same time by accident and I made a screen grab. I had to ask Mark to explain what I'd done. I didn't know my laptop could make screen grabs. And the human brain is the same. Over millennia the average person has forgotten how to press two commands at the same time. How to unlock the door to the data room. If you're persecuted for being too smart, best to play dumb, lock your genius away in the attic and throw away the key. And we know from natural selection, you lose it, if you don't use it."

Wilson was about to ask how the ability to wake from a dream with a business card in his pocket fitted in with the data room concept, when without invitation, an old memory came to mind. The journey back from Scotland to be exact, when he followed the path of a raindrop as it meandered down the window of the train. When his consciousness, his perception of that very moment slipped anchor and took a new mooring in a different channel of cognition. That slight but palpable shift, when he began thinking with, or from, a new part of his brain. An office for certain 'special' mental operations located in a different room, through a door he'd never unlocked before. The *side room,* with its reference library and open access to everything. A *data room.*

The front door of the building burst open and a rush of cold air surged up to the mezzanine floor. Mark and Daisy were back and relieved to see that Sally's *something* hadn't happened and Wilson didn't appear to be in any trouble.

"I've got to go and tend to the butterflies, would anyone like to come?" asked Mark.

Daisy said she'd love to and sent a message to her mum to say she was with Wilson and would be home a little later than intended. Wilson sent a similar message knowing full well it would raise his mother's hackles the moment she read it.

Mark and James led the way through Balthazar's office and out into the stairwell. To the right, an external door opened onto Chapel Street and served as a fire exit for the upper floors. To the left, a staircase zigzagged all the way to the top of the building. The stairs were of grey painted stone with foot worn hollows in the treads. As they made their way to the first floor, Wilson leant over the bannister and peered upwards into a narrow column of space. He expected a sense of déjà-vu or a headache and lights in his eyes, but the migraine was noticeable only by its absence.

Mark inserted a key into the door of 'The Manchester Lepidopterist Society' as Daisy queried the signage.

"Is there really a butterfly society based here?"

"No Daisy, there's only me based here." Mark pushed open the door.

The sauna like heat and humidity hit them instantly and a few seconds were required to adjust to the wan illumination from infrared lamps.

"I need to maintain a constant temperature of seventy degrees and a micro-climate similar to the Amazon rainforest. If not, the protein cases of the pupae cracks and the butterflies hatch too early."

The butterflies had been disturbed by the opening of the door and registered displeasure by flashing the dragon eyes, leopard spots and Zulu warpaint on their flexing wings.

"They're beautiful. You have hundreds of them."

Wilson was equally impressed. "This is amazing, how many species do you have?"

"Seven" said Mark. "If I have more, they all gang up on the weakest, and they die from a lack of cultural diversity. Like people I guess, and just as vicious when they want to be. My air force of brightly coloured Kamikazes. The electric blue one over there is the Palos Verdes, the rarest butterfly on Earth. I have eight of them at the moment."

"That is so beautiful" cooed Daisy, her nose almost touching the glass enclosure. She was mesmerised by the neon shimmer from its wings, as though the insect had been electrically charged with radiant beauty.

"Which is your favourite?" asked Wilson.

"The Brimstone" Mark replied without having to think. "It's the only species of its genus. The butterfly with the yellow wings and the single red spot. Looks like a nurse has just taken a blood sample. Adult Brimstones are leaf mimics and change colour to blend in with their environments; they're like chameleons, not a bad trait to have for an assassin."

"Which is the one you, erm . . . sent to Bradley Givens?"

"Oh, that was a High Brown Fritillary. The big one there with the yellow and brown markings like a tiger's. They're also an endangered species so I breed them here and sell them on to zoos and private collectors."

"See Wilson, that's a High Brown over there, on that branch. Look at the size of the wings. It's huge."

"Yes, the wingspan is almost seven centimetres. They're fast and agile and being so big they can get right into your face, as our friend found out only too well."

Daisy shuddered at the thought of what had happened to Bradley Givens. Flying tigers attacking his eyes.

James popped his head round the door. "Balthazar wants to know if you'd like to join him for a sundowner?"

Wilson checked his watch.

"Fine by me, and I can take you home on the Vespa if you fancy staying a bit longer Daisy?"

Daisy's reply came as a whisper.

"I want to see inside Balthazar's flat. I bet it's really posh."

"James, yeh, tell Balthazar we'd like to. We're coming now."

"You can go straight up," said Mark heading towards a door in the far corner of the room, "I'll be with you in five minutes, I need to check on the eggs that hatched this morning. Balthazar's on the next floor up."

Wilson walked out onto the landing and peered up the stairwell to the third floor. It was getting closer as he led Daisy up the next flight of stairs by hand. Daisy was his wading stick; protection against the tsunami of gushing energy that might flood his system with debilitating charge without notice.

The door to Balthazar's apartment was ajar and Daisy

could hear jazz music playing inside. Wilson let her hand slip from his. Nothing happened. No blinding flashes of light. No hammer blows to the head. He gauged the distance. Two more flights and he'd be standing outside the door to 3b. Wilson turned away from Balthazar's apartment, gripped the handrail of the wooden bannister and tentatively placed a foot on the first step, and then the second.

"Wilson, where are you going? It's this way. We're going in here."

He continued with the ascent.

"Wilson, maybe you're not allowed to go up there."

Four steps. Nothing!

Five, six, seven, eight steps and still no nausea or excruciating pain.

Wilson paused at the last flight. He could see the entrance door now. An ordinary, wood panelled door painted duck egg blue. An innocent looking door with nothing to suggest a trauma would leave you fighting for life if you entered the room on the other side. Though Daisy was no longer by his side, no longer safely within arm's reach, he followed the return and climbed the last few stairs.

James emerged from Balthazar's apartment and stood by Daisy.

"I don't sense that Wilson is with you."

"He's not. He wants to climb to the top for some reason."

Daisy peered up the stairwell and saw Wilson's hand reach the top of the handrail.

"Wilson, where are you going? You can't just wander . . . "

"He's going up to 3b."

"I know James. But he's not asked if . . . say that again!"

"He's going up to . . . " James didn't need to finish the

sentence. He felt the rush of air and heard the yell as Daisy charged up the stairs two at a time as though Wilson's life depended on it. There was a precedent for acting in that way.

Wilson was standing outside 3b with his hand reaching out for the door handle when Daisy dragged him back, body swerved, and assumed a defiant stance in front of the door barring entrance.

"It's okay Daisy. I don't feel the headache. It's not making me ill."

"Wilson we have to go down. Now!" she ordered. "You can't stay here. Don't you realise? Look at the characters above the door. '3' and 'b'. There's another 3B inside there. Just like the one in Stockport Infirmary. You'll die if you open that door."

Wilson was trying to find a context, a reassuring explanation for the need to gamble with his life. What would be the chances of a different prognosis this time? What were the words of Doctor Khan?

People who emerge quickly from a coma like you Wilson, often find they've left something behind in terms of physical or mental function. Or, in rare cases they come back with a new facet to their personality or a new skill.

Or they go blind? Or they die because Daisy didn't rescue them the second time?

Wilson wrapped his arm tightly around Daisy's as if he was about to step off a tall building and she was the only one with a parachute.

"No Wilson, I won't do it. I won't. You'll die in there Wilson. You've not fully recovered."

James appeared at the top of the stairs and passed an instruction down to Mark who was following close behind.

"You might need to get the defibrillator, just in case."

"James no! Help me. He has to go down!"

Daisy's hold on Wilson was as strong as her grip on the newell post as she tried to drag him back down the stairs. She pleaded with Mark and James for help but they didn't seem to recognise the danger. She remembered how Mark Sampson had acted in a similar way when she'd needed help.

Animal fury shone in her eyes as her voice dropped an octave and she growled "I swear to God, if you don't help me get Wilson down those stairs I will kill both of you."

"Stop" said Wilson. And in comparison, *his* voice was in the placid key of calm. Daisy's had been at perfect pitch given the danger she perceived, but appearances can be deceptive. Something in Wilson's self-assuredness made Daisy release him from under restraint.

Wilson turned to Mark and James and then faced Daisy. Her fury was ebbing and a sad resolve, her acceptance of the inevitable, was causing tears to well.

"You're going to die in there Wilson. That's all I can say. You're going to die this time."

"I'm not. You're my wading stick remember? I think it's going to be different today. And I promise not to conjure anything out of thin air, no toy rockets or bangles. None of the magic tricks that do all the damage."

Balthazar came rushing up the stairs carrying a defibrillator in a red case. James raised his hand like a policeman bringing traffic to a halt.

"Promise me Balthazar, Mark, if you hear Daisy shout for help, you'll drag us both out of there."

Balthazar nodded.

Wilson downed a shot of the hazelnut liqueur in Daisy's

eyes and together they entered the offices of 'The Savants' Club' on Floor 3b.

Five minutes later, Daisy emerged and quietly closed the door, as though her child had fallen asleep at the end of a bedtime story. She broke the news to the three people in the stairwell.

"Wilson wants to know if it's okay to stay in there for a few more minutes? And he'd like that drink, a double scotch with a dash of soda and ice. He said it's okay if you've got no ice or soda."

Chapter 42

Aberlour Single Malt

Friday 1st December 2017, 7.00 p.m.

Like a parliament of owls, four heads turned when Wilson entered the apartment and silently debated his appearance. Wilson's face was flushed, as though he'd been jogging and there was a non-specific change Daisy perceived. Wilson looked different somehow. Like a new and improved Wilson had returned. As though he'd acquired a quality that was both imperceptible and indiscernible yet evident nevertheless. As if those minutes in 3b had nourished him with new vitality.

As he plonked himself down on the sofa, Wilson was grinning, as if to say, "see, I told you nothing bad would happen," but a strange intensity to the colour of his eyes told a different story; whatever had happened in 3b was still sparking circuits in his brain.

"Is that my drink?"

Wilson thought it had to be, as all the other glasses were half empty. He downed the glass of whisky and soda with one long gulp and placed the tumbler back on the table.

"I know what Bradley Givens is planning to do tonight and I know how to stop it. We need to go to Tarporley and then McDonalds in Nantwich and we don't have much time. It's a long way on a scooter and to be honest, I'm feeling a bit knackered so I need to take up your offer of help Balthazar.

Also, any chance of a sandwich, I'm starving?"

Tarporley is thirty-six miles south of Manchester and with rush hour traffic thinning on the M56, the people carrier was ahead of schedule. At the Stretton junction, Mark turned left onto the A49 and called James on the handsfree for a heads-up on the general location of The Maltings.

"I'll text you the postcode, but when you reach Tarporley you're looking for signs to Portal Golf and Country Club. Not sure you'll be able to get that close though. I heard on the news they've put up road blocks to keep everyone away from the house. I checked on Google Maps, there's lots of country lanes and they all look snarled up."

"Okay, thanks for that, don't forget the postcode."

Mark checked the rearview mirror. Wilson and Daisy were sleeping. Wilson had nodded off when they'd only been on the road for five minutes, immediately after wolfing down two Pastrami sandwiches.

The A49 sweeps round Tarporley to the West in the manner of a village ring road. The Sat Nav system suggested "take the left turn in two hundred metres." Mark turned into a country lane signposted for Eaton and continued for a mile in keeping with the instructions.

"Wilson! Daisy! We're here."

Daisy woke with a start at the mention of her name and needed a second or so to connect the voice with the dark interior of the car and Wilson's head resting on her shoulder.

"Wilson, wake up. We've arrived" she said.

After a third prod, he sat upright, yawned, and rubbed

his eyes. Directly ahead, looking over Mark's shoulder and through the front windscreen, Wilson could see they were proceeding with caution and Mark's headlights on dipped beam revealed why. Both sides of the narrow road were lined with cars parked bumper to bumper. As they slowly drove onwards, gaggles of pedestrians would stop and reluctantly waddle to one side to allow a safe route through. They passed a camper van with bodywork customised with pentagram symbols and a motorhome in which a couple were drinking wine and watching TV. Daisy saw a woman who looked uncannily like Sally's Auntie Kay trying to reverse her car into a tight space. The driver behind, frustrated by the slow manoeuvring, beeped his horn in frustration.

The people carrier nosed through the foot traffic at snail's pace as though bringing aid to a war zone. But the pedestrians weren't fleeing from the front line, they were flocking to it. To the left, on Daisy's side, vehicles were parked tight up against the hedgerow. An elderly man in a yellow cagoule was caught in the headlights like a rabbit as he ushered his aged companions to one side. Then, through the witches' fingers in a coven of trees, Wilson recognised a rooftop and floodlights.

"Daisy, Mark, look. You can see the house through there, through those branches, where that bank of floodlights is shining."

Wilson moved to the single seat, back-to-back with Mark and continued pointing.

"Just round this bend, as we sweep to the right, there should be a police roadblock to stop us from taking the road that spurs off to the left. There'll be two policemen and a barrier and a couple of spotlights attached to small generator or something like that."

Wilson was both apprehensive about his prediction and eager to discover the truth. Mark slowly followed the curve of the road and negotiated a path through the milling crowds.

"There, over there, look."

Wilson pulled Daisy from her seat but the seat belt pulled back. Daisy released the clasp and moved to the single seat, back-to-back with the empty front passenger seat. She sat side saddle, and open mouthed, as a roadblock with two policemen and a barrier and a couple of spotlights attached to a small generator or something like that that came into view. And the scene wasn't something like that. It was exactly like that!

"And if you look down there, you can see the entrance gates to Bradley's house about five hundred metres away."

The road to the left was free of traffic beyond the barrier and the location of The Maltings was easy to spot because of the map pin in the form of a mobile crane supporting floodlights with the candle power of Wembley stadium. The generator was more like a portable sub-station.

"You can't see the warning signs from here, but there's also an electric fence outside the house. And you see that lamp post half way down the road, the one that's shining more brightly than the others and not quite straight, that's the post Bradley crashed his van into when the first butterfly attacked."

A policeman with a whistle signalled for the people carrier to keep moving to the right. The left turn was off limits. As Mark followed the directive, a curtain of light passed across Wilson's face and Daisy saw the look of boyish excitement. As though Wilson had proven beyond doubt that Santa exists because his stocking was now filled with presents.

Wilson checked the time on the dashboard against the

time on his watch.

"He was listening to a football match. Tonight's Europa League game between City and Sparta Prague which kicks off at eight."

"Who was?" asked Daisy.

"The policeman, the one you're going to meet in McDonalds in Nantwich at half time."

"Wilson, what's happening here. Where are we going?"

"Just trust me. I have to see if this works before I can explain. I have to test something."

"Test what Wilson? You're not making sense."

Daisy was struck by an horrendous thought.

"Wilson, being in 3b has done something to you, you thought you were okay, but I don't think . . . "

Wilson placed a finger on her lips.

"Daisy! Shh! I'm fine. Am I over excited? Definitely! But I feel good, I know what I'm doing."

Mark checked the route map on the Sat Nav and confirmed they'd be in Nantwich for eight-thirty. Wilson sat back, closed his eyes and soon fell asleep.

Daisy shook Wilson awake as Mark pulled into a parking bay close to the entrance to McDonalds.

"Okay, okay" he responded blearily, "I wasn't sleeping, just resting my eyes."

Wilson pressed a button to slide the side door back and asked Mark to find the Man City game on the radio. Then he strode into the middle of the car park and checked his watch for a second time. Daisy and Mark were onlookers as Wilson appeared to rehearse a scenario in his mind like a movie director about to yell 'and action'.

Wilson climbed back into the car and the door slid shut automatically.

"In ten minutes, the commentator, the one speaking now, is going to say something like, 'that was a dismal first half, some serious questions being asked,' words to that effect. It was easier to see the images than hear the sound."

Daisy and Mark nodded but had no idea why.

"Then a police car, a white Ford Focus, will pull onto the car park and stop near the flower beds over there. There'll be one policeman in the car. He'll enter McDonalds, order a milkshake to take out and talk on the phone while he's waiting. That's when we intervene to stop him from driving to The Maltings. He's scheduled to be there for a shift change at ten but we can't let that happen. I'm not sure of the best way to do it. I have a plan, but it's a bit extreme."

"Which is?"

"Reverse this car into the front of his hard enough for the air bag to go off. He won't be going anywhere after that. He certainly won't be on duty outside The Maltings when Bradley decides to . . . well, that's not important right now. The upshot is, we have to stop the policeman from driving off the car park. If you can think of something less clumsy than crashing cars, I'm all ears?"

"I could pretend I've had my bag stolen and tell him I want to report a crime."

"Yeh, but he might radio it in and ask for another officer to come and take over."

Mark found a Swiss Army knife in the glovebox and passed it to Wilson.

"There must be something on there specially designed for puncturing car tyres."

"That was my first idea, but there'll be cameras on this car park. An accidental car shunt ticks all the boxes. The only downside is that you end up with a drink all over your pants."

"And how does that happen?" asked Mark, with an understandable degree of wonderment.

"When Daisy tries to pass the Cola to me in the back. You select reverse, the wrong gear, and as the car travels back you have to brake, which in turn causes Daisy to drop the cup in your lap, so your leg jerks out and the car travels fully back and bang. Whoops! Sorry officer."

Daisy asked Mark if he thought Balthazar would be angry about damaging the car?

"No, not at all! But what about my pants? I only bought them yesterday. They're Armani. And I'll have to sit in a puddle of Cola all the way back."

Daisy gave him an encouraging rub on the arm.

"Well you did say you were here to help."

Time was ticking away as Wilson pointed out the specific bay the policeman would select.

"He parks between that red Golf and the black pick-up. He'll drive straight into the bay so you need to reverse into the one in front and stick out a bit, so you've room to get some momentum when you reverse back. You have to hit him hard enough for the airbag to explode and make sure you're wearing seat belts. When he arrives, enter McDonalds before he does. Order a Big Mac for me and whatever you two want including the Cola. Daisy, flirt a bit in the queue then he might not be so angry when he realises the accident was all down to you."

"Wilson that is such a misogynistic thing . . . "

"Hey!" Wilson raised his finger abruptly as if to say stop. "You're also here to help remember."

Mark turned up the volume of the radio.

"It's started."

'So there's the whistle folks, and to be honest it couldn't have come sooner, a dismal first half for City, three nil down at home, there'll be some serious questions being asked in the dressing room.'

A police car, a White Ford Focus with one occupant then turned into the car park and headed for the space between the red Golf and the black pick-up.

"That's him! Go. And make sure the Cola's in a cup and not a can."

Daisy and Mark entered the restaurant and Wilson was watching as they placed the order on the touch screen. Mark paid with a credit card. The policeman entered, placed his order at the touch screen opposite and stood talking on his phone. He was young, not much older than Wilson in fact and slightly built. No match for Bradley Givens.

Daisy was referring to the ticket in her hand when she spoke to him.

"Are you number six?"

"No, I'm number nine" said the policeman.

Daisy turned to the screen above the counter, scrutinised the pending orders column and turned her ticket the other way up.

"Ah, that's better, sorry, yeh, *I'm* number six. I was reading it upside down."

The policeman gave Daisy the patient smile he normally reserved for confused, elderly people.

The sound of a ping caused Daisy to refer again to the pending column. Number nine was flashing and the policeman collected his order. Daisy blocked his path on the way back.

"You know, it's so annoying when that happens. I should have been served before you cos I'm number six. Weird isn't it? In a supermarket I choose the shortest queue, but then that turns out to be the longest. Or the checkout girl will say . . . sorry, I'm closing, so I'll join another queue and the same thing will happen again. I should report it as a crime."

Ping. Number Six.

"Oh look, that's us. And there goes good old Mark to collect the order. He's not my boyfriend you know, or my dad, he's like a friend; a good old dependable friend. Do you have any friends?"

The policeman was in three minds. Put his milkshake down and question the girl about recent drug use. Ask the bloke some questions about his relation to the scatty girl. He decided on option three.

"Look I'm sorry, I'm going to be late for duty. Enjoy your meal."

The policeman was reaching for the handle of the car door when a human butterfly in the form of Wilson Armitage tapped him on the shoulder.

"Officer, I'm sorry to trouble you but the treads on the tyres on that car in front look dangerously worn to me. If that vehicle is involved in an accident later and somebody gets injured, killed even, well, we wouldn't want that to happen. Can you check them? Would make me feel a lot better."

The policeman was using his special smile a lot that evening.

"Which vehicle sir?"

"This one here. This people carrier."

The policeman, with a milkshake in one hand and car keys

in the other, looked at the tyres. He could see without bending a knee the tread was perfectly legal.

"I think those tyres are brand new. The tread's about an inch deep, I'm not ... "

"Reassuring to know officer, very reassuring to know. Sorry for the trouble, and thanks for the help."

The policeman stood rooted to the spot as he watched good old dependable Mark climb into the vehicle on the driver's side. Daisy was in the front passenger seat leaning out of the window.

"Come on Wilson" she yelled, "that nice policeman will be late for duty and your Happy Meal's going cold!"

Mark may have underestimated the momentum a vehicle can acquire in a distance of less than a metre but the policeman had no such misgivings. The airbag exploded and he suffered a whiplash injury. Wilson and Daisy were searched for drugs and Mark was breathalysed. Since the bumper damage was only superficial however, and the vehicle's papers were in order, the traffic officer had no alternative but to let the man with the wet trousers and the young couple go.

Dev, the injured policeman, told the traffic officer he thought Daisy and Wilson were 'influencers' being chauffeured to a party somewhere. An ambulance took him off to A&E.

If it hadn't been for their *intervention*, at quarter past ten, *that* ambulance would have been ferrying him to the mortuary instead.

Mark drove all the way back to Manchester without speaking. Not because his Armani chinos were most likely ruined, but because the headphones were back over his ears.

Daisy had sent a text to her mum to say she'd be home soon and that she had her key.

"Mark, Mark." Wilson had to shout to make himself heard.

"Sorry Mark, we have to take the same route back. We must go past The Maltings again. I want to check something, it's important."

Mark pressed the touch screen on the Sat Nav and requested the change of route.

"Can you drop me off near that roadblock? I need to ask one of those policemen a question."

Mark found a space fifty metres short and Wilson walked up to the roadblock. Daisy saw him point beyond the barrier towards The Maltings and say something. The police officer replied and Wilson asked him something else. The policeman replied for a second time and shook his head.

Wilson ran back to the people carrier.

"Right, come on. I need to visit 3b again. Only for a minute Daisy, no more than a minute, I promise."

"Wilson what's happening? Look Mark and I have gone along with this because we trust you, but you have to tell us what's going on."

"That policeman in McDonalds was going to die tonight. Bradley was going to force his hand onto live cables coming from the generator outside the entrance gates. But I reasoned if that policeman wasn't here for that specific event, it couldn't happen. The officer I spoke to said there was no change of duty at ten because of a car accident. We made that intervention and changed the future. So now I must go back inside 3b to see how the future has reassembled itself. How the Tetris bricks have changed."

"Tetris bricks? What do you mean? What did you see in there this afternoon?"

Wilson paused, not certain he had the words. Another analogy was required.

"It was like I was meditating and a new part of my brain had switched on and was acting like a . . . a . . . TV receiver. I could flick through all the programmes being transmitted and switch from the past to the present to the future. But Daisy, to sit here and use ordinary words to describe the extraordinary is impossible."

"Try, I want to picture what was going on in there."

Mark turned up the volume on his headphones as they drove away from the roadblock.

Wilson released a dismissive sort of laugh, rubbed his face with both hands, ran his fingers through his hair and then furiously scratched both sides of his head.

"You want to picture what was going on? Hmmph! Give me a minute, I need to think how to do that."

Wilson switched seats, back-to-back with Mark and sat directly opposite Daisy. He took a good few seconds to gather his thoughts.

"Okay, so imagine you're in a swimming pool treading water. The surface of the pool is broken with ripples reflecting light and in the peaks and troughs of the ripples you see images. I saw Dad. He was asking Mum if she wanted a cup of tea. His voice was distant and muffled like it was bubbling up through the water. At that moment, my receiver was tuning in to the present, to what was happening there and then.

"So I stopped treading water and the current pushed me back, faster than the ripple, which I overtook, and then I saw Dad ask Mum if she wanted a cup of tea all over again. I'd followed the present back into the past."

Wilson sensed Daisy was about to break his concentration with a question. "Daisy, I'm doing my best to give you a picture so let me finish." He closed his eyes and continued.

"I swam back up to the present and looking over the ripples, I could tune into things that were occurring at that moment. Dad was now arguing with Mum cos she didn't want that cup of tea. I watched you go down the stairs to Balthazar's apartment after you left me in 3b; I was seeing you in the present, in real time."

"So I swam a little higher up the pool, until the present became the near future. Dad is reading a book in bed then he tries to kiss Mum goodnight but she's still mad with him and turns away. I was witnessing what was about to happen. So I swam even further forward, way, way up the pool until the ripples were more like vibrations on the surface. I was still focused on Dad but I couldn't receive anything. It was as if the future was being pumped into the pool so quickly, it hadn't time to fully form. The water was so agitated I couldn't make sense of it. So I let the jets push me back just a little bit, to a point where the tiniest troughs and peaks broke the surface. They were like embryos of the future, a billion potential moments. I found Dad again. It was horrible. He was old and grey, in a hospital bed with a drip in his arm. And then, on the next ripple I saw Mum, she was connected to him, like on the same wavelength, but she wasn't with him, she was in a place like South Kessock, and most of her hair had fallen out and she was wearing these old, dirty clothes and rocking on a chair. I didn't want to see more, so I drifted back down the pool. As the ripples grew in size, I seemed to be able to dip in and out of the troughs like a bird with wings that never touch the waves, like I was weightless and my mind was free to think of anything. And I can't explain why, but that's when I saw the policeman drive onto the car park. I watched him leave McDonald's, I followed him as he reported for duty and I saw what happened to him fifteen minutes later.

"Our intervention changed that outcome. We stopped a possibility from becoming a certainty. Balthazar said Kim Peek had an incredible photographic memory because his brain was wired differently. Something happened to me when I was in that white room in a coma, somehow I think my brain has also been rewired differently."

Chapter 43

Double jeopardy

Friday 1st December 2017, 11.20 p.m.

Balthazar and James listened in silence to Daisy's description of all that had happened during the evening, as she understood it, and when Wilson returned from 3b, the story continued from his perspective. Wilson's cheeks were flushed as though he'd been walking by the sea on a windy day. Balthazar made him another scotch and soda.

"The policeman's back home now, watching the football highlights on TV with a surgical collar round his neck. *He's* out of danger, but it looks like Bradley's planning to attack another policeman tomorrow night. Same time, same place. I tried to see beyond that but the reflections were all fragmented and ruffled as though a breeze was disturbing the surface. Maybe, because we're stirring things up, the new future isn't able to settle."

Daisy put a question to James.

"Will Bradley Givens be aware of what happened tonight?"

James needed a moment to consider his answer.

"It's impossible to say. The question is, did you intervene to stop an impulsive or a pre-meditated attack? If it was pre-meditated, Bradley may be confused as to why the rota didn't change and that could make him suspicious. Alternatively, your intervention may have nipped in the bud what would have been an impulsive attack. In which case, Bradley has no reason to be suspicious. To be honest, we'll never know."

"Either way, it's ding, ding, end of round one," said Balthazar, rising from his seat, "and I must say, I'm mightily impressed by the way you two have handled the day's events. You've altered destiny not by accident, but by intention, yet you sit here as though it was all in a day's work, just a different, surreal brand of reality."

"Balthazar, my entire life has been spent in the realms of the surreal. Wilson and I have flown above fairgrounds in toy gliders, plummeted ten miles to earth without parachutes, we've brought people into a shared dream, we've seen their memories, I woke up one morning with three solid gold bangles on my wrist. When you refer to a *different* brand of reality, it's actually the same one I normally buy."

Balthazar rocked on his heels with laughter and Wilson gave Daisy a high five before adding his take on things.

"You say brand of reality Balthazar, but to me reality is an abstract thing that changes depending on perspective. Like dream life and waking life. Reality is Daisy and me being here at this moment. Reality is gatecrashing memories to find a missing woman. Reality is drawing buildings from memory with photographic detail or reading a book with an eye on each page or memorising the bar codes in a trolley full of groceries. Or people who can catch a glimpse of the future and see a way to change it. Thank goodness for that stabiliser, that's all I'm saying!"

That was when Daisy realised the time.

"Wilson, we have to go, you said you'd take me back to Macclesfield remember? Plus you've had a drink and we're on a scooter!"

Daisy was right. There was no way Wilson could risk

354

running Daisy back to Macclesfield nor did he want her to catch the train alone. Besides it was probably too late. He checked his wallet.

"I've got fifty pounds. If I go to a cash machine, I'll get some more and go with you in a taxi to Macclesfield and then back home to Bramhall by myself. Then come back for my scooter tomorrow."

Wilson checked with Mark.

"Will the Vespa be okay outside overnight?"

"Yes, it'll be fine, I'll bring it into the compound at the back. But I'm more than happy to run you both home, it's no problem."

"No Mark, you've been driving all night, we'll take a taxi. Come on Wilson, we need to go home. We might have to do all this again tomorrow night and we've still no idea how to snuff-out a non-extinguished spirit."

"You can stay over if you want" suggested James, "we have a spare room!"

"Is anyone hungry?" asked Balthazar, "I'm sure we'll find a restaurant open somewhere in Chinatown and I'll pay. I'm feeling flush, we sold one of those King George sovereigns this afternoon!"

Daisy sent a text to her mother to say she was staying over at Wilson's and would be back early in the morning. Wilson sent a text to Gloria to say the Vespa had a puncture and he was staying at Daisy's. He'd repair it in the morning and be back about ten. Gloria rang Francis about three minutes later.

As a construction of lies was collapsing, Kay was sipping tea, watching Sky News and flicking through the other news feeds on her phone. The trip to Tarporley had been a complete waste of time. She hadn't been able to get anywhere near The Maltings and from what she was reading and hearing, the night was passing by without incident.

Chapter 44

The detectorists

Saturday 2nd December 2017, 12.40 a.m.

Mark found a parking spot on George Street and James, with white cane in hand, led the way to The Happy Moon.

Wilson and Daisy followed closely, primed to leap forward should James stumble from the pavement into the road, but he didn't.

Mark and Balthazar were a few metres behind and much amused by Daisy's 'heart in the mouth' moments.

"The thing is, not only does James know where he's going, he also knows the restaurant will be open even though he's never been to this one before. We usually go to the Yang Sing" said Mark.

James turned back to Daisy but continued walking.

"I've got a nose for Chinese food and can smell a working kitchen a hundred metres away. Chicken in black bean sauce, mmmm, excellent."

Had the waiter been asked the next day about the party of five that arrived just as the last food orders were being taken, he probably would have recalled the following details.

One customer was blind, or certainly had a problem with his eyes. The boy was hungry and ordered a lot of food with half a Peking duck all for himself. They drank Chinese beer and two bottles of red wine. The girl was pretty and some customers followed her with their eyes when she went to the bathroom. Two of the chefs came upstairs from the kitchen to ask her if the food was okay, which they never usually do.

The older man, the tall one, I think he was someone famous, paid the bill and left a good tip. He told stories that made them all laugh. One time, he stood up and walked round the table with his hands on his ears like headphones. Then he pretended to hold something like a sweeping brush. and swished it from side to side. He dropped down on one knee to pretend to dig a hole in the ground and when he stood up, he was inspecting something invisible he'd found, but then threw it away, like salt over his shoulder. Everyone at the table was laughing. They were happy, celebrating. Nice people. Nice customers. Very friendly.

The open-plan flat belonging to Mark and James was in the basement of 247 Chapel Street. It was furnished in an eclectic style and the Kilim rugs, tapestry throws, scented candles and hand-painted ceramics captured something of a market bazaar in Morocco. A breakfast bar partitioned the lounge from the kitchen and the guest room had an ensuite and a double bed.

Wilson's face was bright red and Daisy had to clamp a hand over her mouth to stop from shrieking as Mark showed them how the shower worked and said he was normally up about seven.

"If I'm not, help yourself to whatever's in the fridge. There's tea bags in the cupboard and the coffee's from a capsule – the machine's on the side. I'm sure you'll work it out."

The overnight bags were on the floor either side of the bed. Daisy couldn't control her giggles.

"Wilson, they don't know we've not . . . that this is the first time, that we haven't . . . "

Though procedures commenced with much fumbling and bursts of nervous laughter, Wilson eventually managed to open the 'bloody impossible' bra clasp and no further trespass into this intimate moment is warranted. Suffice to say, a threshold was crossed and both were overwhelmed by the enchanting discovery of the other self.

Time passed in ecstasy.

Then Wilson slept. As Daisy wept.

The boy was now her man.

Chapter 45

Seventy six trombones

Saturday 2nd December 2017, 3.30 a.m.

Tears were drying on Daisy's pillow as Wilson arrived in The Market Square. The Band of the Coldstream Guards in their magnificent bearskin caps, vivid red jackets and black trousers with creases sharper than sword blades, were marching across the parade ground towards L'Ecole. The orchestrated crunch of hobnailed boots on stone cobbles was a percussion section all by itself. Wilson could hear the notes from the trombones but couldn't place the tune.

Orders must have been received from HQ, because the moment Wilson rounded the Clock Tower and his presence in The Market Square became apparent, a gruff voice suddenly yelled, "Companyyyyy. Halt" and the marching came to an abrupt stop.

"To the right. Turrrn."

The bandsmen turned sharply with a spin and a click of the heels.

"Forwarrrrrrd . . . March."

The Regimental Sergeant Major sent his ornamental baton spinning high into the air and as he caught it on the return journey the band set off marching back.

"Left . . . right . . . left . . . right."

As they drew closer, the music reached a completely unnecessary level of din that ricocheted round The Market

Square like rifle fire. Wilson still couldn't identify the music being played because the trumpets were shrieking like banshees. However, as the guardsmen bore down, with chin strips tight under their noses, he recognised the melody and remembered the name of the song.

Frankie Valli and the Four Seasons.

The trumpets were pitch perfect.

Oh what a night!

The entire band turned to salute Wilson as they marched by.

I felt a rush, like a rollin' ball of thunder.

Wilson mock-saluted in return and blushed on hearing the following line.

She was everything I dreamed she'd be, sweet surrender, what a night.

The guardsman playing the tuba and bringing up the rear seemed to make a point of firing out a particularly deep bellow on the word 'thunder' and turned to wink at Wilson. The oil stained hands clamped around valve tubes were a dead giveaway, more so, the trilby hat on his head.

As the band turned sharply right at The Bank building and marched up The Market Square in the direction of the motorcycle workshop, the familiar shapes of two shadow puppets flitted across the window on the first floor. Wilson wasn't surprised to see Big Mac and Short Cake in residence, they'd probably arranged the fanfare and march past just for him.

But for what purpose? To make a tacky joke about what had happened earlier?

Wilson acknowledged the voyeurs with an exaggerated wave and a thumbs-up then perched on the armrest of a bench

361

seat as a state of propriety returned to The Market Square.

Oh what a night indeed! And what a day!

Daisy arrived ten minutes later. She was wearing pyjamas and thank goodness so was Wilson, for that could have been a tricky encounter to capture in words.

They embraced for a few tender seconds without speaking and parted still holding hands. The energy flow brought pins and needles to the tips of Wilson's fingers.

"I think this is when I'm supposed to smoke a cigarette or we go dancing in the Number 11 Club."

"Daisy we might not have a lot of time, so under the circumstances I think the cocktails can wait. I've just seen Mark Simpson and he wanted me to recognise him."

Daisy cast her eye over The Market Square.

"But The Square's empty, there's only us here. Where did you see him? Did he speak to you?"

"Yes, he cracked a joke. And on top of that, in a roundabout way, I think he was making a point about time marching on regarding Bradley Givens. I wasn't meant to follow him but the message was keep moving, keep advancing."

"So how do we move forward when we've no idea of the direction to take?"

It was a good point.

"Big Mac and Short Cake are around here somewhere but we'll be wasting our time asking them for guidance, they'll have been warned against giving assistance."

Daisy dissected the sentence.

"Wilson, what made you choose the word assistance?"

"It's the word to describe what we need isn't it? Why we're here?"

"And it's also connected with the word assistant, which in certain circumstances applies to me."

"Err, sorry, you're losing me."

"It's obvious Wilson. What have I helped you with in the past? I don't really want to say this, but what do I seem to do better than you when we're here?"

Twisted logic had long been the language of reason in The Market Square.

"You mean like pulling someone in?"

"Exactly! I think this empty Market Square is telling us that in order to find this . . . antidote, we must do it ourselves. Or to be exact, I have to! I have to bring someone here. Someone I know, or we both know and once they're here they'll help us find the solution we need."

Wilson saw the light in Daisy's idea but then it flickered and went out.

"There's a major flaw in that thinking Daisy, because we only ever see traces of the past here. Fishing in old dreams and memories won't help us find an intervention for the future. Hold on, what am I saying, that's not true! It worked with Vanessa, we influenced her future, so why can't it work with . . . Bradley Givens?"

"Because of a small but important fact you've overlooked Wilson. Bradley Givens is dead."

"Mmmm. Okay, fair comment!"

"And I hardly know what he looks like!"

"Me neither. I've seen grainy pictures on TV and low res images on my phone. So who do we pull in and . . . hold on a sec. Okay, okay. Bear with me, what if we bring Sally here?"

"Sally? Sally said she's no longer playing a part and it's all down to us now. Sally can't help."

"Yes, but you mentioned a conversation with her, when she told you about finding non-extinguished spirits in an attic?"

"Yes. And she was told to stop by Big Mac and Short Cake. Why?"

"Daisy, you said they told her to stop because she was scaring the living daylights out of them. So maybe Sally can help us with a way to extinguish the non-extinguished Bradley Givens. To 'scare the living daylights out of him.' Let's bring her here and see how she did it."

"No, I'm not going to do that to Sally, she said she can't help, it doesn't feel right."

"So Bradley it is then! I'm going to try and pull him in and in the meantime you come up with a plan for what we do when he's here."

"Just great! Do you think you could find yourself a new assistant?"

The sharpest image Wilson could recall of Bradley was the head and shoulders photo the police released from a fake driving licence. The other images he'd seen online, of Bradley circled in the background of a wedding photo or at a university graduation, had been heavily pixellated. Bradley Givens wasn't referred to as the invisible man without good reason.

Wilson threw in the towel after a couple of minutes of trying to pull him in.

"I can't get a fix. The face I see is so grainy I keep trying to pull in Mr Daley from college. Daisy you have to try."

"Wilson, I don't have enough to go on. I know he was overweight and going bald but then so is my dad. And we certainly don't want to bring him here!"

"Please, what do you have to lose?"

A Mexican standoff ensued until Daisy realised there was no point in waiting for plan B to come along.

"Okay Wilson, what the heck. I'll try just to rule it out."

Starting with the driving licence photo and a disparate set of individual features, she created a mug shot similar to a face created from strips torn from a magazine. As Daisy tried to pull Bradley into The Market Square, Wilson could see from the way her eyelids twitched that something was happening. A connection was being made. After three minutes however, Daisy gave up.

"I can see him but I can't grab him properly. He's digging his heels in. He won't follow me here like the others. I tried Wilson, I really did, five times, but he kept slipping away. He knew what I was trying to do, I could sense it."

"So if it's not Bradley or Sally, who else is there . . . ?"

"I don't know Wilson, let's go through the alphabet shall we, starting with the letter 'A'? A for . . . Auntie Kay?

"Why would we want to pull Sally's auntie . . . ? Daisy that's it! We . . . are . . . complete idiots. I know who we need to bring here and so do you."

Wilson fist pumped the air.

"He told us about this but we didn't listen. Well, it was you actually. He told you. He even gave you all the tools to do the job. He was priming you for tonight."

"Who Wilson? Who is it?"

"Felix! Sally's friend Felix! The boy who died. He left the photo behind in the flat and helped you find it. Don't you understand? He did that for this very reason."

Daisy hated the way Wilson had a knack for putting

two and two together to make five, but he was right, it was so obvious, staring her in the face in fact. The curly hair, the sprinkling of freckles, the broad smile and the dazzling teeth, his school photo might just as well have winked. Sally hadn't been able to pull Felix into The Market Square but Daisy knew if such a thing was possible, she'd be able to do it.

The spirit of Felix was anticipating the call and twenty-seconds later he was there. Except he wasn't.

Daisy felt his arrival before she heard him. A rush of warm air caressed her hand and she snatched it back with a start.

"It's okay, I'm here. You can't see me, but don't worry, this is Felix, Sally's friend. I was waiting for you to reach out to me. I knew you'd find the photo."

The voice was deep, a man's voice rather than a boy's, and carried a dull reverberation, a distortion or disguise, like on television when they want to protect the identity of the person speaking.

Daisy looked around for the source of the voice.

"Where are you Felix? You touched my hand, I felt you. Can you do it again?"

Another surge of warm air, like an oven door being opened, brushed the same hand. Daisy didn't pull back this time.

"Can you do that to Wilson?"

Though Wilson was prepared, he was unable to stop the flinch when the gentlest of handshakes slipped through his fingers.

"I have to stop that now. It takes my energy. I only have just enough in reserve."

The words were delivered slowly, robotically almost.

As he turned in a circle, Wilson was convinced the voice

of Felix was coming from every direction, in surround sound.

"Where are you Felix?"

"You know where I am Wilson, I'm in the spirit world waiting for the moment I can return to The Gateway and continue my journey."

"Is it like our world where you are."

Felix laughed at the connotations of the question, as though a child had asked where Mother Nature lived.

"No. It's not really a world Daisy. It's a state of existence. It's a form of . . . pleasant suspension in time."

"Can you see other spirits. Those waiting to continue the journey like you?"

"Yes, they're all around, but I don't see them in the way you define the word. They don't have physical form. How can I describe it in a way you can appreciate? Oh yes, huh . . . huh . . . huh . . . I know."

Wilson was having difficulty associating the double bass guffaw with the voice of a schoolboy. Felix sounded like Frank Bruno when he laughed.

"Spirits are like those translucent shapes, the floaters that sometimes hover across the moist surface of your eye. They appear like that to me. But not really. Huh . . . huh . . . huh . . . "

"Do you know Bradley Givens?" asked Wilson.

"I'm aware of many spirits. But the term to 'know' as you use it, is not . . . "

"Do you know where he is?"

Felix laughed again.

"Is he in the house where he used to live? In The Maltings? He's there isn't he?"

"Yes, spirits always live at their last known address. He's angry. Huh . . . huh . . . huh . . . And he sits in his chair most of the time becoming even more angry. Huh . . . huh . . . huh . . . Then he does those bad things."

"Do you know why we're here Felix, why we brought you to The Market Square?"

"Huh . . . huh . . . huh . . . You didn't bring me. You can't bring a spirit into The Market Square. This a dream. A shared dream and the energy is not . . . compatible with that of the spirit world. My voice, my touch on your hand, they are merely representations for the purpose of communication. Imagine you are inside and I am outside and there's a barrier I cannot cross."

Wilson and Daisy were momentarily lost for words. They were expecting some remarkable insight to fall into their lap but the words coming from *this* Ouija board spelled out nothing to work with. Perhaps they'd been asking the wrong questions? Pressing on seemed the only option.

"Felix, do you know why we're connected with Sally. And with you?"

"Yes, because of James Chang, nineteen ninety-three to two thousand and fifteen, he was electrocuted on a train track."

As if to make the revelation even more dramatic, a bolt of lightning fit for the climax of a Frankenstein movie tore through the black storm clouds that had descended on The Market Square, seemingly from nowhere. The deafening rip of thunder that arrived a second later made Daisy instinctively duck. The heavens it seemed, were simmering with anger.

"I don't think Felix should have told us that."

"Yeh, I think he hit a nerve."

As if thunder and lightning on demand wasn't intimidating enough, a heavy shower of hailstone was then conjured to send ice marbles bouncing over the cobbles. Insider information can never be allowed to influence odds and the phantom presence of Felix was no longer deemed welcome in The Market Square.

"Huh . . . huh . . . huh . . . You have to go now, to the science room in L'Ecole, hurry. Huh . . . huh . . . huh . . . "

The hail fell with a malevolent clatter as Daisy and Wilson made a run for it. They took the front steps two at a time, burst through the double doors of L'Ecole and stood in the entrance foyer. The old lady was writing in a ledger book with a chubby fountain pen and turned to look through the internal window as Daisy combed slush from her hair with her fingers.

"He's waiting for you in the science room dear."

The lady used the pen as a directional arrow, "it's down the corridor and third on the right."

Layers of rime sat on Daisy's shoulders like epaulettes of ice. Wilson brushed them away and Daisy returned the favour. This behavioural shorthand, the language of primates grooming in the wild, didn't go unnoticed.

"The dominant male . . . will often spend hours . . . plucking ice . . . from the pyjamas . . . of the half frozen . . . "

Daisy gave her ape man a feisty shove.

"Stop with that Wilson Attenborough. Felix is waiting for us in the science room and we can't leave without some idea of a plan to put to Balthazar."

The interior of the science room in L'Ecole was not exactly textbook. There were no rows of benches, no wooden stools, no collections of glass flasks or chemicals labelled in jars on shelves. No rubber tubes connected bunsen burners to gas taps, no tripods stood on gauze mats, there wasn't even a blackboard. This room was more like a set from an episode of *Thunderbirds* or *Wallace and Gromit* scaled up to adult size.

On one wall, a bank of luminous screens carried lines of computer code cascading down like waterfalls of data. But these screens were not functioning, scientific instruments, how could they be, they were made from polystyrene. And a 'control console' in the centre of the room was the design of a child's imagination; the product of cardboard boxes crudely stapled and glued together and painted grey. Needle dials were the faces from old clocks and watches. On/Off buttons were clothing fasteners in various colours stitched in place with needle and thread. A row of slide levers were plastic handles from the tools in a child's gardening set and a keyboard was made from crude cubes of plasticine arranged on a food tray.

To the right, a room within a room had been thrown together with timber and chipboard and resembled a makeshift canteen. The word 'kitchen' was spray painted on a rickety door.

Daisy looked down at the floor, then up to the ceiling, and though these elevations must have been evident, they were in those side margins that never register as a dream unfolds; the feathered-out edges we can never recall when a dream ends.

"Is all this supposed to mean something Wilson?"

Wilson was chuckling to himself; his face lit up like a toddler about to blow out candles on a cake.

"Yeh, it does Daisy. I made all of this when I was about eight for my dad. He'd been working away a lot and I missed him, so it was my idea of a home office. The desk, the computer screens. It took me weeks to build. Mum helped me sew on all the buttons. Dad said it was the best present ever."

"And is this significant?"

"It has to be. We've just been told to come to this room and that's probably why the band also came marching down here, they were pointing me in this direction. That storm moved us along because we were being too slow, or we overstepped the mark by talking to Felix."

"I'm in here."

The voice that beckoned was that of an adult male but not that of Felix.

"I've made coffee. No sugar for you Wilson and a spoonful for Daisy."

Wilson made straight for the kitchen; this voice was easy to place.

The man was sitting at a Formica topped table sipping his drink from a chipped mug.

"Dad! What the hell are you doing here?"

"I could just as easily ask you the same question Wilson."

The kitchen was rudimentary with a sink unit and a wall cupboard and bore an uncanny resemblance to a different kitchen in a flat above a Chinese takeaway in Gatley. A kettle sat on the hob ring of an old gas cooker and steam rose lazily from the spout in wisps.

"Sit down. Your coffee's going cold."

"But I thought you never visited The Market Square, you said you stopped years ago. What happened?"

"You happened Wilson! You and Daisy is what happened. You couldn't let things settle could you? Follow doctor's orders, don't rock the boat, let your mum get back on an even keel. No, you had to add a final flourish to the mayhem you've caused."

"Dad, it's not like that, it's . . . "

"I'm angry with you son. Bloody angry actually. What

you did for Graham was beyond belief, a miracle, but I don't understand why you didn't think it through properly. Someone was always going to be suspicious and put two and two together. And I'm angry because it was also selfish and probably more for your own ego than to right a wrong. He should have been the one to find his mum not you. You're like some self-obsessed glory hunter Wilson."

"Alex, that's not fair, we only wanted to . . . "

"Wilson, when I went to bed your mother was in the lounge staring at a TV that wasn't even switched on; totally unresponsive to anything I said! She's lost her job and she's devastated. And then she found out from Daisy's mother that you lied to her! Look you're both eighteen, you can do what the hell you like with your own lives but don't get your mum involved. You've no idea how fragile she is. She nearly lost her son for God's sake, and with no plausible explanation of how or why. As soon as I heard the phone conversation, I knew I'd find you here. When is this going to end Wilson? I promised myself I'd never come back to this bloody place and look where I am, I'm back!"

Stress and strain were written between the lines creasing Alex's forehead.

"Why did she lose her job Dad?"

"Because she's become the gossip topic of Cheadle village that's why; with a criminal for a husband and a lying son who let things go too far. She built that shop up from scratch. A million pounds she's raised for charity with not an ounce of recognition. You should be ashamed of yourself."

"Alex, we . . . "

"Daisy, I don't know what your role in this is, but everything started to go wrong the moment . . . "

"Dad, you can stop with that right now! None of this is Daisy's fault. In fact, maybe it's all your fault for not warning me about The Market Square in the first place. It's your stupid little experiment that's gone horribly wrong."

They sat in silence and waited for the charged particles of air to settle.

"I'm going to tell Gloria everything, everything about this place and the . . . "

"Dad, you can't do that. Mum won't understand any of this. She'll think she's going mad, it'll tip her over the edge."

Wilson massaged his temples to relax his thoughts and as he did so, reflections from ripples on water, the peaks and troughs of his parents' future arrived with a message that said, *you've already seen where this is going Wilson.*

"Shit. You're going to do it, aren't you Dad? No, in fact you do, do it! I've seen where it leads. You're going to be old and ill and by yourself in a hospital Dad. And Mum will be in a place for the mentally ill with wispy grey hair and she'll be rocking back and forth in a chair that isn't even a rocking chair. I've seen it Dad. That's what's going to happen if you tell her about The Market Square."

"Wilson, what are you talking about? No one knows what will happen in the future."

Exasperated, Wilson pushed himself away from the table and almost toppled over backwards. Stackable plastic chairs are not fitted with casters.

"Dad, something happened to me when I was in hospital; I've come back with a new ability; a special . . . power, for want of a better word. I can glimpse things that will happen in the future and I guarantee you'll drive Mum insane, I mean really insane, if you tell her about The Market Square."

Under normal circumstances, under any circumstances, Alex would have dismissed such a revelation without a moment's thought, but since his son seemed to have a gift for making the astounding real, he kept an open mind.

"So why are you both here tonight then?"

Wilson turned to Daisy then back to his father.

"How long have you got?"

"Wilson, don't play games. What are you doing here, in The Market Square?"

"When Daisy and I discovered the whereabouts of Vanessa, we didn't know it at the time, but all of that was supposed to happen, it was foreseen, destined to bring us to this moment."

"By whom?"

"Alex, that's not important right now, we'll explain another time, but you have to listen to what Wilson is telling you, it's all true."

"Six weeks ago I rescued a girl hit by a car outside Davenport station. I thought nothing of it at the time, but it turns out that Sally, the girl, was meant to be rescued by me so that she'd be waiting in hospital to return the favour. She told Daisy where to find me when I was lost in a coma. That's when our paths merged into one. Look, its complicated to explain and so many strands are woven together that I haven't got my head completely round it myself. We're like pieces in a chess game and all the moves are already known. Pulling Vanessa into our dream led to Sally pulling her teacher into a different dream, which led to the discovery of Felix's photo, which led to Daisy pulling Felix into this dream which led to us being here. After we found Vanessa the police became involved, which caused you to hit Montague, which meant Mum lost

374

her job and complained about my lying in a text, which led to you also being here. Don't you see? Everything has been building up to this moment for months. We all overlap and now converge here."

"But how does, how is my predicament overlapping with a girl I don't know called Sally?"

"Dad, because this is where you come into Sally's story. Where you help Sally and Daisy and me solve a problem and in doing so, you help us solve yours, ours, with the police. Daisy and I thought we were here to see a boy called Felix, to find answers, but I've realised, we're really here to see you. You were always going to be here tonight because you're the one who's going to help us work out what we have to do. Sally knew we'd stay the night with Mark and James and that you'd find out and come here to confront me. That's why she told us to take an overnight bag to Balthazar's office. You were meant to be here. And this setting, a representation of how I saw your work as a kid, an office in some kind of energy control room is a hint from Sampson, a clue."

"Wilson I have absolutely no idea who all the people you're talking about are. A clue to what?"

"A clue to how we can fully extinguish the spirit of Bradley Givens. A clue to arrive at the checkmate move."

"Bradley Givens. Who the hell is Bradley Givens? Oh, you mean the afterlife bloke in the car crash. Wilson, why is it that I had a feeling this was going to come across my desk one way or the other?"

"Dad, he planned to electrocute a policeman last night, but I saw it coming and stopped it. Bradley doesn't have a lot of energy left, he probably can't power light shows anymore, but he can say goodbye Kamikaze style by taking a policeman with him. That will give him the last say in headlines everywhere. So we need to snuff him out quietly, like a candle, that's why you're here. Mark's been dropping hints all the way. Lightning, thunder, the control room model, electrical energy, spirit energy, converting one to another, this is your area of expertise."

Daisy grabbed Alex's arm. "And Felix said that James Chang, someone who also connects us with Sally, was electrocuted."

"Dad, you have to help me formulate a plan and we have to do it tonight, before this dream ends."

Chapter 46

Jump on

Saturday 2nd December 2017, 9.30 a.m.

Mark and James were eating breakfast as Wilson emerged from the bedroom scratching his bed head, yawning and looking somewhat disorientated.

Daisy was taking a shower.

"Sleep okay?"

"Good thanks. I had a really weird dream though."

"Chinese food" said James, 'it gives you nightmares if you eat too late."

"Yeh, but I didn't dream of being chased by a Peking duck."

Wilson was sipping orange juice as Daisy made a capsule coffee. It was the first time he'd seen her freshly showered with flushed cheeks and she looked different somehow; like discovering your girlfriend had a twin.

"James, would it be okay to visit 3b for a few minutes? There's something I need to check for tonight and a good chance we may be asking for help again."

"Wilson, you must. That's why we live in this building. 3b must be referenced."

"We've put everything on the back burner for now," said Mark, "Bradley Givens is our top priority so tell us what we need to do, we're ready."

"Like I said, I'm gonna check 3b first and after that I'm

going to Cheadle with Daisy to ask Sally a few questions. Daisy will catch the train back to Macclesfield and I'll come back here and explain what needs to be done tonight. Is Balthazar in his office?"

"No, he left at five this morning with an urgent issue to resolve. He'll be back later this afternoon."

The Vespa was parked in the compound at the back of 247 Chapel Street and mercifully still had all the rearview mirrors. It was a bright, cloudless morning with a biting east wind as Wilson and Daisy pulled on their crash helmets and fastened up jackets. Sally's text confirmed she would be at home all morning.

"Wilson, I can drive if you want. You sit back and have a rest. I know how to get to Cheadle from here."

"Daisy you've never driven a scooter before."

"Wilson, I've driven an army tank and a Formula One car round The Market Square so don't pretend this is harder than it looks!"

"Er Daisy, I think you just hit the nail on the head. You're definitely on the back."

As they waited for the traffic lights to change at the junction where Bridge Street meets Albert Square, the giant inflatable Santa embracing the clock tower on Manchester Town Hall made a wonderfully comic backdrop to the German market below.

"It's the second day of Christmas Wilson." Daisy had to yell to be heard. "When this is over, *that's* the square where I want to drink glühwein and eat bratwurst!"

Wilson nodded his head in acknowledgement.

The lights changed and the Vespa lurched forward and picked up speed.

Daisy shouted into the rush of air. "I love your scooter Wilson. . ."

Thumbs up from Wilson.

" . . . but I love you more."

Daisy wrapped her arms tight around his waist.

Leanna was in the kitchen sorting the contents of the battery drawer when she heard the Vespa come up the drive.

"Sally your friends are here love" she shouted up the stairs.

Sally was in her bedroom.

"I'll make them a hot drink. They must be perished on that moped."

"It's a scooter Leanna, not a moped."

"Scooter then, whatever."

"Hi Leanna, we we're just on our way to John Lewis. Sally said it would be okay to pop in and say merry Christmas as we were passing."

"And merry Christmas to you love. And you Wilson, nice to meet you. Come on in, you must be freezing. I'll make some hot Vimto with nutmeg to warm you up. It's like mulled wine but without the alcohol."

They sat at the kitchen table sipping drinks. Wilson joked about Daisy's nose being redder than Rudolph's and they laughed at their Vimto smiles like clowns laughing at clowns. Leanna returned to the task of separating dud from good with a battery charge tester. Wilson was taken by the clinical nature of Leanna's decision making.

Surely, amongst the dead batteries being discarded one or two must retain a bit of charge, a few volts in their Outer Shell? The battery equivalent of bangles in The Gateway?

That led to more fanciful thinking.

When a battery dies, not all the charge is extinguished, only the outer layer, what we call the Shell.

We can never totally extinguish a battery. The Durashell exists until only three amps of current are left.

The energy in a battery never dies, it changes from one form to another.

Wilson was reading far too much into the battery screening process and returned to the conversation as Sally was compiling her top five Christmas movies. Daisy's glare was loaded with ulterior motive as she put *Home Alone* straight in at number one on her list.

We need to speak without Leanna being in the room.

Sally got the message.

"Let's go and see Mr Jinx. I've told him about you and he wants to say hi before you go. We're just going up to my room Leanna, we won't be long."

"Okay luv. Does anyone want another mug of Vimto?"

Wilson took the window seat, Sally sat on her bed and Daisy knelt on the floor looking at the framed photo of a family on holiday.

"Sally, remember when you came to visit me in hospital and you said Big Mac and Short Cake warned you about making spirits lose their energy? You said something about using a torch."

"Yes, I used the big one in the cupboard under the stairs and aluminium foil from the kitchen. The torchlight and the shiny metallic surface seemed to confuse them and they took longer to escape."

"Sally, can you explain to us exactly how you did that?"

So Sally took them all the way back to a children's home in Buxton and divulged all she knew about lamping non-extinguished spirits. Wilson had to ask Sally to explain for a second time the connection between fluorescence and substances and substances and spirits, but when the recollection ended, Wilson was convinced his thinking was on the right track.

"I'll see you tomorrow afternoon then" shouted Sally as she stood on the doorstep waving goodbye. Daisy was confused by the parting words and curious as to the how and why, but by then, Wilson had knocked the Vespa into gear and urged her to "hold on" as they pulled out of the vicarage driveway.

Daisy was checking Macclesfield train times on the timetable outside Cheadle station when a message pinged on Wilson's phone. The text was from his dad.

'Told Gloria you went to a house party with Daisy, fell asleep and they let you stay over. Becky, Alderley Edge, big house, marquee in the garden – Daisy's friend if Mum asks. Though doesn't explain why Daisy said she was staying here with you!! Mum fuming cos you lied but I told her you rang me earlier to apologise for not mentioning the party. Make sure Daisy has similar story. Speak later.'

Alex was a meticulous liar if nothing else. Wilson forwarded the message on to Daisy.

"Read that, just in case you come up against the Spanish Inquisition. It's from Dad, it'll make sense."

Daisy's train was due in five minutes and she still had to buy a ticket.

"Wilson, promise me you're not going to do anything crazy or dangerous. It feels like we're heading in that sort of direction again."

"Daisy, I've no idea where this … antidote delivery service is going, but since it seems inevitable, we probably don't have a choice in the matter. I'll call you later."

"Wilson have you thought about last night? I mean about me and you, us together, and what happened?"

"Yeh, every minute since, and I want to make sure last night happens again and that's why I've got to go." Wilson revved the engine and blew a kiss as he pulled away from the kerb. "Go to college. Act normal. Speak later."

Daisy really wasn't in the mood for glazing bloody vases in a Saturday afternoon workshop but threw the overnight bag over her shoulder and went for the train. Francis was relieved to receive the text that said she'd be home for tea.

The parking space for the people carrier was empty when Wilson steered the Vespa into the compound. It seemed that Balthazar was still resolving his issue. Wilson checked his watch. Time was ticking and he still needed to brief Mark and James on the mission for later that evening and then outline his thinking to Balthazar. Gloria would go berserk if he was away for another night.

Chapter 47

The bright idea

Saturday 2nd December 2017, 1.30 p.m.

Mark was on the mezzanine floor talking with Balthazar on the phone. Wilson was conducting a final check in 3b and James was waiting on the landing outside the door, just in case!

"Mark, I'm on my way back, but running late. Everything went as planned apart from the traffic. Apologise to Wilson for me. I'll be there as soon as I can."

Two hours later, through the window at mezzanine level, Mark saw Balthazar drive into the compound. Through the same window, Wilson then watched Mark greet Balthazar and retrieve a black case from the back of the people carrier. The case looked to be of the shockproof, industrial variety that might contain a delicate instrument such as a theodolite *or* a metal detector. Balthazar closed the tail lift with the remote and followed Mark inside through the back door. Mark left the case at the foot of the mezzanine stairs and joined Balthazar with Wilson and James around the table.

"Sorry I've kept you waiting" said Balthazar, "that was something I couldn't put off until tomorrow."

"No, its perfect timing" said James, "Wilson's seen how history tries to repeat itself tonight and we've devised the intervention to ensure that doesn't happen. But you have to foot the bill for any dry cleaning that might be required."

Balthazar was more amused by the deadpan delivery than the joke.

"I don't think you're seeing the bigger picture here James, in the scheme of things a pair of trousers is . . . "

"But they were brand new! It was the first time Mark had worn them."

"Hah hah hah, whatever! So moving swiftly on, where are we up to?"

Wilson then described for Balthazar's benefit what he'd seen unfolding in 3b two hours earlier.

"He's going to attack another policeman, same place, same way, at ten o'clock when the shift rota changes. I can't be involved tonight, Mum's going spare and I need to double check a few things with Dad, so James and Mark are going to disrupt Bradley's plan and we've agreed the way to do it."

Balthazar looked to Mark for confirmation. Mark nodded and said, "no problem, similar plan to last night."

"What I need to talk to you about Balthazar, is an idea for how we might . . . deliver the antidote."

Wilson momentarily lost his train of thought; unsettled by the reality bite of the strange directive he was about to issue to three fully grown men he barely knew. Though he'd never suffered a panic attack he felt the symptoms building until a shot of the special enzyme entered his bloodstream to stabilise the fleeting disconnect.

"Er . . . sorry about that, lost my thread for a second there, I was about to say that what happens next is going to get a lot more complicated in terms of help."

"We're listening, take your time" said Balthazar.

"First, we need to find a way to enter The Maltings tomorrow night, and I'm thinking it has to be with permission and not a break-in, between six and six-thirty when it's fully dark. I've got a list of everything we'll need to take with us."

Mark excused himself and said he needed to fetch something.

"And secondly?"

Balthazar knew what Wilson was about to say.

"I met Dad in The Market Square last night and he helped me develop a plan. I think he was meant to do that. It's a plan based on Sally's experiences of extinguishing spirits, so in a way, that tells me the idea will work because her learning curve was also meant to be. If you follow me?"

The brief smile from James seemed to confirm that was so.

"The big problem is that to implement the plan we're going to need . . . "

". . . firepower." Mark had returned to the mezzanine floor carrying the shockproof case.

"Six FX50 Lightning torches to be exact!"

Wilson was rendered speechless when the lid was raised.

"The FX50 Lightning is the most powerful handheld torch in the world. They're made in Poland to order and you need a special licence to own one. They're so powerful you can fry an egg and ignite paper with the beam."

"Or blind someone," said James, "which is the main reason you can't buy them."

"But how did you know what I was going to say?" Wilson needed stabilising again. "Who told you?"

"You did," said James, "last night in the science room when you hatched the plan with your dad and he mentioned the

FX50. I followed your dream in 3b and once you were set on using the torches it was all down to Balthazar."

"But you can't just go online and order these from Amazon. Where did you get them?"

Balthazar took over from James.

"Once you'd decided on the way forward, I paid a visit to Sampson and his crystal ball did the rest. Early this morning I drove to Luton airport with three butterflies for company and in the short stay car park there was an unfortunate incident in which six unlicensed torches were not exchanged for a suitcase full of cash as intended. Dealing in FX50 torches on the black market isn't without its risks and me lying in wait with three flying tigers was one of them. It's called forward planning. Now, tell me your thoughts for entering The Maltings tomorrow night Wilson."

Chapter 48

Where have you been?

A more fitting way to enter the house would have been through a cat flap, because as Wilson closed the front door, the questioning look on his mother's face made him feel as guilty as a tom after a night on the tiles.

"Mum I don't know what all the fuss is about I'm bloody eighteen for God's sake. I can vote, join the army, leave home, move into a flat. You're making this difficult and it doesn't need to be, if you don't mind me saying."

"Well, Wilson, I do mind you saying! And it's nothing to do with your sneaky little slipping out of the house yesterday without a good morning or a goodbye. Or the ridiculous note. Or the firing up of your scooter halfway down the road so I wouldn't hear the din that bloody exhaust makes, or the lies about staying with your girlfriend or her lies about her staying with you."

"Mum, I called Dad. I told him what happened, I said I'd slept over at an eighteenth in Alderley Edge. I wasn't drunk, I was just tired."

"Wilson, I really don't care what you get up to with that girl but lord knows I should, because she's been nothing but trouble from the moment she walked through the door."

"But Mum . . . "

"Don't but me Wilson. I'm your mother and you'll listen

387

to what I have to say. What I do care about, is the fact you're not doing what the doctors, who just happened to save your life, have told you to do. Rest at home, build up your strength . . . have you looked in the mirror recently Wilson? You've got black bags under your eyes like bin liners, you're as thin as a rake, you look gaunt and emaciated and you're out gallivanting all night as though it's Freshers' Week. I'm your mother, and actually you're right, you can do as you bloody well want, but when you start ruining my life for your own selfish reasons it's me who's held accountable by this nosey parker town of gossip mongers. They talk you know, don't think they don't!"

Alex was nowhere to be seen while all this was going on and Gloria hadn't finished, oh no, she was working up a head of steam and there was nothing Wilson could do other than stand there as the valves blew.

"I've lost my job, so now I'm the laughing stock of the village. Your dad's boss called this morning to say he's suspended without pay until after the trial, and who knows when that will be; plus we've still got the mortgage to pay! And the verdict, which is certain to be bad, will be in all the papers. I daren't ring my own daughters because I've no idea what to say to them. And you think I want to plan for a Christmas of playing Happy Families over turkey dinner and pulling crackers and playing Twister. No chance, I'm not feeling that. I think Christmas is cancelled for this year and you know what Wilson, it's so unfair on Kate and Megan because those poor girls are working so hard at college and not causing any trouble whatsoever. They don't deserve this. To come home to this mayhem. A complete catastrophe because of that bloody Daisy girl and an equally bloody ridiculous Snapchat message story."

"Alright Mum, that's enough, calm down. You've made your point. But if I can get a word in edgeways, no Mum, Mum, give me a minute."

Gloria put her summarising speech on the back boiler, folded her arms and allowed Wilson to have his word in edgeways.

"Mum! I did get that Snapchat message. I promise. But right now I wish I hadn't. Yeh, I know you've both lost your jobs, but Dad's going to be cleared because he's being framed by that idiot Montague and you'll get your job back. And while I'm on the subject, I wouldn't be bothered if I were you. Those charity people treat you like a slave, you don't get paid, have to pay all your expenses and don't tell me that big lazy lump who lords it up as your boss isn't earning a small fortune for doing bugger all in the name of a good cause. Let me tell you Mum, if I get chance one day, I'm going to expose all those fake do-gooders. Plus, there's not only you that's suffered. I've lost all my mates, nobody will speak to me, I'm blocked by everyone on social media and the mate I thought I was helping by going to Scotland has basically said he's gonna kill me if he finds out his mum disappeared because of me! So to be honest Mum, I'm not in a great place myself. And you've got it all wrong about Daisy. So if I want to sneak out of the house to avoid you throwing a fit, just because I want to see my girlfriend and do all the normal things everyone else does, then I'm sorry, I'm going to do it. And you need to get off Daisy's case because if you knew the truth you'd give her a bloody medal."

"What truth Wilson?"

"Nothing! It was a figure of speech."

The irresistible force had dashed itself against the immovable object. Wilson hadn't relished the prospect of clashing with his mother but felt it was handled with a forceful yet light touch. He'd fought fire with fire and now it was time to pour water on the embers.

"Mum, we're gonna have a great Christmas, I promise. All this will blow over and in a few months you'll have forgotten it ever happened."

Wilson was leaning against a radiator in the hallway and Gloria was standing in the doorway of the lounge.

"Where's Dad?"

"Lying low and skulking in the kitchen! Where do you think?"

Wilson settled for the draw with a harrumph and hung up his parka and scooter keys.

Alex was reading a paper at the kitchen table as Wilson poured himself a glass of orange juice from the fridge.

"Well that went well."

"Wilson what do you expect? Your mother has been worried sick and tipped completely overboard by this . . . this boat rocking! Oh, and she's right by the way, you do look like a shadow of your former self,"

"Don't think the boat rocking phrase is right Dad, though I know what you mean."

Wilson pushed the kitchen door shut and returned to sit opposite his father at the table.

"Remember that night I started speaking French Dad?"

"It's not the kind of thing you forget Wilson."

"Seems so long ago. So much has happened. I've discovered so much."

"Yeh, well I did tell you to stop visiting that bloody place."

"Dad, you know as well as I do, you can't ignore it. It's

there. I get it if you prefer to experiment and measure from the outside rather than jumping in the swimming pool. A good analogy by the way for other reasons. But Dad, I'm not backing off. I'm seeing this through and we need to speak but we can't do it here. You need to go back to The Market Square tonight."

"There's no chance Wilson. I've told you, I'm not going back. Last night was a one-off and no more. Deal me out."

"Dad, I need to run everything by you for a final time. I can't do it sitting here in the kitchen. It feels weird, the context is all wrong."

Alex was showing a stubborn interest in his paper.

"I mean it Dad. You have to meet me there tonight. And another thing, in case I forget to tell you, you also need to get Mum out of the house tomorrow afternoon, take her shopping, out for a dinner, go watch a movie. There's a possibility I won't be back until late."

The kitchen door opened and Gloria entered. She was still venting steam.

"There's cottage pie in the oven. Share it between yourselves, I'm not hungry."

Chapter 49

I can't put my finger on it

Saturday 2nd December 2017, 6.30 p.m.

Sergeant Jordan's shift had ended at six and walking from the convenience store with a Chinese ready meal and a six pack of beer, he saw the headline on the cover of that night's Inverness Herald in the paper rack.

'Valiant police chief urged not to retire'

The sub headline read.

'Dramatic breakthrough in the case of 'Abandoned Alice'

Beneath, a photo of a smirking Assistant Chief Constable Montague with his arm in a ridiculously large plaster cast featured prominently.

Sergeant Jordan picked up a copy of the paper and went back to a self-service checkout to pay for it.

He read the story while smoking a cigarette in his car. The article was a pile of preposterous nonsense filled with unsubstantiated accusations about Alex Armitage and his son. It couldn't have painted Montague in a better light if he'd written the article himself; which was probably the case, since Montague's brother was on the board of the company that published the Inverness Herald. Not only did the story perpetuate a ridiculous fabrication, it made Montague sound like a hero.

Jordan threw the paper on the passenger seat, stubbed out

his cigarette in disgust and pressed the button to close the window. There couldn't have been more than a centimetre gap but the Palos Verdes butterfly still managed to glide into the car. It fluttered around to capture Sergeant Jordan's full attention and landed on the nose of the inane, grinning face on the cover of the newspaper on the passenger seat. Sergeant Jordan knew nothing about butterflies but was certain they were not a normal sight in Inverness in the middle of winter. Particularly one as exotic as this with its electric blue wings. Jordan had never seen an insect as visually striking in his entire life. He concluded it must have escaped from a butterfly collector and was unlikely to survive the night. The butterfly then did something extraordinary. It flew up from Montague's face and settled on Sergeant Jordan's hand. The iridescent wings flickered for a moment as though sending a message in semaphore and with a flash of radiant colour the insect returned to Montague's nose. Then it flew back on to Sergeant Jordan's knuckle. He slowly lifted his hand from the steering wheel to inspect the insect more closely. He could see the butterfly's tiny compound eyes and when he extended his index finger the butterfly walked all the way to the tip. The sergeant let his hand gently fall until it was resting on the paper. The butterfly flew from the fingertip onto Montague's nose and quickly returned. It completed the manoeuvre a second time and a third and a fourth as the wing beats became increasingly frenzied.

Sergeant Jordan switched on the engine of his car and drove back to the station with the butterfly perched on his knuckle all the way. If he'd been an expert in butterfly emotions, he'd have said the Palos Verdes looked very pleased with itself.

"Evening Derek, thought you'd clocked off for the night."

"Aye, but I left my reading glasses in the evidence room, I won't be able to do the crossword without them."

The desk sergeant threw Sergeant Jordan the keys.

"Make sure you sign out and if I'm not on the desk, put the keys back in the drawer will you?"

Sergeant Jordan descended three flights of stairs and arrived at a door reinforced with steel plate and round head rivets. He opened the door and entered the evidence room where old case files were stored in document boxes and shelved in alphabetical order. The box for 'Alice the Abandoned' was easy to find. Sergeant Jordan opened the box and placed the contents on a desk. There wasn't much to show for seventeen years of lost existence: medical assessments, reports from the care home in South Kessock, a statement from the ambulance service, twelve photos of women reported missing around the time Alice was taken into care and a bundle of newspaper cuttings. That was it. A typical cold case file. No leads, only well thumbed dead ends. The transcript of an interview with Michael Clarke, taken on the day Alice was identified as his missing wife, was the equivalent of a ribbon tying everything up nicely at the end. Sergeant Jordan double-checked the inventory list with the contents. They should have matched but two items appeared to be missing, including photo number thirteen! He turned to the requisition book, flicked through the pages until he found the day on which the true identity of Alice was discovered and ran his finger slowly down the list of handwritten names and signatures. Montague had been in the evidence room the day after Vanessa was discovered. In fact, his was the last name to have requested the file. Montague had ticked the box to confirm nothing had been signed out.

Sergeant Jordan passed the keys back to the duty sergeant on his way out of the station.

"Were they down there Derek?"

"What do you mean?"

"Your glasses?"

"My glasses?"

"Your reading glasses. The reason you came back."

"Och, they were there on the shelf. See you Monday then."

"Aye Derek, have a nice weekend. See you Monday."

When Sergeant Jordan returned to his car the Palos Verdes butterfly was lying motionless on the passenger seat. The shimmering blue wings piped with indigo had lost none of their vibrancy. He gently wrapped the dead insect in a tissue and on arriving home made straight for the kitchen to preserve the creature in an airtight jar.

Chapter 50

A star is born

Saturday 2nd December 2017, 6.30 p.m.

"I'm not sure Kay will be happy about the tree going up so early. You know how mad she gets when she sees adverts for Christmas at the end of September."

"Leanna, loads of people have trees and lights in their windows, it's the second day of Christmas. If you can open an advent calendar why can't you put a Christmas tree up?"

Leanna agreed that Sally had a point, certainly enough to win an argument with Kay and relented when asked for a third time to help bring all the Christmas stuff up from the cellar.

"If the tree is decorated and looking all Christmassy, Auntie Kay won't make us take it down."

"Okay, come on then, we need to be finished in an hour, before she gets home."

Leanna found a playlist of old festive tunes, 'Let it Snow,' 'Frostie the Snowman,' 'Rudolph the Red Nosed Reindeer,' songs that evoked the Christmas spirit and together they dressed the tree. Sally insisted on hanging all the glass baubles. She was fascinated by the polished metallic surfaces and the 'back of a spoon' reflections.

"These baubles remind me of Mum, especially the red ones. I can see her face shining on the surface."

"Oh Sally that must be so lovely for you. I know it must be difficult when this time of year arrives and everyone else has . . ."

"No, I'm not sad Leanna. I'll miss this though, of course I will, that's why I wanted to see the tree again."

Leanna didn't fully understand what Sally was saying, or the point she was making, and rather than reply inappropriately she decided to change the subject.

"Kay'll be tired and irritable when she gets home. Come on Sal, get a move on with those last baubles then we can put the star on top and I'll clear all these boxes while you vac-up the needles. Your auntie's not been sleeping well and when she sees the tree she'll be super ratty.

"Why hasn't she been sleeping?"

"She's become obsessed with Bradley Givens, you know, the 'spirit' personality haunting that house in Tarporley. The one who supposedly attacked the woman on TV outside the gates. Kay thinks it really happened, a real sign of the afterlife. I think she's getting into the Christmas spirit too early if you ask me. Get it Sally? Spirit? Christmas? Drinks?"

Sally rolled her eyes.

"Like the ghost of Christmas present."

"Ha, Sally! Exactly! And funny you should mention that because she told me yesterday morning that she'd been dreaming about Bradley Givens all night. And in the dream he was here in this house, 'having an influence,' is what she said. Makes me shudder just thinking about it."

"Do you think she had Bradley Givens mixed up with Jacob Marley?"

"Okay Sally stop with that. It's a time for good will to all, including your auntie!"

397

When Kay arrived home twenty minutes later she had to agree with Sally that the lounge looked magical with all the twinkling lights on the tree.

"And this Christmas card, here under the tree, is for you Auntie Kay. But you can't open it until Christmas Day unless I tell you to. Do you promise?"

"I promise."

"Cross your heart?"

"Sally, you're going too far now. I've let you keep the tree up. So don't push your luck. I promise."

Leanna was right, Kay was exhausted. She'd been in meetings all day trying to get fast track funding for a documentary investigating the story of Bradley Givens. 'Invisible man crime wave becomes paranormal phenomenon!' was the elevator pitch.

"It's a story which hammers on the door of every religious belief. The viewing figures would be off the scale."

Her working title was 'True Faith or Fake News'. The funding had been signed off late afternoon and now it was a matter of finding a production team at short notice. Background footage was needed while the house was still there. Someone in the newsroom had heard the local council were planning to knock it down because there had been no planning permission to build the house in the first place. The head of Chester Council Planning Department had been bribed or threatened, apparently.

Along with the tree and the Christmas decorations, two suitcases were also retrieved from the cellar earlier that evening and they now lay open on Sally's bed. She carefully folded all her clothes and placed them in one suitcase but left her school uniform and school shoes to one side. Non-clothing items including books, board games, a scrapbook, an iPad and the holiday photo from the bedside table filled the other suitcase. Then both cases were shoved under the bed out of sight.

Sally lay in bed that night surveying the interior of a room laid bare of all her worldly goods. As though she'd never inhabited the room. Had never existed at all.

Chapter 51

A favour for a favour

Saturday 2nd December 2017, 6.30 p.m.

You wouldn't call Balthazar's contact at MI5 a friend, he was more of an acquaintance.

They'd been at university together and now Andrew Masterson was the head of a small unit of individuals referred to as the human intelligence analysis division. His job description was to investigate how people with extraordinary mental abilities, such as savants and seers, could be beneficial to national security. In shorthand, he was looking for fortune tellers with an uncanny knack for getting it right and his remit was to counter terrorism, uncover espionage and fight major crime activity in the UK.

Masterson was based in a building on the banks of the River Thames in London and reported to the Director General, who in turn reported to the Home Secretary for Her Majesty's government.

"Yes Balthazar, I'm fully aware of the goings-on in Tarporley, I'm actually paid to know about things like that. But at the moment, it's on the outer edge of my orbit. One of my team has been up there and her report says it's all a bit of a hoax. A ghost captured on live television. Come on. Seriously?"

Masterson had reluctantly taken Balthazar's call. It was

getting late and he was planning to take his wife to see the Billy Elliot musical. Whenever Balthazar called he was usually after something; information mostly, a shady secret about this or a shadowy disclosure about that. However, Balthazar fell into the category of individual that his department was most interested in. Balthazar seemed to possess a photographic memory and an uncanny knack for seeing patterns in activity that would normally have slipped under the radar. Like the time he called with details of a plot to bomb University Hospital. MI5 agents eliminated the threat at the planning stage and three terrorists were jailed for life. It had been a red-letter day for Masterson's division. Balthazar had been very specific about what was going to unfold, it was as though he'd been given advance warning or could foresee the atrocity. Balthazar was often a useful source of hard to come by information and that's why Masterson took the call.

"So let me get this straight. You want me to call the office of the Home Secretary of the Government of the United Kingdom, who is about as high as you can get from where I'm sitting, and ask permission for you and a few mates to go and play ghostbusters at some haunted house in Cheshire. Is that the gist of it?"

"I think you're being a little flippant Andy, but if you must put it in a nutshell, yeh, that's about it."

"Jesus Balthazar, could you find something more difficult for me to do? You know that means I have to go over the head of MI5. My boss! She won't be happy if she finds out."

"Why will she find out? All I want is a directive, written on a ministerial letterhead and signed by the Home Secretary's office to allow five eminent psychologists access into the house for a few hours early tomorrow night. To conduct a couple of experiments, scrape protoplasm off the walls, take a few meter readings and find cold spots."

"But the show's over isn't it? All was quiet on the western front last night. The police cordon is keeping at bay all the religious nutters trying to make a point. And Balthazar, I have to say I'm bloody glad, this was starting to rumble in a very dangerous way. Can you imagine if . . . "

"Andy, just get the permission! I seem to recall your last two promotions were a direct result of my assistance. Guidance that you took all the credit for. A favour for a favour. Quid pro quo Starling!"

"Alright Doctor Lecter, let me think about it. When do you need the authorisation?"

"Now Andy! Do it right now. I need the paperwork first thing in the morning. Oh, and ask for a contact number to be included in the directive. If the police become suspicious, I'll need a number for them to call for the all clear."

"Leave it with me, I'll see what I can do."

As Masterson hung up, Balthazar knew he was going to let him down.

A little coercion would be required.

Chapter 52

Blind faith

The occupants of the people carrier parked at the rear of Nantwich police station were in surveillance mode. Mark was providing the commentary for a blind viewer on how PC Pran Sangupta had climbed into a white Ford Focus with a rack of blue lights on the roof and was now on his way to report for the night shift at The Maltings. Mark pulled into traffic and followed the police vehicle along the B5074 as it headed out of town. It was panning out exactly as Wilson had said it would.

"Put the earpiece in and call Balthazar. Tell him we're on the way and check your phone volume is on full."

James made the call and as Mark listened, he was able to plug the gaps in the conversation.

"It's James. He's left the station. I'm just checking I can hear you clearly."

"Yes, we're good Balthazar. Don't worry, it'll be fine."

"A leap in the dark as they say."

"We'll call you when it's over."

"Oh, Mark wants to know if the permission came through?"

"Okay, I'll tell him."

James ended the call to Balthazar.

"No, the permission hasn't come through and he thinks his contact probably won't deliver. Balthazar said he's going to get more ammunition tonight. He said everyone has a murky past and you don't get to work at MI5 without one. Those were his exact words."

Mark was concentrating on the police car and the three vehicles between.

"Mark if anything goes wrong with this, I won't blame you, but I want you to know you'll be paying for the weekend in Paris when I get out of hospital."

Mark reached out for his partner's hand and they met halfway.

"No love, Balthazar will be paying. And we'll be staying at the Ritz in Lady Diana's old room."

They were on the outskirts of Nantwich, half a mile from the roundabout on the A51.

"I think the Spar Wilson described is coming up. Yes, he's indicating to pull in like he said. I'm overtaking now. Get ready."

The people carrier cruised past innocuously as PC Sangupta locked the car door and entered the newsagents for a can of Red Bull, twenty Marlboro Lights and two packs of sandwiches. He was preparing for a long night.

After seven hundred metres Mark kissed James on the forehead, wished him luck, dropped him off at the kerbside, made a quick 'u' turn and sped back to the store. He then drove on for another two hundred metres before making a second 'u' turn. Once he'd pulled up behind the police car, he called James.

"I'm in place, can you hear me?"

"Yes, loud and clear."

"He's just about to pay. Get your white stick ready but

stay back from the kerb, all the cars will stop if they see you're about to walk out into the middle of the road."

"I am back from the kerb, I can feel a wall on the back of my legs."

PC Sangupta emerged two minutes later with his provisions. Both vehicles indicated and pulled out in tandem.

"James, we're on our way, be ready."

Mark checked his rearview mirror. There was a car behind but thankfully it was way off in the distance meaning the driver would have plenty of time to brake and avoid a shunt.

"Start walking away from the wall James, the kerb's about two metres away. That's it, I can see you, wait, slowly, slowly. Now, step out now!"

Mark's call was inch perfect.

Fortunately, PC Sangupta was concentrating on his driving and not trying to open the sandwiches or drink the Red Bull or light a fag. Such an unaccounted for distraction had been a potential flaw in the planning.

Mark saw brake lights glow as the police car pulled up sharply to let a blind man tap his way across the road. For the policeman, it was like one of those moments in slow motion when you see the inevitable about to happen and there's no way you can avoid it. PC Sangupta watched the people carrier grow ever larger in his rearview mirror and braced himself by pushing back against the steering wheel in readiness for the impact.

The inevitable happened and the police car was knocked five inches forwards.

"What the . . . ?"

PC Sangupta didn't know who to blame. The blind man who'd made it safely across or the driver of the vehicle behind who was now remonstrating at *him*.

"You suddenly stopped for no reason. I slammed on my brakes but didn't have chance to stop."

The policeman shook his head and counted to ten as he watched James tap his way up the other side of the road.

Mark returned to the people carrier to switch his hazard lights on and put a warning triangle out. They both inspected the damage.

The people carrier had a small dent in the plastic bumper and paint was chipped. On the Ford Focus, the passenger side brake light was smashed beyond repair.

"I tried to swerve out of the way. That's why I hit your brake light. I'm so sorry, I don't think you can drive this car now, you'll get stopped by the police. Can you call for a traffic officer to come and take a statement? And I'm going to need all your details for my insurance company."

Mark checked the time.

"I haven't been drinking but I need you to breathalyse me as well. I'll need that result for the insurance. It's a shame the blind chap crossing the road has left the scene, I could have asked him for a witness statement. So are you going to claim against me, or do I claim against you?"

PC Sangupta reached for the can of Red Bull and drank it in one go. What a relief! He wouldn't need to spend another night outside those gates shivering with cold and fearful of being assaulted by a demon. Now he had an ironclad excuse for missing his shift.

An hour later, after checking his watch to make sure the witching hour of 10 p.m. had passed, Mark said goodbye to PC Sangupta and the traffic officer and went to collect James from outside the Spar.

Mark helped him into the people carrier, turned the heating on full, furiously rubbed hands and shoulders then wrapped him in the car blanket. The need for warm outdoor clothing had been overlooked during the planning stage.

Before setting off back to Chapel Street, Mark sent a text message to both Balthazar and Wilson.

'All ran like clockwork and we're on our way home. Think the policeman was happy with the outcome!'

It took five minutes for James's teeth to stop chattering.

"Mark, I want to be with you tomorrow night. I know Balthazar thinks I'll be an unnecessary risk."

"He's just concerned about you handling the torches and he's got a point. He doesn't want you waving one around and blinding me. Imagine that, the blind leading the blind."

'Mark, I would never do that, you know I . . . "

"James, I'm joking love. Fancy a Thai takeaway?"

"Yeh, and a decent bottle of vino."

Mark turned up the volume on the music system and they drove back to Chapel Street singing the songs on a Smith's album.

'And if a double-decker bus
Crashes into us
To die by your side
Is such a heavenly way to die'

Chapter 53

Rehearsal

Saturday 2nd December 2017, 10.30 p.m.

"Hey, it's me, you okay?"

"Yeh, just mulling things over. How about you?"

"I'm in bed, about to switch out the light. Mum's at choir practice and Dad's out playing darts. I was calling to see how it went with your mum?"

"Mmm? A frosty reception is the way I'd describe it, but she's calmed down a bit now. She's still furious with Dad though. He's been suspended from work without pay. Hoover's sent me a message to say the lads don't want me involved in the websites anymore so my income will also be drying up. Your Christmas present will have to be a two for one voucher to spend at Greggs."

"That's perfect, just make sure you gift wrap it."

There was a break in the conversation as both minds wandered back to the night before and a certain spare room in a basement flat.

"I wish you were here Daisy."

"Me too Wilson, I was thinking the same thing. About last night."

"The best night ever! And not because of the . . . you know what, it was just being with you, sleeping in the same bed. I'd like every night to be as special as that."

"Wilson, let's get tomorrow over and done with and then we can enjoy every moment together."

"Yeh, I so want that. To draw a line. It's why I went back into 3b yesterday afternoon, to check . . . "

"Wilson, I don't want to hear . . . "

"It's okay, I was fine and Mark's collision went as planned. Also, Balthazar read my mind and solved another problem. I want to go through things with Dad again but it's impossible to speak here in the house. Mum's suspicious enough as it is without hearing us whispering behind closed doors. I've asked him to meet me in The Market Square."

"And will he?"

"I don't know. He went to bed half an hour ago without saying goodnight. It doesn't really matter I suppose, we know what we're doing."

"Okay, so before I nod off, tell me again what you want me to ask Felix?"

Once again, the night passed by without incident outside The Maltings, much to the disappointment of the thinning congregation at the roadblock.

The Market Square however, was a veritable hive of subterfuge and artifice. Wilson's path crossed with Balthazar's and both of their paths crossed with Daisy's. They didn't see each other of course; all three were operating undercover, deep within their own dreams.

Chapter 54

Ships in the night

Sunday 3rd December 2017, 1.30 a.m.

Daisy was the first of the trio to land in The Market Square and mindful that her time could be limited, she made straight for L'Ecole.

A holly wreath with huge red berries was hanging on the wrought iron gates. On entering the foyer, Daisy was confronted by a startling sight. Big Mac and Short Cake were wearing matching red sweaters with snowmen on the front and garlands of tinsel were draped over their shoulders. Short Cake was on a stepladder arranging fairy lights on a huge pine tree and Big Mac was cradling a cardboard box in which his free hand was sifting through glass baubles and adornments. The tree stood over five metres tall and Short Cake was struggling to string the lights around the top.

"Look Daisy. Teacher says, every time a bell rings, an angel gets his wings."

Big Mac had found the decoration he'd been searching for. The golden bell dangling on a loop of cotton around his finger began to shake of its own accord, emitting a fragile, tinkling sound.

There was a discordant aspect to the dressing of the tree that soon became apparent.

Half hidden amongst branches and fronds of pine needles Daisy could see windows, like the quaint, shuttered, wooden windows one might see in a painting of fairytale cottages or the homes of tree elves. The shutters covering two of the windows had been folded back to reveal panels of stained glass portraying winter wonderland scenes of children skating on ice and throwing snowballs.

"What's today's date Daisy?" asked Short Cake as he stretched to frame fairy lights around a window near the top of the tree.

"It's the third of December."

"Thought so."

Short Cake prised open the shutters with a crabby finger and pulled them apart to reveal a stained glass panel depicting Felix as seen in his school photo.

Daisy turned to the lady in the office. She was typing away like an automaton and spoke without looking up or waiting for Daisy's question.

"No, there's carol singing in the music room at the moment dear, you won't be able to hear yourself think down there, so it probably won't work."

Daisy hurried up the stairs and along the corridor nevertheless.

As she descended the flight leading down to the music room, soprano voices singing Christmas carols met her halfway.

"Peace on earth and mercy mild, God and sinners reconciled."

She pulled back the door and slipped inside.

The same man who'd conducted Felix through his violin solo now stood at a lectern waving his baton at the women's choir gathered on the stage. The women were middle-aged and all bore a striking resemblance to Daisy's mother, like doppelgängers in an identity parade. The ensemble was greater than the sum of its parts, disturbingly loud in fact, and Daisy knew she wouldn't be able to focus on the image of Felix, let alone speak to him. She turned on her heels and headed back to The Market Square. Passing through the foyer, Big Mac and Short Cake were nowhere to be seen. They'd made a lovely job of the tree though and the fairy lights in the shape of poppy flowers were a nice touch.

"I did say they were having choir practice and you wouldn't be able to hear yourself think."

The lady in the office maintained focus on her touch typing and was addressing no one in particular when she said, "he's just gone down to the science room."

Daisy didn't catch her words and pushed through exit door on the left, just as Wilson brushed past her coming in, through the door on the right. They didn't see each other of course, because with so much to resolve in such a short space of time, their dreams were being broadcast on different frequencies.

The Market Square was empty as Daisy made her way over the cobbles towards the Clock Tower. Her path crossed that of Balthazar and though there was just a metre of space between them, she didn't see him. Balthazar was conducting background checks on two very important individuals and on a different wavelength altogether.

Daisy chose the bench seat to the right of the statue of Mr Ludlow (or possibly Mr Abingdon) and rehearsed the conversation she'd had with Wilson earlier. There wouldn't be time for another visit if she overlooked even the smallest detail.

Felix responded to Daisy's invocation and announced his arrival by once again caressing her hand with a waft of warm air.

"Felix. Thank goodness you've arrived. I was thinking you could have been banned after our last conversation and the storm. Are you sitting next to me?"

"Huh ... Huh ... Huh ... "

"On my right or left?"

"Huh ... Huh ... Huh ... I'm not left or right Daisy, because I'm not there. I wasn't there the last time. I'm in a flat above a Chinese takeaway if I'm anywhere."

"But I felt you, you touched my hand."

"Yes, but I'm not there and I don't perceive you as you perceive me. This is a dream remember, and I've simply responded to your beckoning."

Daisy knew the conversation might be curtailed by a hailstorm at any minute so moved quickly to the questions.

"Felix, that morning, when I was with Sally and she entered the flat with flowers, she sensed you were there. You heard me call your name and you responded by making that banging noise."

"That was different. That was not in a dream."

"Could you see us?"

"No, I could hear you and sense your presence, where you were in the room, but I couldn't see you in the way *you* mean. We speak the same language but with different words. Huh ... Huh ... Huh ... "

Daisy realised that to have any chance of achieving the night's objectives she had to avoid becoming lost in translation.

"Felix, do you know the colour red?"

"Yes."

"Is red the colour of the Manchester United shirt?"

"That depends."

"On your understanding of the colour red?"

"No, it depends on whether United are playing at home or away. Huh . . . Huh . . . Huh . . . "

"Felix, the home strip."

"It's red. I know what red is."

"So you understand the meaning of the word yes, in my terms?"

"Yes"

"And the meaning of no?"

"Yes."

"Okay. So Felix, do you know why I'm here?"

"Yes. You want me to help you."

"Did Sally tell you she thought her life was building up to something, an inevitable certainty, her destiny?"

"No."

"Well she does. And she thinks Wilson and I are connected with this certainty and we agree with her. Does that make sense to you?"

"Yes."

"Sally knows how to illuminate spirits, only for the smallest fraction of time but for long enough to know they are there. Did you know about that?"

"No."

"When she went too far and consumed their excess energy prematurely she was punished with a car accident and Wilson saved her life and that's when our paths crossed. Actually, she wasn't being punished, it was meant to happen. Felix, I'm sorry, when Wilson explains things it all makes sense, but this is really complicated.

"To get to the point, we believe this certainty, for all three of us, involves extinguishing the spirit of Bradley Givens. Felix, do you follow me?"

"Yes."

"Good, because I'm about to go down a side street now."

"Go on."

"Felix, we also think that because we found your photo in the flat, which you left there, you also have a part to play. Did you lead us to the photo on purpose?"

Felix didn't answer. Rather, he didn't say yes and he didn't say no, nor did he laugh.

"Felix, are you still there?"

"They were three pounds each and Mrs Broughton said she'd pay for mine if I kept it a secret. Mum loved the photo and asked how much it cost so I told her three pounds. And I was going to tell her what Mrs Broughton said when Dad grabbed the photo and started shouting that he didn't have any money and food was more important than photos and he was really mad. So I told him it was free because my teacher knew we were poor and that made him even worse. He threw the photo on the wet floor where Mum had been cleaning and as I went to pick it up, that's when he pushed me. I slipped and hit my forehead on the edge of the cooker and the last thing I remember is pushing the photo underneath where I could see it was dry."

Daisy remembered the layout of the flat and the imagery evoked by the narrative was all the worse for it.

"Felix, I'm sorry about what happened to you."

"It's okay. Shit happens."

"What?" Felix, I'm being serious.

"Huh . . . Huh . . . Huh . . . don't blame me, I got that from Sally. "

415

"Felix, I have to tell you something. I think the wet floor, the push from your dad, you hiding the photo beneath the oven; that was all meant to be. And when Sally first met you in The Market Square, that was also supposed to happen. Did you ever go to the Number 11 Club?"

"Yes."

"Did you ever go to the casino, through the curtains at the back?"

"No."

"Well, if you had, you'd have discovered that bets are placed on the things that happen in our lives. I think you're also included in the bets about Sally, and us, and it's gone on for a long time. We think the betting will only end when Bradley Givens is fully extinguished. Do you understand what I'm trying to say?"

"Yes."

"Hallelujah, because I need you to tell me if what I'm about to ask is possible."

Chapter 55

Ticking boxes

Sunday 3rd December 2017, 1.30 a.m.

The elderly lady continued typing and didn't look up when Wilson tapped on the window.

"I told you as you walked in, he's gone down to the science room."

Alex was drinking coffee at the Formica topped table when Wilson pushed open the door to the kitchen.

"Thanks Dad."

"This is the last time Wilson. I mean it."

"I know Dad, sorry." Wilson took a seat.

"We got the torches. The ones you said. The FX50s. Balthazar acquired six of them this morning."

"Wilson, whoa, hold on a minute. You know you can be arrested for just carrying one of those torches, let alone switching one on? You need a special licence. And you've got how many, six? Acquired from where? And who's this Balthazar character?"

"Dad, listen, none of that is important right now. Tomorrow night we're going to say goodbye to Bradley Givens and I need to be clear in my mind that what we're planning is going to work. And if it does, I promise, it will make the criminal charge go away, not sure how, but I'm certain it will. So I need you to listen to me for two minutes."

"That's what I'm here for son."

"Last night, you told me that it was possible to capture light."

"And I also said that to do that, you needed laboratory conditions, a perfect mirrored surface and a flawless glass ball. It's a theoretical concept, not something you can do in the garage."

"I know that Dad, I was listening. But this is the bit I wanted to check. Sally said when she used a wardrobe lined with silver foil to trap one of the spirits, it made the spirit confused, like it needed time to think about how to escape. And in The Gateway she was told that shining a torch at spirits was the reason they lost their excess energy. So maybe that extra bit of thinking time consumes the last drop of power, flattens their battery to the three ounce mark. My idea is to do the same with Bradley Givens. If we can get into his study and surround him with super powerful light bouncing off silver foil, he won't know where to turn and use up all his charge."

"So you're asking me what Wilson? Do I think if you shine powerful torches at the invisible spirit of a dead person, at something that theoretically doesn't exist, it will make everything okay? I've absolutely no idea son! But given your ability to constantly astound me, I'd say it's more than likely. I will tell you one thing though. If, and this is a BIG if, if these spirits do actually emit fluorescence as you say, which means they are composed of a substance and therefore real, the question of how much energy they possess won't come into it. If you shine six of those torches in a circle, the point at which all those beams meet will be so full of energy that not only would the face of a luminous watch burn out, the battery inside would explode as well."

"I was hoping you'd say something like that Dad."

"I really hope you know what you're doing son. Those torches are dangerous."

"Dad, I'm well aware of that, and don't worry, I'll be supervised by an adult. I've asked Balthazar to buy those masks that welders wear to put over our sunglasses. This is going to change the flow of future events, I'm sure of it. All I need to do now, is make sure the side bet has been taken off the table. I've got to go Dad. See you in the morning."

As Wilson ran from L'Ecole in the direction of Sampson's Motorcycle Workshop, movement in the corner of his eye brought him to a sudden halt.

A man wearing blue overalls was kneeling at the base of the war memorial searching for something in what looked like an old tool bag. He appeared to be preparing for a new inscription, to carve a new name in the granite face, for when he stood and turned to face Wilson, a lump hammer and a mason's chisel were in his hands. They appraised each other from a distance without speaking for a few seconds, and when the stonemason turned to resume his work Wilson continued across The Market Square. He was running low on dream time and Sampson would either be in his workshop or his gaming room. Fortunately he was in the workshop, stripping down an engine, when Wilson entered.

Sampson looked up, smiled, put down the wrench and walked over wiping his hands on a rag. "Hey Wilson, how's it going?"

"I was hoping you'd be able to tell me."

They met halfway. A row of customised Harley Davidson

bikes were lined up like dominoes. Push one over and they'd all fall down.

"We're expecting a full house tomorrow Wilson. The best high-stakes game for quite some time. Marlon Brando's in town and he's brought a few of the wild ones."

Sampson's hand gesture drew Wilson's attention to the Harley motorcycles.

Wilson had no idea what Sampson was going on about.

"So what's the likely outcome for my dad? Black for bad or red for good?"

"Ah Wilson, you know I can't tell you that. We've enjoyed the show so far though."

"Mark, much as I like the way you see fun in everything, this is serious, my Dad could . . . "

"Yes, I know. I know why you're here. You want to know what our position is on the side bet? Will the storm building over Mum and Dad's future suddenly dissolve into bright sunshine?"

"Mark, we had an agreement that if I helped you with the Bradley Givens' problem, you would help me with mine. If that's not the case, all bets are off."

"Ah, if only everything were so simple Wilson! We both know you have no say in this. Nor does Daisy. Or Sally. Or myself for that matter. The course of an outcome, when those dice bounce off the green baize, where they land, how they fall, is all down to lady luck."

"Mark. Are you going to keep your word, that's all I need to know?"

"It appears to be looking that way. A member of the special air service was despatched this morning. Come to think of it Wilson, you've got a busy day ahead. Shouldn't you be home in bed getting a good night's sleep."

"Very funny! But let me tell you this, and it's no joke, I know where you live if you let me down."

Sampson was unlikely to commit to anything further in terms of guidance and so Wilson turned his attention to the bikes.

"Why do you spend time here Sampson? Who buys these bikes? Why are you repairing engines? Shouldn't you be in The Citadel fixing the problems of the world instead?"

"I like to switch off sometimes Wilson. We all need our hobbies. And since you're asking, would you like to buy one? This classic Harley Davidson Fat Boy would suit you to a tee. There's even a pillion seat for driving Miss Daisy. And leather panniers for that special weekend away. Lots of room for your pyjamas and toothbrush."

Wilson smiled at the underlying meaning and was reminded of the tuba playing.

"Can you see stuff like that, if you want to? You know, people's personal moments?"

"Wilson! Absolutely not! What do you take me for? Some sleazy voyeur? What happens behind closed doors, stays behind closed doors. Though one or two of my less scrupulous colleagues do peep through keyholes on occasion. Besides, look in the mirror Wilson. Snooping around in 3b, sifting through people's memories, you'll be needing a little self-censorship yourself. To be honest though, when you get to my age, and I forget how old I am now, you lose all interest in that sort of thing."

"Okay stop Mark, I've got it! Too much information! Anyway, think I'd prefer the Triumph Cafe Racer, the one with the fancy seat. Think that's more my style."

Sampson walked over to the bike and stroked the seat.

"Yep, isn't she a beauty? Hand stitched, quilted leather. Just the job. You'll still need that set of panniers though."

"Can I buy it with a credit card?"

"Absolutely! And you've got unlimited credit in this establishment. No idea how you're going to get the bike home though."

"Mmm, good point. Hey, but I'd want a test drive first and . . ."

Wilson couldn't hold back that first yawn, nor the second one that made Sampson turn and walk away to continue rebuilding the engine. When Wilson's presence dissolved into a fading, transparent tincture of itself, he left the workshop just as Balthazar was walking in.

"Mark, we need to speak. I've got a bit of a problem with Andy Masterson" he said.

Chapter 56

Let's do this

An olive branch had been left on the kitchen table the next morning, in the form of a note.

'Wilson, hope you slept well. Your dad and I have gone to visit Auntie Rita. (Will have to face the music at some time!) And I need to get out of the house. Sorry for shouting at you last night. Dad said you wanted to see Daisy again. Okay. But please, wrap up warm on the scooter and try not to be out too late. Think one night is enough until you're fully better. I know I'm being mollycoddling. I can't help it. Love Mum xxx.'

Wilson had a round of toast clamped between his teeth as he pulled on his parka, grabbed his rucksack and closed the front door. He was running late.

Mark was unloading the people carrier at the rear of 247 Chapel Street when Wilson pulled up. The back door to the building was wedged open and James and Daisy were doing shuttle runs with sheets of plywood board. They were bigger than specified so Mark had bought a jigsaw and a spare set of blades.

"Sorry I'm late folks, slept through my alarm. I was knackered."

423

"It's fine Wilson, perfect timing because I think we're ready to start."

Mark pulled out a trestle table from beneath the mezzanine floor.

"Where's Balthazar? Do we have the permission?"

"No, not yet, he's upstairs on the phone twisting someone's arm. I think it's proving more difficult than he thought. Fingers crossed."

"What about the AV equipment?"

"We can collect it from the rental company anytime after one. Two broadcast quality cameras, three microphones on stands, digital recorders for both sound and visual and the connecting cables with mains leads."

James had been extremely specific with the requirements and even though none of the equipment would actually be put to use, it was important to have authentic props.

"Right, where do we start?" Daisy asked.

"In my opinion," said Wilson, removing his parka and rolling up his sleeves in a business-like fashion, "first we check that we've got everything we need. I made a list last night. Where are the torches?"

"They're in the safe" said Mark.

"Can we check they all work, that they're charged up and we should probably read the instructions?"

Mark retrieved the case from the walk-in safe, placed it on the trestle table and raised the lid.

Daisy was impressed.

"They look like something from *Star Wars.*"

"And more powerful than light sabres according to my dad. Lift one out and get used to the feel of it, but don't switch the bloody thing on. Mark, did you get the welder's masks."

"Yes, Balthazar went out and bought six this morning."

Daisy helped Mark fetch them from the safe.

Wilson pulled one over his head and everything went incredibly dark. The effect was like the sun being eclipsed.

"Is there an instruction leaflet with the torches?"

"Yes," said Mark, "but I'd call it more of a manual. I read it last night. The first page tells you how to switch the torch on and off and charge the battery. The other fifty pages tell you what not to do. I shone one up at the sky last night, only for a second, and I could see the clouds. They're incredible."

"Okay show Daisy how to switch one on."

Daisy took a torch from its moulded compartment, unscrewed the lens cover and passed it to Mark.

"There are two settings. Pulse beam and permanent beam. The pulse beam is what we need, you just press this plastic dimple and as it clicks, the light comes on. Lift your finger, and the light goes off. Forget the permanent beam switch. But first you must power up the torch with this primer switch at the back. Twist it to the red for danger position."

"Okay, wait a second." Wilson dug a pair of sunglasses out of his rucksack and put them on. Then he pulled the visor of the welding mask down over the glasses. He couldn't see the hand in front of his face.

"Daisy, hold the torch out at arms-length and point it at me. Then turn away, close your eyes and press the pulse button, on and off, as quickly as you can. Mark, close your eyes and turn your back, you too James."Then he took five steps back.

"Wilson, you sure this isn't going to damage your eyes?"

"No, I asked my dad. He said with sunglasses and a mask and for one burst with my eyes closed, I'd be okay."

"Okay. Ready? One, two, three, press."

Without eye protection, the intensity of the torch beam would have been equivalent to looking at the sun through binoculars. Mark and Daisy could feel the light coming through their eyelids.

Wilson removed the mask and sunglasses and rubbed his eyes.

"Yeh, that was what you call bright. I can still see a round glow on the back of my eye. They're going to be perfect."

They'd just finished a practice session of lamping each other in sunglasses and welder's masks when Balthazar appeared.

"We still don't have the paperwork," he said, "and Masterson's not returning my calls."

Daisy was first to arrive at the obvious conclusion.

"But unless we have the permission, there's no point in doing any of this."

"Don't worry, there's time. I've got a final card up my sleeve but I'd prefer not to play it unless I have to."

Mark checked the power meter on each torch for full charge as he put them away.

"Why did you get six" asked Daisy, "when there's only five of us?"

"Wilson said he wanted six" said Balthazar.

Wilson was puzzled.

"I didn't say how many we needed. I hadn't worked that out."

"I guess that's the way they come then. In packs of six."

Daisy knew that would be too much of a coincidence but let the matter drop.

Wilson checked the time. It was eleven-thirty and they had a lot of work to do.

"We need to start on the panels, how many boards did you buy Mark?"

"Eight. I know it's more than we need, it's just in case I make a mistake when I trim them down."

"Did you get struts for the back and the aluminium foil?"

"Yes, but we need to make the struts from lengths of timber and attach them to the boards. Screwdriver, hinges and screws are there. Twenty packs of silver foil are in that bag along with three cans of spray mount and a roll of black plastic for the windows. And I bought a jigsaw to trim the boards. What do we think? They're eight feet by four feet now."

"Where's that newspaper with the photo of Bradley in his study?"

"It's on the mezzanine."

Wilson retrieved the paper and placed it on the trestle table.

"Look, here's Bradley's desk and his chair would normally go here. 'He's always in his chair when he's in that room' Felix said."

Wilson continued.

"This trestle table is a similar size, so let's move it nearer to the wall, like in the picture. Mark, can you take one of those plywood boards and stand with it here, longways up. Daisy, grab another board and stand there with a gap of about half a metre between you and Mark. Balthazar, can you do the same on the other side? So, we'll have a sort of Stonehenge arrangement, with five free-standing foil panels and us shining our torches at Bradley from the gaps between. Sally thought spirits tried to escape into shadow, so with five torches like headlights surrounding him and the light bouncing everywhere off the silver foil, there's no escape."

"No! That's not right Wilson. There's supposed to be six torches, not five. It's okay if you don't have a spare torch, I've brought my own."

Sally was walking towards them from the rear of the banking hall. She was holding a torch in her hand.

"You left the back door open, I hope you don't mind me coming in."

"Sally, what are you doing here? You said you couldn't help anymore."

"But I told you I'd see you Daisy. I also have to go. That's how it's supposed to be."

Daisy turned to Balthazar who stepped forward and crouched down, face to face with Sally. He placed a hand on her shoulder.

"Sally, we've got it all planned out. This is not your responsibility anymore. You've done your job, you brought us all together. We'll take it from here."

"But there's something you've not thought about."

"What is it? What have we missed?"

"I can't say. I just know you've forgotten something important. I'm meant to stand here, at the side, with Bradley's chair right in front of me in this direction."

Sally pointed to her rightful place.

"I've seen what the boards look like when you cover them in silver foil, they're perfect. I wanted to try something like this in the attic, but it was hard by myself. Daisy you're meant to stand in that gap there."

Sally indicated the various positions.

"Balthazar, you go there next to Daisy, James you're here and Mark you're over there opposite Wilson and me. So you need to make six panels not five."

"Sally, you can't come with us tonight. It's going to be late when we get back. What will you tell Kay and Leanna?"

"They don't know I'm here, but I left a card under the tree which explains everything."

Wilson glanced at Daisy, they were thinking the same thing.

We were meant to have six torches all along, Sally was being counted in from the beginning.

"You need the panels to be as wide as possible and the people gaps as small as possible. I'll explain the other things when we get there. And I'd rather use my torch."

Sally's directive was delivered with such self-belief that no one doubted her surety.

Sally unfastened all the toggles and removed her duffle coat. She was wearing her school uniform beneath.

"It works best when the silver foil is all crinkly. I think it causes more reflections and that confuses them even more. I'll show you."

Two hours later, six panels covered in silver foil, standing six feet tall and four feet wide, were positioned round the trestle table just as Sally had instructed. The silver foil had been scrunched up before being flattened out and spray mounted. Standing inside the circle felt like being at the epicentre of some kind of solar power generator. The widest gap was the width of Balthazar's shoulders, the narrowest, the width of Sally's. The people carrier didn't have room to carry six passengers and all the equipment. James was starting to panic until Salford Van Hire rang back to say a transit van could be collected from the Stretford branch at four-thirty. Balthazar drove with Mark to collect it.

When Balthazar returned, there was unfinished business to attend to in the Manager's Office. His text message was self-explanatory.

'Andy, if you don't call me back in five minutes, your wife will discover what you get up to between seven and nine on the first Monday of every month in Shepherd's Market behind The Park Lane Hotel. It certainly makes you a security risk. And just to clarify the point, I'm referring to those Monday nights when your wife thinks you're working late to cover for your boss. And if you don't think that's damaging enough, she'll also find out about the 'French affair'. I'm presuming this line is secure, if not, best call me back sharpish.'

Balthazar's mobile phone rang two minutes later.

"Balthazar are you out of your mind? I'm in a meeting. You can't send me messages like that!" Masterson's words were delivered in a angry whisper.

"Andy, I'm not messing around mate. I need that permission."

"Balthazar, I can't just call the Home Secretary on a Sunday and bark out a ridiculous order and expect him to follow it like a boy scout. He's not interested in what's happening in bloody Tarporley."

"Mmm, well he should be. Bring the matter to his attention would you? You never know, you might get another

430

promotion. So to recap, I want permission for six psychologists with expertise in paranormal activity to be in The Maltings from around six until eleven tonight. I need a number to call for clearance if the police say no. We'll be arriving in a people carrier and a Salford Van Hire transit. I can give you the registration numbers if you want."

"Balthazar, I can't do it. And not only that, I won't bloody do it. You can't blackmail me and think that'll get you the okay from the Home Secretary. I can call a special number and have you arrested within the hour."

"Yes, I thought you might say that Andy, so I've got a special number of my own. One that I want you to pass on to the Home Secretary himself, not his office. The magic figure is 34343437. It's the number for his private bank account in Geneva. I know how much is in the account and where it all came from Andy. 34343437. That's an easy one to remember. You've got ten minutes."

Balthazar emerged from his office five minutes later waving a sheet of paper like it was the enemy's flag of surrender.

"We're good to go."

Time was ticking and night was falling as the foil panels were loaded in the transit van. Light reflected from the wrinkled surface in kaleidoscopic colours as Wilson slid the last one into place.

"That's it, we're ready" he yelled, slamming the back door shut.

Mark pulled out of the compound and joined the line of rush hour traffic crawling out of the city centre.

Balthazar followed in the people carrier with James in the passenger seat and Wilson, Daisy and Sally in the back. The boxes containing the AV equipment and the torches were stowed in the luggage space.

"Balthazar, can I see the permission?"

The logo with the portcullis and the address at the top looked very official, but Daisy expected something more ministerial in terms of the words.

To whom it may concern.

This letter gives authority to the bearer and party to enter The Maltings from anytime after six tonight. Six people, two vehicles. Call this office on the number above for clarification if required. Make sure they're out by eleven.

Squiggle for a signature.

The Office of the Home Secretary for Her Majesty's Government.

Chapter 57

Into battle

Sunday 3rd December 2017, 6.00 p.m.

As they made good progress along the M56, at Wilson's suggestion, Sally gave Balthazar a full résumé of her curriculum vitae relating to lamping non-extinguished spirits. When Sally described the method for 'outing' her warrior, for the need to cause a disturbance, to noisily rearrange furniture and the importance of standing in total silence in a pitch-black room, James nodded his head without question, as if to say, 'Yes, that's correct, that's exactly how it's done.'

Balthazar on the other hand, by the nature of his question, appeared to have no past experience of extinguishing non-extinguished spirits.

"What I don't understand is why Bradley won't be aware of us shifting stuff around?"

"He will, they respond to sound" said Daisy, "they can't see us."

Daisy bit her tongue and shot daggers at Wilson. She knew what was coming and it was all his fault because he was the one who'd talked her out of telling Sally in the first place.

'Remember to tell Felix not to give the hand signal until we're ready. Sally doesn't need to know about Felix being involved, we can tell her later.'

Those were Wilson's exact words and now, inadvertently, the truth was about to slip out.

"Daisy how do you know that?" asked Sally. There was a quizzical tone in her voice. "How do you know Bradley won't be able to see us? When I saw those children in the home, and the warrior, it was like they could see me, I could tell from the expressions on their faces. They were looking at me."

"Sally, pass me your torch. Is this the one you used for lamping in the attic?"

"Yes, it's a really good one."

"How do you turn it on?"

Daisy covered the lens with her hand and everyone heard the 'click' as finger shadows were projected down onto the carpet floor.

"When you've been still and silent for a while, they're drawn to the sound of the click. It's the unexpected noise that causes the startled expression, not the fact they've seen you. At the same time, they sense the sudden brightness of light and chase shadows to escape."

"I still don't understand how you can know that?"

"Sally, there's something I have to tell you and I should have ignored Wilson and found time to say this earlier."

"Found time to say what? What do you need to tell me?"

"I spoke to Felix in The Market Square. I thought he might be able to help us."

Sally had to think about that for a few seconds.

"Felix? And could you see him?"

"No, it wasn't like pulling your teacher into a dream. I didn't see Felix, but I could hear him, and he could hear me. I spoke to him."

Daisy could only see the side of Sally's head but knew that somewhere inside, she'd be sifting through memories and thoughts and aligning them with the news she'd just been given.

"Was he okay?"

"Yes, he was laughing."

The smile brightened her profile.

"Yeh, Felix was always laughing. What did he tell you?"

"He told me that Bradley Givens couldn't see us but could hear us. That's how he was able to attack the people outside the gates, he was drawn to their voices, he understood what they were saying and knew cameras would be filming."

"Did Felix say anything about me?"

Daisy shot daggers at Wilson for a second time.

"Yes, he said he was missing you. He told me about the night you went to the Number 11 Club and you were drinking sprite and eating cheesy wotsits because they were his favourite. He asked me if you were okay and told me to say hi. He said to let you know he was in a good place and that shit happens."

Sally burst into laughter.

"Did he really say that?"

"Yes, he said exactly that, and he was laughing as well, with a really deep voice. It was a kind of Huh . . . Huh . . . Huh."

"Yeh, his shoulders always went up and down like that when he laughed."

"I asked him about the photo we found and he told me what happened. It was an accident Sally, his Dad was angry, but Felix doesn't think his Dad intended to make him slip on the wet floor and bang his head."

Sally didn't need more detail. The final piece of the puzzle had fallen into place.

"Felix was meant to hide the photo that day. It needed to stay in a safe place. Felix knew we would come."

Daisy was about to tell Sally how her conversation with

Felix ended, when Wilson cut across her path.

"The most important thing, once we're inside, is to act like we're students, psychology students researching an inexplicable phenomenon. And remember, Bradley is listening, so there's to be no talk about foil panels or torches or where they need to be positioned, just talk about the sound and recording equipment. Also, once we've finished banging about the house, before we enter the study, I'll give you a nod, then we take off our shoes, oh, and before that, check that no floorboards are creaking. I'll put black tape down to show where not to step and . . . "

Daisy placed her hand on Wilson's shoulder.

"We've got it, we know what to do. We've been through it ten times. Don't worry!"

Balthazar smiled at Daisy from his rearview mirror.

The milling crowds and the traffic congestion had abated considerably as they approached the police roadblock. Accepting the afterlife appeared to be dependent on daily reinforcement. Sally could see clutches of people to the left and right of a policewoman with her hands in her jacket pockets standing in front of a barrier. As they drew closer and Balthazar eased on the brake, Sally also saw a man with a video camera balanced on his shoulder filming a female reporter. She recognised the woman without a second to lose and ducked down out of sight.

"Oh flip! Auntie Kay's here. She's with the man with the camera. Auntie Kay's filming the house for a documentary and she'll recognise you from the hospital. Hide your faces, look the other way!"

Balthazar slowed the car to a snail's pace as they

approached the roadblock.

"There's a car blanket underneath my seat. Quick, throw it over your heads."

The policewoman stepped in front of the people carrier, raised her hand to signal the driver to stop and came round to the side.

"Good evening officer."

"Sorry sir, but you'll have to turn round. No one is allowed past this point. There's no access for the public. You can turn the vehicle around over there."

The policewoman then stepped back to give Balthazar room for the manoeuvre.

"We have special permission to enter officer."

He handed over the paper which took seconds to read.

The policewoman looked over Balthazar's shoulder.

"Who's under the blanket? ET?"

"No, they're three of the country's leading parapsychologists."

The policewoman read the words on the paper for a second time. She was unsure of what to do and continued to peer in the back, debating with herself about the possibility of there really being an extraterrestrial underneath the blanket. She studied James's face in profile and when he abruptly turned, she could see he was blind, his eyes were milky white.

"They're having a seance to get in the right frame of mind" he said.

Balthazar rolled his eyes as James said the word seance, as if to send a message to the policewoman that he didn't have a clue what was going on either, and was simply following a ridiculous order on a piece of paper.

"They've got special permission to film and all the equipment's in the van behind us. We're two vehicles. Six people."

The policewoman stepped back to visually inspect the vehicle with the Salford Van Hire livery and then walked away to raise the barrier. The two officers outside The Maltings would have to decide on this. She handed the paper back to Balthazar and fifty metres later he gave the all-clear.

"Okay, you can come out now."

Wilson looked through the back window and gave a sigh of relief. Sally was tittering to herself.

"That was funny, she thought we were ET. Like when he's covered up on the front of that bike."

Daisy placed the tip of her finger on Sally's nose.

"Phone hoommmme."

The second roadblock was still four hundred metres away as the first floor of The Maltings came into view. The bank of floodlights fixed to the upper arm of the crane was bathing the roofing tiles in the equivalent of daylight.

They drove slowly onwards, past the entrances to three or four discretely hidden properties set in private grounds. These were the homes of the stockbroker belt, the mansions of the Cheshire set. Bradley had clearly done well for himself. As more of The Maltings came into view, Wilson realised they had a problem.

"Damn, look how bright everything is. That's going to be an issue."

He was right. If a fleet of alien spaceships had decided to combine all their light rays and illuminate just one property, The Maltings couldn't have been picked out more clearly.

"We'll never be able to block out all this light. It'll be like an operating theatre in that study."

Balthazar pulled to a halt, as instructed by the policeman advancing with his palm raised and passed the self-explanatory document through the window.

"We've been given special permission to film. It's for an episode of *Ghostcatchers!*"

The protocol for such a situation must have been covered at training school because the brick-faced policeman with the jagged scar on his chin read the letter, peered over Balthazar's shoulder, and he wasn't buying it.

"They're savants officer. Kids with special powers. Parapsychologists. They sense things no one else can."

The policeman read the directive for a second time as he stroked the scar on his chin and something didn't feel right. He stared questioningly at Balthazar for a few moments and walked the fifty or so metres back to his colleague to confer. Balthazar tapped his finger on the steering wheel, then drove forward forty metres, turned the engine off and left the car.

The barrier denied access to the driveway. As he approached the policemen, Balthazar's gaze followed the curve of the drive up to a large, red brick property that smacked of tasteless nouveau riche. The entrance porch, a puny sort of portico supported on concrete posts was a pitiful evocation of The Gateway.

Balthazar realised there was another detail that had also been overlooked.

"Is there a problem?" Balthazar was now standing in front of the two policemen, almost toe to toe.

The officers didn't answer immediately. They'd had

nothing to do for six hours and were happy to be suddenly occupied and intrigued by a carload of ghostbusters. The policeman with the scar had taken an instant dislike to the cocky attitude of the driver and was planning to make life difficult, just for the fun of it.

"If there's a problem, you'd better call that number."

The policeman with the scar, tilted his head and gave a wry smile.

Are you trying to order me about mate? Cos if you are, bring it on, I'll have you for breakfast sunshine.

"You've got ten-seconds officer, to either call the number, or let us through."

They were silently fighting with eye to eye combat. Balthazar took a step forward to make sure the officer knew the gloves were coming off.

"Come to think of it. You need to make that call, because I want power back on in the house immediately and these bloody searchlights switching off. And when you speak to the Home Secretary's office, because I know they'll put you through to get approval for the floodlights going off, tell them the bank manager's name at Barclay's Geneva is Francois Vevey. Francois Vevey. That'll pull all the right strings."

With a face of glaring menace the policeman backed off and turned to make the call.

Daisy and Sally looked on anxiously from the car. Wilson gave James a running commentary.

When the call was over Balthazar took the paper from the policeman and returned to the car. He selected forward gear and drove up to the barrier.

Sally saw Balthazar check the time on his wristwatch as

440

he addressed the policeman with the scar.

"When your electrician gets here, I want all the floodlights off immediately."

"Yes sir, I'll make sure it happens. Here are the keys." The cocksure copper appeared to have had the stuffing knocked out of him. His salute was unnecessary as the two vehicles waited for the second policeman to raise the barrier and swing the entrance gates open. They followed the second officer until the drive forked and he veered off to the right, towards the garage and the mains power switches for the house.

"Leave the gates open will you, we don't want to be hanging around when we're done here."

Balthazar took the left fork and followed the drive round to the back of the house.

Daisy pressed every light switch on a panel inside the back door and led James down a hallway with a white tiled floor that led into a spacious, state of the art, kitchen. She settled James on a stool at one end of the breakfast bar and returned to help Wilson and the others unload the vehicles.

The six panels were placed in a row against a wall of appliances and cupboards. The AV equipment was stacked on an island unit. The FX50 torches were lined up on a granite worktop. Daisy rolled out the black plastic sheet for the windows. Mark carried in a white board on which strips of black gaffer tape had been lightly tacked.

They worked in silence and gathered in the kitchen when the unloading was complete. All knew the script and Wilson had the opening line. The timbre of his strong, clear voice mimicked that of an actor on stage.

"Right! Sally and Daisy, you go and check all the rooms

upstairs. Try and sense the presence of a cold spot. We'll check the ground floor and then work out the best location for our . . . movement activated cameras."

Sally held her hand over her mouth to stop the giggles.

"If it's too cold to sense the presence of err, the other dimension, we'll focus on the study. That's the room we saw in the photo on the cover of the newspaper."

It was all very amateur hour and hammed up like an episode of *Scooby Doo*.

Wilson put his finger to his lips to bring everyone to order, made eye contact with Mark and Balthazar and flicked his head in the direction of the second kitchen door that presumably led to the rest of the house and the study.

This door opened onto a spacious hallway, where a grandiose staircase swept in a curve around a magnificent, crystal chandelier and led up to the first floor landing.

"Wow" said Daisy, "this is like the Great Gatsby's house."

Sally and Daisy slowly climbed the staircase as Wilson and the others went off to map out the ground floor.

At the top of the stairs, the first door on the minstrel's gallery opened onto a bedroom so luxurious and opulent, Elton John would have enjoyed a sleepover. The white carpet was as soft and deep as Polar bear fur. The wall of fitted wardrobes could have held a lifetime's clothing for a family of five and the four-poster bed would have been perfect for the princess and the pea. The Rococo style chaise longue, with red velvet upholstery and a frame gilded in gold leaf, might once have belonged to King Louis XV. Funnily enough, it had. Bradley acquired his 'posh settee' when the driver of a Christie's transport vehicle maintained his habit of stopping at Sandbach services for lunch, even though it was against the rules. The vehicle was found abandoned at Knutsford services an hour later and the insurance company had to fork out almost two hundred thousand pounds for the posh settee. And that was in 2010!

Sally opened every cupboard and wardrobe and forced the doors shut with an inconsiderate slam. It was time for Bradley to wake up. Daisy stripped the bed and left the silk sheets and a cashmere throw strewn across the floor.

They tore through the other bedrooms with similar disregard. No opportunity to make a din or disturbance was overlooked. Antique dressing tables were unceremoniously manhandled away from walls. Persian rugs were dragged across floors. Old master paintings in gilt frames were repositioned lopsidedly. When no item of furniture or ornament or soft furnishing had been left unmolested, Daisy and Sally went to find the others and made a hell of a racket as they came stomping down the tiled stairs.

Meanwhile, the other research students, Wilson et al, had completed their own noisy game of 'hunt the cold spot' and only the study was left to search.

Total silence descended when Wilson used sign language to indicate that shoes should be removed before they entered, then the brouhaha returned at twice the volume as directives were issued and orders barked. The enthusiasm in Wilson's voice was very much that of the swot on a field trip.

"Right Daisy. We'll conduct the experiment in here, in this study. It's perfect."

"Yes," said Daisy, "we can put all the recording devices over there. And the camera in that corner focused on the desk. Come on, let's go and bring all our motion sensitive equipment in."

As Daisy and Wilson headed back to the kitchen through

the door to the left of Bradley's desk, Mark remained in the study. He slowly peeled strips of black gaffer tape from the white board and then silently blacked out all the windows using the black plastic sheet. Balthazar glided by carrying one of the six panels.

With much exaggerated puffing and panting, Wilson carried the boxes with the AV kit into the study. Daisy screwed the video camera to a tripod and then dragged it into position, cursing and kicking as it snagged on a rug. Wilson dropped the case containing the sound recorder and volubly complained about the tangle in the cables and the lack of plug sockets and the need to keep dragging stuff out of the way.

Mark was silently taping the gap at the base of the other door leading from the study. Balthazar was aligning the last panel in correct relation to those either side, and that was when static caused Sally's hair to rise and she became aware of the presence of Bradley Givens. She sensed him as she had once sensed the warrior in the dining room. He was a large, overweight man with long, greasy hair swept back over a balding sweaty head. He was slouched back in his chair, dressed in a suit with his hands behind his head and grinning; grinning as though relaxing and listening to a comedy programme on the radio.

Wilson was the first to notice Sally in a trance with her stoney eyed stare focused on Bradley's chair. He waved at Balthazar and Daisy and pointed. Sally caught the wave from the corner of her eye and nodded her head. Daisy led James into position in total silence. Mark took his cue to the left. Daisy to the right. Sally took three steps back and then she too was standing on 'x' marks the spot. Exactly where she was meant to be.

Balthazar positioned the remaining three panels as Wilson floated back and forth with the welding masks, sunglasses and finally, the torches. The entire procedure was conducted in silence. Wilson returned to the kitchen to switch off the lights. He then turned off the lights in the hallway, entered the study and quietly closed the door behind. The scene resembled some form of pagan ritual involving welding gear.

He checked with Sally for a thumbs up. Bradley Givens was still sitting at his desk. Wilson began to think this was going to be easier than planned, he hadn't considered the possibility that Sally would recognise Bradley's presence. He took bearings on the location of the remaining gap between two panels, a gap just wide enough for his shoulders. Stepping backwards, Wilson counted the number of steps and switched off the study light. It was pitch black in a room hermetically sealed against the ingress of a single photon. Transferring his weight gently and slowly, from foot to foot, he moved stealthily back into position and froze when his right shoulder touched the edge of the panel and made it rock. He shuffled into the gap in stockinged feet and then all was ready. Wilson placed his index finger on the pulse button, gauged the trajectory of the beam and stood stock still. Daisy's free hand hung down by her side with fingers outstretched, she was waiting to feel the warm touch of Felix. Mark had placed the torch at the required angle in James's hand and he hadn't moved a millimetre. Balthazar and Sally were waiting for the signal. For two minutes they hardly dared to breathe for fear the thump of a heartbeat would give the game away.

When Daisy felt a breeze slip through her fingers she yelled "NOW" and the room was hit by a flash of man made lightning.

The following transpired in that polaroid snapshot of a single moment.

Daisy saw the presence of Felix through her visor and sunglasses. The close-cropped curly hair, the beaming smile, the button nose, the face from a photo of a clever boy in a school uniform. It was as though a sparkler in dextrous hands had sketched his glowing features against a Bonfire Night sky.

Wilson saw the presence of Bradley Givens. The face from a fake driving licence was portrayed in a fuzzy, fluorescent scribble that captured a triptych of competing emotions in one single portrait. A Francis Baconesque expression of rage, revulsion and terror personified in a spirit with nowhere to run and nowhere to hide. It was all over for Bradley Givens. The antidote had been administered. The tornado extinguished. A battery discharged and residual energy converted from one form to another.

Sally saw the presence of her father through the visor. He was standing by Bradley's side and smiling. One arm was locked round Bradley's neck and the other hand was clamped on Bradley's wrist, forcing him into his seat. On the other side of the chair, the diminutive presence of Felix was a slight, yet sufficient obstacle for the further prevention of Bradley's emergency exit. The rogue spirit was trapped in an electric chair.

If only Sally had been wearing those rubber soled school shoes and not been in stockinged feet. If only she'd not anticipated her father being there and not reached for his hand. If only the extinguished spirit of Bradley Givens had taken a different route to The Gateway instead of following the path of least resistance.

If and only! Two small words, but when combined, the most powerful in the English language.

Energy coursed through Sally's body like lightning down an earthing rod and in doing so it changed *her* from one form to another. When Wilson heard the scream, he pushed the visor from his eyes, reached for the light switch and watched Mark and Daisy catch Sally as she fell to the ground.

The shadow deep in Sally Bennett's soul had been the only place for Bradley Givens to run, the only possible escape route. It was always going to lead directly to The Gateway of course, because that's what the shadow was there for.

Balthazar carried Sally out to the people carrier and wrapped her in the car blanket. Daisy was struggling to find a pulse as both vehicles fled the scene.

The silver foil panels, the torches, the black plastic covering the windows, the expensive AV kit and all the cases and welder's masks were simply abandoned. After watching the cars screech out of the driveway and race off down the road, the policeman with the scar on his chin ran back up to a house in total darkness. The letter had been an order to let the people do whatever they wanted, so there was nothing more to say. At least they'd buggered off early.

It came as a surprise however, to discover that the Home Secretary had ultimate responsibility for exorcising demons, because on entering the study, the officer was of the opinion a satanic ritual had taken place to despatch the devil himself.

Chapter 58

Panic stations

Sunday 3rd December 2017, 9.30 p.m.

Wilson didn't need paramedic skills to know Sally was gravely ill. Her breathing was soft and shallow, her hands cold and clammy and her pupils were not responding to light from the pencil torch on a key ring. She was also unconscious.

Light from street lamps broke over Sally's face in steady waves as they drove out of Tarporley and beneath the wash, Daisy could see the skin was pallid and grey. Wilson had located the nearest hospital on his phone and was giving directions to Balthazar.

Sally was lying across three seats with Daisy kneeling on the floor gently rubbing her hand. Wilson was standing up, shoulders hunched, head pressed against the car roof, urging Sally to hold on.

"The hospital's just a few minutes away, stay with us" he implored.

Sally's bloodless lips opened to release a dry cough and her eyelids parted.

"Balthazar how do I turn on a courtesy light, I can't see a thing in the back?"

Sally turned her head and slowly extended her arm out to Wilson. He dropped to one knee beside Daisy and took her hand. She gave him the faintest of smiles.

"Wilson."

The shallow rise and fall of her chest barely registered and her voice was little more than a whisper.

"Wilson. No hospital. I want to be with Auntie Kay."

Sally coughed again, her eyelids closed and the smile fell away.

"Come on Sally, stay with us, you can do it." Daisy began furiously rubbing the back of Sally's hand, as though trying to reignite life with friction, then she burst into tears. Her mouth was contorted by anguish as she spoke.

"She's only thirteen. She's just a child. What were we thinking? Balthazar, why did you help us, put us up to it? I never thought I'd go through this for a second time."

Half an hour later Daisy's sobs had all but subsided as Balthazar pulled into the driveway of the vicarage.

Daisy ran to the door, kept her finger on the bell and pounded on the glass with her fist.

Kay came running, fastening the tie on her dressing gown as she did so. She gasped and recoiled with her hand over her mouth as Balthazar surged past carrying Sally in his arms. Balthazar kicked open three doors until he found the lounge and placed Sally gently down on the sofa.

Kay flew to Sally's side.

"Oh my God, what's happened? Sally love, wake up, it's me, Auntie Kay, I'm here. Sally, it's all right now."

Kay frantically ran her hands all over Sally's arms and legs and feet and chest and head, feeling for the damage from another car accident and checked her clothing for blood.

"What's happened? I've been worried sick. She left a note to say she was going out and wouldn't be long. Leanna said she's been out all day."

Kay placed her hand on Sally's forehead.

"She's cold, icy cold. Pass me that throw."

Daisy did as instructed and helped cover Sally who was still half-wrapped in the car blanket.

"What's happened? Come on Sally love. Wake up. Talk to your Auntie Kay."

She was shaking Sally's hand more vigorously now and turned to Daisy.

"What's happened? Why is she with you?"

"I think she was hit by lightning" said Balthazar.

"What? Hit by lightning." Kay turned back to her niece. "Jesus Christ! No! No! Where did she get hit? She's not been burned. Where are the red marks?"

"We were driving past and she was . . . "

Sally groaned, raised a knee three or four inches, the throw rose like a tent then collapsed.

"Oh, thank goodness, she's okay. Just knocked out. She's coming out of shock. Come on Sally, I'm here, you're going to be okay. You're a strong girl. Come on now."

When no further response was forthcoming, Kay realised she hadn't been thinking properly.

"We need to call an ambulance. Now! Oh my God, why did you bring her here? Why didn't you take her straight to hospital, or leave her where she was and call an ambulance and wait until they arrived? But there's not a mark on her body. How is it she could have been hit by lightning?"

Kay felt for Sally's pulse.

"You've been taking drugs together haven't you? Grooming her, and she's had an overdose. That's why her skin is grey and she's unresponsive and her hands are sweating, I'm calling the police. I'm going to call the police right now. That's it, that's what's happened."

Kay stood up and began wringing her hands and didn't know what to do for the best or where to turn.

"I need to get dressed. Take her to the hospital, call the police."

Sally coughed twice, the throw lifted again and then Sally opened her eyes. When she saw Kay, she stretched out a hand and her lips parted into a slow smile.

"That's it love, good girl, it's going to be all right. You'll pull through, I'm here. Don't worry, Auntie Kay's here."

Kay knelt down and brought her ear close to Sally's mouth in order to hear the words being mumbled in reply.

"Auntie Kay, don't worry, everything is going to be okay. Don't call the police, or ambulance. My friends helped me. I need to go and . . . meet Mum now . . . and Dad. I saw them . . . they're . . . waiting for me."

Sally was struggling to set her words free.

"I left you a card . . . under the tree. You have . . . to read it now. Like . . . you promised. You crossed . . . your heart."

Sally's hand fell to the floor and streams of tears flowed down Kay's cheeks. She turned to the white envelope propped against the base of the tree. Daisy ducked beneath the branches and handed it to Kay.

"I've got it love. It's here. I'm going to read it now."

The words on the envelope said . . .

'With love to Auntie Kay
(my fabulous other MUM)x'

Kay brushed back tears with the back of her hand and raised the flap on the back of the envelope.

She slowly pulled out the card.

The picture on the front was Sally's drawing of a seahorse with a red nose and a Santa hat covered in glitter. The message inside was handwritten in her neat script.

Dear Auntie Kay,

If you're reading this, it's because I've just asked you to! Or Daisy and Wilson have done so because of an instruction from me! Either way, don't blame them for what's happened or interrogate them on what I've been doing. (I know what you can be like.) So please don't!

I tried to explain to you that something (fairly monumental) was going happen to me. I've known it for a long time, from the moment Mum and Dad died. Their deaths were part of a plan, a certainty in my future, a destiny that nothing could ever change. Going to the children's home was part of the plan. You having that argument with the adoption people was part of the plan. So in a way you also brought this about. But it's more complicated than that. Don't cry — and don't laugh either, I'm being serious!

When I was in the children's home, I learned how to see spirits. The spirits of people who have died but haven't gone to heaven yet. Bradley Givens won't be in the news again. He's gone for good. And I did that. That was my destiny. And now the plan is complete, my journey is over and there's no reason for me stay. So I'm going to find Mum. She's waiting for me in heaven with our seahorses on the beach. I wonder if they'll have red noses at this time of year?

Bye Auntie Kay, you were the best second Mum anyone could ever want. I will be watching to make sure you are okay. Love Sally. X

P.S. I know you'll think Daisy and Wilson forced me to write this letter, so I want to tell you a secret. I know why you didn't get married Auntie Kay. But that man didn't leave you because he didn't love you. He did, with all his heart. On the day the doctor told him his illness would leave him paralysed, he chose not to ruin your life as well. So he chose to let you go. He had to make you think that he didn't care. That he'd abandoned you. But he didn't. He's in a nursing home, I couldn't work out where but Daisy will take you to him if you show her his photo.

Tell Leanna I'll miss her.
Love, Sally. (And don't cry! I'm not.)

Kay folded the card, slipped it back into the envelope and reached for her niece's hand which was hanging limply off the edge of the sofa. Sally was no longer breathing. Kay turned to look at Daisy, then at Wilson and Balthazar. The question 'why?' was on her lips but she knew she would never understand why. Daisy joined Kay at Sally's side and they clung to each other, rocking gently from side to side, sharing an overwhelming and unfathomable sense of loss.

Climbing the steps of The Gateway, Sally's spirit cast no shadow in the light of that new day. The path across the colonnade with its row of towering columns, though well trodden, was not foot worn; for the shell treads lightly as it carries the soul.

Approaching the two nondescript doors, Sally came to a halt, mid-step. A man she recognised from a lifetime ago was standing by the door on the right; the residents' entrance. The man was waving, smiling, calling out her name, urging her to hurry up, to get a move on. A small boy with curly hair was by his side. The boy was also waving and calling and smiling and his teeth were as white as polished opals. Then Sally was running, running faster than anyone could ever run; faster than an angel with winged feet can fly; and she was spinning around in the carousel of her father's arms being raised ever higher and higher; high enough to see her mother standing in sunlight on a beach with sand as white as sugar under a cloudless sky of azure blue. Her mother was on a lovely holiday somewhere and beckoning with laughing eyes and outstretched arms for Sally, her husband and Felix to join her.

Chapter 59

It's over

After weighing all the facts on the scales of culpability; and after untangling the traces of the future that had entwined Sally from the day she was born; it would be difficult to lay blame at the feet of Wilson and Daisy. Sally led them to her denouement just as orbiting planets are drawn to an imploding star.

However, as Wilson lay on his bed in the mausoleum silence of his room, he didn't see things that way. His mind ran back along a time line, looking into the past for the point where a bridge thread might have been cut.

If and only!

If only he'd said 'NO' and sent Sally home when she arrived unexpectedly at 247 Chapel Street.

If only he'd insisted she wait in the people carrier outside The Maltings. She would have been safe and warm in the car. Balthazar had a blanket, they could have turned on the radio. She would have been fine.

If only he'd not taken her on the Vespa to that very first meeting. Or, if Mark had only bought five plywood boards, that would have meant no gap for Sally. She could have stood at the back of the study, out of harm's way as the lights went out for Bradley Givens.

455

Go back to the time of the hospital visit when Sally spoke of forces driving her destiny. Wilson could have feigned sleep. Plugged his ears with wax, lashed himself to the bed frame and sailed blissfully on through the siren songs of her parents' deaths, the discovery of spirits in the attic and the friendship with Felix.

Daisy would have released him from his bindings as soon as Sally had left the ward. She'd have been disappointed possibly, but still alive!

"Did you hear all that nonsense Wilson? That girl's crazy! Let's not get involved, let's not get dragged into this mess. Let her Auntie Kay sort it out." Daisy might have said.

Poor Kay, what would happen to her? What kind of casualty would she become? Long term? Short lived?

Life viewed through the prism of a tragedy often reflects at obtuse angles.

When Wilson slept, it was a featureless, dreamless, empty landscape sort of sleep.

When Daisy slept, it was a fighting with demons and battling with guilt sort of sleep. She had a recurring dream; a dream which involved the same harrowing event being played on a continuous loop. A nightmare in which she and Sally are trying to outrun a vicious, twisting tornado on a vast, open plain of sunbaked red earth. But Sally is too slow and the twister too fast so it always sweeps her off her feet and sucks her up into the sky. And Daisy can see Sally in the grip of the tornado, spinning like a rag doll, screaming for help, being carried higher and higher into the swirling, sidewinding, maelstrom of a dust devil that grows horns and demon red eyes and then eventually swallows her up. Daisy wants to rescue Sally, but there is nowhere to turn for help in an open plain of sunbaked red earth. Nothing can change the story at the end. The tornado with the horns and demon red eyes swallows Sally up every time.

Although Wilson and Daisy are implicitly involved in the death of Sally, they can't be held responsible! They were merely delivering the antidote. An antidote with a thirteen-year-old shelf life on a delivery route that had been keyed into the Sat Nav of their lives. Traces of the future weren't really entwined around Sally at birth, they were just intricately and expertly woven, like a web.

Funnily enough, they say a spider is able to build a web the day it hatches from an egg and I suppose, in a way, Sally did exactly the same. Wilson liked that thought. He felt it connected Sally with morphic resonance, the WiFi of nature and the WiFi of dreams. A tangled web indeed.

The post-mortem was performed the following afternoon in response to an urgent request by the Cheshire police. The cause of death for a teenager with no underlying health conditions could never be as simple as 'died during sleep from natural causes'. But with no evidence to suggest a counter explanation, the pathologist's verdict was just that, 'Death by Natural Causes'. In other words, the catastrophic neutralisation of plasma electrolytes caused by electrical earthing. If only Sally had been wearing those rubber soled school shoes. If only!

The police officers attending the emergency, had seen Sally's bedroom, her belongings neatly packed in suitcases in readiness for a journey; had heard Kay's description of her sad and tragic life; the death of both parents; the bullying at school and the terrible car accident and they drew their own conclusion. Sally had died from a broken heart.

The funeral was arranged for the following Monday at Cheadle Cemetery. Sally was to be buried in the gap between the graves of her parents. A gap just wide enough for her shoulders. Irony is everywhere, should you seek to find it.

Chapter 60

It ain't over, until it's over

Monday 4th December 2017, 6.50 a.m.

Mark and James were lying flat out on the sofas in the Manager's Office and Balthazar was behind his desk, elbows splayed on the desk, head in hands. The three of them hadn't slept since returning to 247 Chapel Street five hours earlier. It was Balthazar's protocol to always conduct a post-intervention analysis, a debrief regarding objectives and outcomes, but quite frankly, none of them could face it. The night's catastrophic events had opened emotional wounds that would take time to heal. Yes, the antidote had been administered. Starved of the oxygen of publicity, Bradley's fires were going out and The Secret was safe. James was able to confirm that.

But all three felt sick to the stomach as they tried to make peace with the directive, the imperative that had brought about Sally Bennett's death. Her future had been in the palm of Balthazar's hand, but it had never been in his remit to bypass the inevitable, only to facilitate it. The spectre of the human sacrifice would haunt them.

Mark was exhausted. The search for deeper meaning in the catastrophe had led him to the heart of darkness and he was lost in self-doubt. Lost like the shepherd in an Old Master painting, beseeching God in heaven to spare the sacrificial lamb. Mark was seeking a benediction, the valediction, that he knew The Powers That Be could never give.

Balthazar sat back in his chair with his hands behind his head. "What a bloody mess" he said, in the oboe tone of the world weary.

The night had taken its toll and no special enzyme would ever be able to metabolise the heartbreaking sound of Kay sobbing. The memory of Sally would follow like a shadow tethered to their souls. Somehow, they were going to have to get through the day, and the one after that, and through all the days to follow. The sound of silence, both strident and melancholic, filled the room for another hour.

Mark pushed his laptop over to Balthazar.

"Come on, sign this off, it'll cheer you up" he said.

The sad story was to have something of a happy ending.

"We've used a proxy server in Poland and an untraceable email address" said Mark.

There was something of the nodding dog in Balthazar's manner as he acknowledged the contents of the email with a grin.

Dear Sergeant Jordan,

Consider this to be a Snapchat, something like the one I sent to Wilson Armitage.

In a locked drawer in ACC Montague's desk you'll find a photo and a video tape. The video shows footage of a woman in Inverness bus station stepping off the coach from London. The photo is a picture of Vanessa Clarke as supplied to the police the day after her husband reporting her missing. A child could see Vanessa and Abandoned Alice are one and the same person. Which is why Montague has removed them from your

460

evidence room. If he'd done his job properly seventeen years ago he wouldn't need to try and pin the blame on Wilson's father!

So what do we have?

Tampering with evidence, dereliction of duty, intimidation, false arrest, negligence, violation of procedures. Might be quicker just to throw the book at him.

One final thing, I suggest you take this information to someone outside the North Caledonian Constabulary, we wouldn't want to see this swept under the carpet. And please make sure it happens. I'll be watching.

Yours sincerely
Gladys's Dad

Balthazar pressed 'send' and as a result, a week later, the following meeting took place.

Chapter 61

Hard facts

Monday 11th December 2017, 10.50 a.m.

Montague was speaking on the phone when Sergeant Jordan and a man and a woman from the Internal Investigation Division of the Metropolitan Police Force walked into his office. He could see from their dour expressions it was a serious matter. Montague brought the conversation with the newspaper reporter to an end by saying he hadn't heard the rumour that he was to be promoted to the position of Chief Commissioner as soon as the position became available.

The man and woman presented their identity cards and Montague had a good idea of why they were there. Sergeant Jordan had overstepped the mark again!

The visitors took seats around Montague's desk and the man spoke first.

"ACC Montague, following the identification of Vanessa Clarke, the lady referred to as Alice, the lady in the . . . "

"Yes, yes, I'm fully aware of the case, and I've been conducting my own enquiries as a matter of fact. Rolling my sleeves up, going back to the coalface with a bit of old school police work. A strange case, but I think I am getting to the bottom of it."

The woman placed a voice recorder on the desk. "You don't mind if I tape this conversation. We like to keep verbal records, saves time, avoids all that report writing later."

Montague thought it unusual and open-mouthed, turned to his Sergeant.

Whatever it is you've done Jordan, you've done it good and proper this time.

"No, not at all, I'm happy to help in any way I can. I have the file here as a matter of fact."

Montague flicked through a small stack of foolscap folders, pulled out the appropriate one and handed it over to the woman. "Everything's here: interview notes, the photos of the lad on the scooter, witness statements. It's all in there."

"Mmm," said the man, "I'm afraid it's not quite that simple, because this isn't the file we're interested in. It's the other one, the cold case file, the one I have here."

From his briefcase, the man retrieved the document box containing all the information relating to 'Alice the Abandoned' and placed it on top of Montague's folder. Then he tapped it three times with his finger.

"This one's the important one! This is the one we want to talk about."

Montague visibly blanched, his face the colour of boiled cauliflower.

"Well," he spluttered, "what can I say about events from so long ago? What's Sergeant Jordan got to do with that? I thought you were here to tell me he's been up to his tricks again, bending the rules?"

"Yes, I suppose you could say that. He's certainly been going behind someone's back, but in the line of duty. To get to the point ACC Montague, have you referred to the contents of this document box as part of your new enquiries?"

"Yes, the day after Vanessa Clarke was identified in South Kessock, I went to check, to err, see if anything had been overlooked. I spent a lot of hours back then chasing all the leads regarding Alice, some of it on my own time, but there was nothing in there I'd missed, or that could have helped, seventeen years ago."

"And did you take anything from the box?"

"Err, no, there was nothing of any significance. Why?"

"So you're certain of that? You only looked at the contents of this box and didn't sign anything out?"

"Yes, that's correct. Why, what's all this about? It's this new file you should be interested in. Is this about Alex Armitage? Has he made a complaint? Besides, I don't understand why any of this would be of interest to the Met."

"No, it wasn't Alex Armitage who made the complaint. It was Sergeant Jordan."

"Sergeant Jordan?"

"Yes, Sergeant Jordan. He received information from an unknown source within the force here in Inverness. From someone who's been 'back to the coalface with a bit of old school police work' you might say. And he brought that information to us."

"So just to be clear, and for the record," added the woman, "you didn't take anything from this box, in particular photograph number thirteen from the missing person images? Or a video recording of passengers arriving at Inverness bus station the morning after Vanessa was reported missing?"

"No, absolutely not. Anyway, there was nothing on that tape. I checked it thoroughly. I remember. I watched it five times."

"Officer Montague, would you open the top drawer of your desk? We have a copy of the key if you don't have yours to hand."

"I'll do no such thing. This is totally preposterous. Barging in here accusing me of . . . I'm an Assistant Chief Constable. The contents of my desk are private. You have no authority here."

"ACC Montague, you're only making things more difficult for yourself, please open the drawer."

After much huffing and puffing, Montague reluctantly took the key from his waistcoat pocket, opened the drawer and feigned surprise at the contents. He placed a photo of Vanessa Clarke and a VHS tape in a plastic case on his desk. The photo of Vanessa had been taken by Michael on a day trip to Blackpool a week before she went missing. She was smiling proudly at the camera with Teaps in her arms. He would have been around six months old at the time. This was the photo never issued to the press. The tape would show the same woman, but with dark hair and unsteady on her feet, alighting the London coach in Inverness bus station.

"I honestly don't know how they got there. Somebody put them there, planted them. They weren't there yesterday. I would have known."

"Officer Montague the two items you have just placed on your desk have been in that drawer for the past week. They were there when the desk sergeant and a locksmith opened the drawer while you were at a conference at Gleneagles."

"This is ridiculous, I am a senior policeman, I . . . "

The man nodded to Sergeant Jordan who then rose to his feet.

"Assistant Chief Constable Montague I am arresting you for tampering with evidence, obstruction of justice, perverting the course of justice and false arrest. You don't have to say anything, but what you do say may be used as evidence in a court of law. Do you understand that?"

The man continued with the charge sheet.

"We also intend to ask that charges of gross misconduct and neglect of duty are considered. From this moment you are suspended from the North Caledonian Constabulary. You may want to get a lawyer Mr Montague, I've spoken to the public prosecutor's office and they are viewing this as a serious matter. If you are found guilty, dismissal from the force with the loss of all pension rights is certain. The charges are also serious enough to warrant a prison term. I need your badge Mr Montague and I must ask you to leave the station with all of your personal possessions immediately."

Chapter 62

Ashes to ashes

Monday 11th December 2017, 11.30 a.m.

There was poignancy in the fact that only four people attended Sally's funeral. She had no parents, no brothers or sisters, no cousins, no mates from netball or friends from school; only Auntie Kay, Leanna and fleetingly, Daisy and Wilson. As her coffin was lowered into the ground, it seemed Sally was having the last word on how lonely her life had been and the first word on the wonderful new journey that was waiting elsewhere.

Kay could almost hear Sally saying, 'No one will miss me. Look, I told you so!'

The strong easterly wind turned a shower into a squall as a huddle of four mourners under two umbrellas hurried across the cemetery grounds towards Kay's car. Over a week had passed since that dreadful night and many words had been left unsaid. The time for remembrance of everything had arrived.

Kay was in the hallway of the vicarage, draping wet coats over a radiator when Leanna gave her a hug that wouldn't let go.

"I'm heading off now Kay, I want to go home and sit in silence for a couple of hours, a bit of me time."

"Okay, love. Thanks for coming today. Sally would have

wanted that."

"I was thinking we could go out tonight, for dinner, just me and you. You've not been out of the house for a week. We could go to Pizza Hut and get drunk, drown our sorrows, raise a glass of red to our angel. What do you think?"

The film of tears blurred Kay's recall of the memory. "Sally's table for three in the window at the front? Yeh, why not?"

"We'll have to order her Pizza Diablo with the extra chilli though. Exactly how she liked it."

"I don't know how she could eat that thing, it was like biting into a volcano. Makes my mouth burn just talking about it."

They were still wrapped in each other's arms.

"Kay, do you think she's with her mum and dad in heaven now?"

"Yeh Leanna, I do. And I don't just think it, I know it and one day I'll tell you why."

Wilson and Daisy were talking quietly in the kitchen when Kay entered wiping tears from her cheek with a tissue. She made three mugs of coffee and sat at the table. The table where she'd once told Sally to keep a rein on Mr Jinx. The table where Sally had been so proud to hear that her Auntie Kay, her fabulous other mum, had won the 'Producer of the Year' award.

Kay took Sally's Christmas card from her bag. "You can read it if you want."

"Kay, we can't. That was personal. I think you're the only person meant to read it."

"Daisy love, you have to read it, I need to ask you

468

something about what Sally has written. Something I don't understand. Please read it."

Wilson and Daisy nudged their chairs side by side and read the message. When they'd finished, Daisy closed the card and passed it back to Kay.

Kay handed over a small photo album in return.

"I've put together the best ones" she said.

The album contained pictures of a man in his mid-twenties. A young man with everything to live for. Grinning at a camera with a bottle of beer in his hands. On his knees looking up at the camera, knackered and relieved to have finished his first marathon. Suntanned on a restaurant terrace on holiday somewhere.

"He was called Philip. I took those photos and we were together for two years. Then one day he didn't reply to a text to meet for a drink after work. I sent more messages and tried to call but he didn't answer. The next day he sent me a message to say it was over, he didn't love me anymore, he'd found someone else and I should move on. And that was it. We were going to get married. He broke my heart and I decided to be wedded to work after that. That's why people think I'm such a cold, heartless bitch."

Kay took the album from Daisy and ran her fingers over one of the images.

"Do you really know where he is. How to find him?"

Daisy turned to Wilson. She had to answer, and with the truth.

"Daisy, how could Sally have found out about Philip. I've never spoken to anyone about him, not even Leanna. I have to believe you can find him. I want to be certain Sally could make miracles happen. Then I can accept that she was an angel on earth, only for a short time. Sent by God to do good things and now he's taken her back, to be with her parents. I need to believe that."

"If you let me borrow the album for a few days, I'll find him for you."

"But how? In what way is that possible?"

"Daisy and I are different Kay," said Wilson, "different to normal people. We can do things and see things nobody else can."

"Are you some kind of savants? People with special talents?"

"Kind of. We're normal during waking hours but come out of our shells when we dream. Sally was the same. We see things in our dreams, things that have happened in the past. We can meet in our dreams, learn things in our dreams."

There was no reason for Kay to dismiss what she was hearing, in fact she needed to hear it. Wilson was saying that Sally's life had a higher meaning, a greater purpose, that Sally had been special, different, a chosen one.

"She always got top marks at school."

Daisy smiled.

"Yes, and she probably wasn't trying that hard. Where did you keep these photos?"

"They were in my bedside table."

"Sally must have looked through them. Saw how happy you were together. She had to show you what she could do in a way you could understand. So she found the memories of Philip in a dream and discovered the truth about what happened. And I can tell you where he is, if you're sure you want me to."

"Really, you can do that? I mean, see memories in your

sleep?"

"Yes, I can, and trust me, I do it loads better than Wilson."

Kay looked at the extraordinary young couple with their crazy ideas, dreams and limitless potential. She and Philip had been like that once.

"Is that why Sally was drawn to you? It wasn't by chance that you met in the hospital was it?"

Daisy placed her hand on Kay's.

"Wilson saved Sally's life when she was in the car accident. He was the unknown boy who came to her rescue and showed the policeman what to do. And Sally then saved Wilson's life. It was all supposed to happen, just like Sally described in the card. That's how we were connected. Our paths had aligned well before she went to see Wilson in hospital."

"But there's more. We saw you Kay. Sally, Daisy and me, we saw you at the police roadblock at The Maltings. We were in the people carrier with tinted windows. You were with a cameraman."

"You had your heads covered by a blanket?"

"Yes, that was us."

"I knew it!" said Kay. "When I arrived home I told Leanna I'd had a strange feeling about that people carrier. When she said Sally had gone out and hadn't left a note, I was going to drive straight back."

Wilson had to tell Kay everything.

"We were there to put an end to Bradley Givens, to extinguish his spirit. I think about that night all the time and if I'd done something to stop what happened, Sally would still be here. I could have insisted that she didn't come. She wasn't included in my plan, but she turned up . . . and . . . "

Wilson's voice was breaking as he confessed his guilt.

471

"You're wrong Wilson. Completely wrong." Kay placed her hand on Wilson's. "If that was truly her destiny, then you had no choice other than to make it happen. Her destiny was also yours."

"But you don't know that with certainty."

"Yes, I do. She wrote me the card, left it under the tree and made me promise not to read it. Sally was prepared for what was coming. She folded away her entire life in this house and put it in two suitcases. She knew she wouldn't be coming back. Wilson, Daisy, please don't blame yourselves. I didn't sleep for three days after her death but now I am at peace with her peace, and that is all I need. She's with her mum now, where she wanted to be, was meant to be.

"Was her sacrifice worth it? To stop every religion being turned upside down, to stop the chaos that would have resulted from the afterlife being proven beyond doubt? I think so. The world is not ready to deal with that. I know I'll see my niece and sister again and I'm happy to wait for as long as it takes for that time to arrive. And I want to meet Philip. I want Sally's miracle to happen."

"I'll call you when I find out where he is, and I'll go with you if you want me to?"

Kay offered to drive Daisy back to Macclesfield and drop Wilson off in Bramhall on the return leg, but Wilson's Vespa was still parked at the back of 247 Chapel Street and had been for over a week.

"If you can give us a lift into Manchester Kay, that would be great. I'm not sure the Vespa will start if I leave it there much longer."

"And I'll catch the train from Piccadilly," said Daisy,

"the weather's awful, it's not a day to be driving over to Macclesfield."

"This is fine Kay, perfect, we'll jump out here."

"Are you sure Daisy? It's pouring with rain. You're going to get soaked."

"No, this is great, I promise."

"But I can take you up to Piccadilly, and then drop Wilson off for his Vespa, it's no trouble."

Kay left them sharing an umbrella outside the entrance to Kendal's department store. Daisy waved and followed Kay's car until it was lost in rush hour traffic. They crossed Deansgate in front of Waterstones and made their way down to Starbucks. Wilson went to order the cappuccinos while Daisy found a table. She removed her trench coat and slipped it over the back of the chair. The shoulders of her black sweater were damp and her Dr Martens sodden.

Wilson placed the drinks on the table, sat down and adjusted his chair.

"That was the same girl who served me the first time, the one from Holland. I spoke to her in Dutch once by mistake."

Daisy sipped her coffee and through a rain streaked window watched the pixellated world go by, her mind elsewhere. The pouring rain seemingly trying to extinguish the spirit of Christmas.

"It doesn't seem like three months ago does it? When you walked through that door in your parka with your crash helmet under your arm."

"When you turned round wearing a bobble hat and dropped your cup."

"That was one of the best moments of my life Wilson."

473

"Knowing what you know now, what's happened to everyone, would you still walk through that door if you had the choice? I mean, would you stop and think and maybe walk away?"

Wilson wiped froth from his top lip with his fingers as he waited for Daisy's answer.

"I don't know. I'm not sure if me walking away would have kept Sally alive. And perhaps we'd still have met but in a different way. So nothing would have changed in the end. But I was thinking just then, looking out of the window, what if I was like everyone else and there was no Market Square? Would I still have met you? Our paths might never have crossed. I come out of one lift as you enter another."

"Sliding doors?"

Wilson held Daisy's hand in his.

"All I know is we met, and I would never want to change that, and yes, that's my final answer."

Wilson nudged his chair closer to Daisy and she rested her head on his shoulder. They sat there, silently lost in thought as raindrops meandered down the window like streaming tears – or the embryos of a river.

At Piccadilly station they huddled together under the umbrella on a platform pockmarked with puddles waiting for Daisy's train to Macclesfield.

"Isn't this the moment where I say, 'so where do we go from here then?'"

"And I say, 'I go that way on the train and you go that way to get your scooter.'"

"Okay. Then I think I said something like, 'what do we do now?'"

Daisy drew closer to Wilson, forcing her body against his.

"And I said, 'I've got your mobile number and you've got mine. So we can meet in Starbucks every day if you want, forever. That's set in stone.' And then I flicked your nose and it was cold and wet. I remember those exact words. I always will."

Daisy's train inched along the platform and pulled up stiffly. Wilson's eyes followed Daisy as she found a seat and removed her hat, gloves and coat. She was waving and pointing to her phone and pretending to text and laughing and waving again. Everything was exactly as it had been the first time. History was repeating itself.

As Daisy's train curved away and out of view, it dawned on Wilson that the replication, this duplication of the night they first met, was a kind of déjà-vu. A 'been there before and done this' prolonged déjà-vu.

And coming up now Wilson, is the bit where you go for your Vespa and drive home. It's expected. Press any, or all of the buttons, it makes no difference, this sliding door always opens on the same floor.

Puppets are not expected to understand, or question the fact, that their next performance is simply a repeat of yesterday's show. So Wilson decided to do something rash, to cut his own strings and bring the curtain down. It was a spur of the moment decision. A last-minute move that made outcomes too close to call and he did it just for the hell of it. Sampson needed to know that his delivery boy was running out of patience. He'd kept his side of the agreement, but now, after a week, the side bet issue had still to be resolved. Wilson felt insignificant and exploited, like one of Sampson's disposable, oily rags, as he stood waiting for the next train to Bramhall. The Vespa was staying where it wasn't supposed to be.

Chapter 63

Out for the count

Monday 11th December 2017, 7.30 p.m.

"Where's Mum?"

"She's gone to a carol concert. Daisy's mother sings in a choir and invited her. She told you this morning."

"Oh yeh, I forgot about that."

Wilson hung up a black leather jacket, wetter than a window cleaner's chamois. The walk from Bramhall village had left him soaked to the skin.

"Why didn't you call me to say you were at the train station? I'd have picked you up."

"It's okay. I needed the exercise. I'm going for a hot shower and dry clothes."

Alex was watching Sky news when Wilson returned to the lounge.

"I don't think Gloria wanted to go to the concert, she's not ready for a relationship with Daisy's family. She bristles whenever you mention her name."

"I know, but she'll have to get used to it. If she makes me choose, she'll lose out."

"Wilson, you're not being asked to take sides. It's understandable she feels the way she does, given the mess we're in."

"But that's nothing to do with Daisy."

Alex decided it was best to end the conversation on the moot point.

"How was the funeral?"

"What can I say? It was the first funeral I've been to and I'm in no hurry to go to another."

"Were many people there?"

"About fifty, mostly people from college and his family."

"Who was it who died? Did I know him?"

"Mr Harris, he was one of the football coaches. Think you only ever came to one game Dad, so you probably won't remember."

"How did he die?"

"I told you, he died in his sleep. From a heart attack."

"Was Hoover there?"

"Err, yes, he was. Teaps wasn't."

"How was Hoover, you on speaking terms now?"

"No, none of my mates are speaking to me."

"Must have been . . . "

"Dad, why are you asking me all these questions. I'm tired to be honest and I'd rather not talk about it."

"Okay."

Alex turned the volume up on the TV.

More bad news about Brexit and then a politician from Glasgow was interviewed about the demand for Scottish independence and a second referendum.

Alex reduced the volume.

"The Bradley Givens story has gone very quiet."

"Don't think it was ever a story was it? Fake news, that's what I've been hearing."

"He got what was coming to him then, did he?"

"You could say that Dad. The torches worked a treat."

Alex switched off the TV and turned to his son.

"Wilson, do you honestly believe that whatever was happening in that house was caused by a non-extinguished spirit? A spirit from The . . . Gateway? The ghost of Bradley Givens?"

"So they say." Wilson wanted his father to let it drop.

"Makes you think though. You know, about the message, if it was true. About the guarantee of an afterlife and a heaven?"

"I don't think about it Dad. I just lock it away in the back of my mind. The idea of The Market Square is enough to drive any sane person crazy. Besides, I've agreed with Daisy, after tonight, I'm really, really, never going back."

"Wilson, are you okay? You've been like a zombie for the past week; ever since you came back late from the . . . extinguishing for want of a better word. Did something disturbing happen that night?"

Wilson's sigh and forlorn expression said everything.

Alex left his armchair to sit by his son.

"What is it, what happened? Tell me."

Wilson covered his face with his hands in an attempt to hide from the truth but there was no holding back.

"Sally died Dad. That's where I've been today. To her funeral!"

The grief came flowing out like a flood of emotion bursting through a dyke wall. A dyke that even the special enzyme couldn't shore up.

When the flow of tears reduced to a trickle, Wilson told his father the full story of what had happened and identified his partners in crime. The five people with blood on their hands.

Gloria was singing 'Peace on earth and mercy mild, God and sinners reconciled' as Alex opened a bottle of whisky and poured out two large measures. All sorts of significance could be ascribed to the words of the carol.

The bottle was a quarter empty when Alex returned to the subject of The Maltings incident fifteen minutes later.

"So is it all over now son?"

"Yeh, it's all over Dad. All over, except for one thing. Someone made a promise they need to keep. Have you heard anything from the police about the court case, about your job? Has anything changed?"

"No Wilson, and now is as good a time as any to tell you. If I end up with a criminal record, I'll definitely lose my job. The chairman of the select committee said I'm required to be 'fully accountable for my actions'. He also said I'd be 'lucky to get a job in a charity shop', which I thought was pretty ironic given the circumstances."

Alex downed the last of his drink.

"And your sisters are home tomorrow. No idea how we're going to explain this to them. Not sure we'll be able to pay the fees for their final year."

"Dad! I'll make sure that doesn't happen."

"So where are you going to get that type of money from Wilson? From your meat pie website?"

"Dad, don't worry, I'll find it. So let's say cheers to that. Here, top up mine will you, in fact make it a double. I've not slept well for a few nights and I want to make sure I'm out for the count when my head hits the pillow."

Chapter 64

A bet's a bet

Wilson stood outside The Bank with a golf ball in his hand. He stepped back off the kerb, out onto the cobbles and took aim. The golf ball felt solid and heavy, the perfect projectile to throw through Big Mac and Short Cake's office window. The crash of breaking glass was followed by the tinkling of shards landing on the pavement below.

Wilson waited for alarmed faces to appear in the jagged hole and when they didn't, he threw another golf ball.

"Can I have my ball back mister?" There was no reply.

So Wilson threw a third golf ball just to emphasise the point and jogged up to Sampson's Motorcycle Workshop without looking back.

The sign hanging in the window read, *'Gone fishing. Again!'*

Right, if that's the way they want to play this, so be it!

The alleyway didn't seem quite so imposing in the daylight; nothing more than the typical, narrow thoroughfare one might stroll down in the side streets of any market town.

The neon sign above the entrance to the Number 11 Club, with its intestinal tubes of glass, rubber hoses and electrical circuitry had also lost its mystique in broad daylight.

Wilson hammered on the door and waited.

Then he pounded again twice as hard.

Still no answer.

So he kicked the door and continued with a repetitive, toe bunging beat until the door was eventually pulled back by Charles. He was wearing a white string vest, drawstring pyjama bottoms and his feet were bare. He yawned and rubbed his stubbly chin.

"I'm sorry sir, but we're closed. Can you come back this evening?"

"Charles, it is evening where I've come from!"

Wilson took a step forward but Charles sidestepped and blocked his path. Wilson returned to his starting position and appraised the obstacle. Charles was over two metres tall and his arms, covered in bouncing dice tattoos, were thick and muscular. He glared down at Wilson like a bull daring a rambler to enter his field.

"Oh come on Charles, don't be like this."

Charles crossed his arms and shifted his stance slightly.

"Sorry sir, we really are closed at the moment."

Somewhat bemused, Wilson scratched his head.

"Charles, I don't want to cause any trouble, but I really need to speak to your boss and I don't have a lot of time."

Charles remained impassive. Wilson tried to humour him.

"Charles, do you know who I am?"

Charles didn't smile. He just stood there looking implacable with his arms folded on his pot belly.

So Wilson rammed the heel of his foot against Charles's knee and popped the knee cap out of joint. As Charles tumbled forwards, Wilson kicked him in the groin, brought his knee sharply up beneath his chin and knocked Charles half unconscious and his gold tooth out.

"Sorry Charles, but you made me do that."

Wilson hurried down the stairs and into the Number 11 Club. The lights were no longer dimmed and in the harsh glare the place didn't look quite so salubrious. The carpet was sticky from spilled drinks. The air smelt of cigarette smoke and stale beer. A vacuum cleaner was whirring away somewhere in the background.

When Wilson arrived at the rope cordon, Charles was standing behind the lectern looking immaculately turned out in his black suit and bow tie. He smiled to show Wilson no hard feelings and his gold tooth.

"Wilson, I do hope that helped relieve all the frustration you've been feeling lately. Allow me."

Charles pulled back the velvet curtains.

"Enjoy the casino sir."

Somewhat flabbergasted, Wilson entered without saying a word.

Nothing had changed in The Citadel of Angels. The glass ceilings rose with vertiginous effect all the way to the hundred and twenty-second floor where they converged on a point of light that sparkled like the North Star. Every gaming table was occupied and as players sought to remedy potential outcomes with interventions, they gave a nod or a smile to Wilson as he strode by.

Approaching the stairwell beneath the escalator, Wilson marvelled at a machine constructed entirely from glass. The foot track, handrail and side panels were all completely transparent and offered crystal clear insight on the internal mechanism of motors and drive gear. Wilson was amazed by the brain's ability to recreate the workings of a fully functioning escalator in see through and by his ability to do it with just an eye movement's notice. He made his way down to the high stakes room.

On reaching the bottom step, the noise from beyond the door suddenly seemed to intensify in the manner of a baying crowd when a boxer enters the ring. Wilson had to force his way inside because the place was packed like a tube train at rush hour. Sampson's high rollers, male and female and of all ethnicity and heritage, were dressed identically in three piece, pinstripe suits cut in a loose fitting, old fashioned style and sported trilby hats. No one paid the slightest attention to Wilson in his pyjamas, everyone was too busy yelling and waving fistfuls of banknotes at whatever was happening on Sampson's gaming table. Cigarette smoke hung in the air like layers of low cloud. A waiter wormed his way through the crowd with a tray of drinks raised precariously above his head. The atmosphere captured something of the illicit buzz of a speakeasy during prohibition. Not that Wilson had been to a speakeasy during prohibition, but he'd read the *Great Gatsby*. It was on his English A Level reading list and the high rollers' room felt something like that. A second waiter was about to enter the scrum so Wilson stepped into his wake and followed. Eventually, he was able to squeeze half a shoulder and then a full shoulder into a sardine space between two women standing four rows back from the action.

Through a gap between bobbing heads, Wilson saw Mark Sampson standing at the far end of the table smoking a cigar rolled with gold leaf. His trilby was pushed back high on his head, shirt buttons were open and the tie was hanging at half-mast. Wilson stood on tiptoe and the view improved. Sampson had a drink and cigar in one hand and he was shaking dice in the other. When he blew on his fist for good luck, the crowd reached a new level of frenzy. Wilson studied the faces of the woman either side. Their skin was perfect, too perfect actually, as though every blemish had been retouched to create a soft focus, doll-like version of themselves, a living selfie.

"Five hundred on the sandstorm" one of them yelled.

"Put me down for a grand on the bridge collapse" yelled the other, waving the crescent of notes in her hand like a fan.

Behind Wilson, another voice boomed out. "I'll take the bridge collapse with two hundred casualties."

Calls for similar wagers filled the air, yet none of the cash being proffered appeared to be changing hands.

There had to be over one hundred people packed into that room. They were all shouting the odds on the likelihood of a disaster, yet from what Wilson could see, there was no bookmaker to accept the bets.

"Double up on the virus epidemic for three fifty."

"Six hundred says the pilot lands the plane."

"Three hundred says he lands the plane, but over fifty dead."

Wilson felt someone force a golf ball into his hand and he managed to free his arm. The time for clubhouse etiquette was over. He pitched the ball over the rough of frantically waving arms in the direction of the green baize and must have found the hole, for the spectators were silenced instantly.

They turned to identify the golfer in their midst, and seemingly in awe of the approach shot, began removing their trilby hats. At the same time, they all found room to take two steps back and in doing so, created a corridor that led directly to the gaming table. The golf ball came bouncing back down this narrow fairway and rolled to within an inch of Wilson's feet.

"You only had to ask Wilson. There's always room for your distinguished presence at this table. And by the way, you nearly destroyed a tower block with that chip of yours."

Wilson now felt an osmotic pressure pushing him forwards and the crowd filled in behind, as though approaching the eighteenth green with his name on the leader board. When he took the vacated slot at the table's edge, what he witnessed on the baize surface was quite simply astonishing.

The model interventions, the toy ambulance, the doll in a nurse's uniform, had been substituted by live events. One such event presented a plane flying through a storm. The aircraft was pitching from side to side with lightning flashes bursting all around and though the plane was clearly flying, it remained within the confines of its red square. As though existing in a self-contained, cameo of real life.

On another square, the span of a road bridge over a river was bucking up and down as though being rocked by an earthquake. Thick smoke billowed from an active volcano on another. One square portrayed a patch of barren, parched earth dotted with wilting vegetation. On another, a petrol tanker had stalled on a railway crossing, and in the distance, a train was rounding a bend. All the squares on the table presented animated snapshots of an impending natural disaster or a man-made accident that was about to happen.

Wilson turned to Sampson.

"So this is where the big bets are placed. You gamble on the likelihood of these events occurring, these major disasters becoming certainties."

"Yes, the choices are pretty basic. There are only two outcomes, good or bad. It's a binary betting decision. The bridge collapses or it's earthquake proof and stands firm."

"So what happened with Bradley Givens? Was nobody backing Sally to live? Or betting on an alternative way for Bradley to be stopped?"

"No Wilson, that was never going to happen. When the likelihood of something becomes so great, like United being seven points clear with two games to go, the betting stops. The betting stopped on Sally just before her mother died. Many years before that, if truth be told, when we caught a first glimpse of Bradley's miscreant future. You rescuing Sally from beneath the car, Daisy rescuing you, the discovery of Vanessa Clarke, your dad being framed, they were bets on the side."

"So you've been gambling with our lives; like we're action figures that you throw away when the fun's over?"

"That's a bit harsh Wilson, we're good souls at heart. And we don't run a book on everything. The comet that hits the earth and raises a dust cloud to snuff out the sun. The virus for which there is no vaccine. We make sure the odds of those things happening are virtually non-existent!"

"So what if I were to suddenly knock this bridge over with my finger?"

Wilson stretched his arm across the table and held his hand above the animated cameo of the swaying bridge.

"I'd say think long and hard about that. You never know what new repercussions might come . . . repercussioning in your direction, and in Daisy's of course!"

Wilson felt hypnotic force in the eye contact as Sampson stared him down.

Wilson withdrew his hand and let it fall to his side.

"Why didn't you help my Dad like you promised? Did the

side bets go the wrong way for him?"

Sampson took a slow draw of his cigar and released fat smoke rings like wispy donuts.

"You mean Alex goes directly to jail and doesn't pass go? Or does he? No, we didn't gamble on that outcome. We're not demons, and if you must know, this room, this ill-mannered mob, this table display, is all down to you. I am not as you see me here, and my colleagues are not as they appear to others, this is simply how we're projected by you in this dream. A creative concept, a notion fed by imagination, a construct that only exists in your mind. Wilson, Wilson, Wilson, you understand so little my friend."

Sampson removed his trilby and began fanning his face with the brim of the hat. It was stiflingly hot in the room.

"Anyway, the upshot is, I think you'll be pleasantly surprised tomorrow and to be honest, I've wondered why you thought you needed our help in the first place. Quis Custodiet Ipsos Custodes? Investigators always need investigating Wilson. You've missed the obvious. You'll understand why when you wake up. Now if it's all the same to you, we'd like to get back to our gaming."

The room then exploded with noise as Wilson found himself being forced away from the table, down the fairway and back to the door. After being sucked out into the stairwell, the door to the high rollers' room slammed shut.

As Wilson made his way across The Market Square, a thought within a dream made him divert to the right to see if the window in The Bank had been reglazed. As he drew closer, to the right of the Clock Tower and beyond the flower beds, he saw Big Mac and Short Cake talking to the stonemason with the tool bag. The three of them were standing by the war memorial deep in conversation. Curious to know what was going on, Wilson wandered over.

"Ah Wilson, how are you?"

Big Mac shifted to one side to create some free space.

"This is Benedict, he does all the odd jobs around here."

Benedict nodded and picked up his bag.

"I'll go and fix that window then. Bloody vandals. The youngsters of today eh?"

Benedict held Wilson in the cross hairs of a glare before heading off in the direction of The Bank.

"So," said Short Cake, rocking on his heels and with a beaming grin on his face. "What brings you to this neck of the woods?"

"I had to see someone about something. A side bet."

"Ah yes, your father's predicament! I think that violent streak may well run in the family. I don't suppose you know who smashed our window?"

"Yes, and so do you. And I'm sorry, I was just angry and upset about what you all did to Sally."

"I know Wilson, but she died to preserve The Secret, as all our heroes do."

"What do you mean, preserve The Secret?"

Big Mac stepped back and pointed to the inscribed face of the war memorial.

"Surely you recognise the significance of this Wilson?"

"No, funnily enough I don't. I know it's always here, but my dreams have never given it any great importance. It never has a part to play."

"Wilson, this is the second most important landmark in The Market Square, shame on you."

"Well, what is it then?"

"If you read the inscription, I'm sure you'll find it self-explanatory."

Wilson read aloud the epitaph of words embossed in gold leaf.

"In memory of the 11s who died to save The Secret."

Then he quickly scanned down the columns of names and read the final line.

"With little to lose, they had so much to gain. The Powers That Be salute you. So what does it mean, what's The Secret? Who are all of these people, these names?"

"They're the fallen. The angels on earth who gave their all so others might live."

"The Secret is the existence of The Gateway and it must be preserved at all costs" added Short Cake.

"So all these people did something to keep the existence of . . . to stop the living discovering the truth about the afterlife? The guarantee that they'd be going to . . . " Wilson nodded in the general direction of the Number 11 Club . . . "up there, when their time on Earth is over?"

"Exactly."

"People like Sally?"

"Exactly."

Wilson began to read down the names of the fallen but the dates were from so long ago. He looked across the columns to the last one and then scrolled downwards to the end. That's when he saw the three recently added names. The names he had seen Benedict making preparations to inscribe.

Wilson dropped to one knee and ran his finger along the bevelled contours of the letters.

Sally Bennett
2004 - 2017

Felix Abdi
2004 - 2015

Edward Bennett
1972 - 2014

"There is no greater honour, no greater honour Wilson" said Big Mac solemnly.

"Where is she?"

"Where she always wanted to be, riding seahorses with her parents" he replied.

"When she's not serving her apprenticeship in The Citadel that is," said Short Cake, giving Wilson a wink. "All's well that ends well. And keep your head down when you swing sonny, that's a nasty slice you're developing there."

Chapter 65

On the twelfth day of Christmas

Tuesday 12th December 2017, 8.45 a.m.

'Wilson, wake up. We have a visitor.'

Gloria was tapping on the window of Wilson's sleeping brain.

That's odd, I haven't heard Mum sound this excited for weeks.

'Wilson, wake up. We have a visitor.'

And who would be visiting at this time? Has Sergeant Jordan come back with more revelations?

Gloria was calling from the foot of the stairs.

"Wilson, wake up. We have a visitor."

The sound rising from the kitchen was of friendly chatter mixed with a dollop of Gloria's fussing voice. Wilson could hear his dad chipping in with whatever was going on and another voice he couldn't quite place. When this third person started laughing, Wilson placed the face. It was Teaps. In the rush to fasten his pyjama jacket and get downstairs, buttons and button holes became hopelessly mixed up.

Gloria, Alex and Teaps were drinking tea round the kitchen table when Wilson entered.

Whoa, it really is Teaps! What's going on? Are we mates again?

"Hey, Teaps, how are you man?"

Wilson was grinning from ear to ear, possibly more from muscle memory than anything else. "What's going on? It's only like, half past eight."

Wilson hesitated before he took a seat, fully expecting cracks to appear in the cheery faces. He wasn't sure he'd properly woken up.

"What's happening, why is everyone looking so pleased? Teaps, what are you doing here?"

Wilson turned to Alex.

"What's with all the smiles, what's going on? Are we playing guess the happy thought?"

"We've received some wonderful news Wilson, just now, from Graham."

"Something to do with Vanessa?"

"No mate, it's nothing to do with Mum, it's about you, and your dad."

"Go on. Tell me. What's happened?"

"Sergeant Jordan called me yesterday. He'd already spoken to my dad, but he called me specially, cos he thought I wouldn't have believed it otherwise."

"Believed what?"

Teaps was more than happy to continue, to deliver the words he'd always hoped he'd be able to say.

"Sergeant Jordan told me he received a message, similar to the one you got, the Snapchat, the one I didn't believe. Whoever sent yours, sent him one as well. It was real Wilson, your Snapchat message was real."

Wilson instantly plugged into the significance and his face lit up like a Christmas tree. Sampson had kept his word.

"I came to tell you straightaway. Wilson I'm sorry for

doubting you, for thinking you'd done something to hurt Mum. And I know you went all that way to check by yourself, in case it wasn't her, so I wouldn't have to face the disappointment of it being somebody else in the home. Mate, I just want to say thanks, from my dad as well."

"Teaps, this is so fantastic. I can't believe it. So who sent Sergeant Jordan the message?"

"He thinks it was someone in the police station in Inverness, someone who'd discovered what really happened. Oh, and there's another thing. Montague has been arrested and suspended from his job. He's in a lot of trouble."

"Couldn't have happened to someone more deserving. Go on, what's he done?"

"They found a missing person photo of Mum in his drawer and some footage of her in Inverness the day after she went missing. If Montague had done his job properly, he'd have known who she was in a few hours."

"In whose drawer? Montague's?"

"Yeh."

Wilson kicked himself.

So that's what Sampson meant when he said investigators needed investigating. If I'd pulled Montague into The Market Square, I could have discovered all of that for myself and Dad would never have been involved. It was staring me in the face all along.

"Sergeant Jordan thinks Montague made up all this and tried to pin the blame on Alex just to make himself look good. He wasn't bothered that Mum had been rescued, or that he'd ruined our lives. He wanted to turn everything to his own advantage, yet he was the one to blame all along. It's unbelievable Wilson. I don't know what else to say."

Wilson turned to his father to have the result rubber stamped.

"So now you'll get your job back right? And the charges will be dropped?"

Teaps answered the questions on Alex's behalf.

"Yes, and Sergeant Jordan said he'll call your dad's boss and explain what happened. He told me to tell you Alex, that you can file a complaint and they'll have to pay you compensation."

"I'm not sure I'll be doing that, but I'm going to call him this afternoon to say thanks. I don't think he ever believed Montague's accusations if I'm honest."

"It's like Christmas has finally arrived. Thank goodness, thank goodness this is all over. I'm so happy I could cry . . . and look . . . now I am crying!"

"And you're laughing at the same time Mum."

Alex excused himself and left for Piccadilly train station to collect Kate and Megan. Gloria was unpacking the last box of Christmas decorations, there would be a Christmas after all.

As Gloria sat on the sofa untangling fairy lights with bifocals balanced on the tip of her nose, Wilson was on the doorstep talking with Teaps.

"So where's your dad been?"

"We came down last night and stayed at his sister's, he spoke with a lawyer yesterday afternoon. He wants to press his own charges against Montague. He's really mad. We both are. He'll be here in five minutes. He wants to say thanks Wilson. And I'm sorry mate, for the things I said in the hospital. You were still recovering from your illness. I don't think I'll ever forgive myself for that."

Teaps took a deep breath to cap his emotions.

"Teaps, we're mates, that's the most important thing. Let's not talk about this again. So what's your plan for Christmas?"

"Ha. Christmas. Good question. Dad's rented a house close to Mum and we're hoping she'll be allowed to stay with us. If that works out okay, we can think about making permanent arrangements. She's not good though, she forgets things, doesn't know where her memories are kept. She keeps asking me who I am and who Dad is. She'll start to make a cup of tea and then forget the kettle's on. You tell her a joke and she'll laugh and then suddenly stop, because she can't remember why she's laughing. So I dunno, if she can be with us for Christmas that's the only present I want."

"Fingers crossed pal, perhaps another miracle will happen, they're coming thick and fast at the moment."

"Yeh, it's just crazy mate."

"What are you doing about college? Are you going back in January?"

"No, I don't think so. Dad wants me to go to London. I told you about Mum's recruitment business, about how the staff kept it going and opened an office down there."

"Yeh, you said."

"They ignored Dad when he told them they could keep the business and kept the profit in a trust for me. They were waiting until I was twenty-one to tell me. I'm going to take up their job offer. I'm certainly not going back to Morrison's and that old flat. Life is moving on and I'm moving with it."

Standing on the front doorstep in pyjamas and slippers, Wilson realised he was saying a last goodbye to a boyhood friend. They were no longer the old Wilson and Teaps. Never again would they kick a football around a school playground, laugh at Hoover's antics on the Playstation, give silly answers to even sillier questions. That former life was ending on a bright winter's morning with batons being passed from boy to man.

It seemed the natural thing to do, to hug. They locked together as though Teaps had saved the penalty and Wilson had scored the winner. The winner in a game that would never be played again.

"When I'm sorted in London, I'll give you a bell and invite you down. I owe you a beer."

"When you're sorted in London Teaps, you won't need to invite me, I'll be there. And you owe me more than a beer."

Chapter 66

The normal night

Tuesday 12th December 2017, 7.00 p.m.

Sam's Chop House wouldn't look out of character in The Market Square; it has a peculiar, olde world charm and there's even stone cobbles set in the pedestrianised street outside. Windows with bottle bottom glass run along the frontage at knee height and draw attention from passersby to the cosy, wood panelled interior below. A bronze statue of L. S. Lowry, Salford's most famous son, sits in a corner, always ready to catch up on the latest news. As you stoop and enter and then step down into the bar, you may struggle to grab the barman's attention because the place is always full. The restaurant at the back, with its high-backed booths in burgundy leather is just as busy. There's something ordinary about the extraordinary in Sam's Chop House; an anachronism that still has its place and relevance in a modern world.

In her text message, Daisy had been very specific with the arrangements and arrived ten minutes early on purpose. She wanted to savour delicious moments of anonymity before Wilson arrived. To be a plain Jane in a black trench coat waiting for her boyfriend to arrive and light up her life. To peer down through the Chop House windows, steamy from the warmth of the people inside, and know the place was also open to her. That she was invited and welcome in the throng of noisy, laughing, shouting, singing, tipsy, fantastic, normal people. People drinking and engaging with friends and trying to get to the bar. People passing round menus and recommending the steak pie or the gammon and egg. People on pub crawls with mates getting another round in. Daisy wanted to be an insignificant part of this wonderfully inconspicuous world, just her and her boyfriend, just for one night.

The sparkling amber eyes, the rosy cheeks and the lovely smile made Wilson stop in his tracks. His feet were saying the girl standing outside Sam's Chop House couldn't possibly be waiting for him.

"Daisy you look different tonight, I didn't recognise you. You've turned all magical and bewitching again."

"I think there's something seriously wrong with your eyes Wilson." Daisy took his hand and pointed out the scene she found so appealing. "Look, we're going down there, doesn't it look wonderful?"

Wilson felt a tingle in her slender fingers and warm hand. They shared the moment before ducking their heads and dashing down the steps to join all the same faced people in the same faced bar.

And so the second night to remember began.

A night of glühwein and German markets and the heady anticipation of what was inevitably to follow. I'm not allowed to elaborate further on the particulars of the later proceedings, I promised Wilson, I'm not some seedy voyeur you know.

Chapter 67

No going back

Wednesday 13th December 2017, 9.30 a.m.

"I needed to experience last night Wilson. To touch base with reality. To enjoy a few hours with no need to look over my shoulder and feel nervous about what's going to come along next."

"I know. I was the same."

They were drinking milky coffee in a café on Bridge Street having checked out of the Premier Inn near the cathedral. Daisy was playing with a spoon in bubbles of froth.

"It's over now Wilson and I'm never going back. We were lucky to escape that place and to live to tell the tale."

"But do you think we can really escape The Market Square?"

"If I'm totally honest, no. I'm not sure we'll be able to make that decision and stick to it. If somebody makes it for us, then yes, we never go back but I can't say for sure that will happen. I hope so. I don't like drinking Champagne that doesn't get you drunk."

Wilson scooped froth from Daisy's coffee with his spoon and gave her a mischievous grin.

"So how's your hangover?"

Daisy smiled as she remembered.

"Just the way I'd want it to be. I've got a splitting headache and I'm glad, because it's real."

"What are you doing today?"

"I'm meeting Mum in half an hour, we're going Christmas shopping. What've you got planned?"

"I'm going to get the Vespa if it's still there, and starts, then I need to get home. I want to see Kate and Megan and speak to my mum. She sent me a message last night to say the charity people called and offered her old job back. Mum told them to get stuffed, which doesn't sound like her. I'm guessing she was celebrating with Dad last night so she might also be a bit worse for wear this morning. I hope she doesn't go back, they just abandoned her. Think she's had enough of all the gossiping as well."

"Ha, I don't blame her."

"And she's going to be okay with you from now on Daisy. She knows she was wrong; that she made you the scapegoat for everything that was happening outside her control. Just being a mum I guess."

"Yeh, don't worry, we'll be friends again."

Daisy was still playing with the froth.

"Are you going to speak to Balthazar when you go for your scooter?"

"No, I'm hoping the gate will be open and I can just start up and be on my way. There's nothing to say. I want to turn the last page on this story. Maybe next year we can call in and say hello."

"Yeh, I'd like to see James and Mark again. We didn't really get to say goodbye."

"I think they'll understand."

"I loved the food we had in Sam's Chop House last night. I think we should go there again. And what was that place called with the band?"

"Matt and Phreds Jazz Club?"

"Yeh, that was awesome."

"So glad they didn't have a jazz flute for you to play."

"Wilson, I promise, I'm taking my own flute if we go there again."

They talked and laughed through highlights of the previous night until Daisy said she had to go and meet her mum and they agreed to speak later. The tricky question of which house for Christmas dinner had still to be resolved.

The compound at the rear of 247 Chapel Street was open and Wilson was wiping rainwater from the Vespa's seat with the sleeve of his parka when the back door opened.

"You weren't going to leave without saying goodbye were you?"

At the sight of Balthazar, a sudden flashback to the scene in Kay's lounge caught Wilson unawares.

"Er, no! Course not. I was just checking. I think the battery might be flat."

"No, it's not. Mark put it on charge. Come in, I want to talk to you about something."

Balthazar walked back into the building leaving the door open. Wilson found Balthazar behind his desk in the office.

"Take a seat. Do you want a coffee or something?"

"No, I just had one with Daisy."

"Is she with you now?"

"No, she's gone shopping with her mum."

"How is she?"

"She's good. Still a bit raw to be honest, we both are. We spoke with Kay after the funeral and that helped."

"You know there was nothing you could have done to change things? You understand that don't you?"

"I don't know. I'd like to believe that. I have to I guess."

"I'm sure, with more time to reflect on matters, you'll see that's the case."

"I hope so, I really do. And if it's true, that it was all inevitable, I need to say thanks Balthazar, to you and James and Mark."

Balthazar waved it away.

"Before you go Wilson, do you have a minute to discuss another matter?"

Wilson shifted in his seat.

"You know that you and Daisy are gifted individuals, one in a million, a million, million maybe?"

"Yeh, I remember the conversation about savants when you said . . ."

"All of that is true. You and Daisy have a special gift, one that can be very useful. A talent that shouldn't be wasted."

"I know where you're going with this Balthazar and I've spoken to Daisy. We don't want to go back to The Market Square."

"I'm totally with you Wilson, totally. I bloody hate the place. That thin one, what's his name . . . ?"

"Short Cake."

"Yes, Short Cake! He gives me the creeps. And I only ever go to the Number 11 Club when I have to find Mark Sampson."

"Balthazar, I don't know where you're going with this."

"Okay, let me get to the point. What are your plans for next year Wilson?"

"Er, finish my A levels and go to uni I suppose."

Balthazar raised his eyebrows.

"Really? You're going to spend three years of your life

pretending to acquire knowledge that you could learn in a week. What's the point in that?"

"It's what normal people do."

"Yeh, I agree. But the fact is you're not normal Wilson, you know that. So you're just going to dumb down and role play for the rest of your life. Like your father?"

"Hey, that's not fair? He's done okay. Adapted his life to stay under the radar. Raised a family, happily married, a good job that suits his . . . skill sets. Why? What's the alternative?"

"Wilson, I've been doing this work for a long time. It has its ups, mostly ups, and the odd down, but only when the Bradley Givens of this world come along. And thankfully that's only happened twice on my watch. The point is . . . now how can I put this?"

Balthazar was bouncing his fingertips together again.

"Why don't you just skip university and go straight into . . . business?"

"Doing what exactly?"

"A bit of this, a bit of that, a bit of metal detecting! It can be highly profitable work, the metal detecting side of things."

"Balthazar, are you offering me a job?"

"Yes, you could say that. But it's more of an apprentice position initially, an opportunity to learn the ropes. You have to walk before you can run as they say. Plus, I'm not due to retire for another couple of years."

"Ha! And if people ask me what I do for living, what will I tell them? What does it say on my job description?"

"You're a dealer in rare coins, you breed butterfly assassins and you help insurance companies find stuff stolen by spirits. I think that would sum it up."

"Oh, very good. I can see my mother loving that. And are

there any perks to this job?"

"Yes indeed, of course! I forgot about the perk. It's *perked* outside. Follow me."

Balthazar abruptly left the office and was talking to himself as he crossed the banking hall, heading for the back door, with Wilson following.

"There are many perks in our line of work Wilson. It's a dream job in that respect. Plus, there's a daytime benefit because this job comes with a company vehicle, well not so much a vehicle, more a mode of transport."

Balthazar led Wilson from the building out into the compound.

A tarpaulin cover was draped over something parked next to the Vespa. Something that wasn't there earlier.

"Think of it as a Christmas present and a big thank you from Mark Sampson."

Balthazar pulled back the tarpaulin.

It was the Triumph Cafe Racer, the one with the hand stitched, quilted leather seat. The beauty Wilson had seen in Sampson's Motorcycle Workshop. Custom made panniers in black leather hung either side of the back wheel.

He stared at the bike in disbelief and then at Balthazar and then at the bike and back to Balthazar.

"This one has exactly the same seat. No. Wait a minute. This is exactly the same bike. This is that bike! Bloody hell. Where did . . . how did you do that?"

"God works in mysterious ways Wilson. Sampson thought it better to deliver it here. He'd have had a hell of job taking it down the chimney. It's all yours. A big thank you for a job well done."

"I don't know what to say. I'm, I'm lost for words.

Seriously? Lost for words . . . speechless. I don't even have the licence for it."

"No problem, we'll keep it in storage until you do. And should you choose not to accept our intern position, don't worry, the bike's still yours."

"I'll kill myself on that thing Balthazar."

"Erm, I don't think so Wilson. Sampson wouldn't have given it to you if there was a chance of that happening."

Balthazar was about to close the back door when Wilson posed a final question.

"How long have I got, to think about the job offer?"

"See you next year Wilson, you've already made your mind up. James told me. He had a quick shufty in 3b."

Kate and Megan rushed out to greet their brother like excited toddlers when they heard the Vespa pull onto the driveway; delighted to be together as a family again; thrilled by the promise of Christmas.

As Wilson was taking off his parka in the hallway, he saw a package on the bureau with his name on it.

"Wilson," his mother shouted from the kitchen, "the postman's delivered something, a book I think."

Inside the layers of bubble wrap there was a note and a Palos Verdes butterfly pinned to a board in a glass frame.

Wilson,
I don't know how you made that happen,
and I don't want to. But I'm so pleased you did.
All the best. Gladys's dad.
P.S. Throw this note in the bin. It's a Snapchat message!